The Wolf and th

Terry Cloutier

The Wolf of Corwick Castle Book 6

Copyright © 2022 TERRY CLOUTIER

All rights reserved. No part of this book may be reproduced,

in whole or in part, without prior written permission

from the copyright holder.

Also by Terry Cloutier

The Wolf of Corwick Castle Series

The Nine (2019)

The Wolf At Large (2020)

The Wolf On The Run (2020)

The Wolf At War (2021)

The Wolf And The Lamb (2022)

The Wolf And The Codex (2022)

Part of The Wolf of Corwick Castle Series

Baine and the Outlaw of Corwick (Spring 2023)

The Past Lives Chronicles

Past Lives (2021)

Jack the Ripper (2022)

The Zone War Series

The Demon Inside (2008)

The Balance Of Power (2010)

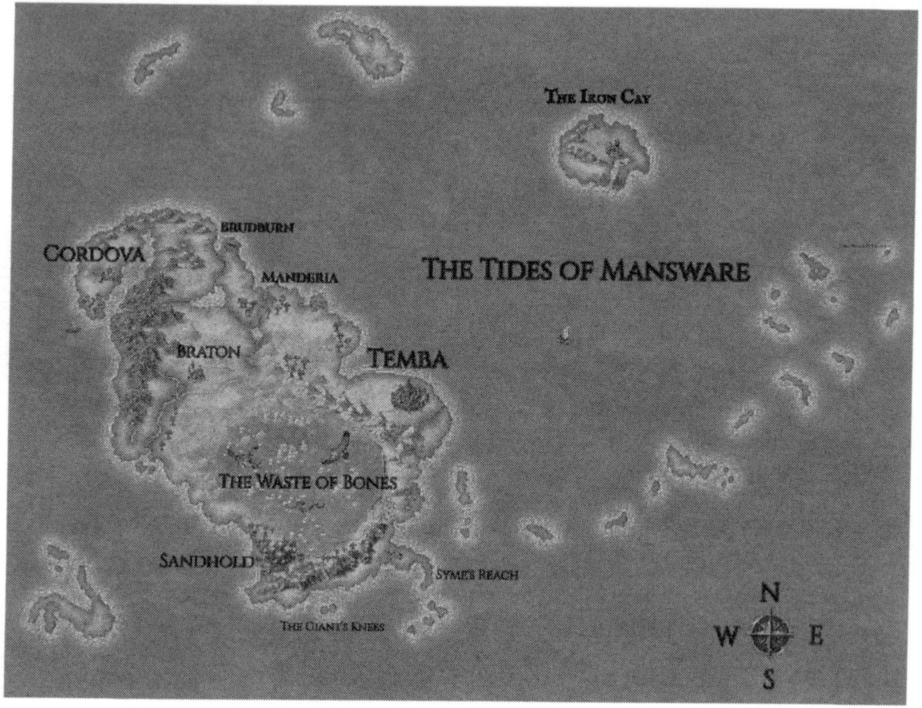
The Iron Cay
Brudburn
Cordova
Manderia
The Tides of Mansware
Braton
Temba
The Waste of Bones
Sandhold
Syme's Reach
The Giant's Knees
N
W
E
S

Table of Contents

PROLOGUE 7
Chapter 1: Beginning 16
Chapter 2: The Tides of Mansware 26
Chapter 3: Sarrey 36
Chapter 4: The Iron Cay 49
Chapter 5: The Fisherman 60
Chapter 6: The Codex 73
Chapter 7: The Auction 83
Chapter 8: Treachery 94
Chapter 9: The Storm 110
Chapter 10: The Temba 120
Chapter 11: Muwa 132
Chapter 12: An Offer To Refuse 142
Chapter 13: A Night Of Madness 153
Chapter 14: Friend or Foe? 168
Chapter 15: Rorian 182
Chapter 16: Freedom 192
Chapter 17: Unwashed Row 202
Chapter 18: Goma 214
Chapter 19: Kish 224
Chapter 20: Tragedy 236
Chapter 21: Lions On The Trail 247
Chapter 22: It's A Long Way Down 259
Chapter 23: Trapped 269
Chapter 24: *Maharas* 279
Chapter 25: The Bone Warriors 291

Chapter 26: An Uneasy Alliance	301
Chapter 27: The Ship In The Harbor	312
Chapter 28: The Circle Of Life	319
Chapter 29: By Land And Sea	331
Chapter 30: The King Of Temba	342
Chapter 31: Spearfish	354
Chapter 32: The Giant's Knees	365
Chapter 33: Reaction To Their Action	377
Chapter 34: The Baggage Train	390
Chapter 35: A Night To Remember	407
Chapter 36: Ravens And Poetry	422
Chapter 37: The Edge Of The World	434
Chapter 38: The Eye Of God	448
Chapter 39: Castaway	458
EPILOGUE	477
Author's Note	483

PROLOGUE

Fate can be a bitch sometimes, I thought wryly as I sat astride my horse and studied the three men kneeling in the dirt in front of me. They were a sorry lot, these three, with their tattered and torn rags that passed for clothing and their long, shaggy hair and beards covered in filth. The faces of the kneeling men were lined and haggard, twisted into mixtures of fatigue, hunger and terror, as they stared at the ground. I knew they had a right to be afraid, for I was tired and irritable and in no mood for mercy this night after the long ride my men and I had just taken. Not to mention the anger and disgust still simmering inside me over what these bastards had done.

I could tell by their expressions that the captives knew what was in my heart and where it would ultimately lead just as well as I did. I closed my eyes in weary satisfaction, relieved that the hunt was finally over and we'd caught up with them. We'd been lucky, I knew. If not for a thorn piercing one of the hiding fugitives' thumbs, causing him to cry out involuntarily, we most likely would have ridden right past the bastards and lost them for good within this vast forest.

I glanced up at the dark sky through the trees, my breath wisping around my head with each exhale. The night was cool, and I could already taste the hint of winter in the air. I sighed. *The gods certainly seem to be favoring me of late*, I thought without any satisfaction. I wondered idly why they even bothered with me anymore. I was an old man now, with nothing left to give this world—or so I believed, anyway. But what if I was wrong? What if more mischief, misery, and heartache were still to come my way before the gods were done toying with me? I shuddered at the unpleasant thought, for truly, how much grief can one man take in a lifetime?

I heard my son, Hughe, clear his throat impatiently and I swore under my breath, wondering how long I'd been sitting there staring up at the sky like some doddering old halfwit. I thrust my fears and thoughts away, angered by my brief show of weakness. Trying to fathom the gods' plans was a fool's errand that would take me nowhere and give me nothing but sleepless nights and ulcers. What would be would be, and there was nothing a mere mortal like myself could do to change that. I glanced at Hughe where he sat his horse, and I nodded to him, then focused my attention back on the prisoners. I didn't bother trying to hide my disdain for them. None of the three would meet my eyes, of course. I suppose I could hardly blame them for that. The shame of what these men had done clearly hung over them like a yoke, the knowledge of their horrific crime a crushing weight that had stilled their tongues and reduced them to mere shadows of what might once have been honorable men.

"What should I do with you?" I growled down at the dejected prisoners. The black mare beneath me shifted at the sound of my voice, shaking her elegant head as if annoyed that I'd even bothered to ask such an obvious question. She was a feisty one that mare, reminding me a great deal of Angry from so many years before. My mount was half the size of the great stallion, but her heart seemed just as large as his had been, perhaps even larger. I'd named the mare Satin, for her gait was smooth and effortless, which was essential when you're old and in constant pain like I was. "Well?" I grunted at the prisoners in annoyance. "Nothing to say to your lord before I pass sentence upon you?"

I waited for several heartbeats, but none would lift their bowed heads or speak. I was hardly surprised. These three knew they were living on borrowed time and that pleading for their lives would change nothing—so why bother? I noticed the thin one with the crooked eye had soiled himself and I wrinkled my nose at the pungent smell drifting across to me. Losing patience, I finally snorted with disgust and looked away, studying the trees that stood like silent sentinels around us. Each one looked identical—tall, dark, and pitiless as they watched and waited for my judgment.

It was nearing midnight now, I guessed, with only a quarter moon and the stars giving off faint light—that and, of course, the torches held by my men who surrounded the prisoners on horseback. I sighed, feeling every one of my many years as I shifted my weight in the saddle, suppressing a groan. My ass hurt something fierce, and my bad foot was sending arcs of fire shooting up my leg, competing with my rear end for prominence. I pushed the pain away as best I could, trying to focus. I had my son and ten men with me, all of whom were far younger and in better condition than I was, yet foolish pride still burned deep within me. I was the Lord of Corwick, and I vowed to show no more weakness in front of them, despite the pain and my overwhelming fatigue.

The mare beneath me suddenly stamped a front hoof impatiently as if eager to get on with it and go home. It was time to end this. "Hughe," I muttered, glancing toward my son, who looked impossibly fit and huge in the firelight sitting astride his horse. I envied him his health and strength.

"Lord?" Hughe replied. My son had a naked blade clutched in his massive hand, and it twitched like a live creature.

"Where is the father?"

Hughe glanced behind him, then made a gesture. Two horsemen appeared. One was a soldier, the other a squat, bald man with eyes that burned hot with hatred as he stared at the prisoners. The bald man's face was badly bruised from the beating he'd taken three days before, but if the discomfort from his wounds bothered him, he showed no sign. The squat man growled low in his chest, the sound primal and full of rage as they drew closer.

"Are these the men who attacked you?" I asked the man, whose name was Ephers Boley.

"They are, my lord," Ephers managed to say through gritted teeth. "Those are the bastards who killed my girls."

I nodded, having expected the answer. Ephers lived in Camwick with his wife and two girls aged seven and eight—or rather, he had lived with them. Now the girls were gone, raped in every vile way imaginable and then murdered by these men during a drunken binge. Ephers and his wife had tried to fight the three attackers off, only to be severely beaten for their efforts, with the wife now barely clinging to life. She wasn't expected to survive, I'd been told. It was a nasty business that had shocked all of Corwick, for Ephers Boley was a well-known tavern keeper, and his children had been popular and liked by all. I glanced again at the prisoners, who continued to stare at the ground in dejected silence. These men had taken everything from Ephers, which I decided meant that their fates should by rights now rest in his hands.

I cleared my throat. "As the Lord of Corwick, I sentence Gauwis of Radthorn, Bertio Fine, and Walda of Camwick to death for the murders of the Boley girls." Bertio Fine, the thin man who'd soiled himself earlier, whimpered at the mention of his name, though the other two did not react. I glanced at Ephers. "How would you like them to die?"

Ephers' eyes burned even brighter with sudden hope at my words. "There won't be a trial, my lord?"

"No, this ends tonight. Right here and right now."

Ephers pursed his lips in wonder. "And I really get to choose how they die, my lord?" he asked.

I nodded. "You do. After what these turd-suckers did to your family, it seems only fitting to me."

I saw Hughe shift in his saddle out of the corner of my eye, guessing that he didn't approve of my ruling. Hughe didn't agree with much I did these days, with his anger over how I'd failed his mother evident in everything he said and did in regards to me. Well, too bad for him. I was still above ground and breathing, which meant I remained the Lord of Corwick, not him. Hughe's day would come soon enough, the gods willing.

Ephers brushed a shaking hand across his bald scalp as he thought, his eyes fixated on the prisoners with almost religious zeal. Finally, he turned his gaze to me. "I once heard a story that you gelded a man for rape many years ago, my lord. A Pith. Is that story true?"

I grinned without humor as all three prisoners' heads lifted in unison, their faces painted in identical masks of horror. "Yes, it's quite true," I said. I glanced at the terrified men. "It's a fate that I believe all rapists should suffer." I raised an eyebrow. "Is that what you wish for these men?"

Ephers nodded immediately. "It is, my lord."

"Then so it shall be," I grunted, relieved that the affair was almost done. I motioned to my men, who dismounted and grabbed the now moaning prisoners by the shoulders.

"I have one more request, though, my lord," Ephers said. His voice was husky now, filled with passion and hatred.

"Which is?" I asked.

"Stake them naked to the ground," Ephers replied. "Then leave me here alone with them."

I frowned. "I'm not sure that's a good idea. What if they manage to overpower you?"

"They will not, my lord," Ephers answered. He dismounted, limping toward me before pausing beside my mare. The bald man lifted his battered face up to me, his fierce eyes now filled with tears. "I beg of you, my lord. Give me this. In the names of the Three Gods, give me the vengeance I need for what they did to my family."

I hesitated, then shrugged. "So be it," I grunted. I glanced at Hughe. "Strip the prisoners and stake them out. Be sure that their bonds are secure and the stakes go deep."

"Yes, Father," Hughe said with a bow of his head. "It will be done."

Ten minutes later, I slipped a razor-sharp knife into Ephers Boley's hand. "I hope you find the peace you seek in this forest," I said to him. "But remember this. What you do here will not bring back your children or your happiness. I speak these words from experience."

"I understand, my lord," Ephers replied. He glanced up at me, his eyes empty of emotion now, like a man with nothing left to live for, which I knew was most likely true. "But it will make them rest easier in the Realm Beyond," Ephers added in a whisper. "That much I know in my heart, and it is enough. Thank you for this, my lord."

The tavern owner looked away, fixating his determined gaze on the three naked men lying spread-eagled on the ground. He started walking toward them as the prisoners began pleading with him to spare their lives and manhood. I knew their pleas would do them little good, for in his place, would I or any other man be merciful after what those bastards had done?

Hughe guided his big horse closer to my smaller mare. He leaned toward me and lowered his voice. "I suggest we leave a man or two behind, Father, just in case something goes wrong."

"Agreed," I grunted. I watched as Ephers Boley paused over the pleading prisoners, the knife in his hand gleaming in the light from a torch thrust into the ground. Finally, I kicked the mare into motion, heading away from what I knew would soon become a gruesome scene. I had seen it many times before and did not need to see it again. "But they won't be needed," I tossed over my shoulder toward my son as the first screams sounded. "Mark my words."

It was early morning by the time we finally returned to Corwick Castle, and the first person I saw within her strong walls was my steward, Walice. The man looked upset, which I knew did not bode well.

"My lord," Walice said as he and Hughe helped me down from my horse. "I must speak with you urgently." The steward glanced sideways at Hughe, his expression cautious. "In private, my lord."

I saw Hughe's features darken, but I chose to ignore it. "We'll talk later," I told my son curtly, dismissing him. Hughe hesitated, then nodded and left without a word, leading our horses toward the stables. I watched him go, aware by the set of his mighty shoulders that he was furious with Walice and me. I could hardly blame him.

"So, what's this about?" I muttered to Walice. "It's been a long night and I'm tired."

I leaned wearily on the steward's shoulder, taking the weight off my bad foot. I'd come a long way in the past few months since my physician, Kieran Ackler, had removed a tapeworm from my skull. But even so, I was far from the man I had once been. Today had been the longest outing yet, and it had sapped my strength more than I cared to admit.

"It's about the *prisoner*, my lord," Walice said meaningfully, his voice no more than a whisper. "He's dying."

I looked at the steward in surprise. It had been many years since I'd thought about the man incarcerated in the dungeons deep beneath Corwick Castle. Few people even knew he was there, including Hughe and my other children. I had meant to tell them at some point, but, as time went by, it had slipped my mind. Finally, I shrugged. "What of it? All men die eventually."

"He's asking for you, my lord," Walice said as if I hadn't spoken.

"That bastard already had his chance to talk to me and he refused," I responded bitterly. "There are no words left between us now. Let him go to The Father and burn for what he's done. I doubt I'll be far behind him anyway."

"That's what I told him you would say, my lord," Walice replied. "But he was quite insistent. He says he's ready to answer *the* question now." I hesitated at that, feeling my eyebrows automatically rise. "What do you want me to tell him, my lord?" Walice prodded after a moment.

I sighed, feeling overwhelming exhaustion pulling me down, though it was quickly becoming replaced by curiosity. Was I to finally learn the man's secret that he'd guarded from me all these years? "Very well," I muttered, knowing there would be no sleep this night for me until I'd dealt with this. "I'll speak with him."

Half an hour later, I stood outside a heavy oak door reinforced with metal. Walice was with me, as was a soldier dressed entirely in black armor. The man was one of the Protectors, a secret group formed specifically to guard and care for the prisoner inside. Each Protector was sworn to secrecy about who was behind that door. Not once had any of them whispered a word.

"Open it," I grunted, motioning toward the entrance. The Protector stepped forward and unlocked the heavy door with an iron key, then pushed it inward for me, his face expressionless. "Wait here," I said to my companions before limping through the archway.

The door closed behind me with a bang, but I hardly noticed. An old man with long white hair was sitting on the edge of a cot at the back of the room with a blanket wrapped around his boney shoulders. He regarded me with red-rimmed, watery eyes. The man made a wheezing noise, which I realized after a moment of confusion was actually laughter.

"It's been a long time, Hadrack," the man said in a gravelly voice. He chuckled. "You got old just like me, I see."

I felt my mind turn back to another time when I was still young, strong, and filled with hatred and the need for vengeance. My wife had just died a noble death in my stead, setting off a terrible war, with much of the responsibility for everything that was happening at the time lying at the feet of the man sitting in front of me. I hadn't known that then, of course, and wished now that I'd killed him long ago and been done with it. I couldn't remember now why I hadn't. I grimaced, feeling my hands clenching and unclenching with the need to right that wrong here and now and wring the bastard's skinny neck.

"Hello, Malo," I finally managed to growl, containing myself. There were answers I still needed from this man, so the joy of his death could wait a few minutes longer. "I wish I could say it's good to see you."

Chapter 1: Beginning

Blood filled my eyes. I blinked and shook my head, trying to see past the red haze that had settled over me like a wet, sticky blanket. The blood stank of despair and death, but luckily it wasn't my own, having spurted in a torrent over me from the neck of a man after I'd caught him with a vicious, two-handed slash. He was a big bastard and had fought well. But when he finally fell to my sword, my opponent took whatever will to resist his companions had left, turning the tide in our favor. Now, the surviving enemy were fleeing from the holding known as Fystone, and I was glad of it, for the fight had been far tougher than I'd believed it would be.

I stabbed Wolf's Head into the ground, my chest heaving as I flung my helmet aside and used my right hand to rub at my eyes. I could hear the aggressive thrum of bowstrings as my Wolf's Teeth shot with their great warbows at the retreating enemy. Knowing my well-trained archers as I did, I doubted any of our foes would make it to the trees that lay two hundred yards beyond the buildings before an arrow eventually found them. My men sounded in good spirits, I noted, joking and laughing as they placed bets on who could bring down the enemy first. And well they should be happy, for the victory had not been assured by any means.

I continued to wipe at my eyes, hissing with impatience to see better as they burned from the dead man's blood. I'd lost my shield just before Jebido had fallen, and I could feel a pinch in my left shoulder with every movement of my arm where an enemy spear had managed to pierce my armor. I thought of my friend, wondering how he was faring. The last that I'd seen of Jebido, Putt and Berwin were dragging him off the battlefield, though the older man had been loudly protesting the entire time that they were idiots and that he was perfectly fine. I hoped it was true.

"The bastards fought well enough. I'll grant them that."

I could finally see properly again, and I turned my still-burning gaze toward Baine, who looked remarkably well-rested, considering we'd been fighting over this godforsaken small holding for over an hour or more. There was a small circle of dried blood on his left cheek, but other than that, he looked uninjured.

"They were certainly brave," I conceded wearily. I glanced down at my armor, which was covered in a thin film of red from head to toe. I could only imagine what I must look like.

"That they were," Baine agreed. He grinned, his handsome, shaven face lighting up with dry humor. "Not that it helped them much in the end. You can't tell the difference between a coward and a brave man when they're dead, Hadrack."

"There weren't supposed to be this many of them here," I grunted sourly. I thought of our scouts, who'd insisted that the holding was lightly guarded and would be a sure thing. I would have brought a larger force had I known the truth. I'd need to have a talk with those men after this. We couldn't afford to make mistakes like this one again. "It was supposed to be easy," I added, wincing as I saw many of my own men lying among the Parnuthian dead. Every lost man weakened me, for I knew there would be no others coming to our aid any time soon. King Tyden and his army were far away and had their own troubles right now, for more than half of the western fleet had been burned under mysterious circumstances in recent weeks. A massive blow to the king's plans for Cardia.

Baine snorted. "When has anything been easy lately, Hadrack?" he asked.

I nodded, knowing my friend had a point. The war with Cardia had already been raging for six months now, and despite having the Swales as our allies, we were slowly but steadily losing ground. Most of our losses had come in the northeast of the kingdom, where the Cardians' sometime-ally, the Parnuthians, had landed a large flotilla of ships in a surprise invasion. No one had seen that coming, including me. With the bulk of King Tyden's army stationed along the western coast, preparing for an attack of their own, the Parnuthians had struck deep into northeastern Ganderland, taking castles, villages, and holdings along the way before we'd managed to redeploy enough forces to counter them. Now, the richness of our lands was being used against us to strengthen our enemy while we grew weaker by the day and the Cardians gloated and prepared.

Things had begun to change in the northeast in the last week, though, I thought with grim satisfaction. Ever since my men and I had arrived on my ships. The king had tasked me to retake the rich farmlands we'd lost, and I was determined not to fail him. The small holding we'd just liberated from the invaders wasn't much to look at and had little to no strategic value, but I knew taking it back was good for morale, if nothing else. The holding was now the sixth that we'd returned to the king's banner, and I was determined to recapture every last inch of land the Parnuthians had seized before I chased those shit-eating bastards all the way back to their stinking homeland.

Baine glanced at the squat stone buildings of Fystone, which had been ruled by a minor lord named Thury Bridgemaker. I had no idea what had become of the lord, though I guessed the chances were good his bleached bones were even now lying somewhere in the trees or grasses close by. "Doesn't look like much," Baine muttered.

"Neither do you," I retorted with a grin. "But we all know different, now don't we?"

"You two going to gab like a couple of old women all day, or can we get on with this?"

I turned, feeling relief as Jebido limped toward us, his weathered face twisted in annoyance. Putt and Berwin were following close behind him, sputtering with worry like a couple of mother hens.

"Are you all right?" I asked my friend.

Jebido waved a hand. "Just a twisted ankle. I've had worse taking a shit in the morning. It's nothing."

Baine shook his head in mock wonder. "Ah, the images you paint, Jebido. I swear you're an artist with words. You should be at the king's court entertaining all the lords and ladies."

Jebido glared at my black-clad friend sourly. "And you're a damn fool." He put his hands on his hips. "What were you thinking earlier? You may be a halfway competent archer, but you're a lousy swordsman as sure as I'm standing here." Jebido thrust a finger at Baine. "You stay back from the dirty work from now on, do you hear me, boy?"

I glanced at Baine in sudden alarm. "You joined the wall?"

Baine shrugged and gave me one of his charming smiles. "It's been a while. I thought I'd get some practice in."

I advanced on Baine, pleased to see the satisfied smile slide off his face, replaced with caution as I towered over my smaller friend. "Jebido is right. If I ever hear of you doing that again, I promise you'll have a lot more to worry about than a few Parnuthians in a shield wall. Understood?"

Baine lowered his eyes, his cocky demeanor gone now. "I hear you, Hadrack. It won't happen again."

"See that it doesn't," I grunted.

"My lord," Berwin whispered in warning. He gestured behind him toward several riders approaching along an overgrown path.

One of the men was fat, with the heavy jowls of his face jiggling obscenely in the sunlight beneath a ridiculous, plumed helmet. I groaned at the sight. The man's name was Rolad Horne, and he was one of the king's observers, sent to offer me advice—advice that I rarely took for good reason. I'd left him four miles behind my advance in a village called Aunsford, where I assumed he could do no harm. My annoyance changed to a smile of pleasure, however, when I recognized the face of the second man, for it was my friend, Lord Fitzery.

"I thought Fitz was up north guarding Gandertown," Baine muttered. "So what's he doing here?"

"I don't know," I said. "Let's go and find out."

I headed down the slight grade that we'd been forced to ascend in our attack on the Parnuthians as the horsemen came to a halt in a bowl-shaped depression where some of my wounded men were being attended. Both Fitz and Horne dismounted and handed off their horses to several young boys before waiting for the three of us to arrive.

"My dear Lord Hadrack," Fitz said, beaming as he extended his hand to me.

I locked forearms with my friend, unable to hide my delight. "It's good to see you," I said warmly. "It's been too long."

"Not since the funeral," Fitz agreed, his expression darkening. The smile returned moments later, though, and he nodded to Baine and Jebido. "It's good to see you both as well. How have you been?"

"Getting fat and lazy, what do you think?" Jebido grunted, looking unimpressed.

I knew he didn't care for Fitz all that much, but the lord seemed unfazed by Jebido's attitude. He laughed. "Same crusty *old* Jebido, eh?" Fitz said. He winked at Baine. "Some things never change."

Baine just grinned. He always enjoyed the sparring between Jebido and Fitz, though in truth, as much as I dearly loved Jebido, I had to admit that he was usually overmatched in a test of wits with Fitz.

"I'm surprised to see you here where there's actual fighting going on," Jebido shot back. He looked the slim lord up and down. Fitz was dressed in untarnished silver and gold armor, with a rich, dark cloak lined with wolf's fur thrown easily over his shoulders. He looked very much the dandy, though I knew different. My friend could be a fierce and deadly fighter when he was inclined. "Not too much action up in Gandertown these days, I hear," Jebido added dryly.

"Oh, you might be surprised about that," Fitz replied with a chuckle. "Why, just the other day, I met these two young chambermaids standing outside the First Holy House with the biggest—"

I lifted a hand, in no mood after the recent battle to watch these two verbally joust with each other. I'd seen and heard it too many times before. "Why are you here, Fitz?" I asked, getting to the point. I glanced at Horne, acknowledging him for the first time. "And I thought I asked you to stay behind in the village where it was safe, Observer."

"I insisted on coming along, lord," Horne answered imperiously. He glanced at Fitz. "Lord Fitzery was sent to bring you back to Aunsford as soon as possible. Since the two of you are good friends, I felt that it was my duty as the king's representative to accompany him to ensure you understood the urgency of that request and obeyed." The fat man pursed his lips, looking suddenly nervous and unsure of himself as I glared at him. "What I mean to say, of course, lord," Horne continued in a shaky voice. "Is that I know how you can...uhm...be rather stubborn about such things." I could feel my face darkening even more with anger. "That is," the fat man hurried to add. "We all know you're a man of honor and are quite loath to leave a battlefield until the fight is won, lord. Your prowess and stamina in battle are legendary, and I was concerned you would discount Lord Fitzery's concerns." Horne glanced at Fitz. "I also know that Lord Fitzery here shares some of your enthusiasm for the...uhm, shall we say, more unsavory arts, so...I...uhm...felt...it...best—"

I stared steadily into Horne's eyes while he babbled, my face now calm and expressionless, until eventually, he faltered and fell silent. It was a useful trick that I'd learned would quickly unnerve the fat man, causing him to lose his train of thought. The gods only knew the bastard could talk forever if it were allowed. Horne was a pompous ass and hugely annoying, but he was also the king's man, so I needed to at least pretend to listen to him from time to time.

"Thank you for that, Observer Horne," I said into the sudden silence, bowing my head graciously. "As always, I am indebted to King Tyden for having the foresight to send someone with your vast experience and wisdom to advise and watch over me." I turned quickly to Fitz, praying neither Jebido nor Baine would burst out laughing. "Now, what's this about? Who sent you to fetch me?"

My friend glanced around, looking suddenly cautious. "That I can't say just yet. The Cardians and Parnuthians have spies everywhere these days." He put his hand on my shoulder. "But trust me when I say it's important and you need to come with us." I sighed at the look of warning in Fitz's eyes, knowing that I'd get no more out of him. Whatever this was about, I could tell it was no joking matter.

An hour later, Fitz and Horne, along with Baine, Jebido, and me, arrived in the sleepy village of Aunsford. The place had once been thriving, growing around a bustling salt mine. But now the mine was exhausted, the last of the salt having been extracted several years ago. Most of the houses and buildings had been abandoned since then, with only a handful of stubborn people remaining to try and eke out a meager existence growing crops in the dry soil nearby. So far, their labors had produced little success. The village was so poor that not even the Parnuthians had bothered with the place.

"There," Fitz said, pointing to a narrow, sun-bleached Holy House with a poorly-patched roof.

I could see nothing but ruins where the bell tower had once stood, while below on the stoop, four House Agents wearing the familiar Blazing Sun surcoats stood guard outside the open door to the building. I noticed there were also men on horseback moving slowly along the skyline to the north, where they could keep a watchful eye on the village. Jebido nudged my arm and pointed south to a group of low hills where still more riders sat their horses watching us. I frowned. What in the name of The Mother was going on?

"Enough of this," I grunted to Fitz as I guided Angry closer to his horse. "Stop with all this secrecy, you bastard. What's this all about?"

"Have patience, Hadrack," Fitz said. He reached out and tapped my arm. "All will be revealed soon enough, my friend. I promise."

I shared a glance with Jebido as Fitz kicked his horse into a trot ahead of us. "The damn fool is toying with us, Hadrack," Jebido muttered under his breath.

"I heard that," Fitz called with a laugh over his shoulder.

"Good," Jebido barked back moodily. "Your brain might be gone to mush, but at least your ears still work."

Fitz snorted with amusement, the harsh sound echoing down the village street as several half-starved dogs came running to investigate us. I saw a small boy standing outside a wooden house with his mother. Both boy and woman shaded their eyes from the sun as they studied our approach and Fitz waved cheerfully to them. "Hello there, young lad." He halted his horse in front of the Holy House and dropped nimbly to the dusty street, then bowed to the woman. "And a good day to you, lady." The boy and his mother stared at Fitz suspiciously, then turned together and went inside without a word.

"Friendly place," Jebido grumbled as the rest of us dismounted.

I let my eyes rove over the four House Agents guarding the entrance, examining them with professional interest. It was something that I did almost unconsciously now when meeting fighting men that I didn't know. All the Agents were big and looked capable, with their features hidden by bulky square helmets. One man stepped forward, his graceful stride hinting at great power and strength. He reminded me somewhat of Malo, for the former House Agent had moved in much the same way.

"Only Lord Hadrack and Lord Fitzery may enter at this time," the man rumbled. His voice was muffled by the helmet, but even so, there was no mistaking the firmness of his words.

"What?" Horne gasped, his mouth dropping open in disbelief. His great jowls rippled like tiny waves as he spluttered. "That is outrageous! I am the king's observer! I demand to be let in this instant!"

The Agent's square helmet turned toward the fat man, his piercing eyes behind the iron pinning Horne like arrows as his hand dropped to his sword hilt. "I believe I was clear, Observer."

"It's all right," I said to Horne, putting my hand on the man's fleshy shoulder. "I'm sure whatever this is about won't take long."

"But I already know what it's about!" Horne protested with a slight whine to his voice.

"Well then," I grunted as I stepped past the fat man and entered the Holy House. "I guess that means there's no need for you to go in after all, now is there?"

I paused just inside the entrance, ignoring Horne's continued protestations behind me while I allowed my eyes to adjust to the gloom. A pigeon took off from the rafters above my head, its wings making a high-pitched humming sound. The bird darted out of the building through a large hole in the wall to my right where a window must have been at one time. I took two more steps forward, focusing on the back of the knave, where three people awaited me in silence. Two of them were standing, while the third sat on a stool between them. I glanced first to the monstrous House Agent with his helmet tucked firmly under his right arm. His name was Guthris, and he'd saved my life at the Battle of Silver Valley. The other person standing was Little Jinny—as I still thought of her—and I couldn't help but smile when my eyes fell on her pretty features. However, those features showed little joy at my presence, which had never happened before, putting me instantly on edge.

"It's good to see you again, Lord Hadrack," First Daughter Gernet said from where she sat on the stool, her hands folded in her lap. "I only wish it could have been under better circumstances."

Chapter 2: The Tides of Mansware

I said nothing as I approached the First Daughter. Behind me, I could hear Fitz's heavy boots clunking on the worn planks of the floor as he followed. I stopped five feet from the seated woman, studying her critically. The First Daughter looked older and frailer than I remembered when I'd seen her last eight months ago, with stooped shoulders and puffy, heavy bags under her eyes. I shifted my gaze to Jin, who gave me a weak smile that quickly fizzled out before she looked down at the floor. I frowned, troubled even more now.

"Please forgive the need for secrecy, Hadrack," Fitz said as he stopped beside me. He sighed, looking suddenly weary himself. "Things have been somewhat, uh, *difficult* lately in Gandertown." He glanced behind him at the open door, where Horne's whiny protests had thankfully stopped. I could see no sign of the fat man on the stoop, guessing that the House Agents had sent him on his way, possibly at the point of a sword. "It's hard to know who to trust these days," Fitz added meaningfully as he looked back at me.

I pursed my lips as I thought about that, still saying nothing. Jebido had instilled in me ever since I was a boy that sometimes it was best just to keep your mouth shut and listen while events unfolded naturally around you. It was a good lesson to remember, though I hadn't always adhered to it in my younger days.

The First Daughter eventually cleared her throat and opened her mouth to speak before a sudden cough caught her by surprise. Jin looked instantly alarmed and started to bend over her in concern, but Daughter Gernet shooed her granddaughter away impatiently. She cleared her throat again, swallowing loudly afterward. "I'm fine, child," the priestess managed to say in a hoarse voice. She smiled wanly, growing more confident in her ability to speak. "Just had some spit go down the wrong way, is all." Daughter Gernet fixed her uncannily intelligent eyes on me. She might be older and frailer, but those predatory eyes hadn't changed at all. "I, too, would like to extend my apologies for the method in which you were brought here, Lord Hadrack," Daughter Gernet continued. She glanced briefly up at the silent House Agent towering over her. "Unfortunately, secrecy and skulking around has become the norm for me of late, I'm saddened to say."

"And why is that, First Daughter?" I asked.

Daughter Gernet waved a hand in the air nonchalantly. "Oh, mostly due to the attempts on my life recently, I'd expect." Her expression remained blank as if she'd just told me about a troublesome corn while I stared at her in astonishment. "It's nothing, really," Daughter Gernet insisted as she patted the House Agent's arm. "But dear Guthris, here, is always the worrier."

I continued to gawk at the First Daughter, unsure if I'd heard her correctly. Someone had tried to kill her? The First Daughter? It was almost impossible for me to fathom.

"It's true, Hadrack," Jin whispered, correctly reading my disbelief. Jin's thin hands were clasped together tightly against the front of her yellow robe. She took a deep breath. "There's been two attempts so far."

"By whose orders," I growled, unconsciously dropping my hand to my sword.

"We'll get to that," Daughter Gernet said. Her face softened. "But first, how have you been? I haven't spoken to you since the funeral. You seemed so lost back then, and who could blame you for it? Such a wonderful girl, that one. A terrible shame."

"I've been just fine," I grunted, not wanting to talk of such things now when I had so many pressing questions that needed answers. "Killing Ganderland's enemies does wonders for returning a sense of purpose to a man," I added in a tone I hoped made clear that I didn't want to talk about Shana or the funeral.

"Indeed," Daughter Gernet said thoughtfully. "And Ganderland is much stronger for that purpose, Lord Hadrack, believe me." The old woman shifted on her stool. "So tell me, what news of the Seven Rings?"

I glanced at Fitz, who just shrugged. The Cardian emperor's inner circle was known as the Seven Rings, and it had been they who had ordered the capture of my wife that had ultimately led to her death. I'd sworn to kill all seven of them, but the Parnuthian invasion had put those plans on hold, at least temporarily.

"Justice will be served," I said tightly. "Be it today, tomorrow, or ten years from now, it will be done."

"Ah, justice," Daughter Gernet said with a faint chuckle. "An interesting word with various interpretations." She winked. "Depending on which side of the issue you sit upon, of course."

"What's that supposed to mean?" I grunted, getting annoyed now. Frustration and Daughter Gernet usually went hand in hand, and this meeting appeared to be no different.

"It means nothing," the priestess said with a sigh. "Just the chaotic mutterings of an old woman, Lord Hadrack. Please disregard my words. I meant no offense." Daughter Gernet finally took a deep breath. "We must all play our part in this little game and pray that The Mother is watching closely while we do."

I shared a look with Fitz. Only a select few people knew the truth about the Master and the First Pair, and my friend, along with Baine and Jebido, was one of them.

"Who is trying to kill you?" I asked more forcefully this time as I circled back to my original question.

"That has yet to be fully determined," Daughter Gernet said, looking unconcerned.

I frowned. "But you have your suspicions?" I guessed.

"Of course we do," the priestess said. "But a suspicion without proof is like a bird without wings, useless and unable to fly."

"It's that bastard First Son, isn't it?" I said, certain that I was right. This sounded like something Son Oriell might try. The man had no scruples and hated Daughter Gernet with a passion.

"Perhaps," the priestess replied vaguely.

So, not the First Son judging by her reaction, I thought, surprised. "If not him, then who?" I asked. "Cardians, maybe?"

"Why would they want me dead?" Daughter Gernet prodded. "They worship The Mother as we do, and I am Her representative in this world." The priestess's eyes were boring into me as she waited and watched while I thought.

"Because your death would weaken Ganderland," I said, though as the words came out, they seemed wrong to me.

"I suppose it would to some degree," Daughter Gernet conceded. "But First Daughters die from old age or other calamities all the time and are replaced without any radical changes in the House. So, why would anyone think this time would be any different? What would there be to gain from my death?"

"I don't know," I admitted.

The First Daughter shrugged. "Nor do we, lord. But I expect the answer will undoubtedly be revealed in due course." She motioned to Jin. "Until then, perhaps my granddaughter can help shed some light on why I summoned you here, hmmm?"

I focused on Jin. "I'm sure you remember the copy of the codex you were sent to find on Mount Halas, Lord Hadrack?" the young priestess asked.

I blinked in surprise while Fitz fidgeted beside me. I glanced at him out of the corner of my eye, but he steadfastly refused to look my way. "Of course I do," I said cautiously. "It was gone. What of it?"

"We believe it has now been found."

I gaped at her. Had they really found Malo after all these years? "Found where?" I demanded a little too forcefully.

"On an island in the Tides of Mansware," Daughter Gernet responded for Jin. "A local merchant there claims to possess it."

For the thousandth time, I cursed Waldin and that damn copy he'd made of the codex as I thought furiously. Was this merchant actually Malo, or had he stolen it from the House Agent and killed him? There was no way to know for certain, but whatever the explanation, we couldn't afford to have the information contained in the codex come to light now with Cardia and Parnuthia breathing down our necks. While it was true that the revelations would cause an uproar in those kingdoms just like in Ganderland, something made me suspect the effect would not be as divisionary there as it would be here. For whatever reason, the two Houses in those countries were much closer aligned and willing to compromise with each other than they were here in Ganderland. Possibly that was due to Ganderland being the birthplace of the First Pair, but whatever the reason, I knew the risk was too great. The codex had to be recovered and hidden again, at least until the war was over. There was no other choice that I could see.

I focused squarely on Fitz, who returned my look and nodded slightly, his face set with determination. I could tell he had come to the same conclusion as me. "How did you learn of this?" I asked, turning back to Daughter Gernet.

"Through our spies in Cardia," Daughter Gernet responded immediately.

"Damn," I whispered as the implications of what that meant dropped on me like a stone.

"Indeed," Daughter Gernet said. She sighed. "It seems this merchant contacted the First Son with an offer to sell him the codex, with the man hinting that the information inside would be well worth it. Son Oriell was reluctant at first, believing it to be nothing but a hoax, but he was persuaded to accept the terms by an interested third party."

"And who might that party have been?" I asked, although a part of me already suspected the answer.

"I'll give you seven guesses," Daughter Gernet responded wearily.

I closed my eyes and took a deep breath. The Seven Rings. It always came back to those bastards. I focused again on the old priestess. "So, you're saying that the Seven Rings and Son Oriell are allies?" I shook my head. "It seems hard to believe, even for a man like him."

"A very ambitious man," the House Agent rumbled in a deep voice, the first words I'd heard from him.

"That he is, Guthris," Daughter Gernet agreed. "That he is indeed."

"What do you want me to do?" I asked, already knowing the answer.

Daughter Gernet leaned forward stiffy. "Why, get the codex before they do, of course. You'll have to hurry, though, for my little birds tell me a ship left Cardia over a week ago, heading south. It will take that ship at least a month, maybe more to reach the Tides of Mansware." The priestess's eyes burned. "You must reach the island first and get that codex for me. I don't know what the Seven Rings have planned for it, but I intend to wreck those plans and piss down their throats!"

I was surprised by the intensity in the old woman's voice. The First Daughter rarely let her emotions show to such a degree. "And what if the codex says something that you don't like?" I asked, thinking that no matter what her worst fears might be, they would amount to nothing compared to the actual truth.

"I will deal with that at the appropriate time," Daughter Gernet answered curtly. I didn't fail to see a shadow pass across her eyes as she spoke, and I knew that despite her ferocity, the old priestess sitting in front of me was terrified by what the codex might contain. *And well she should be,* I thought grimly. Daughter Gernet smiled, though her eyes remained hard and bright. "There is one more thing you must know, Lord Hadrack. My little whispering birds also inform me that an old friend of yours is in command of the Cardian ship."

I felt my heart skip a beat as I waited. "Who?" I finally growled when Daughter Gernet left that statement hanging in the air like wriggling bait on a hook.

"I believe you are familiar with a man named Lord Boudin, are you not?"

My insides went instantly dark at the mention of the name, the need to kill him arcing along my limbs like fire. "I am," I managed to say as I mentally forced my clenched jaw to open and close.

"Yes, I thought that might get your attention," Daughter Gernet said with a faint chuckle. "Do you accept this task that I've set for you, Lord Hadrack?" she asked, though I could tell by her demeanor that she already knew what my response would be.

"Of course I do, First Daughter," I said. I frowned as I thought about why I was here in the northeast. "But what about the king?" I asked. "He gave me clear orders to deal with the Parnuthians. I can't leave now."

Daughter Gernet waved a hand. "You leave Tyden to me. I'll deal with him and those simpering minions of his like that fat fool outside. You just focus on your mission. The Parnuthians and their ilk mean nothing when stacked against the codex. Great things are in play here, Lord Hadrack, things that even I don't understand. But what I do know is everything, and I mean *everything*, hinges on recovering that codex. Do not fail me. Now go." The priestess slumped in her seat after that, looking small and alone and utterly exhausted.

"Come," Fitz whispered to me, turning me away. "We have to prepare."

Less than a day later, I was once again standing on the aftercastle of my huge cog, *Sea-Wolf*, with the salty scent of the sea filling my nostrils and the shrill cries of seabirds hurting my ears. We had a strong wind at our backs, propelling us southward at a steady clip, which I prayed would remain with us. Daughter Gernet's spies had reported that Lord Boudin had left Cardia nine days ago from Leford, a small port city along the kingdom's northwestern coast. Putt had made a rough estimate of the man's course, using our own charts for reference. His best guess was that since the Cardians' starting point was much farther north than ours, we might even now be neck and neck with him, with only the huge continent containing Ganderland and the land of the Piths separating us. It had come down to a race to see who could get to the island first—a race that, hopefully, they knew nothing about—and one that I was determined to win at all costs.

"What do you know about the Tides of Mansware?" I asked Putt. Baine was on the rudder, which had now been elevated to the aftercastle using a complicated pulley and cog system that Hanley had devised. I neither knew nor cared how Hanley had accomplished it. All that mattered to me was that it worked and worked well, allowing me to keep a close eye on Baine. I'd lost him overboard once and had no wish to have it happen again.

"Not much, my lord," Putt admitted. "Few ships from Ganderland sail there."

"Why not?" Baine asked. My friend looked relaxed and at ease, as always happiest when at the helm of one of my ships.

Putt shrugged. "Simple mathematics," he said. "Say a merchant gets brave and sends a trading ship that way. He waits months, but the ship never returns. So, finally, he sends two more, thinking that he's just doubled his chances at success. But those poor buggers don't come back, either. Now the merchant's out three ships, not to mention tons of gold, with nothing to show for it. That's what the Tides of Mansware do. They eat ships like I eat honey cakes."

"I like honey cakes," Baine said dreamily. "Haven't had any in ages."

I frowned at my friend, then focused back on Putt. "Are you trying to tell me that no ships ever go there?" I asked, not hiding my disbelief.

"No, my lord," Putt responded. "Ships still go there, but they're mostly from Cardia. The Cardians have charted the routes to the south extensively. But even so, it's a long journey even for them and fraught with danger."

"We're not going to be dealing with pirates again, I hope?" Tyris asked from where he leaned against the gunwale." The blond archer made a face. "Because I've seen my fill of those bastards for one lifetime."

Putt shrugged. "There are some about, sure. But they'll seem like harmless children compared to the Shadow Pirates." The red-bearded sailor slapped the railing. "Don't worry. Those arse lickers will take one look at *Sea-Wolf* and go the other way, believe me."

"Are there storms then?" Baine asked, looking suddenly unhappy at the thought. I could hardly blame him for that. The horrible memories of the storm we'd all gone through on *Sea-Dragon* years ago would haunt me for the rest of my life.

"Sure enough," Putt agreed. "Like you've never seen before. They call them hurricanes in the south. It has to do with the heat, I expect. It's downright tropical where we're going, which makes for bigger storms."

"Sounds like fun," I grunted. "Anything else we should worry about?"

Putt hesitated, looking down at the deck. "Well, my lord, I've heard talk of—" He paused, scraping his boot along a greasy smear of white bird shit. "I've heard rumors about great sea monsters in the Tides of Mansware that are said to be longer even than this ship." The former outlaw lifted his hands palm outwards at the looks on our faces. "Not that I believe them, mind you. It's just tavern talk, you know. I just thought it bears mentioning."

"Oh please," Tyris snorted. He hooked a thumb at Putt and looked at me. "I think someone's been cutting into the wine, my lord."

"Maybe," I said thoughtfully. "But just the same, we'll post a man at the bow to watch the water when we get there. I'm not interested in taking any chances. Our mission is too important for that."

"Of course, my lord," Tyris said. He glanced at Putt and rolled his eyes, then headed down to the lower deck, where I saw him stop to talk with Jebido, who was still favoring his twisted ankle.

"Monsters in the water, eh?" I grunted at Putt as he came to stand beside me. I couldn't stop myself from smiling. "I've heard tales like that in every tavern I've ever been in, and so has every man on board this ship." I chuckled. "And not one of us has seen one yet."

"Quite true, my lord," Putt muttered as Baine laughed good-naturedly. "And let's pray to the gods that we never do."

Putt's worries would prove to be groundless, of course. There were no monsters to be found on our journey—at least, not in the water, anyway. No, all the monsters we were about to encounter walked upright on two legs.

Chapter 3: Sarrey

Three weeks later, I stood on *Sea-Wolf's* forecastle with Lord Fitzery. The two of us were leaning on the railing together as the ship plowed steadily through the endless waves beneath her great hull with effortless ease. We'd seen nothing for many days since the Pith lands had finally receded into the horizon—nothing but big sky and open water for as far as the eye could see.

"Damn shame about Alesia," Fitz said, glancing sideways at me. "We could have used their help."

I grunted ascent but said nothing, my mood souring as I recalled my last conversation with the Pith queen. Alesia had regretfully declined to join us in our fight against Cardia, despite our friendship and the debt she admittedly owed me for rescuing her and Einrack. The queen had her own problems trying to control a growing fracture between the various tribes right now, she'd said, and was afraid that allying with a kingdom that most of her brothers and sisters despised would do little to help that situation. It was unfortunate timing for us, but there was little that I could do about it. Hopefully, Alesia would manage to bring the Piths together soon and things would change in our favor. For now, though, except for the help of the Swales—who were weak and could only do so much—we were on our own.

I glanced upward at a seabird as it soared overhead, squawking harshly. The sky was virtually cloudless and bright blue, with no signs of any of the raging southern storms called hurricanes that Putt had warned me about. The gods had been good to us on our journey so far for a change. I felt instant discomfort settle over me at the thought, for those gods could be unpredictable bastards at the best of times. I'd learned the hard way that whatever favor they offered us mortals with one hand was usually taken back sooner or later with the other. I hoped this time would be different, though I couldn't shake the feeling that something was coming for us all—something bad.

"What's that look for?" Fitz asked cheerfully, all thoughts of the Piths forgotten. My friend was eating an apple, which was something that he never seemed to get enough of. I wasn't keen on them, preferring my food to have some meat on it. Besides, the pulp kept getting stuck in my teeth and was annoying.

"What are you talking about?" I grunted as I stared down at the water.

Fitz used his knife to cut a wedge from the apple. "You're wearing that, *I'm thinking of killing someone,* face." He grinned and popped the fruit in his mouth. "I do hope it's not me, old friend, for it's much too nice a day to die."

I grinned despite myself. Much like Baine, Fitz always seemed to have a knack for recognizing my black moods and getting me out of them. "You're safe," I assured him. "For now, anyway." I looked up at the clear sky. "But if we get rain, I'd watch your back if I were you."

Fitz laughed and cut himself another wedge. "Duly noted." He sighed and looked out to sea as he chewed. He was dressed in dark trousers and a white tunic, with his long black hair flowing in the breeze. I was surprised to see a hint of grey in his beard at the chin, since Fitz was several years younger than I was. "Do you think we're ahead of them, Hadrack?" my friend asked, looking suddenly worried.

I shrugged, hiding my own worry. "Maybe." I turned to look up at our sail, which was fully spread as a steady wind filled the dark grey canvas. That strong wind had stayed with us for most of the journey, which had surprised even an experienced seaman like Putt. No one could deny that we'd made great time—better than expected—and spirits were high. But would it be enough? My snarling wolf's banner suddenly snapped and crackled from the top of the mast ten feet above Tyris' head, where the archer's keen eyes scanned the ocean from the lookout post. The banner looked like a live beast as it danced madly in the breeze, as though the depicted wolf was eager to rip into tender flesh with its teeth and claws. Soon, I thought, thinking of Lord Boudin—soon. I turned back to my friend. "But if they've got this same wind behind them too, then only the gods know who will get there first."

"Hmmm," Fitz said in agreement. "Unfortunately, true." He spat lightly several times, then plucked a small dark seed from the tip of his tongue and examined it before tossing it overboard. "I still think we should have brought *Sea-Dragon* along with us. If we had, we would have outnumbered the Cardians by at least two to one."

I'd started to shake my head before he'd even finished talking. "No," I said. "I still had an obligation to the king. You know that." I'd left the bulk of my men behind to continue taking the fight to the Parnuthians, led by my capable captain, Wiflem Prest. I'd brought only *Sea-Wolf's* regular crew of six with me along with forty experienced fighting men and archers, although I'd initially been reluctant to allow even that many for fear of weakening Wiflem. My friends had argued for a much larger force, however, and eventually I'd relented, settling on a total amount of fifty, including myself, Jebido, Baine, and Fitz. The number would have to suffice.

"The Iron Cay," Fitz mused dryly. He flung the stripped core of the apple out into the sea with an easy snap of his wrist. "Doesn't exactly sound all that welcoming, now does it?"

I shook my head. Fitz was referring to the island where we hoped to find the codex. The merchant there who claimed to have Waldin's copy was known as The Fisherman, but that's all we knew about him. We weren't even entirely sure *where* The Iron Cay was, either, which had already given me a few sleepless nights. Putt was fairly certain he could find it, but as much as I had faith in the former outlaw's seafaring abilities, a part of me worried we might end up wasting precious days or weeks searching for the island. I had little doubt that Lord Boudin knew exactly where it was, which meant he had the advantage over us. My only hope was that because we had moved so quickly to set sail along with the favorable winds, that we were at least a few days ahead of him.

"Ho!"

Fitz and I both looked up at Tyris, who was waving his arms to get our attention. He pointed off our starboard bow, then cupped his hands around his mouth. "Something floating in the water, my lord! I can't tell what it is!"

I turned, shielding my eyes as I scanned the rolling waves, but I could see nothing. "You see anything out there?" I asked Fitz.

"Not a thing," Fitz grunted. He leaped nimbly onto the railing and steadied himself on a stay line while my men began stirring below us, drawn by Tyris' excited shouts to the starboard railings. "I think I see—something," Fitz muttered. "I'm not sure."

"Maybe it's one of Putt's sea monsters come to gobble us up," I said sarcastically. Fitz laughed as I moved to the inner railing and looked down. My eyes fell on Berwin's lanky form, and I motioned to him. "Go tell Putt to swing a few degrees to starboard. We'll see what this is."

"Yes, my lord."

Less than ten minutes later, *Sea-Wolf* slowed as the crew trimmed her sail. The object was much closer now, a dark mass bobbing on the rough waves that I guessed was perhaps ten feet wide by maybe twice that long. Whatever it was, it was clearly no sea monster.

"Is that a pile of branches on top there?" Baine asked. He and Jebido had come to join Fitz and me on the forecastle.

"Looks like it," Jebido grunted. He leaned over the railing, peering intently.

The object was now a hundred yards away, with *Sea-Wolf* slowing by the moment, yet still knifing through the water faster than I would have liked. I was afraid we might hit the thing at the rate we were moving, but Putt was steering the ship now and he'd anticipated my thoughts, swinging us with a deft hand to port, cutting our speed even more.

We finally reached the object, which was now less than fifty feet away from our starboard bow. I watched as it crested a wave precariously before plunging into the waiting trough, only to repeat the process once again. I'd thought at first that what we were looking at was simply a random pile of driftwood, but now that we were closer, I could see that it was more than that. "Looks like some kind of raft," I muttered to no one in particular.

I could see frayed ropes lashed around individual, waterlogged timbers, with many of the cords looking as if they were ready to split at any moment from the strain. The crude raft remained barely afloat, with more than half its length struggling to stay above the waterline. I grunted in surprise when some of the branches suddenly shifted, revealing a man's brown, startled face looking up at me. We locked eyes for a moment, and I saw fear register there—fear and caution.

I smiled reassuringly at the man, thinking he had probably never seen such a large ship before. I waved a hand in a friendly fashion. "It's all right. We're no danger to you. Come aboard. We have food and water."

The man hesitated and mumbled something, then slowly pushed the branches off himself. He stood shakily, wearing nothing but a soiled white loincloth as he regarded us with dark, hooded eyes. A second form emerged moments later from beneath the branches, this one wearing a tattered, yellow sarong. It was a woman, I saw, and the torn cloth wrapped around her body did little to hide her slim figure.

"By The Mother," Baine whispered in awe. "What a beauty."

"Putt!" I called out. "Lower the skiff and get those people to safety!"

"Yes, my lord!" Putt cried back as men began to scurry along the lower deck beneath his stern gaze.

I'd had a small rowboat fixed to each of my ships on a suggestion from Jebido. It was something few merchantmen had done before us, but now was becoming more and more common on most large ships like ours.

It took my well-trained crew little time to lower the boat and power themselves over to the half-submerged raft. The rest of us on board *Sea-Wolf* watched in fascinated silence as first the man—who looked lithe and strong despite his ordeal—was transferred over to it, then his companion. The woman's sarong rode up her thighs revealingly when she climbed into the rowboat, and I frowned with displeasure as several hoots and catcalls rang out from the lower deck. Jebido and I shared a glance, and I could read in his eyes the question that I was already wondering myself. Was this going to be a problem for us?

It turned out the answer to that was yes, for though we didn't know it at the time, the gods' favor had just turned in a most cruel and unfortunate way.

The girl's name was Sarrey, and her companion—Mondar—was her brother. The two had been abducted from their village by the very thing Tyris dreaded the most—pirates—but they had managed to escape by fashioning a raft. It seemed slavery was very much alive and well in this part of the world, just as it was in ours.

The two fugitives had been out on the water for roughly a week, Sarrey guessed, with little food and only what small amount of rainwater had fallen to keep them alive. Sarrey and Mondar were from a kingdom called Temba, but unfortunately, they had lost their bearings as they'd drifted on the sea and had no idea in which direction their homeland lay. Not that it would have made a difference to me if they knew, anyway, for I had no intention of deviating from our task to take them back. The brother and sister would have to remain with us, at least for the foreseeable future. There was simply no other choice.

I'd given Sarrey and her brother my cabin to use after the first day, more to keep the girl out of sight as much as possible than anything else. There were fifty men on board *Sea-Wolf*, most if not all of whom would become easily distracted and act downright stupid whenever she was close. Only Jebido seemed unaffected by the girl, and though I'd like to say that I too was immune to Sarrey's charms, sadly, that would be something of a mistruth. I loved Shana with all my heart and missed her terribly with every breath I took. Yet my beloved wife was long gone from this world, and I was still here, a strong, healthy man in the prime of his life who could not hide his admiration and appreciation for a beautiful woman—much as I wished otherwise.

I'd questioned both of the Temba about The Iron Cay's whereabouts, but neither of them had ever heard of it, much less knew where it might be. It was disappointing news, which meant I'd have to keep trusting in Putt to get us there ahead of the Cardians.

The first inkling of the trouble to come came on the second day after the rescue when Berwin and a lanky archer named Ryany began quarreling belowdecks in the hold. Jebido was the first to reach them, and he laid into the two men, tearing a strip off their hides and setting them straight, which saved me the trouble of doing it myself. I questioned him after about what had happened.

"So, what was that all about?" I asked my friend as he climbed up from the hold with his face looking flushed and angry.

"What do you think?" Jebido grunted moodily.

"I don't know," I said in an even tone. "That's why I'm asking you."

Jebido hooked a thumb over his shoulder as Berwin and Ryany emerged from the hold, both men looking properly chastised. Neither would meet my eyes before heading off to return to their duties. "Damn fools are walking around with their heads up their arses because of that girl," Jebido responded gruffly. "They look like love-struck puppies. It makes me want to be sick the way they're carrying on." He glanced at me appraisingly, his hands on his hips. "Actually, it's the same look you sometimes get when you're around her."

I blinked in surprise, thinking that I'd been doing a better job of late hiding my thoughts. "I don't give *a look*," I snapped in irritation.

"Uh-huh," Jebido muttered.

"Listen, Jebido," I said. "I know the girl and her brother are a bit of a nuisance. But short of tossing them overboard, what are we supposed to do with them?"

"Don't know," Jebido replied sullenly. "You're the lord. You figure it out."

I frowned. My friend seemed unusually on edge for some reason. "What's eating at you?" I asked.

Jebido sighed, his shoulders loosening a little. He drew me to the railing and lowered his voice. "It's that damn girl, Hadrack. There's something not right about this. Her brother, too, for that matter."

"Not right, how?"

"I don't know. I can't put my finger on it. But something doesn't add up."

"They're no threat to us," I said. "Completely harmless."

Jebido fixed me with a hard gaze. "You sure about that?"

I pursed my lips. Jebido could be cranky and irritable a lot of the time, but I'd learned from experience to trust his instincts. If he thought something was wrong with the Temba siblings, there probably was. "What are you thinking?"

"That they're lying to us," Jebido responded bluntly.

"About who they are?"

"No," Jebido said with a quick shake of his head. "Not that. I think they're lying about what they were doing alone on that raft. The whole pirate explanation just seems very contrived to me."

"Why would they lie?"

"How should I know?"

I thought about that for a moment but couldn't wrap my head around why they would feel the need to mislead us. "What do you think I should do?"

"If it were me," Jebido said, his face hard. "I'd give them a choice. Tell us the truth, or go back out on that raft."

"That's a little harsh, don't you think?"

Jebido shrugged. He patted me on the shoulder as he headed away. "What's more important at this moment, Hadrack? Those two liars or the codex?"

I sighed as I watched my friend walk briskly toward Baine and Fitz, where the two were playing dice near the mast. Jebido's ankle had mostly healed, but I could still detect a slight limp as he moved.

"Your companion seems upset. Is he all right, Lord Hadrack?"

I turned to find Sarrey standing next to me—uncomfortably close, I noticed. I waved a hand as I took a step backward, putting a little distance between us. "Don't worry about him. He's always like that."

The girl was tall, with the peak of her long, curly dark hair almost reaching my chin. She was slim and moved with an unusual grace that I'd rarely seen before, and her eyes were almond-colored and enormous. Her nose was thin and her full lips sensuous, though they were still chapped and peeled from her ordeal on the water. I guessed her to be no more than fifteen years old. Sarrey put her light-brown hands between her small, pert breasts, accenting the protruding nipples through the thin cloth she wore. We'd offered her other clothing, but the girl had insisted on wearing her sarong once it had been properly washed and repaired.

"I just wanted to express my gratitude again for what you did for us, lord," Sarrey said. "My brother and I will be eternally grateful to you and your men."

I bowed my head slightly. "It was the least we could do." I paused, thinking about what Jebido had told me. Was the girl standing in front of me lying? Was there something more sinister going on here? I glanced toward Jebido, where he now sat on a stool, his bad ankle thrust out in front of him. My friend felt my eyes on him and he looked up, his expression stern and uncompromising. I sighed.

"You have a question for me, I think, Lord Hadrack?" Sarrey said.

The words had come out in almost a purr, her voice like liquid gold. I imagined she must be a gifted singer. I pursed my lips, wondering where this was going. "Do I?" I asked vaguely.

"Of course you do, lord," Sarrey said. "You wear your doubts clearly on your face. So please, ask of me what you will."

"Very well, then," I said. I crossed my arms over my chest. "Who are you, really?"

Sarrey smiled, revealing perfect teeth. "I am who I said I am. I am Sarrey of the Temba."

"And Mondar?"

The girl hesitated for just a moment. "He is Temba also, just as I told you."

I nodded. "Did you two really escape from pirates?"

"In a manner of speaking, yes," Sarrey replied.

"What does that mean?"

"On how exactly you would define a pirate, lord."

I paused, caught off guard by the statement. Sarrey was clearly intelligent, more so than she'd initially let on. Putt had told me some of the peoples in the south could be extremely primitive and warlike, but from what I'd seen from this girl and her brother so far, it seemed the Temba were not like that. "A pirate is a person who robs and plunders others, usually for gold," I said.

"But not always just for gold, yes?" the girl asked.

"No, not always," I admitted, thinking of the Shadow Pirates.

"So, lord, would you agree for simplicity's sake that a pirate is nothing more than a person who steals, be it gold, silver, or something else?" Sarrey asked.

I could tell the girl was leading toward something, though I couldn't fathom what it was for the life of me. "Yes, I'd say that's a fair statement."

"Then yes, lord, I escaped from those that I would describe as pirates."

I waited, expecting more, but Sarrey just stared at me. I went over what she'd just said, confused about what her point might be, until a sudden thought struck me. "You just said *you escaped*. What about your brother?"

I expected Sarrey to wave that off, explaining that she'd misspoken, but the girl surprised me by smiling. "You are no fool, Lord Hadrack, and I have come to believe I can trust you."

"Trust me, how?"

"By telling you that Mondar is not really my brother," Sarrey replied, holding my gaze boldly. "He is my lover." I hesitated at that while the girl continued, "My full name is Sarrey del Fante, and I am the firstborn daughter of the King of the Temba, Alba del Fante."

I blinked in surprise. "Why didn't you tell me any of this earlier?"

"I already told you why, Lord Hadrack. We were unsure whether you could be trusted or not. Neither Mondar nor I feel this way any longer."

I took a deep breath as I thought. "So, these pirates kidnapped you, planning to ransom you to your father? Is that right?"

Sarrey laughed in amusement at the idea. "No one tried to ransom me, lord." She shook her head. "No, the pirates I speak of are my own flesh and blood, my mother and my father. They are the thieves who stole my happiness along with my heart, telling me that I must marry a man that I had never even met, let alone loved." Sarrey's face took on a fierce expression. "Mondar and I would rather die than be apart, which is why he helped me escape the Yellow Palace in the middle of the night."

"In a raft?" I asked dubiously. "Why not use a boat?"

"Because a boat can be easily seen, lord. Mondar made the raft himself and he is a fine craftsman. He knew my father's men would be searching for larger ships, not something that sits so low in the water."

"But, where did you expect to go?"

"An island chain many miles east of Temba, lord. Few go there."

"And you planned on living there alone?" I asked. "Just the two of you?"

"Yes, lord," Sarrey said, her eyes shining. I shook my head at the naivety of youth. "If not for a storm that arose suddenly and destroyed our raft," the girl added. "We would have made it, too." She shrugged. "We just drifted with the tide after that, expecting to die out on the water." Sarrey smiled sadly. "It was a fate we accepted gladly, though, because at least we'd be together at the end." The girl hesitated there, and I was certain that she was on the verge of tears. "And then you showed up in your great ship, changing that fate along with our lives."

"You should have told me all this in the beginning," I said reproachfully.

Sarrey grimaced. "My father is a rich and powerful man, Lord Hadrack, and I promise you he would pay a fortune in gold for my return. That is why we lied initially and did not tell you who I was. Since then, however, I have spoken to your crew and watched you from afar, and I know now in my heart that you are an honorable man who gives little thought to gold and rewards. That is why I am here now, telling you the truth."

"I see," I said when she'd finished. I stroked my beard while I mulled over what the girl had told me. Jebido had been right. They had been lying, just not in the way that he'd thought. The news that Sarrey was a Temba princess was unexpected, but I didn't see how it changed anything about our quest for the codex.

"I do not expect to be treated any differently now that you know the truth, lord," Sarrey said, breaking into my thoughts. "All I ask is that you take us with you on your journey, wherever you might be going."

"What of your father?" I asked. "Won't he still be searching for you?"

Sarrey's expression darkened at the mention of her father. "I imagine so, lord. But I have friends in Temba who will have given him misdirection about what happened to me. By the time he learns the truth, it will be too late, so there is nothing to worry about."

I nodded, thinking that she was probably right about that. Unfortunately, Princess Sarrey's confidence that she was free of her father forever was soon to be proven very wrong.

Chapter 4: The Iron Cay

The Iron Cay was not much to look at when we finally did reach it—nothing but harsh, unforgiving rock, hundreds of squat buildings made from sandstone and wood all crammed together, odd, bush-like trees, and white sand. Dark, moss-encrusted outcroppings rose a half mile out from a half-moon shaped bay before curving to join the mainland on either side, with the cliffs forming a natural entrance that I guessed to be about a hundred feet wide. I could make out the remnants of sun-bleached support beams on the rock faces for what must have been a wooden bridge that had at one time spanned the distance between the two cliffs. Now, there was nothing left up there to see other than a pair of tattered black and yellow pennants snapping in the steady breeze.

True to his nature, Putt had sailed us unerringly to the right place, reaching it six days after we'd found Sarrey and Mondar. That was the good news. The bad news was that as we approached the island's entrance, I could see a large cog anchored sideways in the calm waters of the bay, flying a banner that I remembered well from the Battle of Silver Valley—a charging boar on a blue background. There was also a second, much smaller cog floating behind it, I saw with dismay. I couldn't make out the smaller ship's colors, but I knew instinctively that it also belonged to the Cardians. I cursed out loud with disgust. That bastard Lord Boudin had beaten us here after all, and he'd come all this way with two ships, not one like I'd been led to believe.

"Damn the luck," Jebido grumbled. He glanced at me, his leathery face lined with worry. "We're truly buggered now, Hadrack."

I didn't bother to reply. What was there to say? He was right. Instead, I stood on the aftercastle with my balled fists on my hips and my legs spread for balance, smoldering with disappointment and anger as I glared at the island.

"What do we do, my lord?" Putt asked in a solemn voice. "Do I turn us about?"

All eyes focused on me. What to do, indeed? I hesitated, mulling over my options. I was sure Lord Boudin must have spied our ship by now, though I doubted he could make out my banner—yet—for the wind was at our backs, snapping it toward him. But soon, he would know that I was here. I wondered what he would do when he realized it was me. I knew I could lower the banner and turn away before that happened—but then what? The bastard could set sail at any time, which meant I could potentially lose him and the codex on the high seas. I took a deep breath, knowing there was little choice but to proceed. "We go in," I grunted. "This is The Fisherman's domain, not Lord Boudin's. Maybe he hasn't sold the codex to the Cardians yet and we can make a deal for it."

"Very good, my lord," Putt replied with a curt nod. "In we go."

"Lord Boudin getting here first might actually be a good thing, Hadrack," Baine said thoughtfully from where he stood with his hands on the rudder.

I glowered at him and pointed at the two anchored ships nestled close together in the distance. "How exactly is that a good thing?"

My friend grinned, a knife suddenly appearing in one hand as he steered the ship with the other. He made a quick, savage cutting motion across his neck with the gleaming blade. "Instead of trying to outbid those bastards for the codex and losing most if not all of our gold, why not just wait until they have it and then kill them and take it?"

"Just like that, eh?" I grunted. "You make it sound easy. There are two ships over there, Baine, in case you hadn't noticed. Not to mention the owner of this island just might object to such a brazen move."

Baine shrugged, looking unconcerned. "We'll deal with him too if we must. Trust me, Hadrack, this will be easy." He returned the knife to his belt. "It'll be like plucking the heads off of flowers." He laughed. "Weak Cardian flowers."

Putt began shouting at the crew to trim sail as we approached the cliffs guarding the bay. I could see strange boats moving about in the open water east of the island, each with an oddly-shaped sail that reminded me of a crab's claw. The boats had a hollowed-out hull like a canoe, with a boom at either end of that hull extending outward ten feet or so to a log that floated in the water. I realized the log worked to help stabilize the craft, keeping it from tipping over in high winds or rough seas. It was a unique and clever design, I thought absently.

I finally turned my attention back to our destination as we glided between the outcroppings and entered the bay. I noticed identical watermills sat nestled at the base of the cliffs, though neither wheel was turning. It seemed an odd place to build them to me. I shrugged it off and focused my gaze on the Cardian ship, which I saw was almost as big as *Sea-Wolf*. Her decks were freshly scrubbed, and her black hull looked recently painted, which was surprising after such a long journey. Lord Boudin kept a tidy ship, I thought grudgingly. I could see at least a dozen men dressed in dark uniforms moving briskly about on the cog's lower and upper decks. They looked sharp and wholly competent to me, which was not how I was used to seeing Cardians. I felt a twist of unease in my gut. The second ship was smaller and much more weathered but still capable of holding at least fifty men or more.

Fitz sighed from where he leaned against the railing behind me with his arms folded over his chest. "I told you we should have brought *Sea-Dragon* along," he said.

I felt my frustration bubbling to the surface at his words, and I opened my mouth to respond angrily just as a soft voice from the lower deck made me hesitate. "Lord Hadrack, may we have a word? It's important." I moved to the railing and looked down. Sarrey stood near the ladder to the aftercastle with Mondar, one hand holding her hair out of her eyes while the wind toyed with it.

"Come up," I grunted, motioning for them to join me. The two Temba climbed quickly and easily, standing before me moments later. I thought they both looked somewhat apprehensive for some reason, for neither would hold my eyes. "What is it?" I asked, trying not to show my impatience. I had bigger problems than whatever was bothering these two right now.

"Forgive me, lord," Sarrey began. "I should have told you this sooner."

"Told me what?" I growled, wary now.

"Mondar and I lied to you, lord."

I frowned. "I thought we already settled that?"

Sarrey took a deep breath. "Not just about who I was, lord." She glanced meaningfully toward the island. "Also about that."

I followed her gaze, feeling anger rising in me. "You knew where it was all this time?"

"Yes, lord," Mondar replied. The man's voice was deep and pleasant, despite his obvious distress. I'd found myself growing to like and respect him as we'd gotten to know each other better on the journey. He shook his head regretfully. "We are truly sorry for misleading you, lord. *Hisbaros Raboros* is known to all in the southern lands."

"*Hisbaros Raboros*?"

"The Iron Cay in our ancient language, lord."

"I see," I said. "And you lied to me about this why?"

"I will let my Princess explain, lord," Mondar said, lowering his eyes.

"Mondar," Sarrey admonished him, slapping the man gently on the bicep. "I am a princess no longer. You would do well to remember this."

"You will always be a princess in my heart, my love," Mondar replied seriously.

Sarrey rolled her eyes, though she couldn't hide her smile of pleasure as she turned her gaze back on me. "I understand you have business with The Fisherman, lord. Is this true?"

"It is," I agreed.

"I thought as much," Sarrey said gravely, her eyes now filled with warning. "He is a hard man, lord. A man you must tread carefully around."

"Fair enough," I muttered. "But that doesn't explain why you lied to me."

Sarrey sighed. "Because my father and The Fisherman are lifelong friends, lord, and I have met him before. He would surely know me if he saw me. This is why we said nothing. Mondar and I had hoped that you would not be able to find this place and the danger to us would be gone." She lowered her eyes. "It was selfish of us, and I beg your forgiveness."

I nodded, understanding now. "You have it," I grunted, knowing I probably would have done the same thing in their place.

"Thank you, lord," Sarrey said in obvious relief.

The Temba stood together in silence, holding hands. They still looked frightened and miserable despite my offer of forgiveness. It was hard for me not to feel sorry for them. "So tell me," I said in a gentler tone. "What's this Fisherman like?"

"Tough, but fair, lord," Sarrey replied. "But also a man that you do not wish to cross."

"Will he listen to what I have to say?" I asked.

Both the Temba nodded together, although I could tell by the way the girl kept glancing toward the harbor as we drew closer that she was becoming more anxious by the moment. "He will, lord," Sarrey said. "The rules of *Hisbaros Raboros* are clear. All may enter without fear of violence while doing business on the island. None are given preferential treatment, regardless of status. Not even my father, despite being a king and a valued friend." Sarrey frowned. "Troublemakers are dealt with quite severely, lord. Staked out on Bone Beach for the crabs to feast upon, so be warned."

I smiled at that news. I might not be able to touch Lord Boudin while we were here, but he couldn't do anything to me, either. It was a fair deal that I could live with—for now, anyway.

What happened after we left this place was another matter, though, for Lord Boudin was one of the Seven Rings I'd sworn to kill. But before that happy moment arrived, I'd first have to convince The Fisherman to sell the codex to me rather than the Cardians.

"Is there anything else I need to know about this man?" I asked.

"No, lord," Mondar said. "Just be careful and remember that he is a businessman above all else." The Temba licked his lips, looking uneasily at the shore. "Now, if there is nothing else, lord, I need to get Sarrey out of sight before we get much closer. If someone recognizes her, there could be—"

"Of course," I said. "Go back to the cabin and stay there until we leave. I'll have food and water and whatever else you might need brought to you."

"Thank you, lord," Sarrey said humbly. "I am truly sorry we were untruthful with you."

I crossed my arms over my chest, my expression firm. "Are there any more lies I should know about?"

"No, lord," the girl said with a firm shake of her head. "I swear it."

"Then that's all I need to hear," I replied, believing her. "You can go now."

Sarrey turned for the ladder, then hesitated. "Remember, lord, The Fisherman respects men of strength and daring. He does not suffer fools easily."

"I understand, Sarrey," I said, grinning. I'd never met a Cardian yet who wasn't a fool in one way or another. "I'll do my best not to disappoint him then."

Once Sarrey and Mondar were safely tucked away, I had my Wolf's Teeth take up positions on the forecastle just in case of trouble, though I made sure their bows were kept well out of sight. Putt instructed the crew to drop sail, then set them to work at the oars along with the remainder of my men.

Putt glanced at me, then pointed to the west, far from the Cardians. "Seems like good anchorage over there, my lord."

I hesitated. The former outlaw was right, of course, it was a good spot. But Sarrey's words came back to me just then—*The Fisherman respects a man of strength and daring*. I wondered for a moment how far that respect could be pushed as I studied the Cardian cog. I could see only a few figures on her decks. Were the bulk of the crew ashore? Did they have archers? I shifted my focus to the mainland, where a jetty built of small stones and larger rocks jutted out into the water. A group of figures stood at the edge of the dock watching us, with a tall man standing prominently under a canopy held by two other men. The Fisherman, I guessed. I'd been afraid the man offering the codex for sale might actually turn out to be Malo, but the House Agent was far shorter than this man and much stockier. I took a deep breath, realizing that I had an interested audience. I knew the prudent thing to do right now would be to enter the bay quietly and simply anchor. But doing the prudent thing had rarely been my style, and I saw no reason to change that fact now.

I finally shook my head at Putt. "No, sail us directly toward that bastard's ship," I grunted, motioning to the black cog. The former outlaw looked at me quizzically. "How quickly can we turn this thing?" I asked him.

Putt frowned. "Turn her, my lord?"

"Yes," I said. I glanced at the Cardian ship. "Once we get close to them. Can it be done without hitting them?"

"It's risky, my lord," Putt said doubtfully. "Any number of things could go wrong." He scratched at his beard. "But, that said, we'll certainly have better control by using the oars. I wouldn't want to try such a thing under sail."

I glanced at Baine and he grinned back, his eyes alight with mischief. "How close are you thinking, Hadrack?"

I smiled. "Close enough to make those turd-suckers piss themselves. Can you do it?"

Baine laughed and motioned to the rowers on the lower deck. "As long as they do their part, I'll do mine."

"Putt?" I asked, turning to the former outlaw.

Putt made a face as he checked the distance between the black ship and us. Finally, he nodded grimly. "We can do it, my lord," he said firmly. "I can't guarantee just how close we'll be when it's all said and done, but we'll do our best."

"Good enough," I grunted, pleased. "Then get to it."

Putt hurried down to the lower deck, shouting his instructions to the rowers before returning to the aftercastle. I waited, feeling the thrill of action coursing through my veins. It had been too long without any excitement. I knew the timing of this maneuver would have to be perfect, for the men on the port side of the hull would need to reverse their rowing at the exact right moment, while those on her starboard would need to double their efforts if we wanted to pull this off.

I glanced across the ship toward my Wolf's Teeth, who remained at their stations. "No one lifts a weapon against the Cardians without my order," I called to them. "No matter what happens. Am I clear?"

"Clear, my lord!" my archers roared.

"This is going to be fun, Hadrack!" Baine said with an excited laugh.

I patted my friend on the shoulder before moving to the railing beside Jebido and Fitz. I leaned my forearms on the smooth wood as Putt increased the beat of the oarsmen, knifing *Sea-Wolf* faster and faster toward the Cardian cog. We weren't moving nearly as quickly as we might have under wind power, but still fast enough to be seen as a threat, especially with the heavy, steel-plated ram affixed to *Sea-Wolf's* bow. Several black-clad men on the Cardian cog were leaning on the forecastle railing and pointing at us. I could only imagine what they were saying to each other.

"You sure this is wise?" Jebido asked me out of the corner of his mouth.

"What do you mean?" I asked innocently. I glanced toward The Fisherman, who remained motionless like a statue, certain I could feel his eyes on me. I shrugged. "I'm just a simple customer looking to anchor his ship, Jebido. The Cardians don't own the bay, last I looked. And if Lord Boudin takes issue with my berthing so close to him, that's his problem, not mine."

"You certainly do have a pair of balls on you, Hadrack," Fitz said, shaking his head with admiration. "I'll give you that. Let's just hope that big sack of yours doesn't get us all killed today."

I looked up at the sky, which had clouded over in recent minutes. "Well, it looks like rain might be on the way," I said. "Wasn't it you who told me you didn't want to die on a nice sunny day?"

Fitz chuckled and loosened his sword in its scabbard. "That I did, my friend. That I did."

Making a good first impression on The Fisherman was imperative to my plans, and starting a war on his doorstep did not seem the best way to do that. But sailing meekly into the harbor with my tail between my legs like a beaten dog didn't sit well with me either—especially with him watching. I wanted to send a message to The Fisherman and the Cardians that the Wolf of Corwick Castle had arrived—and that he was not a man to be taken lightly. Besides, if my actions somehow caused Lord Boudin's men to do something rash, like attack us, then all the better. The trick afterward would be ensuring things didn't get too out of hand. I still had a codex to purchase.

"Rowers, on my word!" Putt cried, lifting his right arm. He waited then, biting his lips as we bore down on the Cardian ship.

Our bow was aimed directly at the enemy's stern, and I could see the men in black scurrying around her decks in desperation now, certain that we were going to ram them. First, the Cardians' raised the anchor, and then a few random oars appeared from her dark hull. I chuckled as the wooden blades began to move sluggishly in the water, for there were far too few to accomplish much of consequence. That ship wasn't going anywhere fast.

"Hadrack," Jebido grunted, pointing to the aftercastle.

A man had come to stand there, his hands grasping the railing as he stared across the water at me—a man dressed in the black robes of a Son.

Two hulking House Agents stood behind the priest and I felt a moment of doubt, but it was too late as Putt cried out, "Now!"

The rowers on the portside instantly reversed their paddling, even as those on the starboard side kept up their furious pace. The big cog began to turn sluggishly, fighting the move as Baine heaved hard on the rudder with all he had. I looked over at the Cardian ship, which loomed larger by the moment. Our deadly ram was now aimed at an angle toward her center, only turning away one torturous degree at a time in an agonizingly slow fashion. I guessed less than a hundred feet separated the two vessels now, and I cursed, thinking that Putt had waited too long and we were going to strike them in the bow.

I could hear shouts of warning coming from my Wolf's Teeth and screams of dismay from the Cardians as we bore down on the ship, with several of the black-clad sailors leaping overboard in anticipation of a collision. But then, suddenly, *Sea-Wolf's* great stern began to finally swing about with more confidence while the water in the bay beneath her frothed white and angry all along the hull's length. The waves were working with us now, I realized just as the ship heeled suddenly. I grabbed the railing to keep my balance while *Sea-Wolf* shuddered and rocked beneath me and the rhythmic thud of our oars contacting the Cardian ship's hull filled my ears.

"Push off, you lazy bastards!" Putt's voice roared.

I could hear the rowers grunting with effort as they used the square blades of the oars likes poles, pushing us away from the enemy ship. We drifted backward slowly until there was more than a forty-foot gap between the two great cogs, and finally satisfied,

Putt ordered the anchor lowered. *Sea-Wolf* calmed and her hull settled flat in the water as I sighed with relief. We'd made it.

I let my eyes roam over the enemy ship—which I saw was named *Spearfish*. I could see none of the sparse crew now, guessing that they were hiding below decks, anticipating we would board them. I focused my gaze on the aftercastle, where the robed priest still stood, protected by his House Agents. The man's lips were set in a frozen circle of astonishment, but his ugly face was one that I unfortunately, knew well.

"Damn," Jebido whispered.

It was First Son Oriell.

Chapter 5: The Fisherman

"You should let me go with you," Jebido grumbled. "It's too risky going over there alone."

"I won't be alone," I muttered as I brushed at my clothing in what I knew was already a losing battle. "Fitz will be with me."

I figured my boots and dark trousers were passable enough, but the white tunic I wore had stains under the armpits and a tear at the elbow, not to mention a stubborn spot of black pitch on the right breast that refused to surrender to the wet brush I held. I realized my scrubbing was only making things worse, and finally, I sighed in resignation, admitting defeat. I knew I couldn't go to this thing wearing my armor, so The Fisherman and his other dinner guests would have to accept me the way that I was.

"Just Fitz, huh?" Jebido grunted doubtfully. "Are you sure that's a good idea?"

"Don't worry," Fitz said with a wink. "I'll take care of him, Jebido. You have my word."

An hour ago, the young lord had looked just as dirty and disheveled as the rest of us did after spending the last month on board *Sea-Wolf*. But now, I swore Fitz could have attended the king's court and no one would have thought anything of it. Somehow, he'd managed to bathe, clean his clothes, and groom his hair until it shined before tying it back with a fancy black ribbon. Even the man's beard was oiled and combed, I noticed with envy. I couldn't fathom how he'd been able to make the transformation so quickly and easily while I struggled to look even halfway presentable. It was hugely annoying.

"I've been taking care of Hadrack since before you figured out how to piss properly through that little cock of yours," Jebido replied sourly, giving Fitz a dark look.

"And you've mostly done a decent job of it, too," Fitz agreed with a condescending smile. He patted Jebido on the shoulder, ignoring my friend's look of distaste. "But now it's time to let someone else handle the heavy lifting for a change." Fitz's smile widened. "You're not as young as you used to be, you know."

I sighed again, trying to ignore them as I turned to Baine. "How do I look?"

"Which answer do you most want to hear?" Baine asked critically.

"The truthful one," I grunted.

"Like a scoundrel and a killer," Baine replied. He grinned. "But you never know. There might be some ladies ashore who like that sort of thing."

"I'm not going to that man's house to meet ladies," I growled. "I'm going there to get the codex."

"True," Baine conceded. "But I always say it's best to be prepared for every eventuality."

I nodded, not having considered there might be women at this dinner that The Fisherman had invited me to attend. That invitation had come by way of messenger, and I had yet to officially meet my host, which was something that I'd been greatly looking forward to—until Baine had mentioned the fairer sex, anyway. I grimaced, feeling butterflies twirling in my stomach now. I'd always dealt with men fairly well, for I usually understood their motivations and what they were thinking. But women—especially highborn ones—almost always baffled me, for their thoughts usually made no sense to me whatsoever. Even my dear Shana would leave me tongue-tied and shaking my head in befuddlement half the time. I'd been a lord for many years now and should be used to it, I knew, but truthfully, I still had the heart of a peasant and preferred being around those like me. I swallowed nervously, my eagerness to get on with things now dampened.

"Oh, stop looking so glum, Hadrack," Baine said with a chuckle. "You'd think I'd just told you your favorite hound had died." My friend began rolling up the sleeve of my tunic until the tear was hidden, then did the same for the other side. He stepped back to look at me. "There, that's better. It's a little crude but still fashionable enough, I suppose. A shame about that pitch, though."

Putt handed me my sword, and I took a deep breath, nodding to him as I belted the weapon around my waist. It was almost time. "If it pleases you, my lord," Putt said, holding out his open palm. "It was my sister's. I never go anywhere without it. I'd be honored if you wore it tonight."

I looked at the silver broach in his hand, which depicted a rearing horse with a strange horn jutting out between its eyes. I'd never seen anything like it before.

"May I, my lord?" Putt asked, motioning toward the black smudge on my breast. I nodded gratefully and waited as the former outlaw pinned the broach on me, hiding most of the smear.

"Thank you, Putt," I said after the man had stepped back.

"My pleasure, my lord," Putt said, beaming.

Fitz and Jebido had mercifully stopped arguing behind me by now, and I turned to them with a smile, feeling a little more confident with the elegant broach on my chest.

Fitz studied me critically. "You're going like that, Hadrack?"

I felt my smile slip away and regarded my friend coldly. "Do I have any other choice?" I responded gruffly.

Fitz bit his lower lip as he looked me up and down, then finally shook his head. "No, I guess you don't."

I was by far the biggest man on board the ship, and even if one of my men, by some miracle, had better clothing than I did to lend me, I knew it would still be much too small for me. We'd been in a hurry to leave Ganderland a month ago, and I hadn't given much thought to the clothing I was bringing along at the time. Now I wished that I had.

"Do you think that priest will be there?" Fitz asked with a look of distaste.

"I imagine so," I said.

With all the commotion around the two ships earlier that day, I'd been convinced the man on the aftercastle was Son Oriell. But on closer examination of his face just before the House Agents had whisked him away, I realized I was mistaken. The First Son was old and totally bald now, while this man was still young, with a full head of brown, fuzzy hair. But even so, the similarity between the men was too striking to be a coincidence. I wondered if the priest I'd seen was a younger brother of Son Oriell's or perhaps a cousin or some other relative. I made a face at that thought, remembering that sniveling worm, Son Jona, who had been Son Oriell's nephew if I remembered correctly.

"Lord," Tyris said, cutting into my thoughts. "The boat is on the way."

"Thank you, Tyris." I turned to Jebido. "No one sleeps while I'm gone," I told him, though I knew it wasn't necessary. Jebido was well aware of what needed to be done. I realized I was just talking to hear my own voice, preparing myself for what was coming. "And keep a close eye on those Cardian bastards over there," I added in a growl.

"Don't worry, Hadrack," Jebido replied. "I'll see to everything."

I glanced to my right, where I studied the dark hulk of *Spearfish* floating serenely in the waning light. Men were moving about on her deck less than fifty feet away from *Sea-Wolf*, and I could hear faint murmuring as the Cardian sailors talked among themselves. I was pretty sure none of them would sleep this night, either. I wondered for the hundredth time if I'd made the right move or a colossal blunder by anchoring so close to them. Jebido had told me that it was best to keep your enemies nearby so you could keep an eye on them, which I'd done, though I reflected I might have taken his words a little too literally this time.

I heard a sharp whistle coming from the water and moved to the portside, where a long, narrow boat like the ones I'd seen earlier that day glided easily over the calm, glass-like waters toward *Sea-Wolf*. My ride had nearly arrived.

"Remember," I said, glancing at Baine and Jebido. "Stay alert."

"And just how are we supposed to know if you get into trouble over there?" Jebido asked, his voice heavy with disapproval.

I grinned in the semi-darkness. "You'll know, my friend. Trust me, you'll know." I turned to Fitz. "Ready?"

"I can't wait," Fitz said. "I wonder what they'll be serving for dinner? I do hope it's not codfish. I've had my fill of that in recent weeks."

"Mondar told me it will probably be lobster," I said as Tyris flung a rope ladder over *Sea-Wolf's* side. "It's apparently a delicacy in these parts."

Fitz grimaced. "Lobsters are for peasants," he grumbled.

I shrugged and threw a leg over the railing onto the ladder's first rung. "I'm pretty sure the fare The Fisherman serves is the least of our problems right now, Fitz."

"Says the man with an iron stomach who will eat anything," Fitz muttered as he followed close behind me. "But I have a delicate palate, Hadrack. I'm not some burping, farting barbarian, you know."

I climbed down the ladder, ignoring Fitz now as I stepped carefully into the bow of the odd boat, which wobbled beneath my weight. A man with a close-cropped black beard was sitting on the middle bench, staring at me, while a second man stood at the back, holding a long pole. A glowing lantern sat at his feet, giving off faint light.

"Lord Hadrack, I presume?" the bearded man said in a cultured voice. I detected a note of amusement on his face as he regarded my clothing. I nodded, feeling my face flush and glad for the shadows as he gestured for me to sit on a bench facing him. I did so, while behind me Fitz climbed down, then squeezed in alongside me. The bearded man glanced at the young lord, a question on his face.

"This is Lord Fitzery," I explained. "He will be joining us tonight."

"Ah, of course," the seated man said, looking unsurprised. "How wonderful." He snapped his fingers without turning around, waiting with a faint smile on his handsome face as our pilot expertly guided the boat back toward the shore. "And my name is Alfaheed," the bearded man stated, bowing his head slightly. "I am at your service, lord."

"Alfaheed," I said thoughtfully. "That's an odd name."

"As is Lord Hadrack," Alfaheed responded, flashing white teeth. "Perhaps we are both odd men, then, no?"

"Perhaps we are at that," I said with a faint laugh. I felt my confidence building. This was already going well.

"Are you from around these parts, my good man?" Fitz asked in a cheerful voice.

"No, Lord Fitzery," Alfaheed said. "I am Temba. My lands lie many miles from here to the southwest." Fitz and I shared a look, which I could tell Alfaheed had not missed. "You know of this place?" he asked, focusing on me.

I paused, collecting my thoughts as the hypnotic sounds of our pilot propelling us along the water filled my ears. "I've heard of it," I said cautiously. "I'm told it's a beautiful place."

"Ha!" Alfaheed said with a snort, slapping his knee. "Then someone has been feeding you a lie, lord. Temba is many things, but beautiful is not one of them—at least, not in the way I think you mean. No, Temba is a harsh and cruel place to live, lord, which I suppose in its own right can be beautiful."

"How do you mean?" I asked, trying to look interested. Jebido had told me many times that people liked to talk about themselves, and while they were doing so, sometimes they offered up information that you might not have gotten otherwise.

"Ah," Alfaheed said with a sigh. "Everything there can kill you, lord, be it tigers, lions, spiders, giant hornets, or even the puffer fish in our waters. Nowhere is safe in Temba, yet, even so, I yearn to return there with every breath I take."

"I see," I said. "Then why don't you?" I glanced past Alfaheed, noticing we were already almost halfway to the jetty.

Alfaheed's features darkened for the briefest of moments before his smile returned. "Because I serve The Fisherman, lord, and it is his wish for me to remain here by his side. That is how it is, and that is how it shall be."

I nodded, hoping I could learn more about our host. "Tell me about him. What kind of man is he?"

"The Fisherman?" Alfaheed asked. He chuckled. "That, lord, is something every visitor to The Iron Cay must discover for themselves. It is not for me to say."

"I think you mean, *Hisbaros Raboros*," Fitz cut in with a laugh.

Alfaheed's easy-going manner switched instantly, and he stared at the young lord suspiciously. "How is it that you know this name?" he demanded.

Fitz paused, and I could tell by his expression that he realized he'd just made a mistake. "I heard it somewhere," he said vaguely. He shrugged. "Some fishermen we met on our journey told it to me, I think."

"Ah," Alfaheed said after a moment, his face relaxing somewhat. "I understand." He turned his eyes to me—eyes that I could not fail to see had still not lost their hardness or suspicion. "And what is your business here, lord, if I may ask?"

"I think that is something to be discussed between The Fisherman and me," I said. I smiled, matching his hard look with mine. "No offense meant, of course."

"I understand, lord," Alfaheed replied. "No offense taken."

We rode the rest of the way in silence, with the good feelings I'd felt at the beginning of the journey now gone, replaced by a sense of unease. How big a gaff had Fitz just made, and what would be the repercussions of it? I didn't know for certain, though my gut told me I'd have to be doubly careful now in what I said and did. I felt Fitz nudge me slightly with his elbow, though he didn't look my way. I knew it was his way of apologizing.

"And here we are, Lord Hadrack," Alfaheed said, gesturing past me. I turned as the boat's bow scraped loudly against the stone of the jetty. "Would you and Lord Fitzery care to do the honors?"

"Of course," I said. I stood and leaped onto dry land, followed by Fitz, and together, we pulled the odd craft higher up out of the water.

"My thanks, lords," Alfaheed said when he joined us. I glanced at the pilot, who was a short man with a wide, grey mustache. He wouldn't meet my eyes. "Now, gentlemen," Alfaheed continued. "If you will kindly follow me, please? The Fisherman's house is not far."

"Will others be joining us for the feast, Alfaheed?" Fitz asked as we walked along a narrow street. Few people were about, I saw, and those that were refused to look our way. I was glad for my sword, though I had to force myself not to rest my hand on the hilt.

Alfaheed chuckled, his easy-going manner back now as he walked briskly. "The Fisherman has the longest table on the island, my friends, and I have never seen a chair empty for a meal since I arrived here."

"Ah," I grunted, trying to hide my disappointment. "It's always good to meet new people."

"Indeed, lord," Alfaheed replied.

Less than ten minutes later, we reached the top of a winding hill, pausing in front of a large, three-story house. A stone wall that rose slightly higher than my waist separated the property from the road. Several carriages were waiting in the circular driveway, with the drivers chatting together in a small group. Those drivers also refused to look at us as Alfaheed led Fitz and me up a wide stone staircase and into a brightly lit entrance hall. Our boots echoed loudly on the black and white tiled floor, and I paused, waiting uncomfortably as Alfaheed snapped a finger at a servant, instructing her to tell The Fisherman that we had arrived. I could hear the unmistakable sounds of laughter—both male and female—coming from somewhere deeper within the house. I swallowed, trying to control my growing nervousness.

"Gentlemen," Alfaheed said, giving a slight bow. "I am afraid the rules of the house are quite firm." He glanced at Wolf's Head, then held out his hand. "No weapons are allowed beyond this point. They will be returned to you upon your departure, of course."

I hesitated and shared a look with Fitz but saw no way around this. I reluctantly unbuckled my sword, handing it to Alfaheed while Fitz did likewise.

"Thank you, lords," Alfaheed said. "I will guard these as if they were my own. Now, if you will excuse me, I have other duties to attend to. I hope you enjoy your stay here on the island."

"Thank you, Alfaheed," I said. "It was a pleasure meeting you."

"And you, lords," Alfaheed said before turning on his heel and disappearing down a corridor.

"Now what?" I grunted, feeling naked without Wolf's Head on my hip.

"I guess we wait," Fitz said, looking maddeningly at ease. He started to hum and I frowned at him. "Relax, Hadrack," Fitz said with an exaggerated sigh. He lowered his voice. "You've been through this kind of thing a hundred times at King's Court. Just remember to smile a lot and say things like, *That's very interesting*, and *Please tell me more* when these fops start talking to you. They'll eat it up like pudding."

"That's the best advice you can give me?" I whispered back.

Fitz grinned. "That and try not to drink too much." He snapped his fingers. "Oh, and if you can, do your best not to look as if you want to kill someone. That generally spoils a party."

"My dear Lord Hadrack, this is truly an honor!"

I looked up to see the man known as The Fisherman approaching. He was very tall, with wide shoulders, short blond hair turning grey, and a powerful neck. The Fisherman held out his hand to me, and I automatically took it, surprised by the strength of the calloused palm in mine. The Fisherman squeezed hard, and I pressed right back, not reacting except for a faint grin. I knew this game well, and it was one I was born to play. He and I held that pose for a long moment, with his light blue eyes searching my almost gray ones. Our host had to look up at me, despite his height, and finally, he grunted and nodded to himself grudgingly as if affirming some suspicion he'd had.

The Fisherman released my hand and stepped back, his arms hanging loosely at his sides. He flicked his eyes to Fitz. "And Lord Fitzery as well. This night is getting better by the moment."

"Thank you," Fitz said, bowing from the waist. "Lord Hadrack and I are grateful for the invitation on such short notice. It's most decent of you, sir."

"Bah," The Fisherman said with a wave of his hand. "Think nothing of it. There's always plenty of room at my table for a few more mouths." He turned and gestured down the corridor Alfaheed had taken. "Now, if you would care to join me in the library, there are a few people I'd like you to meet before we dine."

"Of course," Fitz said with an easy grace. "Do lead the way, sir."

The Fisherman nodded, heading down the corridor at a brisk walk, his hands now clasped behind his back. Fitz grinned at me and I gave him a black look, feeling like a fish out of water as together, we followed after our host. We turned left into a small sitting room, then through an open doorway from where I could hear the deep murmur of male voices.

"Gentlemen," The Fisherman said as the talking ceased at our entrance. "It gives me great please to introduce you to Lord Hadrack and Lord Fitzery of Ganderland."

There were six men in the room, most with some form of drink in their hands. I felt their eyes probing me and I nodded politely, trying to keep my expression neutral when I saw Lord Boudin among them. He'd been a young man the last time I'd seen him—younger than I'd been. I remembered he'd had massive shoulders even then, but now he looked positively monstrous. His hair was still black and looked as I remembered, but his beard was longer now, with twin patches of gray at the corners of his chin. A formidable man, I realized grudgingly.

I felt The Fisherman's hand on my elbow, guiding me deeper into the room that smelled of dust, mildew, candle smoke, sweat, and cured leather. "I believe you are acquainted with Lord Boudin of Cardia, are you not, Lord Hadrack?"

"I am," I said, allowing The Fisherman to plant me in front of the Cardian. I could tell by his expression that my host was enjoying himself as Lord Boudin and I eyed each other warily.

The Fisherman snapped his fingers. "Ah, that's right. That silly little thing years ago at Silver Valley. That's where you met, is it not?"

"It was, Your Grace," Lord Boudin said. I tried not to show my surprise at the odd title. The Cardian smiled as he flicked his hard gaze back to me. "Lord Hadrack used trickery to get me to surrender to him because he was clearly outmatched. It's hard to forget such a thing."

"I imagine so," The Fisherman said with a chuckle. "But that was then, and this is now, eh?"

"Indeed, Your Grace," the Cardian said. His voice was low, almost bored sounding, just as I remembered it. But there was no boredom in the man's eyes as he stared at me—only hatred.

"Lord Boudin was a young man and quite inexperienced back then," I said. "Making a fool out of him was never my intent." I paused, leaving the words hanging in the air and savoring the moment. I smiled as crimson rose along the Cardian's neck, then looked away and bowed my head to The Fisherman. "But I play to win, Your Grace." I glanced again at Lord Boudin. "In everything I do."

"Of course you do, Lord Hadrack," The Fisherman laughed. He waved an arm at the other men, who were listening to our conversation intently. "As do we all. Why would anyone conceive of playing any game if they expected to lose it in the end?"

"Why indeed," I said softly. A large man of about forty, going soft in the belly, pressed a tankard of dark ale in my hand, then offered another to Fitz. I nodded to him gratefully, then took a sip, still holding Lord Boudin's eyes over the metal rim. I hoped he could read the message I was sending him in my glare—*I'm going to kill you, you bastard.*

"Ah, my old friend," The Fisherman said to the fat man. He grimaced. "How rude of me. I should have offered my new guests refreshment."

"A small thing," the fat man rumbled, waving it off. "You have done the same and more for me in the past." He winked. "And hopefully will again soon."

"We'll see," The Fisherman said with a chuckle. He turned to me. "My old friend, here, arrived not long before you did, Lord Hadrack. Sadly, his beloved daughter was stolen from him and he's been searching for her ever since. He has come to ask for my assistance in locating her, which I will gladly give."

I froze with the tankard halfway to my lips. I didn't dare look in Fitz's direction, praying my friend hadn't let his surprise show. "I hope you find her, Your Grace," I managed to mumble.

"Oh, we will," The Fisherman said, his features hardening. "And woe to the man who took her." Our host turned to the fat man then. "Fear not, Your Highness, we will get Princess Sarrey back. You have my word."

I felt a horrible sinking feeling ripping at my guts as I stared at Alba del Fante, King of the Temba and Sarrey's father. What had I just gotten us into? I closed my eyes, thinking the gods truly must be laughing at me somewhere right now—the mischievous, arrogant bastards.

Chapter 6: The Codex

The woman sitting to my right—Lady Burga Rysor—just might be the most boring person I'd ever met, I reflected ruefully as she prattled on about some second cousin she had that was born with six toes on each foot. As if I cared after the shock I'd just been given in the library. Fitz was sitting across from me at least eight feet away, for the table we sat at truly was just as monstrous as Alfaheed had claimed. My friend kept glancing my way, his expression clearly sympathetic to my plight. There was little he could do about it, though, from where he sat wedged in between an old man who dozed off repeatedly and a young girl of twelve or so with an unfortunate overbite.

"And the poor boy can't even find proper shoes that fit him," Lady Rysor said with a sniff. "They have to be specially made. Can you imagine such a dreadful thing, Lord Hadrack?"

"No, my lady, I surely can't," I said dutifully. I sighed inwardly, remembering Fitz's advice. "That's very interesting. Please, tell me more about this unfortunate lad."

I focused on the bright red, steaming lobster in front of me after that as Lady Rysor chattered on happily. I'd watched the other diners first to learn what to do and grabbed the thing by the head and tail, ignoring the heat as I twisted. I was barely listening to the woman beside me now as I imagined it was her jowly neck caught between my strong fingers. The two parts separated after some work, and I set the head down, then placed the tail between my cupped hands and squeezed. I heard a satisfying crack, flipped the tail over, and, after carefully positioning my thumbs, I pressed down hard. I heard another sharp snap, then was gratified to see a mass of white meat emerge and fall onto my plate. I set the carcass aside, then took a strip of the flesh and popped it into my mouth. I was surprised at how tender and sweet it was. This didn't taste anything like peasant food as Fitz had claimed.

"Oh, goodness, lord," Lady Rysor gasped. "That's no way to treat such a fine lobster." She motioned to a small wooden bowl filled with drawn butter. "You must always dip the meat first, dear."

"Oh, I see," I said. I did as she suggested, aware that melted butter was dripping on my beard as I ate and not caring. The food was intoxicatingly good. "Much better," I said with a nod to my companion.

"Of course, it is, lord," Lady Rysor said with another sniff. She shook her head. "You northerners are such strange people. It's a wonder you've managed to survive this long."

"I can't argue with that, my lady," I grunted.

"I was in Ganderland once for The Walk," the man to my left announced. He was tall and razor thin, with a few wisps of white hair on his age-spotted scalp and a long beard and mustache dripping butter. His name was Lord Fairlot, a Parnuthian, I remembered. The man grimaced. "We took the northern route and landed at Taskerbery Castle. Do you know it, Lord Hadrack?"

"I do, lord," I said politely. If the old bastard knew we were at war with his kingdom at the moment, he gave no sign of it. "It's on the east coast," I added. Mentioning the castle made me think of Wiflem, and I wondered how he was faring against the Parnuthians. The invaders had taken Taskerbery Castle first when they'd landed, and I truly hoped my captain had taken it back by now and killed every last one of the bastards.

"Ah, The Walk," Lady Rysor said loudly to Lord Fairlot, leaning forward so she could see past me. "I've always wanted to go but never had the chance. Was it quite difficult, lord?"

The old man stared at the high, vaulted ceiling above us where a giant candelabra hung. I'd counted over fifty candles on the thing before finally giving up. The lord's eyes took on a faraway look. "It was an interesting ordeal," he finally said with a tremor in his voice. I was surprised to see tears on his cheeks as he returned his attention to his plate.

 I continued to eat enthusiastically while both my companions fell mercifully silent beside me. I let my eyes roam around the room as I chewed. There were perhaps forty guests seated at the table, with a blur of servants scurrying back and forth around us like flies, buzzing as they refilled wine mugs and brought an endless supply of food. I wondered what this feast must be costing The Fisherman. Thinking of the man, I glanced to the head of the table, where he sat like a conquering king. The actual king—Sarrey's father—was seated to his right, while Lord Boudin sat to his left. I saw with dismay that the Cardian and The Fisherman were talking with their heads pressed close together. I growled low in my chest in frustration, wondering what lies that shit-eating bastard was saying to our host.

 I felt eyes on me and shifted my gaze five chairs across from me to where the Son I'd seen earlier sat. I'd learned his name was Son Gylex, but that was all. We'd yet to speak, though I expected that would change at some point this night. The priest nodded slightly as he caught my eye, and I nodded back to him politely before looking away. I thought it was uncanny how much he looked like First Son Oriell as a younger man, and I was even more convinced now that he must be a relative. I'd been surprised that so far, no one had mentioned the stunt I'd pulled earlier that day with *Sea-Wolf*, though I expected that also would change sooner or later.

 I spent the next hour eating a second lobster and drinking small amounts of wine while saying as little as possible to my companions on either side of me. Conversation with anyone else but them was virtually impossible, as the noise from so many people talking all at once was deafening. Eventually, after we'd all been treated to a delicious gingerbread soaked in hot sauce, people began to rise and leave. I was overwhelmingly relieved when Lady Rysor finally exclaimed that she'd never eaten so much in one sitting and had to go home or risk exploding. I glanced at the many layers of fat that her clothing couldn't hide, guessing she was probably lying about the eating part.

I stood, unsure what to do now until I saw Fitz motioning me over to him. He leaned closer to me, putting his lips to my ear. "The Fisherman has invited us to meet him in the garden behind the house to...uh...talk business." He gave me a warning look. "Lord Boudin will be there as well."

"Of course he will," I grunted, not surprised. I knew this was my chance to win the codex, and I intended to make the best of it. I looked around in anticipation, eager to get away from these people. "Where do we go?"

Fitz opened his mouth to reply but hesitated as a black-robed figure stepped in front of me. "Why, it's Lord Hadrack, is it not?" Son Gylex said. The priest's voice was deep, surprising me. I'd expected the same annoying squeak that usually came out of Son Oriell's ugly mouth.

"Indeed it is, Son," I said, bowing my head.

The priest wore a Rock of Life around his neck, held by a thick silver chain. He lifted it off his chest and proffered it to me. "You must kiss the stone, lord," the Son said. "That is the custom these days in Cardia."

"Is that right?" I replied. So the bastard was a Cardian. That was interesting. I glanced down at the stone, making no move to comply.

"The Father is watching and judging you, lord," the priest said impatiently after a moment. "Surely you do not wish to tempt His wrath?"

I grinned. "I've done far worse, Son, and I haven't felt the heat of His touch yet."

Son Gylex frowned, his eyes turning hard. "I have heard many stories about you, Lord Hadrack."

"Have you now?" I replied in mock interest.

"Yes," the priest said. "All manner of dreadful things." He flicked his gaze to Fitz for a moment before returning to me. Son

Gylex lifted his chin to look down his nose at me. "It would appear that they are all true." The priest jiggled the stone aggressively, causing the silver chains to rattle musically. "You insult The Father, lord, and you insult me. Now kiss the stone and say your words, and all will be forgiven. Do this, and I promise I will speak well of you in my prayers tonight."

I noticed some of The Fisherman's guests had stopped to watch the altercation, with even our host and Lord Boudin pausing to look up curiously from where they still sat together at the table. Fitz cleared his throat, signaling with his eyes that I should do as the priest asked. I turned back to Son Gylex and grinned at him while Fitz groaned beside me. He'd recognized the look in my eyes. "You know, Son, you remind me greatly of someone else."

"Is that right?" the priest said frostily.

Son Gylex still held the Rock of Life up between us as though it might help ward off some unspeakable evil—but I knew where the true evil lay. "He's a real ugly son of a bitch, too," I said. "Just like you."

The priest's eyes bulged in shock and his mouth dropped open. "I will see you burn for your temerity!" Son Gylex finally hissed in outrage. He let go of the Rock of Life, letting it thud against his chest as he pointed a finger at me. "Do you hear me, Lord Hadrack!" the man cried. "You will burn for all the misery you have caused this world! Mark my words!"

"Be careful, boy," I growled. "Kissing a polished rock held by a fool might be something Cardians like to do, but in Ganderland, we have our own customs." I leaned forward until our faces were inches apart. "And gutting turd-sucking little bastards like you is one of them."

"I'm curious, Hadrack," Fitz said as a servant wearing a plain white robe guided us through The Fisherman's house toward our meeting in the garden. "Are you actively trying to get us staked out on Bone Beach, by any chance?"

I glanced at my friend, who I noticed was biting into an apple. I had no idea where he'd gotten it. "What was I supposed to do, bend the knee to that bastard and kiss his Rock?"

"Yes," Fitz grunted around the fruit. "That's what you were supposed to do." He swallowed, then sighed, speaking in a long-suffering voice. "By The Mother, Hadrack, I can't decide whether you're the smartest bastard I've ever met or the dumbest." He hooked a thumb behind him down the wide corridor we were walking along. "That stupid little turd back there is meaningless. You shouldn't have let him goad you on like that. We've got a bigger prize to focus on than him."

"I know," I agreed, nodding. "You're right, of course." I looked sideways at my friend and grinned sheepishly, then nudged him in the ribs with my elbow. "But you can't tell me you didn't enjoy the look on that bastard's ugly face when I said I'd gut him, now can you?"

Fitz shook his head as he blew air wearily out of his nostrils before finally, he chuckled. "You're going to get us killed if you keep this up, you know."

"Maybe," I grunted.

We'd reached a set of stout double doors that the servant swung open before he stepped aside, motioning us through. The man wouldn't meet our eyes, which I'd come to learn was a common theme on The Iron Cay. Fitz and I stepped out into a narrow courtyard of flagstones with neatly laid-out flower gardens to either side. A pathway led deeper into the garden, lined by small, perfectly pruned trees where a strange, oval green fruit that I'd never seen before grew. There was only one direction for us to take, so Fitz and I made our way forward while flickering torches on poles lit our way. The night was cloudy and muggy, with light misty rain falling intermittently that did little to help cool us. I was sweating profusely but barely noticed it or the rainfall, my whole being focused on the coming encounter with The Fisherman.

We made our way around a bend, which led us toward a fountain depicting a rearing horse with its rider holding a raised sword. Water poured from the horse's nostrils into the pool below, which I thought was rather novel. I noticed a raised wooden pavilion standing off to one side of the fountain, with its walls and roof protected by thick white canvas. The canvas had been tied back in the front to allow entry, and I could see our host waiting inside for us on a high-backed chair. Fitz and I headed that way, and I was forced to duck when I entered.

"Welcome, Lord Hadrack and Lord Fitzery," The Fisherman said.

"Your Grace," both Fitz and I replied at the same time.

Several glowing metal braziers lit the enclosure, and I noticed Lord Boudin standing in the shadows to the left of the entrance. I glanced his way and he bowed his head slightly with a look of amusement on his face. I returned the greeting, frowning when I saw Son Gylex standing next to him. I did my best not to let my distaste for the man show, though I don't think I succeeded.

"Did you enjoy the feast, lords?" The Fisherman asked.

"We did, Your Grace," I said. "It was beyond our wildest expectations."

The Fisherman beamed at my praise. "I'm glad to hear it, lord."

Alfaheed stood several paces behind The Fisherman's chair, and I nodded to him. The Temba didn't react, his features expressionless. Another man sat on a bench to my right in the shadows, his back pressed against the canvas wall. He was wearing a dark cloak with the hood up, hiding his face. No one paid any attention to him, nor did he introduce himself. I wondered who the man was and why he was there.

"So," The Fisherman said, breaking the silence as he slapped his hands down on the armrests of his chair. "Now that the pleasantries are over, shall we get on with the main event?"

"I would like that very much," I said. I took a step forward, crossing my arms behind my back. "I imagine you already know why I've come here, Your Grace."

"Of course I do," The Fisherman said. "It's my business to know." He shifted his eyes to Lord Boudin and the priest. "But I'm sure you are also aware that I have already offered a deal to someone else regarding this…um…particular item I possess, are you not?"

"I am aware," I replied. I took a deep breath. "Forgive me for being frank, Your Grace, but if that deal was already written in stone, I doubt I'd be standing here talking to you. All I ask is the right to bid on the item. Nothing more, nothing less."

The Fisherman chuckled and nodded. "A fair point, lord. A fair point." He glanced at Lord Boudin, who was shifting his feet uncomfortably. I smiled, realizing that the bastard was suddenly nervous. "And what do you say, Lord Boudin? Should I allow Lord Hadrack this right?"

"Absolutely not!" Son Gylex snapped. He pointed at me. "This man is a sinner and a heathen sympathizer! The codex is irreplaceable, and he should not—"

"That will be enough, Son," Lord Boudin said. His voice was soft and unthreatening, but the hand he put on the priest's arm clenched, and I saw the man wince from the pain. Lord Boudin turned to The Fisherman. "Please forgive Son Gylex, Your Grace. He's had a trying day. He was convinced Lord Hadrack meant to ram my ship earlier. Sadly, the Son is afraid of water and unable to swim. It quite unnerved him, I'm sorry to say."

"Ah, of course," The Fisherman said sympathetically. He glanced my way. "That certainly was quite an interesting maneuver you and your crew performed for us today, Lord Hadrack. I'd never seen the like before. Quite extraordinary." The Fisherman laughed.

"I must confess, I too thought for a time that you intended to ram them, what with that rather large and imposing...um...ram on the front of your vessel."

"That was most assuredly not my intent, Your Grace," I said, trying to look horrified at the thought. "I would never even consider such a thing. Our ship is quite large, and my captain felt the safest berth for her was next to Lord Boudin's two vessels in case a storm should arrive. I've heard they can be rather powerful here in the south."

"Perfectly logical," The Fisherman said, waving away my words. His eyes suddenly turned hard and cold, the real man inside emerging. "But just the same, lord, I do think it was a tad reckless of you to come in so fast. Had an accident occurred, I would have been forced to intercede." The Fisherman leaned forward. "And I promise you, lord, you would not have enjoyed that."

"Exactly the same words I used when speaking with my captain, Your Grace," I said. "I certainly have no wish to incur your wrath. Why my man chose to enter the bay at such speed is beyond me, and I humbly apologize for his error. If it were to happen again, I expect I'd have little choice but to relieve the fellow of his post."

"Were it to happen again, Lord Hadrack," The Fisherman said softly. The chair beneath him creaked as he leaned back. "That man will lose more than just his job." He hesitated. "As will any others responsible."

"A fair and reasonable ruling, Your Grace," I replied humbly.

"Now that that's settled," The Fisherman continued, his expression softening. "I believe I asked Lord Boudin whether or not he objected to a little friendly competition for the item I have for sale."

"I have no objections, Your Grace," Lord Boudin replied immediately. He flicked his eyes to me. "Nor do I have any objections to matching myself against Lord Hadrack in any form, be it here on your charming island or somewhere a little less—" He hesitated and smiled, though his eyes showed no humor. "Shall we say, civilized?"

"Well, there you have it," The Fisherman said in satisfaction. He motioned to Alfaheed, who turned and opened a small chest sitting on a table. The Temba carefully removed a canvas-wrapped object, then unraveled the cloth, revealing a small book bound in red leather. He held it up for us to see as The Fisherman sighed happily, his eyes alight with greed. "Now then, lords, what say we begin the bidding at four hundred gold coins? Do I have any takers?"

Lord Boudin immediately lifted his hand, signaling his willingness to pay. I remained where I was, frozen in disbelief, with my mind unable to process what I was seeing. Only a few men alive had set eyes on Waldin's copy of the codex, and I was one of them. And I knew beyond a doubt that the book Alfaheed held wasn't the same one that the scholar, Rorian had brought to me many years before. It wasn't even close. I clamped my jaw shut to stop myself from cursing out loud.

The codex was a forgery. We'd been duped.

Chapter 7: The Auction

"Do I hear five hundred?" The Fisherman asked, staring at me pointedly.

I could sense Lord Boudin smiling to my left as I hesitated, guessing that he thought I was balking at the amount our host had asked for the fake codex. I licked my lips, glancing over my shoulder at Fitz, whose face was ashen. He'd clearly realized the book was a forgery, too.

"May I have a moment to confer with Lord Fitzery, Your Grace?" I asked. I motioned to the entrance, where I saw the rain was falling steadier now. "Outside, if you please?"

The Fisherman frowned and his eyes flashed with annoyance, but his response moments later was calm and measured, although colder than I would have preferred. "If you must, Lord Hadrack. But I warn you, I am not a man accustomed to waiting." Our host had hidden his disappointment well, I thought, but it was still obvious to me that he'd been hoping for a long and protracted bidding war. My unexpected reaction to what he must have thought to be a low opening bid had just put his dreams of riches in jeopardy.

"Thank you, Your Grace," I said, aware of the slight tremor in my voice. "We won't be but a moment." I turned and grabbed Fitz's elbow, guiding him outside without saying anything else. The rain was much cooler now, which I was grateful for as my mind raced. What in the name of The Mother was I going to do? Fitz started to speak, and I made a sharp motion with my hand, cutting him off, then headed for the fountain. I paused at the outer wall of the pool, welcoming the sound of the water tumbling into it. I doubted with that and the rain that anyone could overhear us talking.

"This is a disaster, Hadrack!" Fitz hissed softly. "That's not Waldin's copy!"

"I know," I grunted. I hooked a thumb toward the pavilion. "But they don't know that."

"Maybe," Fitz muttered doubtfully. "What are we going to do now?"

"I don't have a clue," I admitted. I paused to wipe rainwater from my eyes. "I was hoping you might have thought of something."

"Like what?" Fitz asked with an exasperated sigh. "We're buggered no matter what we do. If we bid on it and win, then what? Who knows what the damn thing might say?"

"Well, we both know it won't be the truth," I responded. "Which might not be a bad thing, considering what that truth actually is." I stroked my wet beard as I thought. "Then again, it could be much worse than we imagine. Let's not forget The Fisherman offered the forgery to First Son Oriell and said it would be well worth his while. What did he mean by that, I wonder?"

"I'm sure nothing good, Hadrack," Fitz said, his eyes filled with worry. "If I were to guess, I'd say it probably names The Father as the more powerful god, not The Mother."

"Probably," I agreed, having come to that conclusion already. "But the only ones who stand to benefit from something like that are the Sons. So, if they're behind all of this, why bother going through with the charade at all? Why go to all the trouble of allying with the Cardians and sending Lord Boudin to sail this far south when it wasn't necessary? The First Son could have just revealed the codex at his leisure with a simple explanation about how it had been found. No one would have thought twice about it."

"I'm sure the First Daughter would have had some serious reservations," Fitz pointed out. "Especially if the forgery says what we think it does and she lost power to the First Son because of it." My friend took a deep breath. "Now that I think about it, doing it this way actually makes a certain kind of sense."

"How so?" I asked, curious now.

"By coming this far on such a hazardous journey, it automatically helps to legitimize the find," Fitz explained.

"But why go to the Cardians, then?" I asked, still not understanding.

"Hmmm," Fitz muttered as he mulled that over. "Maybe because they know Tyden favors The Mother? The First Son probably thought the king would wave it off as a hoax and refuse to send a ship, especially with the war ongoing and half his western fleet sunk." My friend's eyes lit up, and he snapped his fingers as another thought struck him. "Which, if true, might mean that Daughter Gernet finding out about the codex after the fact was no accident, either. What if the Sons correctly guessed that she'd take matters into her own hands when she learned of it and send you, Hadrack? Of course, they would have had no idea you'd already seen the original copy, which means they also couldn't have known that you'd realize immediately that theirs was a fake."

"If all of this is true," I said, watching my friend closely. Fitz was like a fire when he was like this—the more informational fuel you gave him, the hotter and brighter his mind burned. "Where does that leave us right now?"

"Completely buggered, just like I said," Fitz grunted. "Even if you outbid Lord Boudin or lose to him tonight, whatever lies are in that forgery will be revealed one way or another, and the Sons will get what they want—control of the House." He shook his head. "It's pure genius, Hadrack."

"Damn," I whispered, realizing that everything my friend had just suggested made perfect sense. I shook my head at the complex web that the Sons had woven. Had they known all along that the First Daughter would send me here as Fitz had suggested? And if they had, had they sent Lord Boudin on purpose, knowing full well that I was sworn to kill him? Maybe the Sons were hoping that I'd lose control of myself when I saw him, which would automatically set The Fisherman against me. I went cold as another idea struck me. I knew Son Oriell hated me. What if the bastard planned on killing two birds with one stone in all this? Daughter Gernet's spies had told her that there was only one Cardian ship, but they had been wrong. Had that been a simple error, or was this a trap set up to ensnare me? Did Son Oriell hope I'd lose control and go after Lord Boudin and he'd kill me or failing that, I'd end up on Bone Beach as crab food for killing him? I rubbed my face, my head aching as I tried to piece it all together.

"Lord Hadrack?" Alfaheed called from the entrance, cutting into my thoughts. "The Fisherman requests that you return right now."

I glanced toward the pavilion. "We'll be right there," I called out. I turned to Fitz. "Well, whatever is going on here," I said hurriedly. "I don't think we have much of a choice. We need to get our hands on that book and worry about the rest later."

"I agree," Fitz said with a reluctant nod. "But that might be easier said than done." He gestured to the pavilion, where Alfaheed stood watching us impatiently. "If The Fisherman is in on this, you could probably promise him the moon and it wouldn't matter. If that's the case, then the deal is already sealed and this is all just part of their game."

I paused as I considered that, then finally shook my head. "I don't think so, Fitz. Nobody could be that convincing. No, that man wants to sell the forgery for as much gold as possible. I've seen it in his eyes. I'm sure of it."

"Well, if you're right about that," Fitz said, "how did he come to possess it in the first place?" My friend shook his waterlogged head, sending droplets flying in all directions. "It couldn't have been Malo, that's for sure."

I took a deep breath. "I don't know how The Fisherman came to have it," I answered truthfully. "And I don't have time to worry about it now." I clapped my friend on the back through his wet tunic. "What I do know is our host is getting angry and we need to get back in there."

Less than a minute later, Fitz and I stood once again in front of The Fisherman. I felt much calmer and more in control of myself now that the decision was made. I planned on offering the man every last coin I'd brought with me and more if that's what it took to secure the forgery. If Fitz was right and The Fisherman was complicit in this, then whatever amount of gold I pledged wouldn't matter anyway. But if my friend was wrong and I won the bidding, then I'd resolved myself to tossing the damn thing in the ocean the first chance that I got. After that, I'd have plenty of time to figure out some excuse to tell Daughter Gernet about how I'd come to lose it. She would be furious, I knew, but in the end, there really wasn't much she'd be able to do about it.

I took a deep breath as The Fisherman regarded me coldly. Whatever happened in the next few minutes—good or bad—I had no intention of leaving this island without that forgery—even if it meant razing the entire place to the ground.

"I take it you have come to a decision, lord?" The Fisherman said. He sat with his elbows propped up on the arms of his chair, his fingers steepled together as he studied me with wary eyes.

"I have, Your Grace," I said. I glanced to my right at the seated man in the shadows. If he'd moved at all, I couldn't tell. I turned back to our host, thrusting the stranger from my mind. "The Kingdom of Ganderland, backed by the king—" I hesitated and smiled, "and the First Daughter, will gladly pay five hundred gold coins for the item in question."

The Fisherman smiled with pleasure, his long teeth giving him a predatory look. "That is wonderful news, lord. I am delighted to learn that you have not wasted my time along with my hospitality." He turned to Lord Boudin. "And what say you, lord? Do you wish to counter with a bid of six hundred?"

Lord Boudin took several steps forward until he stood beside Fitz and me. "No, Your Grace," he announced. "The Empire of Cardia, backed by the emperor and the Seven Rings—" He paused as I had, "not to mention the First Son, would prefer to offer you one thousand gold coins." He inclined his head. "Which, as you recall, Your Grace, was the sum we originally agreed upon before these Gander interlopers were allowed to participate."

I blinked in surprise at the exorbitant amount, staring straight ahead at The Fisherman, who looked like a man bathing in pure ecstasy. If I'd had any doubts about him before, I had none now. He clearly was not part of this. Lord Boudin's bid had just matched the total amount of money Daughter Gernet had given me, and I decided it was time to get serious and play. "Eleven hundred, Your Grace," I said firmly. I sensed Fitz stiffen beside me but dared not look his way.

"Twelve, Your Grace," Lord Boudin said.

"Thirteen."

"Fourteen."

"Fifteen," I grunted. I glared at Lord Boudin, daring him to go higher.

"Sixteen, Your Grace," Lord Boudin said, though it was done through gritted teeth while The Fisherman squirmed excitedly in his chair like a man in a brothel surrounded by a gaggle of young, nubile prostitutes.

"Seventeen, Your Grace," I growled.

"Eighteen."

"Nineteen."

"Twenty."

I blew air out of my nostrils, getting angry now. I decided it was time to separate the men from the boys. "Forty thousand gold coins, Your Grace," I declared with a flourish, feeling reckless. I saw Lord Boudin open his mouth, and I added, "Plus my pledge that Tyden Raybold, the King of Ganderland, will also pay you a stipend of one thousand Jorqs every year from now until the day you die."

"What?" Son Gylex gasped in obvious disbelief. "That's preposterous! He's lying!"

The Fisherman had reacted to my words as if I'd just struck him across the face, his eyes blinking and his face flushing. He rubbed a hand across his high forehead, losing some of his composure for the first time. Lord Boudin and Son Gylex were conferring together now in heated whispers close to me, but I ignored them, my gaze fixed on our host.

"Well...that's...um...well," The Fisherman said in a strangled voice. He cleared his throat, snapping his fingers at Alfaheed, who hurried to bring him a mug. The Fisherman drank, downing the contents in one shot, then wiped his lips as he stared at me. "So tell me, Lord Hadrack," he managed to say. "Do you, per chance, have forty thousand gold pieces on board your ship?"

"No, Your Grace," I said. "I do not. I have only one thousand Jorqs. But you have my word the rest will be paid once our deal is consummated and I return to Ganderland. That and the guaranteed yearly stipend, of course."

"Your word!" Son Gylex spat in fury. "That's not worth a wet turd lying in the middle of the road."

"Neither are you," I countered with contempt. "In fact, I'd wager you're worth far less."

"Lord Boudin," The Fisherman said intensely, ignoring the priest and me. "Can you match or better Lord Hadrack's offer?"

"I...uh," Lord Boudin muttered. I smiled, for the Cardian looked extremely worried now. "I'm not exactly certain of that, Your Grace."

"Well, I am certain of my offer, Your Grace," I said loudly and firmly. "King Tyden has authorized me to do whatever is necessary to secure the item. Consider my guarantee the same as if it had come from him."

The Fisherman took in a deep breath, looking pained as he thought. He tapped a finger against his chin while his gaze danced back and forth between the Cardian and me. I could see naked greed burning in his eyes. "How much gold did you bring with you, Lord Boudin?" our host finally asked. His tone had gone suddenly cold and calculating, which sent my gut churning with anxiety. What was that old falconer saying about a bird in the hand is worth two in the bush?

"Several thousand, Your Grace," the Cardian answered weakly. He flushed when he saw my smile of relief.

"So, neither of you can pay the full price right now," The Fisherman said thoughtfully. "It appears I am to be paid mainly with promises and flowery words. An interesting dilemma, then, for I must now decide on which of you I trust more." Our host stood stiffly, then stretched while he glanced outside. "Damn rain is making my bones ache." The Fisherman began to pace back and forth in front of us, his hands clasped behind his back. "So, let me see if I understand things as they sit right now. I have competing bids from both Cardia and Ganderland." He glanced at me and smiled. "One of which is considerably larger than the other."

"I am sure the emperor will match the Ganders' offer, Your Grace," Lord Boudin said, though I thought he spoke without much enthusiasm.

"Your vote of confidence does me little good right now, lord," The Fisherman said with a frown. "I require guarantees. Can you give me that?"

"I would need some time, Your Grace," Lord Boudin said feebly.

"As I thought," The Fisherman muttered. He sighed. "So, on the one hand, there is no question that the Empire of Cardia is a powerful foe, were I to chose Ganderland, but—"

"Or a powerful ally, Your Grace," Lord Boudin cut in. "This fact also needs to be considered—carefully."

The Fisherman nodded his head. "Or an ally," he conceded. "But on the other hand, Lord Boudin, your Empire's less than stellar reputation for honoring agreements over the years is something of a hurdle, no?"

"That is in the past, Your Grace," Lord Boudin assured him. "Cardia has reformed under our current emperor."

"Hmmm, maybe," The Fisherman muttered doubtfully.

"Lord Boudin is only offering you twenty thousand empty words, Your Grace," I said, trying to take the initiative back. "With the vague promise of more empty words to come if you choose him. This is nothing more than a shell game he's playing with you, Your Grace, with the pea already sitting firmly in his pocket."

"I do not speak empty words or play silly games, Your Grace," Lord Boudin said with a barely controlled sneer. "I'm afraid it is my colleague here who whispers whatever it is that you wish to hear in hopes you'll be blinded." He turned to me, a challenge on his face. "I wonder, Lord Hadrack, what you would have done if I'd matched your offer just now? Would you have pledged fifty thousand gold coins? Sixty, maybe? It's easy to toss around fantastical numbers when you have no intention of actually paying them."

"Are you not one of the Seven Rings?" I shot back at the Cardian. I glanced down at the red ruby ring on his left hand, symbolizing his status.

"What of it?" Lord Boudin said with a frown as he unconsciously balled his hand into a fist.

"What of it?" I scoffed. I turned to The Fisherman. "Your Grace, everyone knows the Seven Rings are the true power behind the emperor." I stabbed a finger at the Cardian's chest. "This man has the authority to match my offer, but he refuses. He is trying to swindle you, hoping that you will believe him and, by doing so, get the codex at a bargain price while making a fool out of you in the process. Our offer is superior, and I swear to you on my life that it will be paid in full."

"A life that's worthless because its time is almost up," Lord Boudin spat with contempt. "I'll see to that."

"Like your brother did?" I taunted him. Lord Boudin's brother had been a provincial regent based in Bahyrst, a Cardian city that I'd traveled to in search of Einrack after pirates had abducted him. The regent had actually been killed by Jebido, not me, though I doubted Lord Boudin knew that—or cared.

"You sniveling piece of cow shit!" Lord Boudin snarled. "I should slit your throat right here and now."

I smiled contemptuously and turned to The Fisherman, ignoring the furious lord now. "You know, Your Grace, there are two things I've learned about Cardians in my many years of dealing with them."

"Oh, and what would that be, Lord Hadrack?" our host asked, looking interested.

"First, they are all greedy bastards, Your Grace," I answered. I glanced at Lord Boudin and grinned again at his dark look. "And second. Every one of them is a coward at heart."

"Your Grace!" Son Gylex protested. "This is unacceptable behavior! I demand that you—"

"You demand?" The Fisherman snapped. He pointed a finger at the priest, whose ugly face was turning white as he realized his error. "Just because you wear that robe, Son, does not give you the right to demand anything here. This is *my* island, not yours, nor your god's, for that matter! Speak to me like that again, and I assure you I will gladly risk my soul with The Father and stake you out on Bone Beach!"

"But I—"

Alfaheed suddenly stepped forward with a knife in his hands and death in his eyes. I hadn't seen The Fisherman make any kind of signal to him, but it hardly mattered. Son Gylex squeaked in fear at the sight, lifted the hem of his robes, then scurried out of the pavilion into the rain.

"And that is how you deal with an annoying little mouse," Alfaheed announced into the silence before he sheathed his knife and returned to his original position.

"Thank you, Alfaheed," The Fisherman said. He shook his head. "Why is it that the noblest profession we mortals can ascend to in this world often seems to attract the worst dreck humanity has to offer?"

"Because the gods have a twisted sense of humor, Your Grace," I replied.

The Fisherman laughed heartily at that. "I think you're right, lord." The amusement eventually faded from the man's face, though, and he nodded, his features all business once more. "Well, lords, my decision has been made." Our host stepped forward and offered me his hand without any warning. "We have a bargain, Lord Hadrack. The codex in exchange for forty thousand Jorqs and a stipend of a thousand per year until I die."

"Agreed," I grunted, taking the man's strong grip in mine while Lord Boudin cursed beside me.

I tried not to think about how I'd get Tyden and Daughter Gernet to live up to the bargain, especially considering the item they'd just paid such a steep price for would never reach Ganderland. That little problem, however, was soon to become the least of my worries—by far.

Chapter 8: Treachery

The Fisherman was a man of his word, as was I, and after Alfaheed had returned Fitz and me to *Sea-Wolf* with the codex, I'd had Putt bring out the two chests from the hold that contained Daughter Gernet's gold. Now those chests sat open on the deck, with the coins glittering in the light of several lanterns as Alfaheed examined them. Movement on my ship had all but ceased when the money chests had been unlocked and opened, with my men staring at the fortune inside in awe and amazement and, I didn't doubt, a fair amount of longing. I knew few of them had ever seen so much gold in their lives before, nor probably would do so ever again.

I'd warned Sarrey and Mondar to stay well hidden while their fellow countryman was on board the ship, though it was probably nothing but wasted words. Those two didn't need any encouragement from me not to be seen. I hadn't bothered to mention to Sarrey that her father was only a few hundred yards away onshore, seeing no reason to frighten her anymore than she already was. I'd inform her later, I promised myself, once we were far away from this place.

"Well, Lord Hadrack," Alfaheed said from where he crouched on one knee in front of the chests. He lifted a handful of coins and let them jingle musically in a stream back into one of the chests, then closed both lids and stood, looking satisfied. "All seems to be in order here."

"I'm glad to hear it," I said.

The Temba picked one of the chests up easily and carried it to the gunwale, lowering it down to a man waiting on the ladder. He did the same for the second one, then turned to me and offered his hand. "It has been a pleasure doing business with you, lord."

"And with you," I said as I shook the man's hand, eager to be rid of him so I could go over the forged codex. It didn't really matter what it said inside, of course, since I planned on destroying it anyway. Yet still, I had to admit that I was curious.

Alfaheed nodded and let go of my hand. "When will you be setting sail, lord?"

"At first light," I responded, trying not to show my impatience.

"That is good," Alfaheed said. "And may I ask how long it will be before the rest of the payment arrives?"

I pursed my lips as I thought. "Nearly a month for us to return to Ganderland, then a week or two for the gold to be gathered, then another month back."

"Ah," Alfaheed nodded, looking unsurprised. "Will it be you returning, lord?"

I shrugged and adjusted Wolf's Head on my hip, glad to have the weapon back where it belonged. "That is up to the king and the First Daughter. I just do what I'm told."

"As do we all, lord," Alfaheed grunted. He moved to the railing and flipped a leg over it. "As do we all." The Temba began to climb down the ladder, then paused with just his head and shoulders showing above the railing. "The Fisherman is a good judge of character, lord, and he is convinced that you are an honorable man and will hold up your end of the bargain. That is why he is letting you take the item with you now. I recommend that you do not disappoint him. He is not a man who likes to be proven wrong, so be warned, his claws are long and sharp and can reach even faraway Ganderland."

"The money will come, Alfaheed," I promised, while inside my head, I said a silent prayer that it was true. "I gave The Fisherman my word," I added. "And the Wolf of Corwick never goes back on his word."

"Then all will be well," Alfaheed said with a grin before disappearing from my sight.

I stood where I was until the Temba's boat was almost halfway across the bay, heading for the jetty before I signaled for

Baine, Fitz, and Jebido to join me on the aftercastle. Putt and one of the crew were up there already, and I sent them away, waiting until we were alone before I cracked open the forged codex. I could feel my heart beating faster as Baine brought a lantern closer, with all of us hunched over the pages while I flipped through them carefully, one by one. I frowned, pausing after the sixth page to glance up at Fitz, who I saw was mirroring my expression. I knew Jebido and Baine had never actually read the codex, but Fitz had, and I could see the growing puzzlement in his eyes.

"What's wrong?" Jebido grunted, switching his gaze between Fitz and me.

I didn't answer him and instead turned a few more pages until I was absolutely certain, then I cursed.

"Are you going to tell us what's wrong, or are we just supposed to guess?" Jebido demanded.

I took a deep breath, more confused than ever as I tried to understand. "It's the same."

"What?" Baine muttered. "What do you mean?"

"The words," I explained. "As far as I can tell, the words in this book are exactly the same ones that I read years ago."

Jebido blinked in surprise. "You mean this really is Waldin's copy after all?"

Fitz took the book from me, and he shook his head. "No," my friend said thoughtfully as he slowly turned the pages. "The ink is completely different from what I remember, and it's been written on inferior sheepskin." Fitz pointed. "See all the fine hairs here? Parchmenters usually use lime to remove hair from the hide, but this looks like it was done with fermented vegetables or something like that. That's why it looks this way. The pages of Waldin's copy were done by a master parchmenter, and he used a much finer hide than this, probably calf or lambskin."

"But that makes no sense," Baine said. "How can the book and ink be different, but the—" He paused for a moment as sudden realization struck him. "Oh," he muttered, looking alarmed now. He focused on me. "Does this mean what I think it does, Hadrack?"

"I'm afraid it does," I growled. "Whoever wrote this book had to have had the original to copy it from." I looked down at the decking as I felt anger flickering along my limbs. I knew only one person who could have done this, though I couldn't fathom why he would have. "Malo," I whispered through clenched teeth. "It could only have been that bastard."

"Malo?" Jebido repeated. He shook his head. "The man might have been an ass most of the time, Hadrack, but he was a loyal one. I don't see him doing this. What reason would he have?"

"Actually, there might be one," Baine cut in. "Just not a malicious one. What if Malo was afraid something might happen to Waldin's copy, so he made another one?" Baine shrugged at our blank stares. "Well, it's possible, isn't it?"

"If he did that," I said. "Then how do you explain the copy ending up in The Fisherman's hands and not the original?"

"That I don't know," Baine admitted as he rubbed his chin.

"Uhm, Hadrack, I think you'd better read this," Fitz said in a warning tone while offering the open book to me.

He used his finger to point out a passage, which I read slowly and carefully. I closed my eyes after I was done, the anger gone now, replaced by a sudden, almost overwhelming weariness. The book wasn't identical to Waldin's after all, it turned out, for, in this version, there was no mention of the Master or the Realm Beyond. All it stated was that The Father was the more powerful god, just as we'd suspected would be the case all along. Now I was really confused. I'd never liked Malo, but I had always respected him and knew he was fiercely loyal to the Daughters and the House. The man I'd known years ago would never have written something that he knew would jeopardize either one. That's why he'd disappeared with the codex in the first place, after all. So what did it mean? What was going on here, and who was responsible for it?

I took a moment to explain to Baine and Jebido what Fitz and I now knew, and when I was done, the four of us stood in silence as we tried to work things out.

"It had to have been the Sons, then, Hadrack," Fitz finally said. "Just as we thought. They're the only ones who stand to gain from this news getting out."

I smoothed my beard as I thought, feeling strangely uneasy. We'd missed something. I was certain of it. But what? I glanced toward the silent Cardian ship across from *Sea-Wolf*. I could see several of her crew patrolling the decks with torches, but everything else seemed calm there. Was it too calm?

Lord Boudin had been furious about losing the bidding, storming from the pavilion in a tantrum after vowing that things were far from over between us. I rarely agreed with the bastard, but I knew he was right about that. I had a score to settle with him, and I wasn't going home until it was satisfied. I fully expected Lord Boudin to follow us when we sailed in the morning, guessing that he'd try to attack us on the high seas once we were free of the island. It was something that I was looking forward to with great anticipation. The Cardian lord's cog was admittedly formidable, but even so, I knew I could trust in *Sea-Wolf* to outmaneuver it and the other ship as well. I planned to disable the smaller ship's sail first using my Wolf's Teeth and fire arrows, then, when the vessel was out of action, go head to head against Lord Boudin. The bastard would probably still have more men than me, even without his second ship, but they were stinking Cardians, who I'd willingly match my battle-hardened troops against, outnumbered or not.

I glanced again at *Spearfish*, that uneasy feeling something was wrong getting stronger. What if the bastard did something unexpected, though? What if he didn't wait until morning? Would he dare attack me at night while we were at anchor and risk The Fisherman's wrath? Sarrey had told me there were upwards of three hundred soldiers on the island that The Fisherman could call upon, along with a small fleet of those strange, canoe-like boats.

Would Lord Boudin chance an attack anyway, despite those men? I didn't know for certain, but I was taking no chances.

I leaned over the inner railing. "Putt!"

"My lord?"

"Weigh anchor. We're moving."

"Yes, my lord."

Twenty minutes later, *Sea-Wolf* again lay at anchor, this time more than five hundred yards away from the two Cardian vessels near the cliffs guarding the entrance. If Lord Boudin tried something in the middle of the night, we'd easily see him coming long before his men could hope to reach us.

I was alone now with Baine, the two of us leaning against the portside railing on the lower deck. Fitz had gone down to the hold with a lantern and the codex, determined to read everything in it to ensure there were no more surprises in store for us. Jebido had gone to bed, anticipating a long and possibly bloody day ahead.

"There's one thing that's been bothering me about all of this, Hadrack," Baine said.

"Only one?" I grunted. It was almost midnight, and I could feel the long day pushing down on my shoulders, yet I knew I was still too edgy even to consider trying to get some sleep.

"If the Sons are behind the forged codex, that means they have Waldin's original as well, right?"

"Probably," I said. "Chances are they found Malo somehow and killed him for it. It's the only thing that makes any sense."

"Which means they know the truth just like we do."

"That depends on who you mean by *they*," I said. "My guess is only a select few know, same as us. If there were more, I'm sure it would have come out by now."

"So, the First Son, then," Baine said with a nod. "He'd have to know."

"Yes," I replied. I motioned to the anchored Cardian ships. "And maybe that turd-sucking relative of his over there, too. Maybe that's why he's here."

Baine followed my gaze. "What about Lord Boudin?"

I sighed, feeling pain throbbing at my temples. "Maybe him too. Anything's possible. But if he does know, why did he react so badly to my winning the codex? If whoever is behind this wanted me here in the first place, shouldn't everyone be happy now? Nobody knows we're aware it's a forgery, nor that I intend to destroy the damn thing. As far as everyone else is concerned, I'm planning on handing the codex over to Daughter Gernet, which must be what they want."

"It doesn't make any sense," Baine said.

I clenched my hands on the wooden railing, frustrated at not understanding what was happening. I shook my head. "I feel like a hound dog trying to catch its tail, going around and around and around and getting nowhere." I rubbed wearily at my eyes.

"Maybe you need to sleep on it," Baine said sympathetically. "You look exhausted."

"Maybe you're right," I agreed.

My head was pounding now, and I said goodnight to Baine, then made my way to an open bedroll near the forecastle. I lay down and closed my eyes, certain that I wouldn't sleep—but sleep found me soon enough, quickly followed by a dream.

I was a boy again, throwing small rocks at the many stumpy-legged marmots that infested our fields while my father and older brother cleared bigger stones. I struck one of the squirrel-like critters and it squealed in pain, dashing back down its burrow while I giggled with delight. My father paused to watch me, removing his hat to wipe the sweat from his brow. He was so young, handsome, and strong looking, despite his withered leg, and he laughed at my antics. A scream suddenly sounded, echoing over the fields, and my father's face changed to fear. The cry sounded again, but I couldn't tell where it was coming from. Was it Jeanna? My mother? I didn't know. I called out their names, turning around and around, searching for them, but no one was there. Even my brother and father were gone now. I hadn't seen them leave, and I started to cry, feeling helpless and alone.

The scream came again, louder and filled with such horrible anguish that it pierced my subconscious. I sat bolt upright, brought back to the present as the men around me rose from their beds, cursing and shouting questions. The horizon to the east was stained a faint pink, I saw, signaling dawn was approaching.

"To arms!" I heard Putt cry out. "To arms!"

I flung the blanket covering me aside and snatched up Wolf's Head, then stood as more screams sounded from the stern. I felt dread inside, realizing that they were coming from a woman.

"Sarrey!" I shouted, breaking into a run.

I could see men crowded around the cabin door, and I pushed my way through them and made my way inside. A lantern sat on the floor, lighting the small room as Fitz and Jebido held a distraught Sarrey back while she railed against them with her fists. I cursed as I stared at the bed, where Mondar lay with his face turned away from me and bright red blood staining his naked chest. The poor bastard's throat had been slashed open from ear to ear.

"What happened?" I demanded.

"I don't know, Hadrack," Jebido said, sounding shaken. "We just got here." He held onto one of Sarrey's wrists as she fought to break his hold. "Easy, there, lass," he said gently. "Easy. We're not trying to hurt you."

"Let me go!" Sarrey spat at him. "Let me go!"

Fitz and Jebido both glanced toward me, and I nodded. They released the girl, and she instantly lunged toward the bed, collapsing across Mondar's prostrate corpse while weeping uncontrollably.

"Lord!" Berwin called out anxiously

I turned and strode back out of the cabin as the sound of bowstrings and shouts arose from the aftercastle above me.

Berwin immediately pointed to starboard. "Someone just jumped overboard, my lord. That way."

I rushed to the railing, where I could just make out a disturbance in the water seventy feet away. The sky above was still dark and cloudy despite the dawn coming, but lights from shore reflected off the water, revealing a shadowy form for the briefest moment before it disappeared beneath the waves. I cursed as arrows smacked all around where the figure had been, knowing instinctively that my men had missed. The form resurfaced moments later, twenty feet to the right of where we'd last seen it. Again the bows thrummed, and again the figure dove out of sight unscathed.

One of my men jumped on the railing, about to dive in, but I called him back, for I saw that it was already too late. I watched bitterly as a man dressed all in black hauled himself out of the water onto the shore. He looked back at us, but I could see nothing of his face other than a white blur. The bows above me sounded again but the man was already gone, having disappeared into the bushes that ringed the shore. We'd lost him. I glanced toward the Cardian vessels. Men were stirring there, I saw, with lanterns and torches lighting up the decks. I could also hear the sounds of clinking metal as they donned armor and grabbed weapons.

"Putt!" I roared.

"My lord?"

"Weigh anchor right now! Get us out of here!"

"Yes, my lord."

I could already see activity among the squat buildings further up the island, with torches and men hurrying through the cramped streets toward the shoreline. Some had already reached the beach and were dragging their sleek canoes into the water. I wondered what in the name of The Mother was going on as I searched the faces of my men? "Tyris!" I shouted. "Where are you?"

"Here, my lord," the blond archer called out from the forecastle.

"Get all your men up top." I pointed to the boats. "Don't let those bastards get near us!"

"Yes, my lord!"

"And keep your eyes on those turd-sucking Cardians. I want to know the moment they make a move."

"Of course, my lord."

"Looks like we just stirred up a real hornet's nest," Baine commented as he moved to stand beside me.

"It does at that," I agreed. "The question is, why?"

Behind me, the crew worked to raise the sail while others hurried to unplug the oar-holes and unlash the oars from the sidewalls. My Wolf's Teeth were now stationed all along the aftercastle, watching in silence as at least twenty canoes glided smoothly through the water toward us. I could see many more of the odd boats shoving off from the beach. I sighed. It looked like things were about to get interesting. The wind was blowing straight into the bay, which meant the sail was virtually useless, leaving *Sea-Wolf* moving sluggishly toward the outcrops and freedom under the power of her oars alone. Putt would have to tack back and forth across the bay if we wanted to use the sail at all, but there clearly was no time for that. I cursed, knowing we wouldn't make it and were in for a fight.

"You better get up top," I said to Baine. "We're going to need a steady hand on the rudder."

"Right," Baine grunted, his tone all business.

I drew Wolf's Head and waited after he left, while above me, I heard Tyris' sharp command of, "Nock, Draw, Loose!" Moments later, a scream arose before a man in the lead canoe twisted and tumbled into the water, followed moments later by a second man in a different boat. I grinned mirthlessly as a third man fell before our pursuers had had enough, cutting away to either side where they were out of range. My Wolf's Teeth had just bought us some much-needed time. Would it be enough?

I glanced around the lower deck. Twenty of my men were working the oars, with the rest fully armored now and carrying shields, guarding the gunwales. The Fisherman's men would find it a tough task to get aboard if they persisted in their attack, and those that managed it wouldn't last long. I shook my head, wondering how it had come to this. How had The Fisherman learned about Sarrey and Mondar? And more to the point, why had he sent an assassin to kill the man? But, even as I asked myself that question, I felt my insides go cold. I swore softly under my breath. The Fisherman hadn't known about Mondar at all, I realized. The assassin hadn't come for him this night—he'd come for me.

I heard Jebido cry out in warning behind me and I whirled to see my friend standing at the cabin entrance holding his right eye. He pointed toward the forecastle. "The girl, Hadrack! Stop her!"

I looked that way, confused, not understanding what was going on as Sarrey raced up the forecastle ladder. Whatever was happening, the urgency in Jebido's voice was unmistakable, and I didn't question it. I started to run, pushing soldiers out of my way as I called Sarrey's name. The girl paused to look back at me when she reached the top of the ladder, and I could see nothing but anguish on her features in the lantern light.

"Forgive me, Lord Hadrack," she called out before I lost sight of her.

I reached the ladder and clambered upward, breathing heavily now as I reached the top. Then I froze. Sarrey stood on the railing at the bow, clinging to a stay line with her long hair whipping about her head.

She put out a hand to stop me. "Stay back, lord. This is how it must be."

I took a step forward, my hands out to my sides. Now I understood. "Don't do this, child. This isn't the answer. Trust me."

"You're wrong, lord," Sarrey said. She glanced down at the water foaming below, and I could see the sheen of tears on her cheeks. "Without Mondar, there is no reason to live. He was the love of my life."

"There is always a reason to live," I said gently. I heard someone climbing the ladder behind me and glanced at Jebido as he came to stand beside me. I could see four bloody trails that started at his forehead and ran down his eye to his cheek where the Temba's fingernails had raked him. I took another step toward the girl. "It's easy to give up," I said. "Not giving up is the hard part. Believe me." I put my hands to my chest. "I, too, lost the love of my life not that long ago. But here I stand, for better or for worse."

Sarrey blinked, studying me critically. "And have you found joy in anything you have done since that time, lord?" she asked. "Does your food taste just as good now as it did before she died? Does the air you breathe smell just as sweet? Does the sound of the birds singing in the trees give you pleasure, or does it give you endless pain, knowing she will never hear it again?"

I lowered my head, for there was no answer I could give her that wouldn't come out as a lie.

"As I thought," Sarrey said with a knowing look. She smiled sadly. "I am sorry for your pain, lord. But you have chosen to live with it, as is your right. I, on the other hand, choose differently, which is also my right."

I opened my mouth to argue, but before I could utter a sound, Sarrey turned and, without another word, jumped. I cried out and lunged forward, arms outstretched, but I was far, far too late. I leaned over the railing afterward and looked down in dismay, just able to see the girl's head bobbing in the water as *Sea-Wolf* slid slowly past her. Sarrey didn't wave her arms or struggle in the least, and a moment later, she dipped below the waves.

"The girl made her choice, Hadrack," Jebido said sadly as he came to stand beside me. "Just as she said. There's not much we can do about it."

I felt a familiar stubbornness rise in me, angry at the needless waste of a young, promising life. "Oh yes, there is," I growled at my friend.

I turned and raced for the ladder, sliding down the rails using my hands and feet before shouting at the first man I saw to bring the longest rope we had. I sprinted for the aftercastle and tore up the ladder, then ran to the stern and leaned over the gunwale. I spied Sarrey moments later, floating limply in the water near *Sea-Wolf's* hull. For a moment, I thought one of the oars must have struck her unconscious as she passed them, but then I saw her move feebly. I closed my eyes in relief. "Thank The Mother," I whispered.

"The rope, my lord," my man said, holding it uncertainly. "What do I do with it?"

I grabbed an end and tied it around my waist just as Jebido climbed up to the aftercastle, out of breath. He saw what I was doing, and his bushy silver eyebrows rose in astonishment. "Have you gone mad? We're in the middle of a battle."

I grinned. "Then I guess I better make this quick." I took off my brother's Pair Stone from around my neck and handed it to my friend, then unstrapped Wolf's Head and set it down while instructing the soldier to tie off the other end of the rope. Then I moved to the gunwale and hopped onto the slick wood of the railing. "Don't forget to pull me in when I get her," I grunted at Jebido.

I heard my friend say something, but I'd already leaped outward, keeping my feet together and my hands extended above my head as I hurtled downward like a stone. I hit the water hard and fought against the swirling tide before finally I surfaced and sucked in needed air. I looked up at *Sea-Wolf*, which was already moving away from me faster than I would have liked. The rope around my waist was long, but I knew it would play out quickly, which meant I didn't have a lot of time if I wanted to save the girl.

I treaded water as I turned in a circle, searching for Sarrey before I heard a shout and glanced up to see Jebido leaning over *Sea-Wolf's* railing with his hands cupped to his mouth. He pointed to his right urgently and I looked in that direction, certain I'd just seen a brief flash of something in the water. I struck off that way using strong, steady strokes. Moments later, I saw a body wearing a yellow sarong floating face down. Alarmed, I redoubled my efforts until I reached the motionless girl. I got a hand on Sarrey's arm just as I felt the rope tightening around my waist, knowing what that meant. I rolled the Temba over, lifting her head clear of the foaming water and holding on to her just as *Sea-Wolf* began to effortlessly drag us behind her. I slapped Sarrey's cheeks and called out her name, relieved when the girl finally coughed and spat up seawater. She was alive.

Sarrey's eyelids fluttered several times and then opened as she sucked in air. She looked confused for a moment, then seeing me holding her, alarmed. "No," she gasped out. "Let me go to him!"

Sarrey struggled to break my grip, but the girl had no strength left and could do little. I held onto her with my arms underneath her armpits and hands locked together over her chest as I floated on my back. I craned my neck to look at *Sea-Wolf* behind me. I could see Jebido and Fitz desperately working at pulling in the rope, and I mentally cheered them on. The big cog had almost reached the twin outcrops and freedom as my men shouted at me from the decks and waved their bows and swords in victory. I smiled with relief, letting my body stay limp while we were hauled along like hooked fish, knowing Sarrey and I would be safe again on board *Sea-Wolf* in just a few minutes.

I looked to my left, feeling my smile slowly fading, replaced by puzzlement as I saw frantic activity around the watermill. I could see soldiers with torches standing on the beach near the waterline, pointing at *Sea-Wolf* and waving their arms. None had bows, however, and I couldn't for the life of me fathom what they were doing or hoped to accomplish. That's when I heard a horrible screeching sound coming from both watermills before the wheels began to turn slowly. The screeching was followed by a hiss moments later as something impossibly long and dark began to rise from the water between *Sea-Wolf* and me.

My first thought was that it might be one of Putt's sea monsters, and I felt my heart jump into my throat. But it wasn't a monster at all, although I almost wished it had been when I saw a network of heavy chains appear, spanning from one outcrop to the other. The top of the chains in the center of the waterway remained below the waves, however, trapped there beneath *Sea-Wolf's* heavy stern. I held my breath, watching as the big ship slowed while the rowers fought to break her free. Had the chains snagged the rudder? Finally, with a squeal of wood and metal, *Sea-Wolf* shuddered and pulled away, sending the freed barrier beneath her springing into the air with a rattle of chains and torrent of water.

I cried out in surprise and pain moments later when Sarrey and I were yanked roughly backward through the waves, with the center of the rope around my waist now suspended high up on the barrier halfway between *Sea-Wolf* and us. The big cog had come to a stop, wallowing on the tide as the rowers tried to keep her in place while eager hands hauled at the rope, though it didn't seem to be moving much. I craned my neck upwards and looked closer, noticing in dismay that the rope was hooked in the chains and stuck fast. I could hear howls of anger and frustration coming from my men as they worked to free me, while at the same time, cheers from The Fisherman's men as their canoes knifed through the water toward us.

I knew I had only moments before those boats arrived, and I fumbled desperately with the rope around my waist, trying to untie it with one hand while I held Sarrey with the other. If I could get free, I was confident I could swim beneath the barrier to freedom, even with the girl in my arms. But the rope was wet and had tightened from the towing and, try as I might, I couldn't work the knots loose. I shouted out loud in anger and frustration when a shadow fell over me as a canoe slid in beside the girl and me. I looked up at the face peering down at us, feeling the bitterness of defeat washing over me.

"You should never have come here, Lord Hadrack," Alfaheed said in an almost regretful tone just before something struck me on the back of my head.

I knew nothing else after that.

Chapter 9: The Storm

I awoke to pitch-darkness and the sounds of rain and wind—lots and lots of wind. I groaned, reaching for the back of my head, which ached like nothing I'd ever felt before. The moment I made contact with my skull, I winced as red-hot pain flared down my neck and spine to my toes. I felt instantly nauseous and I groaned, my vision blurring as I rolled onto my hands and knees and vomited. When the heaving was mercifully over long minutes later, I waited with my eyes closed, breathing in and out until the dizziness had mostly cleared. I cautiously crawled away from the mess I'd made, my mind registering that the floor beneath me was a combination of dirt and reeds. My forehead bumped into a wall moments later, and I hissed in pain, even as I began to run my hands over the wooden boards. They felt damp to the touch and smelled of mold, but I could tell they were too solid to break through, especially in my condition. I wasn't surprised. The Fisherman wasn't stupid enough to have locked me up in a house of straw.

I carefully sat on the floor with my back propped against the wall, extending my feet out before reaching for my wound again. This time I probed the area using a great deal more caution. I realized cloth bandages had been wrapped several times around my head, and after I took my hand away, I could feel blood on my fingers. The building around me shook just then as the wind howled in frustration and rain pelted against the roof in waves. I sat where I was, stewing in my anger in the darkness as I thought about the unlikely events that had led to my imprisonment. I knew the gods had conspired against me once again, and I was sorely tempted to jump to my feet and scream my rage at them. Perhaps when I was a younger man I might have, but now I just sat in brooding silence, conserving my strength as I waited. Sooner or later, someone would come for me, and when they did—well, we'd just have to see what happened then. I had no weapons, of course, but my captors had surprisingly left my hands and feet free. I planned on making them regret that mistake.

I closed my eyes and lowered my chin to my chest. I'd decided my first course of action would be to find out where the doorway was. But before that could happen, I needed the hammers smashing against the inside of my skull to diminish just a little—which meant, for now, I had to rest. What had happened to Sarrey? I wondered. Had she survived? Was she even now reunited with her father, as distasteful as I knew that would be for her? And what about my ship? Where were my men now? Had they managed to get away, or worse, had they turned back for me, and the Cardians and The Fisherman's men had overwhelmed them?

I breathed out noisily in frustration, wishing I had the answers as the wall behind me vibrated, fighting to resist the howling wind outside. Something began making a sharp rattling sound far above my head, and I looked up, guessing it might be a loose shingle or board. I could see nothing there but endless blackness before, with a wrench and shriek of triumph from the wind, part of the roof tore loose. Rainwater immediately began pouring down on top of me and I cursed, fighting nausea again as I rose to my feet and stumbled away, coughing and spitting.

The wind was making a high-pitched whistling sound around the gap in the roof as it fought to do more damage, which it did a moment later as another piece began to thump wildly before it tore off with a snap, widening the hole. I pressed myself against the wall, wondering if the entire building was about to come down on top of me. That's when I felt the wooden support beam behind me. I turned with sudden hope and ran my fingers up its length, searching for the crossbeam I knew had to be there. I had to stand on my toes, but my questing fingers finally found the bottom of the heavy beam jutting out a good three inches from the wall. I smiled. Maybe the gods hadn't completely turned against me after all. I lowered my arms, took three quick breaths, and then looked up, preparing to leap just as overwhelming dizziness and nausea hit me like double punches. I wobbled on my feet like a drunkard, gagging and swearing in frustration at my weakness as I waited until the feeling passed, but the moment I looked up again, the nausea returned. Now what?

I closed my eyes, taking in great gulps of air as I leaned against the wall, waiting for the room to stop spinning once more. Finally, feeling somewhat better, I resolved to keep trying until I made it. I kept my eyes firmly closed this time and leaped upward, ignoring the beginnings of nausea as my fingers came into contact with the top of the crossbeam. I clutched at it, suspended above the floor while my head swam and my stomach churned. I fought against both and started to work my way to my right along the beam, sliding one hand along, then the other while the rain poured down on me and the swirling wind tugged with glee at my hair and beard. I felt the bandage rip away from my head moments later and fly away like a frightened bird, but there was little that I could do about it.

Once I was under where I believed the hole to be, I paused there, preparing myself as rainwater sluiced down on me in a stream from higher up on the roof. I lowered my head and took a deep breath, then with a groan of effort, I thrust my right hand upward, searching for anything to hold on to. My fingers instantly smashed into something hard and unyielding, and I cried out in surprise, almost losing my grip and falling. I managed to grab the crossbeam with both hands and I waited, suspended with my shoulders aching. After a couple of breaths, I tried again. I felt my hand go through the opening this time, and I fumbled around desperately until I latched onto something round, solid, and soaking wet. My prison had a log roof, it seemed.

I held on to the thick, slippery log with my right hand and let go of the crossbeam with the other, dangling above the floor and kicking my legs wildly before finally contorting myself enough to get the other arm through the opening. Now, using both my hands and praying I wouldn't lose my grip on the slick wood, I pulled myself upward, ignoring the pelting rain that stung my face and the wind that tried to dislodge me. My upper body passed through the opening, and I wriggled further out onto the roof with my legs still inside. I reached outward blindly until I found another log and wrapped my hands around it. I could feel my thumb and fingers digging deeply into the wet chink of mud and chips wedged between the log and the ones to either side of it. Grunting with effort, I dragged myself out of the hole, and when I was finally free, I lay face down on the roof, blowing like a winded horse as the storm seethed in outrage and tore at my clothing.

The pain in my head had receded during the treacherous climb, or perhaps I'd simply forgotten about it, I don't know, but now it came back with a vengeance. I grit my teeth against the pounding and slowly dragged myself to the edge of the rain-soaked roof, fighting the slickness of the wood and the wind that fought to blow me over the side. I opened my eyes, using a hand to protect them from the rain as I peered downward. I could see little other than a water-logged, muddy street below me and a shadowy building opposite with shuttered windows. One of the shutters came loose with a crash as I watched, revealing lantern light from inside that lit up the street. I heard a muffled curse coming from inside the house before an arm appeared and dragged the shutter closed again.

I saw no other movement anywhere else, guessing that everyone in the village was sheltering inside the buildings against the storm. No sane person would be out in this, after all, which suited me just fine. I shifted around until my legs were hanging out over the roof's edge, then used my arms to slowly propel myself backward until, eventually, I was dangling from the eave. I let go, landing in a crouch on the balls of my feet in a puddle, where I froze, listening. I waited, holding my breath, but heard no outcry at my escape. I nodded. So far, so good. My head had cleared somewhat, I was pleased to note, though my stomach still felt unsettled. I looked around, wondering what my next move should be.

I guessed there had to be guards watching the building where I'd been locked up, but where were they? I pressed myself close to the structure, protected somewhat from the rain by the eaves, and then I started to move by feel along the outer wall. I reached a corner and paused to peer around it as a river of water washed across my boots, heading toward the street. I was in an alleyway between two buildings. The wind was stronger here, shrieking down the passage, and I started to shiver in my wet clothes. I kept going, still not certain what I was going to do, just as I heard muted voices coming from ahead. I reached another corner of the building and cautiously snuck a look around it, able to discern a shadowy form standing beneath an overhanging porch that was shedding rain like a waterfall. A second man stood in an open doorway with the light from inside silhouetting him. One of my guards, I guessed.

"You want to talk to him now?" the man in the entranceway asked, sounding surprised. He had to shout to be heard. "In this?"

"I do," came back the loud reply. The voice was one I didn't recognize, although the outline of the man's body seemed familiar to me, despite his heavy cloak. I realized a moment later that it was the man who'd sat in the shadows during the bidding for the codex.

"The Fisherman told me not—" the guard began.

"I just spoke with him," said the second man, cutting him off. He pointed behind him, gesturing with a finger to the west. "The Fisherman granted me access to the prisoner. Now, if you really insist on going all the way up to the Hill in this storm to ask him if it's all right, be my guest. Just don't blame me for what happens when you do."

The guard paused for a moment as he thought about that. "Wait here," he commanded. The man disappeared inside, then was back less than a minute later. I figured he'd had to ask a superior what to do. "You can speak with him."

"What?"

"You can speak with him," the guard shouted. "But make it fast."

"Of course," the man on the porch said, giving a slight bow. He stepped inside, and the door slammed shut behind him a moment later, cutting off the light.

I knew my escape was only moments away from being discovered and that I had to act fast. But what could I do? Stealing one of the canoes along the shore was certainly an option, but then what? I quickly discarded the idea. I was no seaman, and trying to get away in one of those strange boats in this storm was asking for a quick death. I glanced to the west, where the stranger had pointed moments before. He'd called the house where The Fisherman lived the Hill. If I could get up there and somehow get my hands on that traitorous bastard, then maybe I could use him to negotiate my way out of here. It seemed like the only chance I had.

I turned and started to run through the mud and puddles while the storm raged around me. No one saw me or tried to stop me in those first few minutes, and for that, they should thank the gods, for I was in a killing mood this night. I reached a street with a boarded-up Holy House that I remembered seeing on my way to The Fisherman's dinner with Fitz and Alfaheed. The Temba had told me the Son had died of old age years ago, and the Daughter had lost her life swimming in the tide pools on the island's windward side. The House had been abandoned ever since. I knew I was getting close.

"What in the—?"

A dark form suddenly appeared to my left from an alley, and I reacted without thinking, cutting the man's words off as I grabbed the front of his waterlogged cloak and dragged him toward me. I lifted a knee, directing it as hard as I could into the startled man's groin. Then, as he stumbled and cried out in pain, I twirled him around and, using both my hands, took hold of his head and gave it a savage twist sideways. I heard a satisfying crack before the man went limp in my arms. I lowered him into the muck, then took off his cloak and put it on, glad to have its warmth. I fumbled in the dark after that as I hurriedly searched the body. I grinned when I felt a sword on the dead man's hip. The weapon was short and oddly curved, which seemed to be a style favored by The Fisherman's soldiers. At that moment, it was priceless to me.

I glanced up at the raging skies. "Thank you," I whispered to the gods. "I take back all those harsh things I was thinking about you earlier."

I moved on, my confidence soaring. I now had a warm cloak and a weapon. Things were indeed looking up. I knew The Fisherman's house was less than four blocks away from the Holy House, and I made my way forward with a swagger in my step, walking down the middle of the street as if I owned it. Maybe my escape had been discovered by now, and perhaps it hadn't, but either way, I knew anyone looking out a window wouldn't care much when they saw me—except maybe to think that the soldier out there was either drunk or insane to be moving about on a night like this. As for my potential pursuers, I thought, who among them would expect me to go inland? I grinned, knowing they'd all be searching the shoreline for me, which would take time—time that I intended to use to my benefit.

I finally reached the Hill, where the distinctive outline of The Fisherman's house was easily recognizable from the other much smaller buildings around it. I ran forward and crouched behind the stone wall that separated the house from the street. I could see the circular drive was empty, with only one poor bastard standing on the stoop guarding the door. The man waited beneath an extended roof, huddling in his cloak with nothing but a small lantern in his hands for company. I heard him curse as the rain intensified, and I grinned. This was going to be easy. I made my way along the wall to the right until it ended, then took another peek. I was now more than forty feet away from the house, with the guard partially obscured by a column that supported the roof.

I clutched my curved sword tighter in my right hand, then began to run in an awkward crouch, heading at an angle away from the house. I could see the darkened roofline of an outbuilding in the distance, and I sprinted toward it, not stopping until I reached the safety of the structure's exterior wall. The sharp smell of shit and horse sweat assailed my nostrils almost immediately, telling me that I'd found The Fisherman's stables—not that it mattered, for a horse wouldn't do me much good on an island as small as this one.

I waited, watching the house in case there might be more guards patrolling along the perimeter, but I saw nothing. It was time to go. I took a step, then hesitated as my foot came into contact with something, sending it spinning away with a clunk. I bent down, searching until I found the object, quickly realizing that I'd kicked over a wooden bucket. I started to toss the bucket aside, then changed my mind, clutching the rope handle firmly in my left hand instead as I began to run toward the house. I was grateful for the sound of the wind and rain as my boots splashed through thick mud and deep puddles. My head still hurt with each plodding step, but nothing like it had earlier, and I noticed with surprise that my stomach felt almost normal again.

I'd already closed the distance to less than twenty feet from the house, the entire time careful to keep the column between the guard and me. When I guessed I was ten feet away, I threw the bucket high in the air, sending it soaring through the rain over the roof of the stoop, where it landed with a crack on the wet ground on the other side. The guard naturally turned that way, lifting his lantern just as I leaped up behind him. The man whirled, his surprised expression in the wane lantern light almost comical as I slashed sideways with my sword, cutting open his neck. The guard made a strangled, gargling sound, dropping the lantern, which I'd anticipated. I caught it deftly before it could fall and stepped back with my sword dripping blood. I waited, watching without pity as the dying man clutched at his neck as he tried to staunch the bleeding. I knew it was a wasted effort. The guard's eyes bulged as he stared at me in horror and he tried to speak before slowly folding at the knees and then pitching face-down on the stone.

I set the lantern beside him. "Sorry, friend," I whispered. "Tell The Father I say hello."

I moved to the heavy double doors and listened but heard nothing. Hopefully, the entrance hall on the other side of these doors would be empty or more blood would flow. I knew I'd have to move fast, for the moment I opened the door, the sounds of the storm would be amplified greatly, which meant someone was bound to come and investigate. I tightened my grip on my weapon, took a deep breath, then thrust open the door and burst inside to find the entrance hall well-lit but abandoned, just as I'd hoped.

I quickly closed the door, shutting out the storm as I listened. I could hear music coming from somewhere in the house, but nothing else other than my ragged breathing and the water from my hair and cloak dripping on the elegant black and white tiles beneath my feet. I paused, wondering where to go next. Where would The Fisherman be at this time of night during a storm like this? The music sounded like a harp to me, but with all the tiles and marble around me, I couldn't tell where it was coming from.

I glanced down the corridor which led to The Fisherman's library, guessing that would be a good place to start the search. I took two steps toward it, then paused as I heard sharp footsteps echoing down that same corridor. I pressed myself against the wall and waited with my sword poised to strike. An older female servant of at least forty appeared, humming softly to herself. She saw me, and her eyes went round, her mouth already opening to scream. I wrapped my big hand over her mouth, silencing her, then pressed the sword to her belly.

"Where is The Fisherman?" I demanded in a whisper. The servant stared at me, terrified as she trembled in my arms. I felt sorry for her, but I needed to know and didn't have time for niceties. I had no intention of harming the poor woman, of course, but she didn't know that. "Tell me," I growled in my meanest voice, pricking her with the end of my sword. "Or I swear by The Mother I'll disembowel you right here and bathe in your blood."

The servant moaned in terror as I cautiously released the pressure on her mouth.

"Well?" I grunted.

"In the dining room," the woman managed to say.

"Ah," I said with a smile. "Then I think you'd best take me there, don't you?" The servant bobbed her head up and down frantically as I put a hand on the back of her neck and pushed her ahead of me. "One sound out of you," I whispered in her ear. "And I'll snap your scrawny neck like a chicken bone. Understand?"

The woman nodded again, leading me toward the dining room where I'd eaten only a few short hours before. I stepped inside, then slowly released my grip on the servant's neck. I swore, barely noticing as she scurried away with a terrified squeak.

"Ah, there you are, Lord Hadrack," The Fisherman said with a patronizing smile. He was sitting at the head of the dining table just as before, but now, instead of half-drunken guests surrounding him, there were at least fifteen armored men standing at the ready, all with their swords drawn. I could hear the clink of armor behind me as more men blocked my exit. I sighed, then spun the curved sword around in my hand and offered it to the closest soldier.

I was The Fisherman's prisoner once more.

Chapter 10: The Temba

The Temba ship was called a catamaran, which was a large, double-masted, and double-hulled sea-going vessel the likes of which I'd never seen before. Thick, roughly hewn wooden decking connected the twin hulls, with a hut erected between two bright red, crab-like sails to shelter the ten-man crew from the weather. The rest of the space was crammed with chests, caskets, and supplies tied down with netting. I'd spent most of the last twelve days since my recapture chained to the front mast of the catamaran while we sailed southwest on our way to the land of the Temba, only getting released briefly each morning and night to relieve myself. I had no protection from the elements where I sat on a narrow platform between the double bows and was mostly ignored by the Temba except for their sour-faced captain—a man named Chaba—who hated me for some reason that I couldn't fathom.

A slave boy named Tako would bring me water twice daily and sit with me and talk when permitted, but apparently, I was not to be given any food. The boy had a kind heart, however, and he'd tried sneaking me some fruit on the second day, only to get caught in the process. Chaba had been quick to punish Tako for his daring, forcing me to watch as he'd stripped him naked and whipped his back and buttocks with a willow branch. After that, I'd made the boy promise he'd never take the chance again despite his initial assurances that he was used to such beatings.

While it was obvious by the many old scars crisscrossing his back that the boy spoke the truth about the beatings, I'd seen the look in Chaba's eyes and was afraid the next time Tako would suffer much worse than just some strokes from a branch. I'd explained to the boy that a man can survive a long time without food if he has water and that I knew the Temba king didn't want me dead—at least, not yet, anyway. Tako had been as good as his word, and there had been no further incidences since, which I suspected had greatly disappointed that mean bastard, Chaba.

    The Temba king's royal entourage consisted of a hundred men on four large catamarans, which their captains were careful to sail well within eyesight of each other in a straight line during the day. At night, all four vessels would be lashed together like a floating fortress before the men would gather around metal braziers placed on stone slabs to drink honey wine, sing songs, and swap lies long into the night. Each morning when the sun was beginning to kiss the sky, the ships would be untied, and King Alba would lead us onward, sailing with his daughter in an enormous, yellow-painted catamaran called *Akuwaei*. Tako had told me the name meant *Deep-Water-Horse* in the ancient Temba dialect. My catamaran was the smallest of the four and was called *Tunias*, which meant *Wandering-Spirit*.

    The Temba spoke the universal language of our world just like everyone else did, of course, for that was one of the laws decreed by the First Pair that all must obey. But they always named their vessels in the old language, which was permissible, and would occasionally interject the odd Temba word or phrase when they spoke that I'd struggle to interpret. Tako was helping enormously with that.

    So far, we had seen no signs of any of the monstrous hurricanes that plagued the Southlands, although it had rained heavily several times, leaving me cold, shivering, and miserable where I sat exposed. I couldn't imagine how these ships could survive this far out to sea if a great storm came, but Tako assured me they would weather it easily because of the double hulls. After what I'd gone through on the much larger and sturdier *Sea-Dragon* years ago, I had my doubts. I hadn't talked to Sarrey since our capture, though I had seen her more than once during the nightly gatherings. The girl never joined in the merriment, looking lost and forlorn as she walked the decks. I suspected that if not for the two guards that constantly shadowed her wherever she went, she probably would have flung herself into the ocean by now.

"What kind of a knot is this?" I heard our captain shout. "Are you really this stupid, or are you just lazy?"

I glanced over my shoulder at the commotion as Chaba scolded one of the crew—a quiet fellow named Sumisu who had always seemed sympathetic to my plight and had offered me extra water once. *Wandering-Spirit's* captain had a volatile temper and was prone to lashing out at anyone for even the smallest infraction, and I'd seen the same thing play out numerous times before. The Temba all worked naked except for a white loincloth, and their skin was the color of dark copper. They were all short and stocky men with black, shoulder-length hair, powerful arms and shoulders, and colorful tattoos on their backs. Chaba saw my eyes on him, and he laughed when I looked quickly away. The bastard sometimes liked to beat me with a club when angry, and I saw no reason to give him an excuse now. I'd already spent many hours thinking about how I would kill Chaba when the chance came—if it ever did. The wishful exercise helped to pass the time if nothing else.

Tako appeared a few minutes later with a water jug, his expression grim as he knelt beside me. "What's that look for?" I asked.

The boy held the jug to my lips and I drank gratefully, for it was unbearably hot in the full sunlight. "*Gulana* says we will arrive in Temba soon." *Gulana* was a term of respect for a captain or ship's master.

I pushed the jug away, having drunk my fill. "Good," I grunted. "I'm looking forward to having some solid ground under my feet again."

Tako looked down, not meeting my eyes. "They will kill you, *Hasama*."

"I told you not to call me that," I scolded, though not with any real anger. *Hasama* meant lord, and Chaba had forbidden anyone to use the title when addressing me.

Tako shrugged. "*Gulana* will sleep for a short time before we make landfall. He will snore soon and make a lot of noise. He won't know."

I grinned. The boy was right, Chaba snored louder than any man I'd ever heard. The only things that rivaled the sounds he made in his sleep were his belches and farts. "Can you stay with me, then?" I asked, feeling a sudden need for company.

Tako nodded. "Yes, for now." His expression darkened. "You will be dead soon, *Hasama*. This makes me very sad."

I shifted position, ignoring the discomfort where the iron manacles around my wrists had rubbed the skin raw. I was wearing only a simple white loincloth like my captors and had similar marks from the shackles on my ankles. "Tell me what to expect," I said.

"This thing they speak of has not happened in many, many years, *Hasama*," Tako said. "Since long before I was born." I frowned and waited, not liking the sound of that. "The king will have you—" Tako hesitated, searching for the words. He made a sawing motion with an extended finger. "What do you call cutting off the skin piece by piece?"

I pursed my lips, my eagerness to reach Temba quickly extinguished now. "Flayed alive?" I whispered.

"That's right," Tako said somberly. "You are to be taken to King's Square near the Yellow Palace and made an example of. I'm sorry to say there will be much pain before you die, *Hasama*." The boy made a face. "A terrible death."

"Indeed," I said.

"*Yashi*!" one of the crew called out impatiently. *Yashi* was the Temba word for turd.

"I must go," Tako said anxiously. "I'll come back when I can, *Hasama*."

I took a deep breath after the boy left, holding it in as I tried to control my accelerating heartbeat. Flayed alive, I thought as I let the air out of my lungs. I shuddered at the fate that awaited me. I'd get away somehow, I vowed. Seven men still needed killing before I went to the next world to be with Shana. I thought suddenly of The Fisherman, feeling instant hatred. Make that eight men. The bastard had sold me to Sarrey's father for a single gold coin and had laughed while he'd done it. Our deal for the codex, The Fisherman had said, was voided because I'd given Sarrey sanctuary on my ship and offended his dear friend, King Alba. Honor and friendship, The Fisherman had lectured me, were everything to him, even more so than gold. I'd argued that I'd upheld my end of the bargain and hadn't known who the girl was, but neither The Fisherman nor the king had believed me, or if they had, cared all that much.

The thousand Jorqs from Daughter Gernet would be kept as a penalty for breach of contract, The Fisherman had declared, and my ship would be hunted down and my men killed, with the codex being sold to Lord Boudin per the original agreement. I ground my teeth in anger as I pictured the look on the Cardian's face before he'd left in pursuit of *Sea-Wolf*. I doubt I'd ever seen a happier man in my life. I had no idea what had happened since then, but I had confidence in my men and was convinced they were out here somewhere, maybe close by, searching for me. I knew it was a faint hope, but it was all I had at the moment.

I sat brooding for several more hours, dozing off and on under the full force of the sun until a sharp horn the Temba used to communicate with each other sounded from the ship ahead of us. One of the crew on *Wandering-Spirit* answered the call, followed by the last catamaran in line. I peered ahead curiously. I could see the king's double sails on the horizon and the unmistakable outline of land beyond that. It appeared we'd finally reached Temba.

"Are you well, *Hasama*?" Tako asked. I hadn't heard him approach.

I nodded as the boy crouched beside me again. "I'm well."

Tako looked toward the approaching coastline. "The gods have favored us with strong winds. We will arrive before *Satista* now. This is a good thing."

"*Satista*?"

"Prayer," Tako explained. He motioned to the sun overhead. "To The Mother and The Father. All men in Temba must kneel and give thanks to the gods Above and Below when the sun goes down. Even our great king." He grinned. "This is a time of peace and reflection, *Hasama*."

"I see," I said, feeling sudden hope. "So, no execution, then?"

"Execution, yes," Tako said. He smiled shyly. "Just not when we get home. Maybe later tonight. I don't know for sure."

"Well, that's something, at least," I muttered.

An hour later, I sat transfixed, staring at the largest settlement I'd ever seen. I'd always thought that Gandertown was the biggest city in the world, but now I knew better. I looked at Tako in amazement. "But," I managed to mumble. "I thought the Temba were just one tribe?"

Tako grinned. "We are one tribe, *Hasama*," he agreed. The boy winked. "Just a very big tribe, yes?"

"Yes," I said in wonder.

I could see perhaps a mile in each direction along the coast, but there were few trees, only high walls and tall, elegant buildings made of gleaming yellow sandstone. It was hard to comprehend the sheer enormity of the place. Mountains rose to the south of the city, with an immense bronze statue of a woman and a man standing together on the tallest peak. Each of the figures held a strange, spear-like weapon with blades on either side in one hand while shielding their eyes with the other as they looked out over the city.

Tako saw my curiosity, and he nodded. "*Maharas*," he said. The boy paused as he thought. "Guardians, *Hasama*. They keep our lands safe. No enemy has taken Temba since they watch over us."

"I can see why," I grunted, hugely impressed. I guessed all it would take was one look at those giant statues—which I estimated rose three hundred feet or more—and most invaders would turn away in terror. Any people who could build something so large and majestic must logically be formidable foes.

Hundreds of small canoes, flat barges, and colorful catamarans of all sizes were sailing in the waters, with any in our path quick to move aside as the king's procession drew closer to land. Our four ships were now tied together, with the king's vessel surrounded protectively by the other three at the front and sides. We were on the left side. Archers with oddly curved bows had formed along the perimeter of the decks, watching the water and land ahead with hard eyes.

"Well, that's interesting," I muttered to myself. Perhaps not all was well here, after all.

"We go to the Royal Docks, there," Tako said, cutting into my thoughts as he pointed east.

I could see a monstrous stone pier towering above the water with a crowd of people waiting there for us. The king's yellow and black banner emblazoned with a bright orange lion's head was in evidence everywhere, and I could already hear faint cheers echoing over the water from that direction. I looked away, studying the many small canoes floating around us that I'd first seen at The Iron Cay. Tako had told me they were called outriggers. Most of their occupants were watching us with blank faces, and I noticed that not one of them was cheering their king. I compared that to Ganderland, where King Tyden couldn't go anywhere in the realm without a roar of approval following him. The people of Ganderland loved Tyden wholeheartedly, but it seemed that was not the case here in Temba regarding their ruler. It might be nothing, I knew, but maybe I could leverage whatever was going on here to my advantage.

I motioned to the archers. "What's that about? Is the king in any kind of danger?"

Tako grimaced. "The White Ravens make much trouble in Temba lately. They say the king is a sinner and must be punished."

"White Ravens?"

Tako rolled his eyes. "They are very strange people, *Hasama*. They shave off all the hair on their bodies and wear white robes. They say The Mother and The Father are false gods. That there is only one true god—the God Beyond." The boy shook his head ruefully. "The king was not worried about them in the beginning. He tolerated them, saying a few crazed rats was not a problem. But now, many people believe this nonsense, so more rats are scurrying around in the night than ever before. The king blamed the White Ravens for Princess Sarrey's disappearance, so he tortured some of them to get the truth. Others he threw in prison. That made the common people very angry, which has brought a great deal of violence to the city lately. That is why the archers watch. To protect our king."

I mulled that over as we drew up to the dock, where I could see a small group of brightly dressed dignitaries waiting patiently. I noticed the men were surrounded on three sides by soldiers holding round yellow shields with an orange lion's head painted on them. They also carried similar spears like those that I'd seen the statues holding. A large crowd had gathered behind the soldiers waving yellow and black banners, but though they were cheering their king loudly, I could tell by their expressions that their hearts weren't in it. This was a show and nothing more, I realized.

Two men dressed in bright white robes with shining, shaven heads caught my eye, standing on the balcony of a building that overlooked the dock. Each wore what looked like a six-pointed silver star around their neck. The men watched the king's arrival with expressionless faces as Alba del Fante and his daughter disembarked from their ship, then made their way up a long wooden ramp. The archers and soldiers followed afterward, while the ships' crews remained. I studied the robed figures on the balcony curiously, then turned and glanced to the west, where an outrigger sat some distance away. I'd noticed more of the white-robed bald men sitting in that boat on the way in but hadn't thought much about it at the time.

I knew the fact these so-called White Ravens were echoing—at least partially—what I'd read in Waldin's copy of the codex wasn't a coincidence. They clearly knew the truth. But who had told that truth to them? The Sons? The Piths, maybe? I shook my head as I thought. Neither seemed likely to me since the truth about the Master wouldn't benefit the Sons at all, and as for the Piths, I knew them better than anyone. If the tribes had made contact with the Temba at some point, I would have heard about it from Alesia—which left only Malo to consider. Could the former House Agent be allied with the White Ravens? I snorted at the thought. Except for Einhard, Malo was probably the most stubborn and principled man that I'd ever met. He would never have breathed a word about what was in that codex. I was certain of it. Yet, someone must have.

"*Yashi!*"

Tako looked over his shoulder fearfully at Chaba, who stood six feet away on the decking, glaring at us with his hands on his hips. The captain was fully dressed now, wearing black leather armor, lambswool trousers, and a leather helmet. He motioned behind him with his chin. "Go help the others with the supplies. I will take care of the *Ramata*."

Tako had told me *Ramata* meant northerner, though he hadn't been able to meet my eyes when he'd said it. I suspected ever since then that the name was a little more insulting than he had let on.

Chaba held up a key after Tako hurried away. "You are going to be a good little whipped dog, yes?" he asked me.

I could see the contempt in his eyes, and I just looked down, not bothering to say anything. The Temba snorted, thinking me weak and cowed after my long days tied up without food. He was right about the weak part, but I wasn't cowed, far from it. The captain carried a curved sword—called a shotel—stuck carelessly in his belt at the back. The sword reminded me of the sickle my father used to cut wheat with on our farm. If I could get my hands on it, maybe I could show that bastard just how cowed I was.

Chaba knelt, unlocking my ankles one at a time. I casually glanced behind me past his bent form. The rest of the crew were untying the cargo from the deck, and none were looking my way. Tako was helping them, and he must have felt my gaze on him, for he looked up. Our eyes met, and I made a barely perceptible motion toward Chaba with my head, hoping the boy would understand. Tako hesitated, looking suddenly apprehensive, but he quickly recovered and nodded in determination. I took a deep breath, waiting as Chaba unlocked my left wrist.

"You are going to die soon, *Ramata*," the captain grunted. I could smell the stink of his breath on me. The Temba favored a fruit called durian, which gave off a scent that reminded me of pig shit. I suspected it tasted like it, too.

"We all must die sooner or later, great *Gulana*," I said, keeping my eyes lowered. "I must pay for the insult that I have given your king. I understand this now."

Chaba hesitated, looking at me with a mixture of surprise and suspicion. I lifted my head, staring at him with what I hoped was an earnest expression. "So, you finally learn some respect, eh, *Ramata*?" he eventually grunted. "This is a good thing." He laughed. "Much too late, of course, but still a good thing." The captain inserted the key in the lock on my right wrist. "I didn't think dogs from the north could be taught proper manners. It would seem I was mistaken."

"I have spent these past days watching you, great *Gulana*," I said meekly. "And I have seen how a real man must act. Thank you for showing me the path to honor before I die."

"Quite so," Chaba replied, looking pleased. He turned the key, and the lock gave a sharp click before the manacle popped open.

I glanced at Tako, who stood poised and waiting for my signal. I nodded. The boy immediately whirled, using a small knife to efficiently sever a section of roped netting that held down a tall stack of wine barrels. None of the crew had noticed what he'd done, I was relieved to see. Tako dropped the knife, leaned his thin shoulder against the top barrel, and then pushed. He pretended to be startled moments later when the barrels tipped over and fell before they started rolling wildly across the deck. Several of the crew were in the path of the heavy caskets, and they dodged out of the way just in time as at least five barrels hurtled past them and over the side of the catamaran and into the water with a great splash.

I heard several of the Temba curse their bad luck, and I smiled when Chaba looked back at all the commotion with an expression of annoyance and growing rage. I grabbed the bastard by his long hair before he could stand and yanked him toward me, twisting aside and smashing his forehead into the unyielding wood of the mast. Chaba groaned, stunned as I grabbed the hilt of his sword and tore the weapon free from his belt. I put the blade to his throat.

"All men die!" I hissed in his face. "Remember?"

Chaba opened his mouth to call out to his men, and I didn't hesitate, cutting from left to right across his neck. The Temba gagged, his eyes round with disbelief as he died. I would have greatly enjoyed taking a moment longer to savor his death, but I knew I didn't have the time for it. I stood, my legs wobbly from sitting so long, then tossed aside the sword and dove clumsily headfirst into the water as deep as I could. I struck out toward the west until I saw the blurry outlines of an outrigger floating above my head. I was quickly running out of air, and I used my hands to guide me along the submerged hull, then surfaced on the far side of the boat away from the view of the catamarans and dock.

I had no idea what I was going to do next just as an offering hand appeared over the boat's railing. That hand, I saw, was attached to a man wearing a white cowl partially covering his head, revealing bright eyes, fleshy lips below flushed, rounded cheeks, and a bald forehead. I was startled to note that he had no eyebrows. A White Raven, I realized.

"Why, hello there, little fish," the man said. He looked over his shoulder, then turned back and smiled kindly down at me. "The Lions didn't see which way you went, little fish, but it won't take them long to figure it out. My brothers and I offer you sanctuary. Do you wish to take it?"

"Yes," I croaked, sucking in air. For really, what choice did I have?

And that is how I met Muwa, the White Raven, and began one of the most harrowing adventures of my life.

Chapter 11: Muwa

  I spent the next hour confined in a false bottom located beneath one of the benches at the back of the White Ravens' boat. I guessed that the tight space had originally been designed for smuggling goods and would normally have been too narrow for a man of my size to fit. But I was nearly naked and had lost a great deal of weight in the last twelve days, and because of that, as well as my overwhelming desire to keep my skin on my body, I was just able to squeeze myself inside.
  The White Raven who'd originally offered me his hand had helped pull me onto the outrigger, where I'd lain in the boat's belly shaking and dripping water while the other two had raised the sail enough to shield me from the eyes of the king's men. I'd worried that with all the people in the ships around us and along the shore, there would be countless witnesses to what we were doing. But the Ravens had assured me that no one would talk. I wasn't sure how these strange men could be so certain of that, but I didn't have any other option except to take them at their word.
  I was forced to lie in my hideaway like a contortionist with my arms pinned beneath me, and my knees turned away from my hips and drawn up. The outrigger constantly rocked back and forth on the waves, and I fought a losing battle to keep my nose, cheek, and right shoulder away from the rough wood of the trapdoor above me. I quickly gave that up as hopeless, resigned to the painful jarring and scratching with each lap of the waves. Besides, I had other things to worry about, for there was little air inside my lair and it was surprisingly hot despite my being submerged beneath the waterline. I could see through a small hole in one of the boards above me, but my line of sight was limited to the bottom of the bench and a bit of blue sky, which didn't do me much good.

Eventually, I just closed my eyes, trying not to think about what would happen if the Temba found me. I realized my current plight was very reminiscent of when Baine, Jebido, and I had been forced into cages many years ago after the fall of Gasterny. Of course, there were no Cardian captors to contend with this time, but instead, a bunch of white-robed religious fanatics whose motivation for saving me remained a mystery. I wondered if I was better or worse off now than I had been then. Only the gods and time could answer that question.

The Temba had begun swarming the area with ships and soldiers after my escape, starting a highly coordinated search of the shore and every barge, catamaran, and outrigger within a half mile in both directions along the coast. As the search proceeded, the Raven with the round face and kind eyes sat above me, describing what was happening in a monotonous tone. My first concern was what had happened to Tako, but as far as the Raven could tell, the boy's hand in my escape had gone completely unnoticed. I dearly hoped things remained that way, for I owed that lad my life. Someday, I hoped to repay Tako for what he'd done for me, but first, I'd need to stay out of the clutches of the Temba.

Our outrigger had been one of the first boats searched, since it was the closest vessel to *Wandering-Spirit* when I'd escaped. I'd been convinced the king's men would find the secret compartment easily and drag me out kicking and screaming. But after coming alongside us and questioning the Ravens about what they'd seen, the soldiers had left without actually coming aboard. The White Ravens had few possessions or gear with them; nothing but netting and a few frayed ropes coiled in the outrigger's belly. The Temba had poked these with their spears, but not with much enthusiasm, as it was obvious that if a man were hiding beneath them, he would be easily seen.

The Temba had left to search elsewhere, but not before instructing the White Ravens to stay put and remain at anchor until further notice. That further notice came nearly an hour later when a ship pulled alongside us once again. This time, a soldier came across, sending the boat into fits of rocking despite the outrigger's stabilizing float. I was worried that someone must have finally talked and my hideout was about to be discovered, but the man didn't even ask the White Raven sitting above me to move off his bench. It seemed their enthusiasm for the task was waning, and he was just going through the motions.

"What news, Lion?" I heard the Raven ask. "Has the foreigner escaped the net?"

"There's been no sign of him, *Galata*," the soldier grunted. "He couldn't have escaped, though. Where would he go? No, the bastard most likely drowned and was swept out to sea."

"Well, then his soul is with the One True God now," the White Raven said. "I will pray that He forgives this poor, unfortunate man of all his sins and welcomes him to the Realm Beyond."

The soldier snickered. "Sure, old man. You do that." I heard his boots clumping on the boards above me, and then the boat rocked as the man jumped back onto his ship.

"Fear not, my little fish," the Raven above me said softly after the Temba had left. "*Satista* approaches, and soon you will be safe. The Lions have lost the scent and are sniffing in all the wrong places. By the grace of the One True God, you will be free to swim again within the hour. This I swear to you."

"Thank you," I whispered, my voice hoarse and strained.

"Think nothing of it," the Raven replied. "My brothers and I are here in the service of God, and giving you sanctuary is all part of His plan." The man paused and, when I didn't respond, added, "So, what should I call you, my little fish? What name does the One True God whisper to you in your sleep?"

I hesitated for only a moment. "Lord Hadrack," I answered. I figured the White Ravens and the entire city would learn my true identity soon enough anyway, so why start our relationship off with a lie?

"Ah," the voice responded, sounding pleased. I knew immediately that I'd made the right decision, for it was clear by his tone that he'd already known who I was. I wondered how. "A man of honesty," the Raven continued. "How refreshing. Sadly, that has become something of a rare commodity these days. It is a pleasure to meet you, lord. I have, of course, heard much about you, even here in faraway Temba. My name is Muwa, by the way."

"Oh, I thought that it was Galata," I said. "Isn't that what the soldier called you?"

Muwa chuckled. "He did call me that, lord. But *Galata* means white slug. The Lions find it amusing to denigrate our faith in this way. It hardly matters, of course, for we are stronger than anything they can do to us or say about us. They are like blind children, you see, and God has tasked us with showing them the light. Soon, they will begin to see and then they will understand."

I felt the boat start to move forward through the water then as the White Ravens took up the oars. "And may I ask, lord," Muwa said. "How has it come to pass that you have drawn our mighty leader's ire in such an unfortunate fashion?"

I remained silent for a moment, wondering what to say. Finally, I decided to keep telling him the truth, or at least a version of it, anyway. "I sailed here from Ganderland on a trading mission," I said. "We came across a half-sunken raft in the water, where we found the king's daughter and a man named Mondar barely clinging to life. Apparently, a storm had capsized them."

"How interesting," Muwa said as if I'd just told him I'd seen a squirrel eating a pine cone. I guessed he already knew about that, too. "Please, do go on, lord," Muwa prompted.

"I had no idea who the two were at the time," I said. "We pulled them from the water, more dead than alive, then continued to our destination."

"And what might that destination have been, lord?"

"The Iron Cay," I answered, though I suspected my questioner also knew that.

"Ah, I see," Muwa replied. "And while you were there, lord, I imagine our king discovered his daughter was on your ship and accused you of taking her. Is that a proper summation, would you say?"

"Yes, it is," I agreed. "I was snatched from my ship by that bastard Fisherman and sold to your king for a single coin. He planned on having me flayed alive in King's Square later today."

"Oh, how dreadful, lord," Muwa stated in a disapproving voice. "Please forgive some of my...uhm...shall we say, less enlightened countrymen. The world has become such a dark and soulless place in recent years, filled with endless wars, rape, debauchery, and other sins too numerous to mention. That will change when the Enlightenment arrives, but until then, we must let our faith in God give us strength. Don't you agree?"

"Uh, of course," I said, wondering what the Enlightenment was.

"Don't you want to ask me, lord?" Muwa added as if he'd read my thoughts.

"Ask you what?"

"What I meant by the Enlightenment, of course."

"Maybe once we're out of this, you can explain it to me," I said. I sensed Muwa was ready to start preaching and hoped to put it off as long as possible. I was curious, actually, but I was also exhausted, starving, and hurting from head to toe.

"I look forward to it, lord," Muwa said graciously. "Now, we are almost to shore. Is there anything else that I can do for you?"

"Getting me away from the king's men is more than enough," I said. "I am forever in your debt."

"Bah, think nothing of it, lord," Muwa said with a snort. "My brothers and I are here to serve." He paused then as if an idea had just occurred to him. "Although perhaps someday, should the need arise, you can do something for us in return, lord."

"Such as?" I asked, instantly on my guard now.

"Oh, one never knows for certain until that moment arrives," Muwa said cagily. "Now, does one?"

"No, I guess one doesn't," I muttered, low enough that I doubted the man heard me.

Muwa had informed me that a covered wagon was already on its way to us, though how he'd gotten the word out was a mystery to me. At the moment, I only cared about getting free of that compartment. I had twin points of fire burning along my shoulder blades, and I'd lost the feeling in my feet half an hour ago.

"Ah, here we are," Muwa said as the outrigger bumped and scrapped against what I assumed was a dock.

I waited, listening, but other than one of the Ravens tying us off before sitting down again, no one else moved. "What's happening?" I finally whispered after long minutes of silence had passed. "Why aren't we moving?"

"Patience, lord," Muwa said. "I understand you are in some discomfort, but there are Lions in the streets. In fact, I can see two of them standing by a fishmonger's stand less than fifty yards from us right now. One of them is an ugly beast of a man, too, and he's looking this way. But, if you can't take it any longer, lord, then by all means, please come out of there and stretch your legs. Just don't blame me for what happens next."

"I'll wait," I grunted sourly, disappointed. "So, do you have a plan to get me away from here?" I added, trying, and failing to hide my annoyance. Muwa's attitude was quickly getting on my nerves. "Or am I going to have to spend the entire night in this thing?"

"I do have a plan, lord," Muwa assured me, sounding relaxed and at ease. "Trust me. This was expected. We just need to wait a little longer. Besides, I'm rather enjoying the cool breeze coming off the water after such a hot day. Can you feel it?" I frowned at that, wanting to remind Muwa that it wasn't his skin the king planned on hacking off, but I bit my tongue. The White Ravens were the only friends I had at the moment, and it was best not to antagonize them. "Brothers," Muwa finally said to his companions. "Aidar has arrived. Go now, and may the One True God watch over you."

"One god, One heart, One mind," the Ravens chanted in unison.

The boat began to rock back and forth as the men climbed onto the dock. I heard the whisper of their sandalled feet heading away across the wooden planks just as Muwa started to whistle. I had to force myself not to curse out loud, trying to control my impatience and temper. I managed to wait for what I guessed was five minutes, listening to the Raven's inane whistling before finally, I couldn't take it any longer. "What's happening?" I demanded. "What's taking so long?"

"It's almost time for the fun, lord," Muwa said, sounding amused.

"What fun?"

As if on cue, I heard an excited voice shouting, "There he is! The *Ramata*! I see him! Hurry! He's getting away!"

Cries of surprise instantly sounded, and I could hear running feet heading away from us. Muwa snickered. "The king's men are fearsome fighters, lord, but alas, they have little between the ears." Moments later, I heard a thud above me as Muwa removed the bench, then lifted the trap door away. I blinked in the waning sunlight as dusk approached while the Raven smiled down at me. "Shall we go, lord? Or have you changed your mind about staying in there?"

"Help me up," I grunted, twisting my shoulders to stick out a hand. Muwa chuckled, grabbing me in a powerful grip. It seemed effortless for the Raven as he pulled me out of the compartment, where I crouched in the outrigger's belly on my hands and knees. I took a moment to savor the fresh air and my freedom.

"There is little time, lord," Muwa said. He held up a white robe. "Put this on. We must hurry. *Satista* approaches. We must be gone before then."

I stood shakily and did as the man asked, letting him pull the cowl low over my face as he fussed. The robe was much too small for me, but it would have to do. Satisfied, Muwa jumped nimbly onto the landing, then reached back and helped me to cross the two-foot gap of open space between the boat and dock. I was glad of the Raven's strength, for I was all but used up and probably would have fallen into the water without him.

"Keep your head down and follow me, lord," Muwa whispered. "No matter what happens, you must get in that wagon."

The White Raven turned then, hurrying away with his hands thrust inside the sleeves of his robe. I emulated him, ignoring the pains in my legs and feet as the blood started to flow again. The dock was thirty feet long, though it felt like a thousand to me. I was certain I could feel hundreds of pairs of eyes on me as I tried to keep up to Muwa but could see very little from beneath my cowl with my head bent. We finally reached the end of the wharf, and I chanced a glance up. A covered wagon pulled by a brace of matching black horses awaited us on the street twenty feet away. I noticed a very tall and thin White Raven standing by the open door, with another sitting up in the driver's seat. The skinny man wasn't wearing a robe, but I recognized him as one of the Ravens who'd been in the outrigger with us. I guessed the robe I wore belonged to him.

"You there!" a commanding voice suddenly rang out from further down the street. "Stop!"

I looked that way, feeling my heart starting to thud rapidly against my ribs. Two soldiers were coming toward us, both carrying spears with a curved sword blade on each end. I was to learn the hard way that the Lions were experts with these weapons, which they called a *duelata haisha*, or double-bladed glaive.

Muwa glanced back at me. "Keep going, lord!" the Raven hissed. "Get in the wagon! I will deal with this." He turned to face the approaching soldiers, spreading his arms to his sides. "A good day to you, Lions? What can I do for you?"

I didn't hear the reply, as I'd already reached the wagon and had begun climbing inside with the skinny Raven's help. A curse suddenly sounded, and I paused halfway into the cab to look back. One of the Lions was on his back, looking stunned. Had Muwa hit him? The second Lion growled and whirled his glaive at the Raven in a blur of speed. I winced, expecting to see the man cut down, but Muwa leaped nimbly backward, and the blade hissed past his midsection. The Raven darted into the opening, using his balled fist to strike the Lion hard on the side of his helmet. The man staggered but had the presence of mind to swing backhanded at Muwa's head with his glaive. That also missed, for the Raven dropped smoothly to the ground beneath the weapon, then used his leg to sweep the Lion off his feet. I stared in astonishment. I'd never seen anyone move so fast in my life.

Muwa glanced back at us, and I could see the annoyance on his face. "Go, brother!" he shouted at our driver. "Get him away from here!"

I looked down the street, grimacing. Two more soldiers were hurrying down the road.

"Get inside, lord," the Raven behind me grunted, pushing me forcefully through the door.

I stumbled and fell, lying facedown on the floorboards between two opposing benches while the Raven climbed in on top of me, then slammed the door shut. He banged his fist against the roof, and a moment later, the wagon started to move, quickly gaining speed.

"My apologies, lord," the thin Raven said, helping me to my feet and onto a bench as the wagon rocked and bumped along the uneven cobblestones. "I meant no disrespect."

"But what about Muwa?" I asked. "We need to go back and help him."

The Raven sat down opposite me, and he smiled, looking unfazed. "Do not concern yourself with Muwa, lord. He has the One True God on his side, so he cannot fall." The man winked. "Perhaps instead, you should pray for the Lions, for they will need all the help they can get. Not that it will change the outcome any."

I nodded doubtfully, but there was little that I could do in my condition other than to go along with it. I settled back on the bench, feeling utter exhaustion weighing me down as I closed my eyes, rolling with the motion of the wagon. I must have slept for a time, for dusk had fallen when I opened my eyes. I glanced at the skinny Raven, who still sat across from me and was staring at me intensely. He smiled when he saw my gaze on him, though I found his expression more unnerving than comforting. With his bald head, long nose, and sunken eyes and missing eyebrows, I thought the man reminded me of a great bird of prey about to tear into fresh meat. Was I the meat?

"We have arrived, lord," the Raven announced when the wagon came to a halt a few moments later. "You are safe and are now a free man."

I stared at my companion, who offered me another of his predatory smiles. He was right, of course. I was free of the Temba, at least for now. But judging by the Raven's expression, my presumed safety in this strange land might not turn out to be everything that I'd hoped it would be.

Chapter 12: An Offer To Refuse

I was dog-tired and weaker than a newborn kitten as I climbed down from the wagon. It was dark out now, and I paused to look around cautiously while the thin Raven stepped down behind me. I was standing on a narrow street with tall, darkened buildings to either side. A man lay stretched out along one wall of a house fifty feet away—whether dead or asleep, I couldn't tell. A second man plodded past us with his head down, pushing a barrow filled with chamber pot waste collected from the streets. I smelled woodsmoke on the wind and the sharp, tangy stench of animal hides and piss, guessing that there must be a tannery nearby. A hound started to bark to the north, followed by a woman's high-pitched laughter. I heard a man shout and a bottle breaking, then the barking stopped and all was silent.

The thin Raven said something to the driver that I didn't hear, then he took my arm and gently guided me aside as the wagon headed off. I swayed with exhaustion, glad for the Raven's support. "We're almost there, lord," he said. "Then you can finally rest."

I nodded. "What do I call you?"

"I am known as Kish, lord." The Raven motioned toward a three-story building with a peaked roof, where I noticed a man standing in the shadows of the arched entrance. "This is where you will be staying for now until better accommodations can be found." Kish whistled, and the form broke away from the wall, hurrying toward us. I wasn't surprised to see that he was dressed in a white robe, though it was covered in filth. "This is Theny, lord," Kish said, introducing the man. "He will help you to get inside."

I didn't protest as Theny put an arm around my waist, supporting me as I half-walked, half-staggered with him toward the building. Theny was tall and extremely strong, with wide shoulders and few teeth in his mouth. He reeked overwhelmingly of onions, piss, and sweat, though I doubted that I smelled any better after my almost two-week ordeal. Once inside the building, Kish took up a lit candle, then led us down a corridor to a flight of stone stairs. We reached a landing, then turned right, making our way along a narrow arched passageway that smelled of decay and something long dead. The brick ceiling was low and brushed against my head, and I could hear water dripping all around me while rats scurried away from beneath our feet.

Kish glanced back at me, with the skin stretched tightly across his shaven skull looking almost ghoulish in the flickering candlelight. "I imagine this is not quite what you are accustomed to in your grand castle back in Ganderland, lord," he said. I thought I'd detected the hint of a sneer in his words. "Please accept my apologies. It was the best that we could do under the circumstances."

"It's perfectly fine," I said. "Trust me, I've seen far worse."

Kish looked pleased at that, and he turned around, his footsteps echoing loudly in the confined space. He cursed a moment later, and then I heard a squeal as he kicked a rat away that had the temerity to stand its ground in his path. "I hate rats," I heard him mutter under his breath.

I saw the thin Raven shudder, but he continued onward without pause until we reached another set of stairs. We climbed down them, then exited through an archway into a large room with a dirt floor and wood ceiling supported by heavy beams darkened with age. A table and several benches were the only furniture, and Kish put the candle down on the worn wood of the tabletop. Theny guided me toward the table and hooked a corner of a bench away from it with his toe, and then he helped me to sit.

"Theny," Kish said when the big man straightened. "Please get some food and proper clothing for our guest."

The big Raven bowed his head in acknowledgment but said nothing. He headed back through the entrance while Kish busied himself lighting more candles.

"So," I said, feeling increasingly uneasy. Something told me that I needed to get away from these people while I still could. This seemed like the perfect opportunity. I just wished I had more strength. "What happens now?"

Kish looked up as he dripped hot wax into a brass bowl, then fixed the candle he held in place. "Now, lord?"

"Yes," I said. "I have a feeling you people didn't help me escape out of kindness. What do you really want from me?"

Kish blinked in surprise, and his eyes turned wary, which confirmed my suspicions. These people were up to something. The Raven forced a smile, which only helped to make him look even more untrustworthy. "Kindness is God's way, lord. We merely do as He asks of us. There are no ulterior motives in what we do. We are mere servants to a bigger order."

I stood suddenly, clearly catching Kish off guard as he quickly stepped backward. "Then you and your companions have my everlasting gratitude," I said. "But I think I'll be on my way now."

"On your way, lord?" Kish asked. His voice was smooth and controlled, yet I could tell the man was anxious and trying not to show it. He kept glancing toward the arched entrance. "But, where will you go? The Lions will tear the city apart now that they know you didn't drown."

I realized he was right. Someone had distracted the Temba soldiers by claiming that they'd seen me, which meant the whole city was probably on the lookout for me by now. I silently cursed. The ploy had admittedly been a good one, but now that I thought about it, maybe it was meant to have a duel purpose all along. While it was true the ruse had gotten me away safely, now I was completely alone and hunted in a strange city with only the goodwill of the White Ravens standing between me and capture. I was indebted to these men, and they knew that, with my life now held in the palm of their hands. As far as leverage went, I couldn't think of anything better than that. The question was, what did these people hope to gain from me?

"Yes, that's certainly unfortunate," I finally said. I gave the man a challenging look. "Or maybe convenient, depending upon your point of view."

"I can't imagine what you mean by that, lord," Kish replied.

"No?" I grunted. I decided to push the man a little and see what might happen. "Then maybe you're even dumber than you look."

Kish flushed at my words, his eyes turning mean. This man wasn't nearly as intelligent or polished as Muwa, I realized. There was a whip-like rawness to him, with seething anger and resentment bubbling just below the surface that I knew could be used against him.

The Raven finally forced himself to smile, revealing sharp teeth like a fox. His eyes remained hard and mean, though. "I understand you are tired and upset after your trying ordeal, lord," Kish said soothingly. I took a step away from the table, and the thin Raven moved with me, putting himself between me and the archway. He lifted his hands, palms outward. I noticed those hands were unusually large and shaped like spades, though the skin looked soft and callous-free. No manual labor for this one. "But there is no reason for hostility," Kish continued. "We are the One True God's messengers, sent here to help you. My brothers and I are not your enemy."

"Says you," I growled. The Raven wore loose wool trousers and a white tunic, for I still had his robe on. A blue, six-pointed star hung around his neck, supported there by a leather thong. He had no weapons that I could see, and though Kish was taller than most men, he was reed-thin. I guessed at most he weighed a hundred and fifty pounds. I took another step. "Get out of my way."

"I'm afraid I can't do that, lord," Kish said. He'd put his back squarely to the arch, making it clear that I'd have to go through him if I wanted to leave. I had no problem with that.

"Last chance," I grunted. I was still weak from hunger and fatigue but had little doubt that I could deal with the skinny Raven in short order. Kish remained where he was, watching me warily. I could tell that he was leery of a confrontation, but there was also steel-like resolve in his features as well. The man would fight to keep me here if he had to. I moved until I faced the Raven, with less than two feet separating us. "I am going up those stairs," I said grimly. "If you try to stop me, you will regret it."

"And why, Lord Hadrack, would anyone care to stop you?"

I glanced toward the entrance, where Muwa had appeared with his hands thrust deeply into his sleeves. I hadn't heard the round-faced Raven arrive. Kish sagged slightly in relief, but he did not change his expression or move aside. Muwa entered the room wearing a pleasant smile as Theny followed behind him, carrying a medium-sized wooden chest.

I motioned to Kish. "Ask him. He's the one that said I couldn't leave."

"I am sure it was all just a simple misunderstanding, lord," Muwa said airily. "You are not a prisoner by any means. You are our valued friend." He nodded to Theny, who placed the chest he held on the table, then opened it and began removing some articles of clothing, followed by a loaf of bread, several mugs, and two flared green bottles of what I guessed was wine. Then, judging by the intoxicating aroma, he removed a meat pie wrapped in cloth. I felt my mouth start to water, unable to take my eyes off the food.

"So, lord," Muwa said as he came to stand before me. I had to force myself to look at him while my stomach grumbled. "Since you are not a prisoner, you are free to leave whenever you feel like it. I promise you, none here will try to stop you." The Raven motioned to the table. "But, I should mention that Theny went to a great deal of trouble to bring you this meal, and it would be a shame to waste it. You are clearly tired, lord, and no doubt starving. So, why not partake of this feast, and then, if you still feel inclined, take the clothing we have for you and go. Neither the One True God nor we, His servants, will judge you harshly for it."

I studied the Raven critically. "You mean that?" I asked, feeling my resolve weaken as the maddening smells swirled around me.

"Certainly, lord," Muwa said. He gently took my elbow and guided me closer to the table. The Raven pulled the cloth away with a flourish. "Veal pie with hard-boiled eggs, lord." I could see someone had decorated the crust with dough, forming a crude cow head in the center of the pie, which informed the diner what was in the filling. Muwa uncorked one of the bottles and poured some dark red liquid into a mug before handing it to me. "Wine from Cordova, lord. I hope it is to your liking."

I automatically took the mug, annoyed that my hand shook from fatigue.

"Please, sit, lord," Muwa said. "You look worn to a frazzle."

The Raven helped me onto the bench, and I didn't resist before he moved around the table and sat. I looked down at the contents of my mug, wondering if it was poisoned. I shrugged, discounting the idea as I downed it in one gulp. If the White Ravens wanted me dead that badly, then all they had to do was find the closest Lion. I smacked my lips at the taste and smiled with pleasure.

"How was it?" Muwa asked.

"Damn good," I answered truthfully.

"Excellent, lord," the Raven said, looking pleased. He poured himself some wine, then glanced up at our companions. "That will be all, brothers. Thank you."

Both Kish and Theny bowed, then headed toward the arched entrance.

"Kish," I said abruptly.

The thin Raven hesitated and turned. "Lord?"

"Get in my way again like that, and you'll be meeting your god sooner than you would like."

Kish and I held eyes, neither willing to look away until finally, Muwa cleared his throat, breaking the standoff. The skinny Raven gave me one last look filled with loathing, then he followed Theny up the stairs.

"Was that really necessary, lord?" Muwa asked, looking amused.

"Maybe not," I grunted with a shrug. "But it made me feel better."

Muwa laughed and slid a wooden spoon over to me. "Eat, lord." I took the spoon, then started to cram food into my mouth like a hungry bear while the Raven refilled my mug. He added more wine to his mug, then set the bottle aside. "When is the last time you ate?" Muwa asked sympathetically.

"The Iron Cay," I managed to say around a mouthful. The pie was cold but delicious. "I had lobster," I added.

"Ah," Muwa said. "The Fisherman is famous for that, among other things. I can't say I've developed a taste for it, though." I nodded as I ate, thinking of Fitz and wondering where my men were now. The Raven frowned after a moment as he watched me devouring the pie. "You might consider taking a little more time between bites, lord. I imagine your stomach will revolt soon if you keep gorging yourself like that." I hesitated, caught between overwhelming hunger and the realization that the man was right. Muwa tore off a chunk of bread and offered it to me. "Here, try this. It should help fill you and keep your stomach down."

"I don't think I'll ever be full again," I said, meaning it. My belly felt like an enormous hole—one I was determined to fill with every scrap of food on the table.

Muwa chuckled. "I understand, lord. I have been where you are now."

I studied the Raven curiously as I bit into the bread. "Is that right?" I said.

"Oh yes," Muwa agreed. "They rarely feed you at Kenningwood."

I bit off another piece of bread, then washed it down with wine. "Kenningwood?"

"It's a form of prison, lord," Muwa explained nonchalantly. "A place where some are sent to reflect upon their sins. I was incarcerated there for ten years." He glanced down at himself, then chuckled. "I have, sadly, put on some weight since those unfortunate days. Though to be fair, the One True God does not measure us by the pound, but by the weight of our faith."

"I see," I said as I spooned a healthy portion of pie into my mouth.

"I was something of a troublemaker in my youth," Muwa continued. "A boy that was foolish and easily swayed. So much so, in fact, that I became involved in a doomed plot to overthrow the king."

I looked at the Raven in surprise. "How come they put you in prison?" I asked. "I would have just taken your head."

"Quite so," Muwa said. "All those involved with me did eventually die, I'm sorry to say. Though not in such a crude manner as you suggest." He took a sip of wine, smacking his lips in appreciation. "But for me, the king chose leniency."

"Why?" I grunted, wondering where all this was going.

"I expect it was due to his relationship with my father."

"And what was that?"

Muwa shrugged, looking slightly embarrassed. "They were cousins, lord."

I gawked at the Raven. "You're Temba royalty?"

Muwa chuckled. "I was, yes. But now I am a servant of the One True God. Nothing more or less than any of my brothers."

"Oh, I doubt that," I said. I hooked a thumb over my shoulder. "Something tells me you're a lot more than that fool Kish out there." I put my spoon down, trying to ignore the growing ache in my belly. I hoped I wasn't on the verge of throwing up. I pushed the almost empty pie plate away, then leaned forward with my arms folded on the table. "So, now that I've eaten and we've become such good friends, why don't you tell me what this is really all about."

Muwa stared at me, not blinking as he thought. Finally, he sighed. "You were right, of course, lord. We do want something from you."

"What a surprise," I said sarcastically. "And what would that be?"

Muwa stood, putting his hands back into the sleeves of his robe as he began pacing. I belched loudly twice, which seemed to help the discomfort. I started toying with my almost empty mug of wine while I waited until, finally, the Raven stopped and leaned on the table. "Why did you come south, lord?"

"I told you—" I began.

Muwa snorted, shaking his head. "No, what you told me was only partially true. The rest was a lie. You are as much a trader as I am a whore in one of the city's boy brothels."

I hesitated at that. Did Muwa know the real reason I'd come? I decided to stay with the lie and see what happened.

"Oh, in the name of the One True God, lord," Muwa said in exasperation. I guessed he'd read the intent in my eyes. "Do not insult me by continuing with such ridiculous tripe. It belittles you. Just tell me the truth, and then we can both be free of it."

"If I agree to tell you," I said, still weighing my options. "Then first, you need to give me something."

"Agreed," Muwa said. He sat again, clasping his hands on the table with an expectant look on his face.

"Who leads the White Ravens? You?"

Muwa shook his head. "No. I am just one feather on the body, not the brain."

"Who, then?"

"He is known as the Eye of God."

I mulled that over. "And what do you and this Eye hope to accomplish?"

Muwa smiled in contentment. "Enlightenment, lord."

I nodded, having expected that answer. "Whose Enlightenment?"

Muwa spread his arms wide. "Why, the entire world, lord. The job of the Eye and the White Ravens is to spread the word of the One True God and expose the lie."

"What lie?" I asked breathlessly.

"I think you know the lie of which I speak, lord."

"You're talking about the codex," I said.

Muwa beamed. "Precisely. The very codex that you were sent here to acquire."

"You knew all along?"

"Certainly."

"How?"

Muwa smiled modestly. "You do not need to wear a robe to be a brother in the White Ravens, lord."

"Spies?"

"An unfortunate word, lord," Muwa said. "I would prefer patriots to the cause."

"But how could you have gotten word about me so fast? We hadn't even made landfall yet."

Muwa shrugged. "Ravens come in all sizes and colors, lord."

"Messenger birds?" I asked in surprise.

"Indeed, lord. As I said, my brothers are everywhere—even on The Iron Cay and the royal ships."

"You weren't at the docks by accident, then," I said, understanding now.

"No, lord." Muwa grimaced. "We knew you were coming. Although, we did have a different reception in store for you. But it seemed you chose to take matters into your own hands." He smiled. "In the end, God ensured that we were both successful, and so, here we are."

"Why me?" I asked. "Why go to all this trouble?"

Muwa tapped a finger on the table as he studied me. "My patriots tell me you saved Princess Sarrey's life, not once, but twice. Is that true?"

"Yes," I said cautiously. "Why? What of it?"

"They also tell me that she is quite taken with you, lord."

"She's just a child," I protested.

"And heir to the throne," Muwa said pointedly. "King Alba's elder sons are both dead. Princess Sarrey does have a younger sister, but that one has barely begun to walk and is no threat. The path to the throne for Princess Sarrey cannot be contested unless—The One True God forbid—King Alba was to sire another boy." Muwa grimaced. "Unfortunately, I've heard the queen is newly pregnant and is already carrying low. Which, as you know, often means a boy."

I pursed my lips. "What has any of this got to do with me?"

"You are quite possibly the most famous man in the known world, lord. A warrior renowned and revered for his fighting prowess, not to mention implicitly trusted by your king. You are also a close personal friend to the First Daughter, who I am told always listens to your wise counsel. Princess Sarrey, on the other hand, adores you and is the heir to the most powerful kingdom in the Southlands—at least for now. There has never been a sounder match, wouldn't you agree?"

The Raven's lips twitched in amusement as dawning realization of what he wanted hit me like a hammer blow. "You can't be serious," I said.

"We are deadly serious, lord. In exchange for our help, the White Ravens would like you to agree to marry Princess Sarrey."

Chapter 13: A Night Of Madness

"I won't do it!" I exclaimed. I could feel rage crackling along my limbs like fire as I glared at Muwa. For his part, the Raven just stared back at me steadily, not saying anything. "Did you hear me, you bastard?" I finally demanded.

"I heard you, Lord Hadrack," Muwa said with a slight incline of his bald head. "May I ask why not?"

"Why not?" I repeated in disbelief. "Why do you think?"

"Is the girl not beautiful?"

"What has that got to do with anything?"

Muwa smiled condescendingly. "Then you admit her looks please you, lord?"

I shook my head in disgust. This man had no shame or decency. "I had a wife, Muwa. The best a man could ever hope for. I have no wish to take another. So, whatever your game is here, you can forget it. I'm not playing."

The food was firmly entrenched in my stomach now, and though my belly was making odd gurgling sounds, I was fairly confident that what I'd eaten would stay where it belonged. My strength was returning as well, I was relieved to note. I suspected that I would need it in the next few minutes.

"Ah," Muwa said with a nod. "Of course, Lady Shana. A woman whose great beauty was only surpassed by her great intellect, so I've heard."

I felt a sharp pang in my chest at the mention of my wife's name. I could still picture Shana clearly in her last moments, her beautiful blue eyes filled with equal parts sorrow, love, and determination as she looked down at my broken body. If only I had understood sooner what she planned on that cliff, maybe I could have stopped her somehow. I had been horribly wounded and barely able to move after my battle with Captain Bear, but even so, I would have gladly slit my own throat to keep her from doing what she had. The anger I felt at my failure that day was always brimming close to the surface in me, and I decided to let some of it out. I leaned aggressively toward the Raven with my balled fists propped on the table.

"You don't get to say my wife's name," I growled. "Do so again, and I promise I will end your life right here and now."

Muwa pursed his lips as he stared up at me. I saw no fear in his eyes, only interest and perhaps a little bit of respect as well. "My sincere apologies, lord," the Raven finally said. "I meant no offense toward you or your wife, I assure you." He shifted his bulk on the bench, then took a sip of wine. I noticed his hand was rock steady while he did so. "I admit this...uh...offer of ours must come as a surprise, lord. This setting was not how I had hoped to pose it, of course, but alas, that is God's will. That said, I am truly sorry to cause you additional distress after what you've been through recently."

"Really?" I grunted sarcastically. "Because you don't look sorry in the least." I shook my head. "Maybe you've forgotten something important in all of this, Muwa."

"Such as?"

"Such as I was brought here by the king to be executed, remember? I doubt that order has been rescinded, especially now that they suspect I'm still alive. The last time I looked, flaying the skin from a man strip by strip doesn't exactly make him a good candidate for matrimony."

"Circumstances can change, lord," Muwa said in an even voice.

"What are you up to, you bald bastard?"

"Give me your word you will help us, and I'll gladly tell you."

I snorted, sick of the back and forth. We were getting nowhere fast and that ended now. I tore off Kish's robe and tossed it aside, then the soiled loin cloth beneath it. Regardless of what this man said, I had no intentions of helping the Ravens. I held Muwa's eyes with mine the entire time, expecting him to protest over what I was doing. But my companion just regarded my nakedness expressionlessly, saying nothing. I turned to the clothing the Ravens had brought me, sliding on a pair of rough cotton pants with drawstrings at the waist and ankles.

"Have you thought about what such a liaison could do for you, lord?" Muwa finally asked me as I tied the pants. "For you and your kingdom?" If he was alarmed by my actions, he showed no sign of it.

"Do for us?" I said mockingly. "Or for you and your little birds?"

I didn't wait for him to reply, slipping a black, long-sleeved cotton shirt over my head with laces at the neck and down both sleeves. I was pleased with the fit and glad there was no need to make adjustments.

"Why not both?" Muwa asked. "You can help us, and we can help you. It's a fair bargain, lord."

"Usually, when someone insists that a bargain is fair," I said with a snort. "It's because they are trying to cheat you." Muwa sighed as I picked up the last article of clothing, a sleeveless brown doublet with four horn-shaped buttons and a wide leather belt at the waist held by loops. I put the doublet on and tightened the belt, feeling better than I had in weeks now that I was properly clothed. "Do you intend on trying to stop me from leaving?" I asked the Raven.

"I gave you my word I would not, lord."

"That's lucky for you," I grunted, satisfied. At least I wouldn't have to fight my way out of here. "What about boots?"

"Under the table, lord," Muwa answered in a resigned voice. "They're calfskin, I understand. I hope they will suffice."

"I'm sure they'll do just fine," I said, bending to drag the boots out. I'd been so focused on the food earlier that I hadn't noticed Theny had put them under there. I sat on the bench and eagerly pulled on the boots, which were soft and supple with wraparound fronts that laced along the sides. They fit perfectly. I'd been barefoot for so long that I'd forgotten what a good pair of boots felt like. I stood, stamping my feet to settle them, then glared at Muwa. "I'm going now. You have my gratitude for saving me, but that's it. I'd like to say it's been nice meeting you, but that would be a lie."

The White Raven frowned. "How long do you think it will be before the Lions find you, lord?"

"Why, are you planning on telling them where I am?"

Muwa looked surprised. "Why, of course not, lord. We did not go to all the trouble of snatching you from their jaws just to throw you back in."

"I'm glad to hear that," I said. I knew instinctively that the Raven was being honest with me. I looked around the bare room. "I don't suppose you have any weapons handy?"

"I do not carry weapons, lord. It is not my way."

I nodded, remembering how Muwa had dealt with the Temba soldiers earlier that day. "You've had training," I said, more statement than question. Muwa's eyebrows rose. "The way you handled those Lions, I mean. That was nicely done. You must have had training."

"Indeed, lord," Muwa replied. "In the kennels of Kenningwood, you either quickly learn to protect yourself, or you die. I did not die."

"No, you didn't," I said thoughtfully. "What about those Lions back at the docks?"

Muwa stared at me steadily. "They made their choice, lord." He shrugged. "Besides, I couldn't risk them associating you with us. That would have been very bad for our cause right now."

I grunted in acknowledgment, impressed. A man that could kill four armed soldiers with his bare hands alone was someone to be respected, even feared. Perhaps it was a good thing that I didn't have to fight him.

"Are you certain I can't change your mind, lord?" Muwa asked as I took a step toward the entrance. For the first time, I thought I detected a note of uneasiness in his voice.

I shook my head. "No. Whatever your plans are here, I want nothing to do with them. I have my own problems."

Muwa let air out of his nose in exasperation. "Unfortunately, lord, you have everything to do with what is happening here." He reached into his robe, withdrew a gold coin, and then flicked it to me. "If you insist on going, then take this with you and reflect carefully on it."

I caught the coin, surprised. It was heavy and well forged, perfectly round with a thick edge. I'd never seen one made of such fine quality. I turned the gold over in my hand. One face depicted the profile of King Alba del Fante with wreaths around his head, the other a roaring lion's head. Surrounding the lion were the words: *Strength. Power. Resolve. We are Temba.*

"That coin you hold in your hand is much like this very moment, lord," Muwa said solemnly.

I frowned. "How so?"

"Flip it high in the air and let it fall, and one side or the other will always land facing up when it hits the ground. This can't be disputed. Which leaves us with two possible outcomes resulting from one single action."

I sighed, in no mood for philosophy. "Do you have a point?"

Muwa took another coin from his robe, holding up the king's profile. "Let's suppose this room represents this side of the coin, lord. Let's call it peace, prosperity, and harmony with the One True God." He showed me the other side. "And this represents whatever awaits you outside. Let's call it death, destruction, and anarchy. You represent the single action, with only two possible choices open to you."

I nodded, understanding now. "You're threatening me," I growled.

"On the contrary, lord," Muwa said. "I am just explaining the realities of your current situation. You are the one in control of your fate, not me, for you are the holder of the coin. You may flip it any way you like, but there are no guarantees on how it will land. One pathway is muddled in secrecy and distrust, at least from your perspective. But I assure you it is safe. The other is shrouded in the unknown and is more dangerous than you can even fathom. I urge you to pick the right path."

I glanced to the entrance and the darkened stairwell. "What's waiting for me out there?"

Muwa shrugged. "Nothing good, lord. Not for you, nor for anyone else who stands in our way this night. It is unfortunate and not what I would wish for personally, but sometimes the blood of innocents must be spilled before changes can occur."

"What changes?"

"Why, Enlightenment, of course, lord. The time has come for the people of Temba to learn the truth. Tonight is the first step toward that goal. This is why I urge you to stay. With your help, we can mitigate the damages and fewer people will have to die. Agree to marry the princess right now, and I promise you will not only be saving your own life but hers as well."

"You're going to kill her?" I demanded.

"That's up to you, lord. If you choose wisely, you and she can lead long, productive lives here in Temba."

"As what?" I snorted. "Your puppets?"

"Your term, lord, not mine. Princess Sarrey looks up to you and will listen to what you have to say. The Mother and The Father are false deities, we both know this, but the claws of their false existence run deep through many generations. Educate the girl about the truth, and once she is Enlightened, many of the Temba will follow her lead. You can avoid thousands of senseless deaths this way, lord, so I beg you to consider it."

"And if I don't?"

Muwa shrugged. "Then we will have no choice but to burn everything down and rebuild from the ashes, lord."

"You bastard," I growled. I could feel my hands clenching and unclenching, sorely tempted to leap on the Raven and pummel him out of existence.

"It would not change matters, lord," Muwa said, guessing my intentions. "Even if you were to overcome me, which in your condition is highly unlikely, the Enlightenment would continue regardless. It is already underway and cannot be stopped, only blunted somewhat by your choice." The Raven held up the coin and tapped the king's face. "You have the ability to save many lives tonight, lord, but only as long as you choose wisely." Muwa slowly spun the coin around between thumb and forefinger. He placed the gold on the table with the lion's head facing up and gleaming in the candlelight. "The One True God's wishes cannot be denied, lord. One way or another, you will do as He wants, whether you are aware of it or not. We all must play our part." Muwa lifted his hands in the air. "For you see, lord, the God Beyond controls both faces of the coin and will triumph regardless of whether you choose the easy or the hard way. I, of course, would prefer the easy way but am more than prepared for the other if need be."

"Is that right?" I grunted, unimpressed. I put the coin he'd given me on the table, covering it with my hand. "There's one important thing you haven't considered in all your planning, Muwa."

"And what might that be, lord?" the Raven asked curiously.

I lifted my hand, showing the coin balanced perfectly on its edge. "What happens when I tell your God to shove a pike up his ass." I turned and walked out then, with the Raven's eyes burning into my back. He never said a word, and even if he had, I wouldn't have listened. Perhaps, in hindsight, maybe I should have. For I was about to step into a world of mayhem and madness the likes of which I'd never even imagined could exist.

There were no signs of Kish or Theny when I reached the street. I paused in the shadows by the doorway, listening, but all was quiet. Were there Ravens waiting close by to deal with me? Or had Muwa been truthful and they were letting me go? I tensed as something moved to my right, slinking away in the darkness down an alley. I had a quick impression of a sleek body, dark fur, and a tail in the weak moonlight, and then it was gone. A cat, maybe, or a fennec fox? Tako had told me the city was overrun with the big-eared foxes, many of which had migrated from the deserts surrounding Temba. Whatever it had been, cat or fox, it had certainly not been a Raven.

I relaxed slightly and made my way onto the street, heading north with my eyes constantly roving the buildings and alleyways. Nobody was around except for the same man from earlier lying in a heap exactly where I'd last seen him. If he'd moved at all since I'd gone inside earlier, I couldn't tell. A shuttered window with a broken slat sat above the prone body, allowing faint candlelight coming from inside the house to shine down on him. The man was big, with long black hair going gray and a wispy beard. He was wearing a soiled cloak with a rip down the back, and as I passed him, I hesitated. I moved to stand over the man and prodded him with the toe of my boot.

"Hey," I whispered. I kicked harder when the figure didn't move. "You there. Get up." Nothing. I looked around, then crouched and rolled the man onto his back, almost gagging at the overwhelming stench of shit, sweat, and wine. I was surprised to see that he was still breathing, though erratically.

"Get away from me," the man muttered in a slurred voice. "Ain't got nothing left, you thieving *capatis*." I didn't recognize the Temba word, though I doubted it was complimentary. The drunk mumbled something else that was unintelligible but he didn't open his eyes. Moments later, he started to snore, which was fine with me.

"Sorry about this, friend," I grunted as I worked to get the ragged cloak off him. "But I need this right now more than you do."

I stood and put on the cloak, wrinkling my nose at the smell, but there was little choice. So much for my clean clothes. I bent down afterward and searched the man's body, looking for a weapon. But there was nothing on him, not even a money purse. I guessed by what the drunk had said that someone had already taken everything he owned. I stood again, lifting the hood of the cloak to hide my face, then continued north. I had no idea what I was going to do yet, but for now, I just wanted to put some space between the Ravens and me.

I walked with my head down, holding the cloak closed with my hands, for whatever buttons or ties there might once have been on the garment were long gone. I reached a side street and hesitated there, torn between continuing north or taking a new direction. That's when I heard the first shout. I pressed myself into the darkness against the closest building, not moving as a man appeared coming from the east. I blinked in surprise. He was completely naked and carried a bloody knife in one hand and a woman's severed head in the other. The man staggered and fell to one knee less than thirty feet away from me, then lifted his eyes to the darkened sky and howled. I felt the blood run cold in my veins at the eerie sound. A moment later, I heard the distinctive crunching of heavy boots approaching before four Lions appeared, holding shields and glaives.

The naked man whirled, laughing in a deranged cackle as he watched the soldiers trotting toward him. The Lions stopped twenty feet from the man, then cautiously spread out with their glaives ready.

"What have you done, Oluf?" one of the soldiers asked. The man was young, and he sounded unnerved—unnerved and a little frightened.

"Done?" the man shouted wildly. "What have I done, you ask?" He giggled as he lifted the decapitated head by its long hair and shook it at the Lions. "Why don't you ask Fat Mara here what she did, eh?" The soldiers all shared an uneasy glance. "Or rather," Oluf added with a sneer, "what the bitch didn't do."

"You killed her, Oluf," the same Lion said, speaking as though he were talking to a half-wit. *Perhaps he was*, I thought—*a clearly violent one*. "We can't let you get away with that. You have to come with us."

"She refused me," Oluf said, now with a whine to his voice. He was swaying on his feet and looked ready to fall at any moment.

"That was her right. She was part of the guild. You had no cause to murder her."

"Bah," Oluf grunted, waving the head around wildly as blood sprayed from the severed neck. "She's just a damn whore, you stinking *Yashi*." He lifted the gruesome head, turning the slack jaws and bulging eyes to face him. "Now ain't ya, my pretty? Nothing but a damn fat whore with a used-up cunny and a talented mouth. Well, maybe not so fat anymore, eh?" The deranged man giggled again, then cupped his other hand to his ear, nearly cutting it with the knife he held in the process. "What's that you say, Mara? Here, right now? Oh, you're a naughty little bird, you are. A fine, naughty bird." Oluf glanced at the Lions, who seemed reluctant to approach him. He shrugged and cackled. "Well, why not, lass?" He tossed aside his knife, then lowered the head to his waist and inserted his manhood into its gaping open mouth.

I felt my stomach start to churn with disgust as the man began thrusting himself in and out of the dead woman while the Lions watched in horror. Finally, the young soldier who'd spoken earlier grunted an oath, then leaped forward, using his glaive like an axe as he took the man's head off. Olaf's limp body fell sideways, with his head landing on the dirt road with a soft squishing sound a moment later. I noticed with a queasy feeling that the whore's dead mouth was stuck firmly around the decapitated corpse's still erect manhood.

    The Lion who'd struck the blow lowered his glaive and kicked Fat Mara's head away with a curse of disgust. He looked up moments later as more screams and shouts arose from the west, where I could see the unmistakable glow of a fire. "Now what?" the Lion grunted. He motioned to his men. "Come on, lads. Something tells me this is going to be a long night."

    I waited until the soldiers were gone, then made my way cautiously toward the still-twitching corpse. I knelt and picked up the forgotten knife Oluf had tossed aside, then hid it within my cloak. I stood, hesitating as the sounds of breaking wood arose from the direction the soldiers had gone, followed by several men entangled with each other bursting out through a doorway of one of the buildings. The combatants landed on the road, clawing and spitting at each other like crazed wildcats. A small crowd surged out through the same entrance after them, shouting encouragement and obscenities at the two fighters. More people appeared from other buildings at the noise, and within moments, a wider brawl involving bottles, knives, and clubs broke out on the street. I saw one woman jump on a man's back and tear off his ear with her teeth before spitting it out. She howled at the moon like a wolf afterward, clinging to him like a leech, but the man was busy bashing in another man's face with a club and didn't seem to notice his injury or that she was even there.

    "What in the name of The Mother is going on here?" I whispered.

    I remembered Muwa's dire warnings about my leaving. Did any of what was happening right now have to do with the Ravens, or was this just a typical night in the sprawling city? I thought of Sarrey and what might await her. Had the Raven been bluffing about his intent, or was he really planning on killing her? I pictured Muwa during our conversation. He'd been calm and relaxed the entire time, but fiercely determined as well. I knew in my gut that what he'd told me had been no bluff. The girl was in danger. Tako had told me the Yellow Palace was only a half mile away from the Royal Docks. I had little doubt it would be heavily guarded, as would the princess, but maybe I could get word to the girl somehow and warn her. I knew my chances were slim, but even so, I had to try.

I turned my back to the expanding brawl, heading east toward the docks. I came to a building burning briskly on the next block, with several still forms lying out front of it. The corpses looked like they'd been severely beaten, and I saw a half-naked man laughing as he pissed on the flames. He was so close to the fire that I could see his pants, hair, and beard were all smoking from the heat, but he didn't seem to notice. I shook my head and kept going, keeping my head down and trying to control my rising panic and superstition. What madness was this that could turn people into such crazed, unfeeling, unthinking beasts?

Several riders on horseback appeared then, galloping down the street toward me at full speed with dark cloaks billowing behind them. The men were whipping their mounts in terror and looking over their shoulders, but I saw nothing coming after them. I darted into an alley and crouched behind a crate as they passed, not knowing what to expect. Moments later, I heard a roar that seemed to shake the ground, then a huge beast with a shaggy mane appeared, loping down the center of the street after the riders. It was a lion, I realized in awe. I could only stare in amazement at the big cat. Tako had told me that Alba del Fante kept a pet lion in the Yellow Palace, and I wondered if this was it.

The lion kept going past the entrance to the alley, and when it was gone, I quietly stood and stepped back onto the street. I looked to the west. The riders had disappeared into the gloom by now, but the lion stood a hundred feet away, crouched low on all fours with its back to me as a man appeared from a stable carrying a saddle. The man saw the big cat and he dropped the saddle, but rather than run like any other sane person would, he began waving his hands wildly over his head while he sang and danced in front of the confused animal. The lion quickly got over its confusion, and it crouched even lower, its tail twitching and the great muscles in its back legs bunching. I knew what was coming, and I hurried away just as the beast pounced, wincing as a shrill scream pierced the air. Madness. Everywhere was madness.

It took me at least an hour to reach the docks, and what I saw during that harrowing journey will stay with me until my final days. Death and destruction lay everywhere, with screams of mortal agony coming from all directions, buildings on fire, bodies lying in the streets and alleys, and danger lurking around every corner. Burn it all down, Muwa had said. On one street, I witnessed a crowd of beggars in tattered rags pull two soldiers from their horses, then kick and punch them with their fists and feet until nothing was left but meat, blood, and bone. On another street, I found a woman cackling to herself as she shoved the end of a broom handle up the arse of a naked man bent over a water trough. Thankfully for the poor bastard, I could tell he was already dead. The woman paused in her task when she saw me, and I grimaced at the crazed look in her eyes. I thought she might come at me then, but after I showed her the knife I held, she returned to her gruesome task, humming as if she was only doing the wash and not buggering a corpse.

I was only two blocks from the docks when an old man attacked me with a shovel, wielding it like an axe. He had blood rolling down his face from a wound on his forehead and was ranting about dogs who talked and trees that walked. I had no wish to kill him, so I clubbed him on the chin with my fist, which sent him spinning to the ground. I figured that would be the end of it, but the old bastard bounced back to his feet moments later, cursing me as he attacked again. I dodged the swung shovel easily, then struck him another solid blow to the head. The old man collapsed a second time, only to immediately jump back to his feet, screaming every vile word I'd ever heard at me. I was worried that the noise the crazed old man was making would draw others, so I reluctantly used the knife on him, putting him out of his misery.

The docks were lit by torches and calmer than I'd expected when I got there, almost deserted, although I could see the remnants of burning hulks in the water where several catamarans had been set on fire. Bells were ringing continuously in alarm from deeper within the sprawling city, and I could see a large group of people gathered to the south on an open stretch of beach waving torches and shouting. I could also hear screams of pain coming from that direction, but the mob had their backs to me and were more intent on what was happening in front of them than me. I was grateful for that.

I headed northeast toward the Royal Docks, which I could see were also lit up by torches. As I drew closer, I could hear the sounds of a battle raging above me on the pier, with steel striking steel and the screams of pain and aggression mixing with the incessant bells. I paused, wondering what to do next just as a cry of fear sounded in front of me. The cry was quickly followed by running feet pounding along the planks toward where I stood. I looked around, then slipped into the shadows of an overhang built over a fishmonger's stall, clutching my knife tighter. I peeked around the support post, watching as the shadowy outlines of a boy appeared, gasping for air as he ran. I could hear the eager voices of men whooping and laughing as they pursued the boy, and I cursed under my breath when moments later, a large form loomed over the fugitive, shoving him off his feet. The boy cried out, landing hard on his face, while above him, the man laughed. He kicked the child in the side, chuckling when his victim groaned, then flipped him over with his boot.

"That'll teach you to run from me, *Yashi*!" the man growled. He lifted a club in his right hand, holding it up in the firelight. I realized in surprise that I knew him. He'd been one of the crew on *Wandering-Spirit*. His name was Paserma, if I recalled correctly. "Now I think it's time we make you bleed for what you did to Bwari, eh?"

"Please, please don't hurt me!" the boy pleaded, raising his hands defensively. "I didn't do anything!"

I felt anger settle over me—anger and determination—for I knew that voice well. It belonged to Tako.

Chapter 14: Friend or Foe?

"Thank you, Mother," I whispered to the sky, knowing that she had guided me here to this spot at this exact moment. Tako needed my help, and I needed no better encouragement than that to act.

I leaped out from my hiding place, roaring at the top of my lungs as I charged the man hovering over the terrified boy. Paserma looked up as I bore down on him, his flat features turning in a heartbeat from cruel anticipation to blatant fear, while Tako scrambled away to safety beneath him. I could see four more shadows loping along the decking behind the Temba, though they were too far away still to have a chance at saving him. I felt my lips pull back from my teeth in a wolfish grin. Better they worry about themselves when the time comes.

Paserma had the presence of mind to swing his club at my head as I reached him, but he was no warrior and I'd been expecting it, so he might as well have not even bothered. I easily ducked the clumsy attack, and my skull—which my opponent was clearly attempting to crush with his club—was long gone by the time the blow came. All the Temba managed to accomplish was hit empty air above me and maybe swat a few dozen gnats that swarmed the area around us into oblivion. Paserma's momentum from the miss turned him sideways and off balance, leaving his right side open and vulnerable—the most precious sight a fighter can hope to see. I growled with pleasure and stabbed upward viciously, angling the blade beneath his ribs and piercing his liver. Paserma screamed, the sound high-pitched and strangely feminine.

The Temba was no coward, and despite his mortal wound, he still tried to swing backhanded at me, though the attempt was weak, slow, and ineffective. I let go of the knife and easily blocked the blow with my right arm, forcing the club down, then grabbed the hilt of the knife again, where it remained buried in the Temba's side. I pulled the short blade out, then rammed it back a second time, widening the wound as sticky hot blood gushed over my hand. Paserma shuddered, whimpering now. He dropped the club and fell to his knees, where he swayed, trying to stop the dark red blood from pouring out of him. He might as well have tried plugging the White Rock River with a thimble. I grabbed the Temba by his long hair and he didn't resist me other than to cry out in pain. I dragged him to the edge of the dock and kicked the doomed man into the water where he wouldn't get underfoot for what I knew was coming next.

"*Hasama!*" Tako cried out in warning.

The four crewmen had slowed their advance but were still coming on, though more cautiously now, as they saw what had just befallen their companion. They spread out, with the two on the outer edges carrying spiked clubs while the ones facing me head-on were armed with curved shotel swords. I knew those two would be a problem and hoped they didn't know how to use their weapons effectively. If they did, things could get interesting. I stooped and picked up Paserma's fallen club, spinning it expertly in my left hand while I held the crimson-stained knife low in my right. I crouched, waiting as I studied my adversaries. I recognized all of them from *Wandering-Spirit*. None of these men had mistreated me during my time on board, and for this, I was willing to offer them a chance at life.

"Turn around and go back," I said. "No one else needs to die here tonight."

"You killed Paserma," one man said in an accusatory voice. It was Sumisu, holding a sword awkwardly in his left hand as he faced me. The sailor had always struck me as sensible and intelligent, and I hoped because of that I could reason with him rather than fight.

I gestured to Tako, who was hiding behind a piling. "He would have killed the boy. There was little choice."

"That *Yashi* took Bwari's eye," Sumisu said with an angry snort.

Tako stood up at that, and I saw he held a fishing gaff in his hands now. "Bwari took his own eye!" the boy shouted defiantly. "I had nothing to do with it!"

"Lies!" Sumisu snapped. "What man would do such a thing to himself?"

"You'd be surprised," I grunted. I motioned to the burning city. "Look around you. Does what's happening here look normal to you." I heard the other crewmen muttering uncertainly, but Sumisu still appeared unconvinced. I sighed. "Your people are at war," I added, trying to break through to him. "And you don't even realize it."

Sumisu's sword lowered a fraction—a good sign. "War with who, *Ramata*?" he demanded.

"*Hasama*!" Tako responded angrily. He pointed the fishing gaff at me. "This man is Lord Hadrack of Ganderland. You call him *Hasama*!"

Sumisu didn't even glance at the boy. "War with who?" he repeated.

The Temba hadn't shown respect by calling me *Hasama*, I noted, but he also hadn't repeated the previous insult, either. I hoped that was another good sign that I was finally getting through to him. "The White Ravens," I replied.

Several of the crew snickered. "The *Galata* are nothing but dung-eating sheep," Sumisu snorted dismissively. "Spineless cowards hiding behind their white robes while spouting nonsense and blasphemy. They cannot fight."

Don't be so sure of that, I thought, picturing again how easily Muwa had dealt with the Lions earlier. "Trust me," I said to the Temba crew. "They are the ones behind this. I don't know how they caused this madness, but somehow they did." I pointed toward the Royal Docks above us, where I could still hear the battle raging. "The White Ravens are planning on murdering the king and the royal family."

Sumisu glanced up at the dock for a moment, his expression turning to alarm as he faced me again. "This is truth?"

"I swear it by the First Pair," I said. "The White Ravens are the ones who helped me escape earlier today and I learned their plans. I got away from them and came here to warn Princess Sarrey." I spread my arms, holding the club and knife low. "I didn't have to do that, Sumisu. You know that. I could have easily run the other way, but I didn't. Instead, I came back here to try and help the daughter of the man who has ordered my death. That's got to count for something." I waited as the Temba tried to make up his mind while the bells wailed to the south as the city burned. "Look," I finally said in exasperation. "We're wasting time here. Either we all fight it out right now, or you get out of my way. I'm fine with either choice."

Sumisu glanced back at his companions, then lowered his sword. He took several steps forward until we were face to face. The Temba was short, but he had massive shoulders and arms earned from years of hard labor. "We will not fight you," he stated.

"Good," I grunted. I motioned for Tako to join me. "Then we'll be on our way."

Sumisu put a hand on my chest, stopping me. I tensed, but the Temba just regarded me steadily. "I think that maybe you could use some help, *Hasama*. Five men are better than one. What do you say?"

I grinned back at him in relief. "I'd say I couldn't agree more."

Sumisu knew the city well, and he led us down refuse-filled alleyways and along cross streets lit by burning buildings, avoiding the Royal Docks. The route was longer than if we'd gone straight as the crow flies, but with the ongoing battle above us, we'd had little choice. Most of the streets were deserted now, with nothing left but crumpled buildings and the twisted corpses of men, women, children, and horses littering the ground. I wondered where everyone still alive had gone. Our way led us steadily upward, and finally, we reached an arched wooden bridge that extended over a narrow canal. There was little smoke from the fires by the bridge, and we paused there to catch our breath, able to look down on the Royal Docks now from our lofty vantage point. The sight was sobering, for below was nothing but utter madness, with citizens fighting citizens and Lions battling other Lions in a wild melee that spanned the length and breadth of the stone dock.

"Look there," a Temba said, pointing. He was older than the others, with a noticeable limp. I knew his name was Roge.

A line of Temba soldiers three deep had formed a shield wall along the western part of the Royal Docks, blocking access to the brick road that led to the Yellow Palace. I could see that magnificent building rising in the distance through layers of thick black smoke that billowed upward from the many fires burning around the imposing walls protecting it. The structures inside those walls were tall and domed, and though I couldn't see them from where I stood, Tako had told me there were countless courtyards and lush gardens throughout the palace grounds. *Or at least, there had been*, I thought sourly, *until this night had come*. The Lions were facing off against an equal number of soldiers, each of which I saw sported a blue, six-pointed star painted over top of the lion's head on their shields. The Ravens had clearly brought many of them into the fold of their fanaticism.

Sumisu glanced at me, his eyes glittering and hard like ice chips. "You were right, *Hasama*," he growled. "The *Galata* are behind this." The Temba spat over the side of the bridge. "Traitors all."

I nodded, saying nothing as Sumisu led us away across the bridge at a fast trot. The Temba had given me his sword, confessing that he was uncomfortable with the weapon, preferring my knife and club. I clutched the shotel in my hand as we ran, praying to The

Mother that we'd reach the palace in time. Less than fifteen minutes later, we came to a block of buildings opposite the palace untouched by the flames, where we crouched along a crumbling stone retaining wall. The palace walls were made of yellow sandstone and towered at least twenty feet above the ground. I saw with a sinking feeling that the wooden gates were thrown wide open but looked undamaged. I wondered why.

Bodies of citizens lay everywhere on the street and at the entrance, many of them transfixed by arrows. A major battle had obviously been fought here, but in the end, I guessed treachery from inside had done in the defenders. Individual, scarecrow-like figures were wandering here and there along the walls and on the street. Some looked bewildered and were crying, while others would stop to pound their fists against the sandstone for a time, turning it red with their blood before moving on and doing it all over again. Most seemed heedless of the fact that the gates were open not far away from them.

"The gods have abandoned us to madness," I heard one of the Temba mutter.

I turned to Tako, who was crouched down beside me. "I think you'd better stay here until we get back," I said to the boy. "It'll be safer."

"Safer, *Hasama*?" Tako whispered with a shake to his voice. I could see the fear and dread of the unknown in his eyes. He looked down the street and shuddered. "I don't think so."

I followed his gaze, grimacing. A young girl of about seventeen was on her knees beside one of the corpses, and as I watched, she shoved her hands into an open wound in the man's chest, then began wiping the blood on her face and body while making a keening sound of ecstasy. The girl was plain-looking but obviously highborn, wearing a rich, black and silver dress with flared sleeves and a pointed hood that hung down her back. She began licking her fingers, then paused to look our way as if sensing our presence behind the wall. I could see her eyes gleaming with insanity and I swallowed nervously, relieved when she finally lost interest in us and returned her attention to the corpse's open wound.

"All right," I grunted, more unnerved than I cared to admit. *Maybe the gods had abandoned us,* I thought. I squeezed the boy's shoulder. "You stay close to me, then. Understood?"

"I understand, *Hasama*."

I nodded, then glanced around at Sumisu. "Where would Princess Sarrey normally have been at this time of night?"

Sumisu shrugged. "Hard to say, *Hasama*." He pointed toward the left wing of the palace, which was shaped like an upside-down U. "But perhaps the household quarter would be the best place to start looking."

"It's as good a place as any," I agreed. "Lead the way."

We made it across the street without incident, but once through the gate, that quickly changed. A guardhouse stood to our left, but it was a smoking ruin with several dead soldiers lying in front of it. A small group of men stood in a circle within the inner courtyard, egging on one of their companions as he humped a woman who lay on the ground on her back with her skirts thrown up past her waist and her legs spread. She pleaded for the man to stop, pounding her fists against his back, but he paid her no heed. The man's trousers were around his ankles, and as his hairy buttocks rose and fell, I had a sudden vision of another woman being raped in a similar way when I was just a boy—my sister, Jeanna.

I felt instant outrage just as I had then, and I charged without thinking, not knowing or caring if the Temba would follow. The laughing watchers didn't hear me approaching over the girl's cries, and I tore into them like a wounded boar out for blood. The shotel I held was an unfamiliar weapon to me, shorter than I was used to and curved, but it was damn sharp, nonetheless. I spat curses at the men as I swung left and right, cutting deeply into one startled man's arm, then slashing at the neck of another. Both men fell—one dead, one severely wounded. I hardly cared. I forged onward as my foes broke like frightened rabbits beneath the teeth of a hunting wolf. I heard a thud and glanced behind me, smiling grimly as the Temba joined the fray with their clubs. Even Tako was laying about with his gaff, wielding it like a veteran warrior.

    I reached the girl and her eyes widened with both hope and fear as she saw me looming over her attacker. For his part, the man seemed oblivious to what was happening around him as he thrust himself into her. I grabbed his long, greasy hair with my left hand and hauled him off the girl, flinging him to the side as he screamed in pain and protest. The man rolled and tried to get to his feet, but his trousers were impeding him and he fell comically on his face. I didn't laugh.

    "Get away from here," I growled at the girl. She needed no further encouragement, pausing to lower her skirts to hide her nakedness before she was up and running toward the gates.

    I focused back on the rapist as he groaned and fought to push himself to his hands and knees. I waited until he had, then kicked him hard in the stomach. The man cried out, falling to his side, where he lay gagging on his own vomit. He tried to say something as I dropped to one knee beside him, probably to plead for his life, judging by his eyes. I had no interest in listening. I put the point of my curved sword against his vulnerable throat, then shoved upward before ripping it sideways and tearing his windpipe out. Blood splattered my cloak and face, but I hardly noticed.

    I stood as the others joined me. "We must go quickly, *Hasama*," Sumisu said under his breath. He pointed north toward an archway cut out of cedar hedges that led to a garden lit by a large bonfire. "It is not safe out here."

    I could see a crowd of people milling around inside, shouting and knocking over statues and upending stone benches. I nodded, needing no further encouragement. We headed for the household quarter at a run, stopping only to cut down a few of the demented—as I was starting to think of them—that were foolish enough to try attacking us on their own. We reached a series of wide stone steps and raced up them, pausing at a set of tall mahogany doors gilded with gold leaf panels. One of the doors was open inward several inches. I waited, pressing my ear to the crack, but heard nothing beyond except the occasional faraway scream or oath.

"Be ready," I grunted to the Temba. I glanced at Tako. "You come in last and keep your head down." The boy nodded, his lips pressed together in a tight line of determination. "All right, let's go."

I stepped back and kicked the door open, then darted inward, only to find a large entrance hall that was completely abandoned, with hundreds of candles in bronze sconces protected by metal cages burning along the walls, lighting the interior. Several bodies of older women wearing colorful, flowing sarongs lay on the marble floor in front of me, with the spreading blood stains pooling beneath them cruel evidence of their final moments. An enormous crystal Blazing Sun hung from the center of the arched ceiling forty feet above our heads, while an equal-sized gleaming black Rock of Life sat on a white pedestal directly below it. A man in a red robe lay sprawled by the pedestal's base, his hand stretched out and pointing toward a wide corridor that led away from the hall to the north. A similar passage headed off to the west, with a set of stairs rising on my right and left.

"Which way?" I asked Sumisu.

The Temba shrugged. "I don't know, *Hasama*. In my twenty-three summers, I have yet to be invited to attend a party here."

"Well, you have now," I muttered.

"*Hasama*," Tako said. I turned to him and the boy pointed to the stairs on my right. "I think that way."

"And what makes you say that, *Yashi*?" Roge asked with a snort. "You're a slave and a stupid one at that. What do you know of such things?"

"Probably more than you do, piss-drinker," Tako retorted with contempt. Roge seemed taken aback by the boy's aggressive attitude and he flushed but did not react. I doubt any of them had heard Tako talk back to them before. The boy looked at me, his eyes pleading. "I don't know why, *Hasama*, but something tells me we will find the princess this way."

I hesitated, then shrugged. "That's good enough for me. Let's give it a try."

I led this time, taking the gleaming marble steps two at a time until we reached the second floor. I paused there. A soldier lay stretched out on the landing with his back propped up against a wall by an archway. His chin was on his chest, and his hands were clasped over a wound in his stomach. I thought the man was dead at first, but then he moaned, fighting to lift his head as I cautiously approached. A round shield lay on the marble by his left side and a sword on his right. I was pleased to see the shield did not have a six-pointed star painted on it. I knelt by the man and put my hand on his shoulder.

"What happened?" I asked.

"There were too many," the man whispered. "Just too many."

"What of the king?" Sumisu demanded as he came to stand over me. "Where is he?"

The soldier groaned, shifting position. "Dead, I think. I saw him fall, but I can't be certain."

Sumisu grimaced. "What about the queen?" he asked.

The soldier shook his head, and his voice caught in his throat as tears began to fall. "They cut her to pieces. We tried to get to her, but—" He stopped there, pausing to turn his head away from me as he spat. I glanced at the spray of blood on the floor. This man didn't have much time.

"What of the princess?" I asked urgently. "Have you seen her? Is she alive?"

"Which one?"

I hesitated at that. I'd forgotten Sarrey had a sister. "Both," I replied.

"I don't know about Princess Magret," the man said. "I never saw her. But Princess Sarrey was still alive not that long ago. She might be still." I felt overwhelming relief as the soldier coughed up blood, oblivious to it staining his lips and beard. "She was heading for The Court of Lions the last I saw of her. We were trying to protect her rear."

"Where is this Court of Lions?" I asked.

The soldier motioned weakly down the corridor behind him. "That way. Just follow the bodies. Third passage on your right. Take the stairs, then go through The Room of Bliss." He leaned forward and grabbed my arm, surprising me with his grip. "You get Princess Sarrey out of there, you hear me?" the man demanded fiercely. "Princess Magret, too, poor child. You get them both away from this madness."

"I will," I said firmly.

The soldier shook his head, his eyes burning with pain and resolve. "No, swear it to me."

"I swear it will be done," I promised. "On my life as a lord and a man, you have my word." The soldier nodded in relief then and lay back against the wall, clearly exhausted. I saw the light fading from his eyes and I squeezed his shoulder. "Go to The Mother now, friend," I whispered. I needn't have bothered, though, for I saw his soul had already fled his body and gone to Judgement Day. *Will the rest of us be far behind him*? I wondered.

I stood, motioning to the others to follow me as I started to run down the corridor. More twisted bodies lay on the polished marble, leading away like a trail of breadcrumbs just as the soldier had promised. I counted twice as many six-pointed stars on shields lying among the dead as lion heads. The king's soldiers had clearly fought ferociously for their princess every inch of the way. I could only hope their sacrifices had been enough.

I reached the third passage and headed down it, barely slowing as I leaped over the dead bodies of four men entangled with each other like lovers. The passageway had a series of small, rounded alcoves to either side, where plush couches and chairs sat surrounded by giant urns filled with flowers and plants. Small metal braziers burned in each one, giving the areas a warm, welcoming glow that was belied by the twisted and torn corpses lying everywhere inside them. I reached the end of the passage and paused at the head of the stairs for the others to catch up to me.

"*Hasama*," Sumisu said, offering me a shield he'd had the foresight to pick up. I saw he carried one for himself as well, along with a shotel, as did all the Temba except for Roge, who favored a glaive. I noticed even Tako was holding a sword.

I nodded in approval and took the shield gratefully, glancing around at the men with me. "Stay close together," I instructed. "Like this." I grabbed Roge and another man, pushing them together. "Keep your shields locked like so and always face the enemy head-on. Stab between the breaks with your sword. Whatever happens, don't panic. You do that, and we all die. Understood?"

"Understood, *Hasama*," the Temba said together.

I could tell they were nervous and scared—who wouldn't be?—but not one of them refused to meet my eyes when I looked at them. These men weren't professional soldiers, but I knew they would give me their best and not run, which was all I could ask of them.

I turned to Tako and put my hand on his shoulder. "You will stay here."

"No, *Hasama*, I can—"

"It's not a debate, boy," I growled. "You will stay here and guard the stairs. Understand me? I don't have time to argue with you."

Tako searched my eyes, but he could see no wavering or weakness there, and eventually, he looked down, defeated. "Yes, *Hasama*. I will do as you say."

"Good," I grunted. I headed for the stairs. "The rest of you, follow me. And may the gods watch all our backs."

The stairs were wide and covered in luxurious red carpet with a gold diamond inlay. Several dead soldiers lay crumpled against the inner wall, and as I reached the landing at the bottom, I could hear the sounds of battle coming from ahead. I kept moving, entering an impressive-sized room dominated by majestic marble columns supporting a golden domed roof. A massive cistern of red and white veined stone sat in the center of the room, surrounded by many smaller ones at fixed intervals. A naked woman's body lay draped over the edge of the larger cistern, one leg in the water, the other out. Her neck had been slashed from ear to ear, though her eyes remained open and staring at nothing. I thought she looked surprised at her death.

I could see silk draperies hanging between a pair of intricately carved wooden columns at the end of the room. The fabric was sheer and the color of sand, blowing in a light breeze as faint moonlight filtered through. I knew we were close. I ran toward the thin barrier and swept the cloth aside, pausing there as I took in the scene before me. A raised terrace of white stone protected by wooden trellises led down to an open courtyard, which was dominated by rows of hedges forming a wide circle around a fountain in the middle. Pathways of cobblestone cut through the hedges to the south, east, west, and north, all heading toward the center.

The fountain was formed of ten exquisitely crafted white marble lions supporting a curved basin of water—also white marble—on their backs. Water poured from the open mouths of the lions into bowl-like reservoirs at their feet, but I barely noticed, for my attention was fixated on the woman and the man who stood in the upper basin knee-deep in water, clinging to each other. I counted fourteen soldiers holding torches surrounding the fountain, laughing and taunting the pair as they poked and prodded at them with their swords and glaives.

The girl was Princess Sarrey, I was relieved to see, but even so, I cursed as I stared bitterly at the man with her. He was dressed all in black, using a long sword to swat away the soldiers' weapons with surprising speed and skill. I'd thought at first glance that it was Baine up there, but that hope had been short-lived. No, it wasn't Baine at all, and though his face was illuminated only by firelight and I hadn't seen him in many years, I knew him just the same.

It was that bastard, Rorian.

Chapter 15: Rorian

"Come on!" I said to the Temba. "Stay close to me, and when the fighting starts, make sure you keep your shields up."

I didn't wait for a reply, heading to the terrace before jumping to the uneven stone walkway below. The soldiers hadn't noticed my small band yet, but I knew that would quickly change. Rorian was looking our way, and I was caught off guard when his expression changed from surprise at our appearance to instant rage when he recognized me.

"Youuuuuu!" Rorian roared, pointing and shaking his sword at me. "You did this, you bastard!"

I frowned, wondering what that was all about. Rorian and I had never been friends, having crossed swords once in anger. But that was long in the past. It was he who had brought me Waldin's copy of the codex and changed the war with the Piths. If not for that, I shudder to imagine what might have happened to the Kingdom of Ganderland. And though I hadn't seen Rorian since then, we had parted as uneasy allies—as unlikely as that seemed—rather than enemies. Which made the man's reaction to seeing me even more puzzling, though I knew there was little time to dwell on it now. Blood and death were close at hand, and I needed to focus only on that.

I locked gazes with Rorian for one long moment before he was forced to turn away to swat aside a soldier's probing sword. Then, with the kind of blazing speed that I remembered well, the scholar twisted his wrist and his blade flashed in the firelight, cutting open the man's cheek and sending him reeling away with a cry. Rorian's northern sword was much longer and heavier than the soldiers' shotels, giving him a decided advantage in reach over them. The double-bladed glaives some of the Lions carried were longer than the curved swords, but as a thrusting weapon, they were far from ideal. Because of this and Rorian's cat-like reflexes, he'd been able to keep them back so far. I doubted it would last much longer.

Several of the Lions had noticed our approach by now, and I heard their warning shouts as those closest to us turned to face the new threat. Rorian, ever the opportunist, took that momentary distraction to wreak havoc on them, cutting down two of their number from behind before they could put distance between themselves and the madman above them. That delay bought us the time we needed, though, and I led my men down the footpath between the hedges at a dead run, heading for the narrow entrance that opened onto the diamond-shaped courtyard surrounding the fountain. That was where I'd decided to make a stand.

The soldiers began to form a line to face us well clear of the scholar's great sword, leaving three Lions to keep him occupied. I'd seen the man fight before and I grinned, thinking they should have left at least twice that many. Even that might not have been enough, though.

"Hold!" I cried out to the Temba when we finally reached the courtyard.

The area ahead of me was laid with giant gray flagstones, each as long as I was tall and half again as wide. Four enormous metal braziers burned around the perimeter in line with the hedges, each one raised on a block of stone steps. I knew our position wasn't ideal, but at least our flanks to either side were protected by thirty feet of well-trimmed hedges that rose just past my waist. The enemy could use the other footpaths to go around and threaten our rear, of course, but that would take them time. I was betting that whoever led these Lions would be reluctant to divide his remaining men to do that—at least at first. But if he did, I would have little choice but to attack those who stayed.

By now, the Lions knew they weren't up against a full-out assault by professional soldiers. Instead, they faced one man wearing a beggar's robe and four Temba sailors dressed in nothing but white loincloths—normally easy pickings for armored soldiers. Not surprisingly, all the Lions carried shields with six-pointed stars, and they began banging them with their weapons as they shuffled forward in a tight shield wall. I could see no flaws in their approach, and I grimaced. These men were clearly well trained and competent. The coming fight would not be an easy one.

Sumisu was on my left, with Roge to my right and the other two Temba on the outer flanks. All the men looked nervous but determined as they watched the approaching Lions warily. "Shields together," I said, keeping my voice calm and steady. No man would fight at his best if his leader showed signs of weakness and panic. "Stay close and do what I do."

We formed ranks awkwardly, the thud of our wooden shields locking competing with the crunch of the enemy's boots as they trudged forward in perfect formation. I crouched and waited, breathing deeply in and out to control my heart rate as the others emulated me. I had fought in shield walls more times than I could remember and knew what to expect, but for the poor bastards standing with me now, it would be their first time—maybe their last. The smell of sweat and fear filled my nostrils, the sharp odor mixing with the drifting smoke from the braziers and the pleasant scent of cedar.

The Lions were less than thirty feet away as I glanced past them toward Rorian, who continued to spin around and around in the water-filled bowl so he could keep an eye on his guards. Sarrey clung to his back, her expression filled with dismay and terror. I knew the scholar was only biding his time before he attacked and guessed that he'd wait until the fighting between the Lions and my band began in earnest before he made a move. I almost felt sorry for those men left behind to deal with him—almost.

The soldiers were twenty feet from us now, most wearing ridged leather helmets with nose guards. "Remember," I said to the Temba. "Whatever happens, do not drop your shields, and do not panic. If we fight together, we will win. Otherwise, we die."

"We hear you, *Hasama*," Sumisu grunted. He forced a grin, although it was weak and didn't last long. "We have come this far and will not fail. The gods watch over the princess and us. I can feel it in my heart."

"I hope you are right," I muttered, not convinced the gods were even paying attention. We were outnumbered almost two to one, a fact that I would have gladly accepted if Baine and Jebido were here with me. But they weren't, and all I had were untested sailors, though there was no denying the Temba's strength and bravery. Would it be enough?

The Lions halted with fifteen feet separating our opposing forces at a signal from a soldier in their center. That man lowered his shield casually to look at us. The Lion was short like most of his people, but he was built like an ox, with broad shoulders and a bushy gray beard. "Will you yield, Unbelievers?" he asked. "And save us the trouble of slaughtering you?"

"Would you in our place?" I threw back at him.

The older man grinned. "Of course, I would, friend. It's sheer folly to stand against us. You know this as well as I do." The Lion gestured with his glaive. "Look at you and your pathetic rabble. There is no hope for any of you. Throw down your weapons and denounce your false gods in favor of the One True God. There is always room in the new order for all manner of men, both friend and foe alike. Do this, and I will be merciful. I promise."

I lowered my shield, letting the man get a good look at me. "Promises from a humper of goats mean very little to me," I retorted. The Lion's jaw cracked with anger at my words, and I laughed. "Do your worst, shit-eater. I have met and killed a hundred men just like you. I have no doubt I'll kill that many again before Judgement Day finally comes for me."

"Oh, I think that day is already here," the Lion growled. Several of the men around him snickered.

"Then let's get on with it," I said with a shrug. "For never let it be said that the Wolf of Corwick Castle wasted words when there was real fighting to be done."

The Lion blinked in surprise. "You lie. You are no lord, let alone *that* one."

"Do not judge a man by the clothes on his back," I said. "Judge him by his deeds. Ask the White Raven Muwa if you doubt what I say." I could hear some of the soldiers muttering uneasily now. It seemed my name had a fair amount of weight, even this far south. "Enough talk," I grunted, sensing some of the Lions' courage wavering. "I haven't killed anyone in a while and I'd like to change that." I nodded my head to the Temba flanking me. "As would my Wolf Pack. I'm sure you've heard of these war dogs. Deadly fighters, each and every one of them. It was they who sunk their teeth into the North's forces and broke its back during the Pair War." I grinned, while beside me, the Temba shifted uneasily. I didn't dare look at them, afraid their faces might reveal the lie. "Now those teeth are coming for your throats, Lions, so be warned."

I had no illusions that any of the soldiers would actually turn and run. I just wanted to plant some seeds of doubt in their minds. From such things, sometimes great things can grow. It was the best that I could do under the circumstances.

The leader finally smiled, then spat, the spinning glob landing with a wet slap on the stone two feet away from me. He lifted his shield. "Kill them all," he growled. He sneered. "Except for his *lordship*, of course. He's mine."

So be it, I thought.

The Temba tensed around me as the Lions resumed their march. We were outnumbered nine men to five, but sometimes overeager troops will lose their focus when closing on an enemy shield wall and rush forward wildly during the last few feet. I was hoping for that, for those were usually the first men to die and might help even the odds. But unfortunately, the Lions didn't do that, and they came on slowly and steadily with frustrating discipline.

I sensed rather than saw the Temba to the right of Roge move moments later, but before I could shout a warning, the sailor screamed and ran forward, colliding with the Lions' shields as he hammered his shotel against them. I cursed as the hooked tip of a sword snuck out from between two shields like a striking viper, then retreated, taking the Temba's left eye with it. The man screamed and dropped his sword, falling to his knees before another thrust from a glaive pierced the side of his neck and he fell.

"For Princess Sarrey!" Roge screamed, breaking the line.

"Princess Sarrey!" the other two sailors cried together in response, joining him as they surged forward.

I shouted a curse in frustration as my wall disintegrated, knowing I had no choice now but to join the Temba. "Kill them!" I screamed. "Kill the bastards!"

I sprinted forward with the others and crashed into the line of shields, which wavered under our attack but did not break. I'd headed for their leader, but Sumisu beat me to him, bellowing like a madman as he used his shield like a ram, smashing it over and over again against the Lion's shield. I braced myself behind my own shield, using the power in my legs to push against the wall ahead of me. I felt resistance and took a quick step back, causing the Lion who I'd faced off against to stagger forward off-balance. I dropped to one knee in front of him, sweeping the shotel at the man's ankles. My blade sank deep and the Lion screamed as I twisted the weapon deeper into his flesh, then tugged, using the curved blade to my advantage. My opponent immediately collapsed on his back, creating a gaping hole in their line that I quickly took advantage of.

I jumped into the breach, taking a moment to kick the fallen man in the face to keep him occupied before I hammered my shield against the side of the Lion to my left, knocking him off balance even as I slashed my sword against the hip of the man to my right. That soldier cried out and fell, though not before he'd grazed my shoulder with his blade. I felt blood start to flow but ignored it as I blocked an attack from the man to my left that I'd knocked off balance. That Lion died moments later when Roge slashed him open from head to groin with his sword.

The Temba paused to grin at me, and then he sagged when a Lion pierced his side with his glaive. Moments later, I saw another of the Temba get hacked down, leaving only Sumisu and me still standing. Three Lions were dead or wounded, with six left who could still effectively fight, including their gray-bearded leader. I saw him smiling arrogantly behind his shield and I growled. The odds had now changed to three to one, with that fact made even worse now that the fight had moved into the open courtyard, nullifying the protection on our flanks from the hedges. We were in trouble.

I glanced at Sumisu, who was bleeding from wounds on his forehead and left arm. "Get behind me," I grunted.

The Temba obeyed, pressing his back to mine as we waited with swords and shields up while the Lions circled us warily. Four held glaives, the other two shotels. I took a quick glance toward Rorian, but he remained in the bowl with Sarrey, watching us with hard eyes. I wondered what he was waiting for.

"So, *your lordship*," the leader of the soldiers said with a chuckle as he came to a stop facing me. "Have you changed your mind about surrendering?"

"No, I haven't," I said. "But I have changed my mind about something else."

"Oh, and what might that be?"

I smiled at him coldly. "I don't think you're a humper of goats after all. You're too ugly, and they're too smart to let you come anywhere near them with your pathetic little cock. Just like every woman you've probably ever met."

The Lion flushed beneath his helmet, and I grinned, guessing I'd hit a nerve. The man opened his mouth to respond angrily, and that's when I moved. I darted forward, extending the shotel in my right hand outward in a lunge, catching the Lion off-guard. My blade slipped past his shield and pierced his leather armor below his left armpit, going in at least half an inch before he managed to spin away with a cry. The soldier next to him was quick to react, swinging his glaive in a blur over his head before sweeping it at my head. I was off-balance and barely managed to get out of the way, having to drop to the ground and roll while his blade whirred over me. I came to my feet in one smooth motion, then dodged sideways as a second Lion stabbed at me with his sword, missing my midriff by mere inches. I slashed him across the back and he fell screaming, then barely got my shield up in time to block a second attack by the glaive-wielding Lion. His weapon clanged off the metal boss of my shield and deflected away as he cursed. I crouched low, using my right leg to sweep him off his feet. I pounced on the fallen Lion and punched down at his face—once, twice, and then a third time—using the rounded end of the hilt of my sword until his features were nothing but a bloody, wet mess.

    I stood when the man stopped struggling, breathing heavily from the exertion as I glanced around for a new target. Sumisu was down on one knee to my right on the steps leading to the brazier with his shield raised to protect himself as a Lion with a glaive attacked him. The leader of the soldiers crouched on the stone on his knees twenty feet away from me, holding his side and spitting blood. To my left, the last able-bodied Lion stalked toward me with murder in his eyes. The soldier clutched a shotel in his right hand, but his shield was gone. I smiled in anticipation as I crouched and waited for him, spinning my sword in my hand. Behind him, I could hear the sounds of metal on metal as Rorian joined the fray. *About damn time*, I thought.

    A scream arose from the fountain as one of the Lions there spun and dropped, his face a crimson mess, while Rorian whirled among his foes in a dark blur, impaling a second Lion with his sword. The scholar yanked his blade free of the dead man, then advanced on the last Lion, who hesitated for a heartbeat, then turned and ran to the west and disappeared through an arched opening. I laughed as the soldier coming for me cursed the man for a coward.

"Follow his example and live," I grunted. "Or come and meet your death." The Lion's eyes beneath his helmet had lost their murderous tinge, and were now filled with indecision. We stood ten feet apart, not moving until the man's features finally hardened. He'd made his choice. I sighed. "So be it," I muttered as the soldier advanced. When he was close, the Lion swung overhand at me, chopping down. It was all too predictable, and I easily shunted his blade aside with my shield, then rammed my sword into his midsection. The man gasped, his eyes bulging in surprise as I twirled away from him, tearing out his innards with the hooked blade. I didn't bother to look back as the Lion fell with a clatter to the stones, knowing he was done. I glanced toward Sumisu, surprised and relieved to see he'd somehow gotten the better of the soldier he'd been fighting. The Temba was sitting astride the Lion's chest, his strong sailor hands wrapped around the man's neck as he choked the life from him.

I knew Sumisu didn't need my help, so I headed toward the leader of the Lions, who was fighting to get to his feet. The man saw me coming and he began to curse me, with frothing pink blood bubbling at his lips. I guessed I'd nicked a lung.

"You bastard," the Lion managed to gasp as he finally gained his feet. He still retained his shield and fought to bring it up while lowering his glaive, aiming its wicked blade at my heart.

"I warned you," I grunted impassively.

The Lion screamed something then—I don't know what—and he charged, clearly hoping to catch me by surprise as I had with him earlier. He didn't. I easily slipped to the side as his glaive punched empty air, then chopped down with my shield, knocking the double-bladed weapon from his hand. The Lion staggered, wheezing as he clumsily swung his shield for my head. I leaned backward almost casually, feeling the wind brush me as the wood and iron swept past a foot from my face. I grabbed the Lion by his bushy gray beard, yanking him forward onto the point of my sword. Blood spurted and I waited, holding the man as the light slowly faded from his eyes.

"The One True God forgives you," the Lion whispered before he died.

I shrugged and let the soldier fall. Whether the man spoke true or not mattered little to me at that moment.

"Are you all right, *Hasama*?"

I glanced at Sumisu, who'd come to join me. The Temba was bleeding in half a dozen places, but even so, he looked content and pleased with himself. And well he should. "I am," I said. "And you?" I asked, gesturing to his wounds.

"I'll live." Sumisu glanced toward the fountain, where Rorian was helping Sarrey down from the bowl. "The princess!" he said before rushing forward to help.

Together, the two men lowered the girl to the flagstones, and when she was down, Rorian strode toward me. I smiled wearily as he drew closer. "It's been a long time," I said.

The last I'd seen of Rorian, he'd looked like a walking scarecrow, frazzled and wasted away to the bone because of what he'd learned from the codex. The scholar was that no longer, looking fit and healthy, although I noted that his hair and beard had gone completely gray. I felt my smile slide away as the man approached. I could see the promise of violence in his eyes as he glared at me—violence and an unshakeable hatred.

"You murdering bastard!" Rorian hissed.

Then he attacked.

Chapter 16: Freedom

I had only enough time to lift my shield before Rorian was on me, moving at an astonishing speed, much like the lion I'd seen earlier that evening. His great sword rang off the metal boss of my shield, scraping loudly in the courtyard and setting my teeth on edge from the force of the blow. I fell back, bewildered and using all my skills just to remain alive as the scholar rained furious blows down on me left and right. Rorian's face was the color of red-hot coals, burning with seething rage as I ducked beneath a vicious blow that would have taken my head. I twisted away, knowing what was coming next, narrowly missing getting kicked in the face. The scholar was off balance for the briefest of moments from the kick, and I used the iron rim of my shield, smashing it just above the furious man's knee. I'd hoped to disable him long enough to figure out what was going on, but Rorian just grunted from the blow as I danced away, looking more angered that I'd managed to hit him than anything else. He paused, flexing his leg and testing it while he held his longsword two-handed in front of him. I saw no weakness there, much as I wished otherwise.

Despite that, I was glad for the respite so I could get my wits about me. "Have you gone mad?" I demanded. I held my sword low, reluctant to bring it into the fray—yet. Killing Rorian wasn't something I wanted, but I'd do it if I had no other choice. What I really wanted was answers. Why was he here? And more importantly, why was he so bent on killing me? "What's the matter with you?" I spat.

"What do you think, you bastard?" Rorian growled. His lips were pulled back from his teeth in a savage snarl, and he suddenly darted forward lightning-like with his sword, which I managed to deflect away with my shield. The last time we two had fought, I'd been young and relatively inexperienced. I was that no longer but instead a seasoned warrior, and I could see the scholar was quickly coming to realize that fact. Most men would have died under his first furious onslaught, but I was unharmed, which clearly had given him pause to think. The rage that had dominated the scholar's actions earlier was now slowly being replaced by cold calculation and a business-like manner, which made the man more dangerous than ever. The initial jolt of energy I'd received from Muwa's food was starting to wane, and I could feel infinite weariness settling into my bones. I knew I needed to get through to the scholar soon, because if this fight dragged on much longer, I was afraid I would lose.

"I think you've lost your damn mind!" I snapped. "What did I do to deserve this?"

"What did you *do*?" Rorian shouted incredulously. He shifted to his left, and I matched him, keeping my shield close to my body. I laid the flat of my sword on the shield's rounded rim, pointing the blade toward my adversary threateningly. I had no wish to use the weapon on the scholar, but he didn't know that. "I know who you really are, Lord Hadrack!" Rorian spat. "And we both know what you did. So don't try acting innocent with me!"

I shook my head. "Rorian, I swear I have no idea what you're talking about."

The scholar pointed at me. "You killed them!"

I blinked in surprise. "Killed who?"

"Thera," Rorian said, his voice catching. "My children. Even my grandchildren, you heartless bastard."

I gaped at the man. "Your wife? Your family? You think that I killed them?"

"I know you did!" Rorian hissed. He surged forward, his sword whirling in a blur over his head before he struck. Once again, I retreated, using both shield and sword to parry his vicious attack. I sidestepped a thrust that would have disemboweled me and managed to pin his sword hand beneath my left arm, then lashed out crossways with my right elbow, catching the scholar in the face.

It wasn't as powerful a blow as I would have liked, but even so, Rorian stumbled backward in surprise, his nose pouring blood.

I waited, knowing I didn't have much time before he attacked again. I could feel my shield arm shaking from fatigue. *You need to end this*, I told myself. *Just talk, and maybe he'll listen.* "I'm sorry for your family, Rorian," I said. "I truly am. I know what it's like to lose people you love, including a wife."

Rorian hesitated. Now it was his turn to look confused. "Lady Shana is dead? Truly?"

I nodded. "Eight months ago."

The scholar paused to wipe the blood from his nose. "I hadn't heard," he said grudgingly. "A fine woman." His eyes flashed. "Much too fine for a bastard like you."

"On that, we agree," I said with a tired sigh. I lowered my sword and shield slightly, though not all the way. Rorian was remarkably fast despite his age, and I needed to remain cautious. "Whatever you've heard, or whatever you think you know," I said. "I did not kill your wife or your family. I've never even been to Afrenia."

Rorian rolled his eyes. "You don't say?" he grunted sarcastically. "I know that. You got your little white birds to do the dirty work for you." I opened my mouth to protest, but the scholar cut me off. "Don't try to deny it, either. You sent them to kill all of us, but they missed me." Rorian grimaced. "I found one of the bastards here in the city, Hadrack, and he told me everything at the point of a sword. I know you're the Eye of God, and I know you're the one behind all of this!"

I felt my mouth drop open in disbelief. "What?" I managed to say. "That's ridiculous!"

"No," Rorian said, his eyes narrowing with determination. I could tell he was moments away from attacking me again. "It's the truth, you turd, so prepare to die!"

"Stop this at once!"

Rorian hesitated, looking over his shoulder as Sarrey strode toward us. The scholar frowned when she stepped between him and me. "You will lower your weapon, sir," she said to him in a firm voice.

"But—" Rorian began.

"You *will* lower your weapon, sir," Sarrey repeated, her eyes flashing. It was a command filled with steel given by a princess—someone who was used to giving orders and having them instantly obeyed. This was a new side to Sarrey that I hadn't seen before.

Rorian grimaced, giving me a baleful glare, but he slowly lowered his sword as ordered. Sumisu came to stand with the princess, though he was careful to take a wide berth around the scholar, glancing at him suspiciously.

Sarrey spun on her heel, then put a hand on my chest as she looked up at me. "Thank you, Lord Hadrack. Sumisu told me what you did. Once again, it would seem that I am in your debt."

"It's nothing," I said, keeping a wary eye on Rorian. "I just did what any man would."

Sarrey smiled sadly. "You are being modest as usual, lord. Unfortunately, there are too few men like you in this world."

I motioned to Rorian, who I could tell was clearly itching to renew our little dance. "How do you know him?"

Sarrey glanced over her shoulder at the scholar. "I don't. Not really, anyway. All I know is he's a merchant that came to speak with my father. When the revolt began, he fought with us against the traitors." She raised an eyebrow at me. "And how do you come to know him, lord?"

"We're old friends," I grunted.

Rorian just glared at me, his jaw muscles working as he tried to control his rage. I knew the moment Sarrey stepped from between us, the scholar would strike again. I had very little energy left and needed to ensure that didn't happen. I glanced at the girl. "Can you please inform my friend that I have nothing to do with the White Ravens." I fixed my gaze on Rorian, then motioned to the dead Lions and their painted shields. "If I was this so-called Eye of God, would I have slaughtered my own men?"

Rorian pursed his lips at that, but his eyes still burned like molten lava.

"I do not know who this Eye of God is," Sarrey said, turning to Rorian. "But I assure you, Lord Hadrack would never do what you accuse him of. He is not that person."

"What do you know of such things?" Rorian growled. He examined Sarrey from head to toe. "You're nothing but a child—the spoiled daughter of a king. You were still sucking at your wetnurse's teats when Hadrack and I met. You know nothing about him, and you certainly know nothing about me."

Sarrey met Rorian's challenging glare with one of her own as she advanced on him, stopping less than a foot away. "I may be young," she said with ice in her voice. She gestured to me without glancing my way. "But I know a good man and a hero when I see one." She looked the scholar up and down as he had her. "I also know an ass when I see one as well."

"*Hasama!*" I turned to see Tako racing toward us, waving his thin arms. "Men come this way, *Hasama*! Many men with stars on their shields."

I cursed under my breath, knowing we should have been gone from here long ago. I handed my shield and sword to Sumisu. "Please step aside, Sarrey," I said, moving toward Rorian.

The girl's eyes widened, and she began shaking her head. "No, lord, he will—"

"It's all right," I said. I reached the girl, gently pushed her out of the way, and then stood before Rorian. I held the man's eyes, reading the temptation in them to gut me. I prayed that he wouldn't. "We don't have much time," I said. "So listen closely. We've known each other for many years, Rorian, and in all that time, have you ever known me to act without honor?"

Rorian hesitated. "You once threatened to kill my wife," he finally grunted. "Remember? On that beach?"

"I did," I admitted. "It was the only way I could get you to surrender. And do you remember what you said to me after you threw down your weapon?"

Rorian grimaced. "That you wouldn't have done it. I told you I could tell by the look on your face."

"Exactly," I said. "I swore to you then that I didn't make war on women, and that's still true. Nor do I make war on children. I did not do this thing you accuse me of, Rorian. I swear it to you before the First Pair." I took a deep breath. "But, if that's not good enough for you, then cut me down right now. Just know that if you do, you'll have to live the rest of your life with the knowledge that you killed an innocent man. A man that considers you a friend." I could see Rorian wavering, indecision and doubt draining the anger from his eyes.

"*Hasama!*" Tako said urgently, coming to pull at my sleeve. "They come!"

"Well?" I said to Rorian. "What's it to be? Will you strike me down in cold blood, or will you join me in finding out who this Eye of God really is so we can kill the bastard together?"

"You didn't do it," Rorian whispered. It was more a statement of fact than a question.

I shook my head. "No. I told you that."

Rorian searched my eyes, then he finally nodded, coming to a decision. "Then let's go find the man that did, Lord Hadrack." He smiled, though his eyes were filled with deadly promise. "But if I find out that you have lied to me in any way, I promise your death will be long and painful."

"Fair enough," I grunted, relieved. "Now, let's get the princess out of here."

Sarrey was the only one who knew the palace well, having spent her entire childhood roaming its many opulent rooms and corridors. She led us at a run toward the west where the cowardly Lion had fled not that long before. We passed through the archway, then turned right down a corridor open to the night sky except for massive stone lintels that spanned the passageway every ten feet. The moon was three-quarters full, helping to light our way as we slipped in and out of the shadows cast by the beams overhead. We finally entered a small garden dominated by a single rounded tree in its center, and we paused there cautiously, but the space was empty of people. Elegant buildings with blue and yellow facades rose on three sides of the garden, each with a multitude of stone terraces leading into what I assumed were living spaces. Sarrey headed unerringly for one of the lower balconies to our right, where she paused below it. I guessed the terrace was perhaps seven feet above the ground.

"You're the tallest, lord," the girl said to me. She pointed above her. "We need to get up there. Can you lift me?"

I grunted ascent and moved to put my hands around her waist. She was so thin that my fingers almost touched together. "Are you sure about this?" I asked. "What's up there?"

"Freedom," Sarrey replied.

I nodded, then lifted the girl, finding she weighed next to nothing despite my fatigue. I held her high as she wrapped her hands around the base of one of the narrow, finely sculpted stone balusters, then let her go when she began pulling herself upward. I waited, watching nervously and poised to catch her, but Sarrey climbed hand over hand quickly and confidently to the rounded stone railing, then crawled over it to safety.

I grabbed Tako next and tossed him high. The boy flew upward and latched onto a baluster with ease, scrambling upward like a monkey. I motioned to Sumisu. "Now you." I took the Temba's shield and sword and handed them up to Tako, then stooped, cupping my hands so the shorter man could step into them. I lifted the Temba upward, surprised at the man's weight. I glanced at Rorian as Sumisu nimbly climbed up and over the railing to join Sarrey and the boy on the balcony. "You or me?"

"You," Rorian grunted.

I nodded and handed my weapons up to Sumisu, then jumped, grabbing the base of the baluster. I was halfway up when I heard shouts and the sounds of running feet coming from the east. I glanced back the way we'd come, just able to make out the faint glow of torches coming from the corridor.

"Move!" Rorian hissed. "Get out of sight. I'll catch up to you."

I needed no further encouragement, powering myself up and over the railing as Sarrey and Sumisu helped me. We crouched low on the stone afterward, then began to crawl toward the open entrance to the building. I glanced back once as men in armor appeared in the garden, but there was no sign of Rorian anywhere. I hoped the bastard would get away somehow, more because I still had a hundred questions I wanted to ask him than anything else.

We entered the building on our hands and knees, with the room in almost utter darkness except for a small patch by the entranceway lit by moonlight. I could feel a plush carpet beneath me and smell the distinct scent of a spice the Temba called *cassia* tickling my nose. The sailors had chewed sticks of it on my way to Temba. "Where are we?" I asked in a whisper.

"The dwelling of a friend," Sarrey responded. "He's gone south to the city of Sandhold and won't be back for some time."

I nodded, trying to get my bearings as I looked around. I could just distinguish the faint outlines of furniture to my left, but that was about all. "Are you planning for us to stay here?" I asked doubtfully. If I were the Lions looking for us, the first thing I'd do is start searching buildings.

"No," Sarrey said. She took my hand and stood. "Come along. We're getting out of here."

I let Sarrey lead me, still holding her hand, while Tako clung to my cloak and Sumisu brought up the rear. I was as good as blind in the dark, but Sarrey moved with easy confidence, taking us down a hallway that smelled strongly of incense. We reached another, much larger room with six huge arched windows on the outer wall that allowed the moonlight to filter through despite the sheer satin curtains covering them. I looked up at the vaulted ceiling twenty feet over my head, decorated with wood and painted ceramic, impressed. A blue marble table sat in the center of the room, sitting on multicolored tiles that lined the floor in an intricate floral pattern. A vase with drooping flowers sat on the table, and luxurious couches and chairs lined the walls, each separated by a table with gold leaf inlays. I could only marvel at the richness displayed in the room.

"Who is this man?" I asked in wonder.

"Vizier Banta," Sarrey explained.

"What's a vizier?" Tako asked in a whisper.

"He offers counsel to my father," Sarrey replied.

"He's an advisor," I said, understanding now.

"Yes," Sarrey agreed. "I've known him all my life. He's been like a father to me, more so than my actual one."

I nodded. "All right. So how does being here help us? The Lions will start searching these buildings any time now."

I hadn't realized Sarrey was still holding my hand, and she let it go, then moved to the center of the room, where she began fiddling with the vase on the table. I frowned, about to comment, when I heard a sudden click. Sarrey turned to look at us, her face in the moonlight lit with satisfaction. "This is how I escaped the castle before. Only Banta and I know about it." She put her hands on the edge of the round table and pushed downward, then waited as the table slowly shifted to the side, revealing a large hole in the floor beneath. I moved closer and looked down at a spiral staircase made of iron.

"Where does this go?" I asked.

"To Unwashed Row," Sarrey replied. "It's the poorest part of the city and the least likely place they'd look for us."

I hesitated, thinking of Rorian. If the scholar somehow managed to escape the Lions and made his way back here, there was no way he'd know the secret stairway was there once we closed it behind us. Did I care? I thought about that, deciding that I actually did. We weren't friends despite my claim to him otherwise, but I knew I couldn't just abandon the man without at least trying.

"Is there anything around here that I can write a message to Rorian on?" I asked Sarrey.

The girl paused as she thought, then nodded. "I'll be right back."

Sarrey returned moments later with some parchment and an inkwell, and I quickly scribbled down a few hasty words.

The Mother is always watching with kindness and mercy from Above. But do not fear The Father and his wrath should you end up there, for despite his fires, sometimes salvation lies Below. Waldin

I placed a corner of the note under the vase, then nodded to the others that I was ready. The cryptic message wasn't much, but it was all I could think of on short notice. The reference to Waldin should alert Rorian that what was written was more than it seemed. The scholar was one of the smartest men I'd ever met, and I had to depend on his ability to decipher what I meant. It would have to do. Now, it was time to worry about getting Sarrey away from the city.

After that, once the princess was safe, I vowed I was going to find the Eye of God and kill the bastard—whether Rorian was by my side or not.

Chapter 17: Unwashed Row

Unwashed Row was perhaps the most depressing place I'd ever had the misfortune to set my eyes upon. Maybe on a different night without madness and death lurking around every corner, it might have been less harsh, but I doubted it. Filth and refuse lay everywhere, with big-eared foxes, rats, feral cats, and wild dogs eagerly filling their bellies on the many dead people and animals lying in the streets while black clouds of flies rose and fell among the bodies in swarms. Normally the night scavengers would be forced to compete for whatever meager scraps had been left behind by men. But on this night of all nights, there were plenty of choices for all, with an abundance of fresh meat available to be had for even the smallest and weakest among them.

The tunnel leading from the Vizier's dwelling place had been long and winding, filled with cobwebs and beady, red-eyed rats, with a steady stream of cold, putrid water that reached up to our ankles flowing along the floor. It had taken the four of us at least an hour to traverse the tunnel, which I was told had been dug hundreds of years ago to smuggle in whores and contraband to court officials after a pious and overly conservative king had outlawed drinking and any forms of sex except between man and wife. He should really have known better. Now the tunnel was used by the Vizier to come and go as he pleased, though why he needed to do so was a mystery that Sarrey couldn't explain. I'd asked her what she knew about the strange events occurring in the city that night, but she could offer little to what I already knew. Sarrey's time in the palace since we had arrived from The Iron Cay, she'd told me, had mostly been spent under lock and key, only coming out once to eat at a formal dinner. That's where she had been introduced to Rorian.

I thought of the scholar, wondering if he'd seen my note and was following us or was even now just another of the many corpses feeding the scavengers.

"You should get some rest, Your Majesty," Sumisu said reproachfully.

The Temba sailor had taken it upon himself to cater to the girl's every need, hovering over her like an overprotective mother. We'd found an old barn wedged at the back of a darkened alley to take refuge in, where we planned to stay until things settled down outside. None of us had been too enthused with the idea of waiting, of course, but after attempting to make our way through Unwashed Row earlier, it had quickly become apparent that it was too dangerous. Whatever malady had taken hold in the city was still ongoing, and rival wild mobs of people roamed the streets everywhere, burning and looting buildings and brawling with each other. We'd nearly been caught by one such pack and had ducked down the alley and found the barn by accident. Now we lay hidden in a rickety loft filled with dust-covered, moldy hay, with my biggest fear being that some half-crazed fool would stumble upon the building and set fire to it.

"How can I sleep with that going on?" the girl asked with a weary snort.

Sumisu nodded sympathetically as screams and shouts of pleasure and pain continued to echo from outside without letup. The Temba had discovered a moth-eaten old horse blanket on the lower level, and now he was attempting to find enough clean hay to fashion a bed for the princess. I could see he was having little luck. I sat with my back against a support post not far away, my sword across my legs. I'd never been so tired in my life. Sumisu was to take first watch, so I leaned my head against the wood behind me, then closed my eyes.

"*Hasama?*"

I reopened my eyes a crack, focusing on Tako, who crouched in front of me.

"Hmm?" I muttered.

"I don't think we should stay here," the boy said, his face filled with worry. "It's not safe."

I sighed, shifting my bulk as I opened my eyes further. "I agree," I said. "But what choice do we have? If we go out there, we're bound to run into trouble. At least in here we can rest and regain our strength."

"The Row is not a good place to be at the best of times, *Hasama*," Tako continued. "Very bad men live here. If they find us—"

"They won't," I said, trying to soothe the obviously frightened boy. "We've been here an hour already, and nobody has come down the alley."

"The morning will be much worse, *Hasama*," Tako said. "Once people awaken and start chores, they will be everywhere. I was born in this place, and I know how they react to strangers." He glanced over his shoulder at Sarrey, then turned back to me and lowered his voice. "If they recognize the Princess, *Hasama*, it will go very bad for her. There is little love for the Royal Family here."

I frowned, trying to make my tired brain work. "We can't fight our way through those people out there, Tako," I said. "We barely got away from the last group." I leaned forward and patted the boy's shoulder. "Besides, I'm so tired right now I doubt I could even lift a sword. I need to rest, and I suggest you do the same."

"But—"

"No," I said, cutting him off. "Whatever is happening out there has to end at some point. We just have to wait it out. We'll deal with things after that."

"Will you at least consider leaving before first light, *Hasama*?"

I nodded drowsily, letting my eyes close once more, not even having the strength to argue anymore. "Uh-huh," I managed to say before sleep took over me.

I awoke with a start much later to the smell of food. Tako crouched before me again, holding a half loaf of flat black bread under my nose that I could tell was made from hazelnuts. He grinned shyly in the half-light, and I realized with a lurch that dawn was fast approaching. "What's this?" I mumbled as my stomach gurgled with sudden desire.

"Our little adventurer went out and scrounged it for us," Sarrey said, chewing on some of the bread herself. By the looks of her, I guessed she'd just awakened herself, though I thought she was staring at me strangely.

I shrugged the girl's odd expression off as I glared at the boy in alarm. "You did what?"

Tako shrugged. "I told you, *Hasama*, I was born here. I know where to go. Besides, no one even notices someone like me."

"You shouldn't have taken the chance," I said reproachfully, though that didn't stop me from taking a bite. Black bread was the lowest form of bread possible, made by the poor with whatever grains were available. I thought it was one of the most delicious things I'd ever eaten.

"Tell him what you told us," Sumisu said to the boy, his face etched with fatigue and worry. I felt suddenly guilty, knowing I'd slept the entire time and had left him to keep watch.

"I spoke with a man I know," Tako said. He gestured to the bread. "He's the one who gave me that. He told me his wife and two sons were all dead, killed earlier tonight in the riots."

I took another bite. "And?" I grunted, knowing there was more.

"The man's name is Luiga, and he was at his home, nursing a broken ankle. His wife and sons went out earlier that day to Ranlay's Square for *Satista*, but because of his foot, he couldn't go, so he prayed at home." I frowned, unsure where this was going. "Luiga's wife returned after prayer, but the sons did not. She told him there were White Ravens at the ceremony, carrying caskets of Blessed Wine. Not long after that, she started feeling sick. Luiga tried to help her, but he said she started screaming crazy things at him, then ran out the door. He tried to follow but didn't get far on his leg." Tako grimaced. "What he saw outside made him turn around and go back inside his house."

I nodded, knowing what the man had seen. We'd all seen it. "This Blessed Wine," I said. "Is it normally used during the ceremony?"

"Yes, *Hasama*," Sumisu answered for the boy. "Each worshiper takes a sip from a communal cistern, then kneels on a holy stone and says his words to the gods." The Temba looked thoughtful. "Bwari left for *Satista* with some of the other crew while the rest of us were ordered to stay and watch the ship. None of the others came back except him." Sumisu glanced at Tako. "You were telling the truth. Bwari did take his own eye."

"The Ravens must have put something in the wine," Sarrey said. "It's the only thing that makes any sense. They probably did it all across the city."

"But what could make people go mad like that?" I asked. I felt much better now that I'd gotten some sleep and had some food in my belly. I stood and stretched.

"I have no idea,' Sarrey admitted.

I moved to the outer wall facing the alley and peered through a large crack in the planking. I could see no movement outside, nor did I hear anything, though there was a noticeable glow in the sky to the east. "The sun will be up soon," I said. "We'd best be on our way." I moved out of sight of Sarrey, then relieved myself against the barn wall.

"Where do we go, *Hasama*?" Sumisu asked when I was finished.

I stooped and picked up my shield and sword. "I don't know. But Tako is right. We can't stay here. Hopefully, whatever the Ravens used in the wine will have worn off by now."

"And if it hasn't?" Sarrey asked.

I shrugged, feeling more confident now that my strength had returned. "Then we deal with it." I paused, thinking. "Our best chance is probably to head for the harbor." I gestured to Sumisu. "Can the four of us sail *Tunias* alone?"

"Yes, *Hasama*," the Temba said. "It will be difficult, but—" He paused there as if reluctant to continue.

"But what?" I prodded.

"The Lion traitors and the Ravens will be watching for just such a move, *Hasama*. They must know we are in the city, which means we only have two options—find a ship and sail away from here or stay hidden."

"They can't watch the entire harbor," I said.

Sumisu looked doubtful. "They don't need to, *Hasama*. All they have to do is put ships on the water and stop any boat that's leaving the shore."

I grimaced, knowing the Temba was right. With all the rioting in the city, there was still a chance that the Lions had lost control of the wharf, at least in places along its more than one-mile length. But what if they hadn't? We'd no doubt have to fight all the way to get there, and when we did, we might just end up delivering ourselves into the White Ravens' hands anyway.

"We could go inland over the mountains," Sarrey suggested. "They won't expect that."

Both Tako and Sumisu just gaped at her. The Temba sailor finally shook his head. "That is madness, Your Majesty. We would surely die out there alone without food and water."

"I went there once before," Sarrey said stubbornly. "Several years ago with my father and Banta. We didn't lose a single man."

"And no doubt you traveled with a heavily armed escort and plenty of provisions, Your Majesty," Sumisu said, careful to keep his voice free of scorn. "But as you can see, we don't have that luxury. You know as well as I do that danger lurks everywhere inland for a small group like ours."

"Do you think it's any safer for us here?" Sarrey asked, looking annoyed now. She turned her gaze to me. "When I ran away from the Yellow Palace, I met Mondar in Unwashed Row and—" The girl hesitated, her voice cracking. She looked down at her hands, clearly trying to maintain control of herself. She finally looked back up at me, and I could see tears brimming in her eyes, mixed with a steel-like resolve. "Mondar and I went southeast to the Red Sparrow River that flows near the mountains, where he'd built the raft. That's how we made it to the ocean."

"Are you sure you want to try something like that again?" I asked doubtfully. "Because it didn't work out so well the last time, as I recall."

"No, lord," Sarrey said. "I don't want to attempt fashioning a raft. I want to continue south through the mountains to join the same road that my father and I took around the Waste of Bones." She flicked her eyes to Sumisu, whose eyes had gone round, then back to me. "I want to go to Sandhold. I believe the people there might be willing to help us."

"No, Your Majesty!" Sumisu gasped, looking even more horrified now than he had before. "The Bone Warriors will boil us alive and eat our flesh!"

"Nonsense," Sarrey said with a laugh. "That is just some silly story used to frighten people so they won't be tempted to go inland and end up dying in the desert."

"Who are these Bone Warriors?" I asked.

"Wards of the desert, lord," Sarrey said. She glanced at Sumisu and smiled. "They are fierce fighters, yes, but they don't eat the flesh of their enemies. Admittedly, they have no liking for us Temba, especially Lions. But they are not the ones I wish to speak with anyway. Besides, Banta is in Sandhold."

"Can we trust this man?" I asked.

"We can, lord," Sarrey said. She smiled bitterly. "The Vizier is sworn to serve the king, who is now dead, as is my mother and, as far as I know, my little sister as well. Which means I rule Temba now." She frowned as a thought struck her. "Or I would rule if not for the White Ravens and their ilk who have overrun my city like a plague." The girl's eyes flashed, and her face took on a severe look, making her appear far older than her years. "We will find Banta in Sandhold, lord, and when we do, he and I will come back here and deal with these traitors. After that, I will sail to *Hisbaros Raboros* and find those responsible for my beloved's death and make them pay in pain and blood. I swear this to be true before the gods."

I glanced at Sumisu, who looked ill at the prospect of heading deeper south, then Tako. The boy appeared frightened as well.

"And what about me?" I asked. "What would you have me do?"

Sarrey stood and came to me, putting her hands on my chest. The girl was undeniably beautiful despite being disheveled and dirty from our flight. "I hope that you will join me in this quest, lord. I know it is much to ask, but I feel the gods have thrust us together for a reason, and that reason is to eradicate any trace of these white vermin and their minions from my lands." She stared into my eyes, the fierceness of her features gone, replaced once again by that of a young, vulnerable girl asking for my help. "So, will you stay by my side, lord?"

"My ship and my men are still out there, somewhere," I said weakly. "I need to find them."

"Yet, even so, lord," Sarrey whispered. "Will you help me regain what is rightfully mine?"

"My kingdom is at war and needs me," I protested, though with little conviction. I'd never been able to resist a woman in need.

"Yet, even so," Sarrey repeated.

I could feel the girl's eyes burning into my soul, and finally, I sighed, defeated. "All right," I said. "I'll help you win the city back." I thought of Rorian with regret, knowing if the man were somehow still alive, he would never be able to follow our tracks now. I glanced at Sumisu and Tako. "It's settled. We go south, and may the gods watch over all of us."

Getting out of the city took us several hours, and the sun was already up and glinting off the Yellow Palace by the time we finally reached the outer limits. I'd given my beggar's robe to Sarrey before we'd left the barn, and though it was much too large for her, at least with the cowl up it was almost impossible to see her features clearly. That's not to say the journey through the winding streets of Temba was easy, of course, for it wasn't. Whatever the White Ravens had put in the Blessed Wine had begun to run its course by sunrise, but unfortunately for us, the madness was still far from over.

My small band only made it several blocks before the first attack came, though it was not what we'd expected—a pack of roving dogs rather than men. We managed to kill three of the beasts and run the others off without sustaining any injuries, and buoyed by that, we'd continued on, only to be set upon by a toothless old woman wielding a broom on the very next block. She'd been hiding in a recessed alcove and had dashed out at us, striking Sarrey on the shoulder without warning before we could subdue her. Sumisu had been incensed by the attack, and I'd had to physically restrain him from cutting the old woman's throat. He had given her a solid punch in the stomach when we left, though, sending her wheezing and gasping to the ground. After what she'd done to the princess, I thought it was more than fair.

Two blocks later, we were assaulted by a large group of young boys throwing rocks, and they only scurried away after Sumisu and I had charged at them with our swords and shields. Tako had taken a stone in the eye, swelling it closed, and I'd had one glance off my wounded shoulder, reopening the cut. That was our first half hour. The journey went on like that, with nary a block or two passing without some incident occurring. At one point, we heard the roar of a lion, but it had come from the east and sounded far away. By the time my little band finally reached the open plain bordering the city, we were sporting bruises and wounds in half a dozen places. I considered it a miracle that we'd made it out in relatively one piece.

Of the four of us, Sumisu had taken the worst wound—a nasty cut to his lower leg from a spiked club, which had slowed us down considerably. He was lucky it had glanced off the bone rather than shattering it, but the injury still left him barely able to put any weight on his leg. The Temba had begged us to leave him behind, but I wouldn't hear of it. The man had given everything he had and more to ensure we all survived, and I had no intentions of abandoning him. Both Sarrey and Tako had adamantly agreed, and Sumisu finally gave up and accepted my help to support him.

Now, after another hour of travel, we four sat crouched on a knoll in a thicket of small scrub trees covered in vines overlooking a field filled with rows of strange, bush-like plants that Tako told me were called lima beans. Apparently, they were a staple for the people here, for the plants thrived in the hot climates of the south. However, what interested me more than the lima beans was the sod buildings we could see off in the distance nestled in a small valley. I knew our little band would need provisions if we hoped to make it to our destination, and I was hoping we could find them there. I was also hoping for a horse or two, but I had no real expectations on that score. The buildings looked poor and rundown, and I could see no evidence of a corral or stable among them.

I glanced at Sumisu, who had cleared some space with his sword and lowered himself to the ground with his bad leg stretched out in front of him. I'd torn a strip of cloth from the beggar's robe to bind the wound, but I could see long streaks of fresh blood staining the sailor's leg around the crude bandage. The Temba's face was bathed in sweat, and the pain he was experiencing was reflected in his eyes. "How are you doing?" I asked.

"I'll be fine, *Hasama*," Sumisu responded. He smiled weakly. "I could use a few minutes to catch my breath, though."

I nodded and stood. "All right. Everybody else stays here and rests. I'll go check out those buildings down there and see what I can find."

Sarrey got to her feet. "I'll go with you, Lord Hadrack."

I frowned. "I don't think that's such a good idea, Your Highness. Someone might recognize you."

"I'll keep my hood up," Sarrey said dismissively. "Besides, whoever lives there is much less likely to feel threatened if a woman is with you." She took in my dirty, bloodstained clothes and ragged hair and beard. "You don't exactly look like the friendly sort at the moment, lord."

I opened my mouth to protest, but the girl had already pushed herself through the branches and out into the open. I glanced at the Temba and boy. "Take care of him," I grunted at Tako as I headed after Sarrey. "We'll be right back."

"*Hasama*," Sumisu called after me. I hesitated. "Don't let anything happen to her—please."

"I won't," I promised him. "You have my word."

I strode after the princess, quickly catching up to her with my longer strides as we made our way through the neat rows of lima beans. I could see woodsmoke rising from a hole in the roof of the biggest building, which was at most only fifteen feet long by ten wide. A light brown mongrel with a white belly lay in the dirt near the building's entrance, stretched out in the sunlight. The animal suddenly lifted its head and looked our way, having heard us or caught our scent. The dog leaped to its feet, bristling, then began to bark, followed by a man appearing from the building's entrance. That man was old and bent, with a pointed silver beard that hung to his waist and a gleaming bald head. He shaded his eyes with his hand, waiting and watching as we drew nearer while the dog continued to bark. The animal never moved from its spot or bared its teeth, though, which I was grateful for. We needed whatever help this old farmer could offer us, and I doubted being forced to slaughter his dog would help endear the man to our cause.

Sarrey and I were less than fifty feet away from the building when I heard the old farmer mutter a surprised oath just as I heard a familiar rumble like thunder behind me. I turned, feeling my stomach lurch as seven riders crested the knoll, breaking around the thicket to either side as they galloped toward us.

The mounted men were flying a Lion banner and were led by a man wearing flowing white robes.

Chapter 18: Goma

"Get inside!" I shouted at Sarrey, shoving her toward the sod house. The girl stood frozen for a moment, staring at the approaching horsemen in disbelief, then she began to run. I was right behind her, while ahead of us, the old man was shaking his head with his hands lifted toward us, palms out.

"I want no trouble!" the farmer kept insisting over and over again, his eyes wide with fright. "I want no trouble!"

"Too late for that, friend," I grunted when we reached the yard. The dog was running around us in excitement, barking endlessly, while the thudding of the horses' hooves grew louder by the moment. I glanced back. The Lions were fifty yards away and closing fast, hurtling along the rows between the lima beans while thick trails of dust streamed behind them. The bald Raven was in the lead with his white robes flapping in the wind. I cursed when I recognized the man's triumphant, grinning face—it was that skinny bastard, Kish.

"Go away!" the old man cried, blocking the entrance to his home with his arms spread. He flicked his hands at us as if trying to shoo away troublesome flies. "Whoever you people are, just leave me be in peace."

"Move out of the way!" I growled in his face. "Or I'll move you."

"You have no right!" the old man insisted. "This is my home!"

Knowing there was little time left to argue, I grabbed the farmer by his great beard and dragged him out of the way, ignoring his cry of pain as I flung him aside. I shoved Sarrey through the opening just as the farmer's dog leaped at me, growling and taking hold of the flap on my left boot with his teeth. I kicked the animal away only to have it come right back, fangs bared, saliva foaming at its jaws as it advanced on me, though more warily this time.

"Call off your dog!" I shouted at the old man, who had fallen to his hands and knees in the dirt. The horsemen were only moments away from entering the yard, and I groaned with dismay when I saw two figures heading down the knoll behind them at a run. Tako and Sumisu! The Temba sailor was limping and struggling over the uneven terrain, but he still managed to keep up with the boy. I felt nothing but fear for them both, well aware that the mounted riders would make short work of them the moment they were noticed. The dog took another step forward, growling with the hair on the nape of its neck standing straight up. I knew I wouldn't have time to dispatch it before the riders were on me. "The woman inside is Princess Sarrey!" I screamed at the farmer. "Call off your damn dog!"

The old man's eyes went round in surprise, and he glanced toward the doorway in shock as Sarrey appeared with the cowl of her cloak lowered. "Do as he says right now," the girl commanded in a voice that brooked no argument.

The farmer hesitated, his expression filled with indecision before finally, he nodded. "Carron, that's enough!"

The dog immediately became less aggressive, transforming from a slobbering savage beast into an obedient, faithful pet in the blink of an eye. I stooped, lifted the old man up effortlessly, and then pushed him through the doorway. "Protect Her Majesty with your life," I grunted before I turned to face the mounted men as they came to a halt in the yard with clouds of dust swirling around them. The old farmer said nothing, but I saw the indecision and fear on his face switch to fierce determination. He whistled, and the dog followed him into the house, though it was careful to go around me warily. Moments later, the flimsy wooden door slammed shut, leaving me alone to face seven men on my own.

"Lord Hadrack," Kish said moments later with an air of contentment about him. He shifted in his saddle, leaning forward on the pommel. The sun gleamed off the sweat on his bald head while the Lions hastily dismounted around him. The youngest of the soldiers—who couldn't have been more than sixteen—took the horses' reins while the rest spread out in the yard holding swords or glaives. "It's good to see you again," the skinny Raven added with a condescending smile. "Did you enjoy your evening of freedom?"

"I've had better," I grunted.

Kish laughed. "Yes, I imagine that's true."

"How did you find us?" I asked, trying to keep the bitterness from my voice.

The Raven shrugged. "It was Muwa's idea, actually. He correctly guessed that you would do something unexpected after we lost you in the palace, so he sent patrols to the south." Kish took in a deep, self-satisfied lungful of air. "It would seem the One True God has favored me by answering my prayers and allowing me the honor of finding you."

"Careful what you wish for," I growled.

I shifted my shield on my arm, studying each of the five Lions opposing me. Three were much older than me, with graying beards and scarred faces, evidence of past battles. Two of them were armed with glaives, the other a shotel. All three watched me with expressionless, almost dead eyes. I could tell by the easy way they held their weapons that they were all experienced warriors. These men would be dangerous, I knew. The other two were young and cocky, filled with the restless energy of youth and brimming with overconfidence as they grinned at me in anticipation. I decided I'd kill those two first and then the other three. I'd leave the young lad holding the horses and the White Raven until the end.

"Yes, well," Kish said, looking unfazed. "As much as I am enjoying this, we have a task at hand. I recommend you throw down your weapon, lord, and come with us. There is a trial to be held, after all."

I frowned. "What does that mean? What trial?"

Kish feigned surprise. "Why, for the untimely deaths of King Alba and his wife, of course. Surely it hasn't slipped your mind that you murdered them?" I just gaped at the Raven as he smirked. Kish flicked his eyes to the closed door. "Not to mention poor Princess Sarrey, who you savagely raped before slitting her throat. A terrible tragedy that, and one that will surely require restitution once the trial is complete."

"You bastard," I grunted, understanding now.

"Muwa did try to warn you, lord," Kish responded. "But you foolishly chose to ignore that warning. If you had just cooperated with us to begin with, this, uhm, unpleasantness would not have been required."

"If you want my sword, you ugly little worm," I spat. "Then why don't you come over here and take it?"

Kish grinned, though his eyes remained hard and cold as he regarded me with obvious dislike. "I am a man of God, lord, not a warrior. I was born to serve His needs above all things, not fight. Besides, I am a gentleman at heart and truly abhor violence." He glanced around at the Lions. "Luckily for me, my companions have no such reservations, as you'll soon find out."

I took a deep breath, flicking my eyes past the mounted Raven for less than a heartbeat. It had been enough to pick out Tako and Sumisu making their way forward in the dirt on their bellies between two rows of lima beans. The Lions hadn't seen them yet, and I felt sudden hope. If I could distract Kish long enough for them to get closer, we might have a chance at getting out of this.

"Do you really think anyone will believe your lies?" I asked Kish.

"Why wouldn't they, lord? Let's not forget that before your escape, you were set to be executed for abducting Princess Sarrey. Angered as you clearly were by that more-than-just sentence, it's perfectly logical, from your point of view, anyway, why you would take your revenge out on the Royal Family in such a brutal fashion." Kish pursed his lips. "Your reputation as a violent and headstrong individual is well known, lord, even here in the south."

"Uh-huh," I grunted. Tako and Sumisu had made it to the edge of the beanfield, with nothing left between them and the Lions now but open, dusty ground. Now was the time to act. "I think we're done talking," I said. "I'm never going to surrender, so why don't we just get on with it?"

"A splendid suggestion, lord," Kish agreed, looking unsurprised. He wheeled his horse around, moving back to give his men room. I felt my heart leap in my throat, but both Tako and Sumisu had recognized the danger at the same time and ducked beneath the plants. The Raven didn't see them.

The Lions began closing in on me, and I shifted to my right slightly, moving away from the door so they would have their backs to the boy and sailor. Kish's horse shook its head and snorted nervously as if knowing what was coming. The metal bit in its mouth jingled musically. I heard movement to my left moments later, startled to see the old farmer's shadowy features appear in a narrow open window cut from the sod. He lifted a bow in his gnarled hands for me to see and then surprised me by winking. I grinned, feeling better and better about our chances.

"The boy holding the horses," I whispered to the farmer out of the side of my mouth. "Start there."

I had no idea how accurate the old man would be with his shaky arms, but if nothing else, the distraction should surprise the Lions long enough for me to get among them. As it turned out, I needn't have worried, for I learned later that the old man had been shooting a bow his entire life. The first arrow hissed out from the house like a striking snake, catching the lad holding the horses high in the shoulder. He cried out and spun around, losing his grip on the reins. A second arrow followed the first, slapping into one of the horses' flanks, causing it to shriek in pain, which sent the rest of the animals into panicked flight. That's all I needed.

I roared, charging forward at the confused Lions, while behind them, Sumisu and Tako burst from their concealment, dashing toward Kish, who was fighting to control his startled horse.

I had just enough time to see Sumisu grab hold of the Raven's robe and yank him from the saddle, then I was in amongst the enemy. The first youngster died with a stunned look on his face before he could even raise his sword, and the second one a moment later as I smashed the edge of my shield into his stomach, knocking the wind from him. The Lion grunted, opening his mouth to cry out even as the point of my sword slipped inside. I twisted my wrist and yanked, using the hooked blade to tear half his face away as blood shot upward in a spray around me. The young man shrieked in horror and fell writhing to the ground, making an awful keening sound that almost made me feel sorry for him. I mercifully put him out of his misery with a quick stab downward.

 I half-crouched after that, breathing easily as I waited for the remaining Lions to make a move. Things had gone my way so far, but the element of surprise was over now, and I knew I still faced three formidable foes. I saw out of the corner of my eye the youth struggle to his feet, wobbling unsteadily and moaning as he tried to yank the bolt from his shoulder. A thrum sounded from the house moments later and another arrow appeared, this time lodging in the center of the young soldier's chest. The lad looked at the shaft sticking out of him in surprise before his eyes rolled in his head and he fell again, this time for good. I focused back on my adversaries, who had wisely put themselves between the archer in the building and me. The old farmer had proven surprisingly accurate, and I prayed that continued, not relishing an accidental shaft striking me in the back.

 "I don't want to kill any of you," I said, lying. There was no way I could allow these men to live and report back to Muwa about what had happened. If the Lions were foolish enough to throw down their weapons and save me the trouble of fighting them, then all the better. I glanced toward Kish, unable to suppress a smile. Sumisu straddled the Raven's narrow chest, striking him left and right in the face while the thin man wailed and tried to block his punches. Tako danced around the pair, kicking at whatever exposed body parts he could reach on the fallen Raven. "That one, though, that's different," I said, nodding to Kish. "He's not leaving here alive."

The oldest-looking of the three Lions frowned, shifting his gaze briefly to the struggling combatants. He glanced at one of his companions, a squat man with a trim beard and a bulbous nose. "Karal, see to the White Raven."

The soldier named Karal licked his lips, glancing toward the sod house nervously. "What about that archer?"

"The One True God will protect you," the older Lion grunted.

I snorted at that. "If any of you take even one step that way, our deal is off," I said.

"We never had a deal," the Lion growled back.

I shrugged. "Then, by all means, *Karal,* do what you must."

Karal took one more wary look at the house, then started shifting away from us sideways. He turned his shield toward the building and made his body small behind it, leaving only his feet, the top of his helmet, and part of his lower body visible. I knew it would be a tough shot, even for someone like Baine. I hoped the old farmer was up to it. A moment later, the bow from inside thrummed again, and I breathed a sigh of relief as Karal cried out, then collapsed with a shaft transfixing his leg just below the knee.

I sprung into action, charging toward the older Lion, and as he hastily brought up his shield, I pivoted away from him, swinging at the second man. That soldier was slower to react, and I slipped past his guard, cutting a long slash down the side of the man's armor before I spun away. I didn't know how much damage I'd inflicted but had little time to worry about it, for the older Lion was on me now, cursing me as he attacked. I backpedaled, off balance as the glaive the soldier held whirled, striking at me with both blades in a dizzying array of speed and prowess. The only thing that saved me from that initial onslaught was my shield, which thumped and rocked on my arm, absorbing the wicked blows as I continued to retreat.

Find his pattern, I told myself. The Lion grunted and attacked, narrowly missing me as I dodged aside, then he grunted again, using the reverse side of the glaive to slash at my head. I ducked and somersaulted away, coming up in a tight ball even as I swung sideways at the man. But the Lion was quick as a cat, and he leaped over my blade and I struck nothing but air. I bounced to my feet as the soldier and I regarded each other with wary respect. I looked past him. Karal was still on the ground, holding his leg, and I was relieved to see the Lion I'd hit moments before was lying motionless in the dirt with an arrow in his back. The old farmer had come through again.

"*Hasama!*" Sumisu called out as he hobbled toward us. He still carried his shotel, but his shield was gone. Behind the Temba, Kish lay on his back, unmoving, with his arms spread wide. Tako stood guard over him, the point of the glaive he carried positioned at the Raven's throat. The older Lion moved so he could watch the Temba sailor and me simultaneously, though he had to know doing so would make him vulnerable to an arrow.

I saw movement in the window of the sod house moments later, and I shook my head. My blood was up now, and I was determined to finish this myself. "Don't shoot," I called out. "This bastard is mine." The door creaked open moments later, revealing first the old farmer holding his bow and his dog, then Sarrey looking relieved and worried at the same time. I glanced over at Sumisu. "You stay out of the way, too," I ordered, focusing back on my opponent.

But Sumisu kept coming anyway, ignoring my words as he limped forward determinedly. He paused when he reached Karal, who quickly tossed his weapon aside and begged for mercy, but the Temba had no such inclination. After it was done and Karal lay still, the sailor hobbled closer, moving awkwardly on his bad leg to flank my opponent. I noticed the cloth I'd wrapped around Sumisu's wound was gone, and the gaping tear in his leg was now matted with dirt and blood. Sumisu took several more steps toward the

Lion, and I frowned in annoyance, about to warn him again not to get too close, but our opponent was no fool. The man had seen an opportunity, and, like any good fighter—he took it.

I saw the muscles in the enemy soldier's shoulders tense, and I shouted a warning, but it was too late. The Lion charged at Sumisu, his glaive whirling. I cursed and started running, knowing I would be too late even as I did. Sumisu realized his danger and he lifted his sword awkwardly to block the soldier's attack, stumbling backward and almost falling as his bad leg gave out beneath him. It was a move made in desperation and worthy of praise, but the man had no real training in warfare, unaware that, much like in the game of chatrang, the initial attack was rarely the one that mattered most—it was what came next that did. The Lion disengaged contact and spun, whirling the glaive around and down in tandem with his body, catching the Temba sailor by surprise in his unprotected right side.

Everything had happened in the blink of an eye, and I cried out in anger and frustration as Sumisu fell. I launched myself at the Lion as he prepared to strike the killing blow, forcing him back and away from the fallen Temba. The soldier retreated from my fury as I used all my skill with sword and shield, pounding away at him left and right, not giving him a chance to breathe. I could see the old farmer aiming our way with his bow, but I knew he wouldn't let fly and risk taking the chance of hitting me unless he had a clear shot.

That clear shot never came, however, and finally, after long minutes of back and forth and both of us weakening from fatigue, I deflected a counter strike away with my shield that decided things. The Lion reacted slowly to bring his guard back up after his failed attack, and I took advantage and lunged into the gap, puncturing deep into his left thigh. The man cried out in pain and he fell to one knee, but I knew he wasn't finished and that the glaive was coming next. Off balance and not having time for anything else, I head-butted the man in the face, sending him reeling to the ground, where he lay stunned and bleeding.

I kicked the weapon out of the Lion's hands, then stood over the fallen warrior, my sword at his throat as I glanced over at Sumisu. Tako was crouched over the sailor's body, and he looked up at me, then slowly shook his head. I cursed at the waste, knowing the Temba's death was entirely my fault. If I had only let the old farmer put an arrow in the bastard to begin with, Sumisu would still be alive.

"It was a good fight, Lord Hadrack," the Lion said to me with a weary sigh of resignation. "And it was truly an honor to cross blades with you." He shifted his eyes to Sumisu's body. "I am sorry for your friend. All I have ever been is a soldier, and I only did what I was trained to do."

"I know that," I replied, understanding what he was saying despite my anger. "I would have done the same," I whispered.

Then I killed him.

Chapter 19: Kish

We buried Sumisu beneath a pile of rocks near a stand of old cypress trees not far from the farmer's house, though we left the dead Lions lying where they'd fallen for the scavengers. There just wasn't enough time for us to deal with them even if I'd wanted to, which I did not. Staying the extra half an hour it took to lay Sumisu to rest was risky, but Sarrey, Tako, and I had all agreed it was the least we could do for him. I knew Kish and his patrol would be reported missing soon, which meant more Lions were bound to come this way looking for them. We needed to be long gone from this place before that happened.

The old man's name was Goma, and though he was poor and had little in the way of food, he offered us whatever he had. That, coupled with the water skins and few provisions the Lions had brought with them, would have to do. The good news was we now had six horses—the one that had been struck by an arrow was too lame to take with us. The bad news was I knew no matter what we did or how fast we traveled, the Lions would keep coming after us. I couldn't hide what had happened in this place, nor was I experienced enough in woodcraft to conceal our trail from our pursuers when we left here.

I thought suddenly of Sabina, the girl who'd helped Malo and me track down Rorian long ago. Her extensive skills would have helped immensely right now. I hadn't thought about Sabina in many years, and I wondered if she'd gotten married and was a mother by now. Part of me hoped that she had found happiness somehow, despite how things had ended so tragically between us. I was surprised to realize the animosity I'd felt toward her wasn't as strong as it had been in years past. Time blunts even the harshest of memories, it seemed.

"That's the last of it, Your Highness," Goma said regretfully to Sarrey before handing me some dried meat wrapped in a dirty cloth and a small leather sack half-filled with withered dates. "I wish I had more to offer you."

"Your generosity will not be forgotten, sir," Sarrey said. She placed her hand on the old man's shoulder. "Nor your bravery, I assure you."

Goma looked embarrassed at the praise, and he lowered his eyes. "It is my duty to help you, Your Highness. I only wish I had understood your danger sooner and had not acted like a scared rabbit."

Sarrey laughed. "Nonsense, you were magnificent. I doubt we'd be standing here now if not for you." She leaned forward suddenly and kissed the farmer on his wrinkled cheek, and I thought the old bastard was going to drop dead from sheer astonishment. Sarrey finally turned away, pretending to ignore Goma's red face as she bent to pet the man's dog on the head. She turned to me afterward. "I'll take those, lord," she said, indicating the food I held. I handed her the dried meat and dates, then watched her walk toward Tako, where the boy waited, holding the horses' reins. I noticed he kept probing gingerly at his injured eye, which had turned an angry shade of purple and had swollen to the size of a goose egg. I frowned, worried the injury might be far worse than I'd thought at first.

Finally, I took a deep breath, focusing my attention on Goma. "You should come with us," I said, although I already knew what the response would be. "You would be welcome."

"I cannot, *Hasama*," the old farmer replied with a firm shake of his head. "I told you both my sons went into the city last night with their wives and children for *Satista*. I must be here when they return."

I'd described to Goma everything that had happened since my arrival in Temba while we'd buried Sumisu, including in detail the madness that had struck the city. I knew the chances the farmer's family would return unscathed were remote at best, but I hadn't had the heart to tell the old man that at the time. I was feeling torn about whether I should do so now or not.

"It's all right, *Hasama*," Goma said, his deep-set eyes filled with knowledge and sorrow as he studied me. "The conflict you feel in your heart right now is clear to me, and I thank you for it. You are a good and honorable man. But I am an old and tired one that has seen much death and misery in his lifetime. There is nothing you can hide from me that I don't already suspect. My family are most likely all dead. I know this already, so there is no need for you to voice it. But if I am wrong and even one returns home before the soldiers come back, then I must be here to help them."

"I'm sorry," I said, meaning it. Our relationship had begun badly, but in Goma, I now recognized a kindred spirit despite the differences in our ages. I wished I'd met the man sooner, for I would have greatly enjoyed sharing drinks with him in an inn while I listened to his life story. Unfortunately, the gods rarely give a man what he wishes for. I sighed in resignation as I glanced around the yard at the twisted, blood-soaked bodies. Green blowflies were already buzzing industriously around the corpses, looking to lay their eggs in the wounds, and overhead I could see several vultures circling with predatory interest. I gestured to the dead. "If nothing else, I wish we had more time to bury them for you."

"You've already been here too long as it is," Goma said. He glanced at the bodies and spat. "Let those bastards ripen in the sun and stink for all I care. They are all traitors and deserve no better for what they've done. Besides, I expect I won't live long enough to smell them rot, anyway." I nodded sadly, knowing that he was probably right about that. Once more Lions arrived, they would undoubtedly take their revenge out on the old farmer for what had happened here. "Take these," Goma added, removing his bow and an arrow bag filled with shafts off his shoulder and offering them to me. "You might need them, *Hasama*."

"I can't," I protested. "That's all you have to defend yourself with."

Goma thrust the bow and bag into my hands. "You can accept them, and you will, *Hasama*. Your job is to keep the queen alive, not worry about the fate of one worthless old man. These will help make that happen. The gods have already sealed my destiny, and that bow will do me little good. Judgment Day has finally come for me, and I will not hide from it."

I took a deep breath, then slung the bow and arrow bag over my shoulder before offering my hand. "It's a shame," I said as the old man's warm, dry hand wrapped around my forearm and we shook. "I think we would have been good friends in another place and time."

"So do I, *Hasama*," Goma agreed. "So do I." He gave my arm one last squeeze, then released me, motioning to the horses. "You'd best be getting on. You've got a long ride ahead of you. I wish you luck."

I nodded, knowing there was nothing left to be said. I headed for the mount I'd selected, a gray, dappled horse with a black mane, a black tail, and surprisingly intelligent eyes. Sarrey and Tako were already mounted and, as I swung into the saddle, I glanced at Kish, who sat brooding on the same horse he'd ridden earlier. I'd seriously considered slitting the man's throat at first, but in the end had decided to keep him alive—at least for now. Once we were safely away from here, I had questions for the bastard. The Raven glared at me with little love, and I couldn't help but smirk at his bruised and battered face, courtesy of Sumisu. Kish's hands were fastened securely to the pommel of his saddle with rope, and for good measure, I'd also tied his ankles beneath his horse's belly.

"You'll pay for this, Lord Hadrack," Kish hissed between his teeth. "If it's the last thing I do, I'll see that you pay for this."

"Maybe," I replied, swinging the gray around while holding the reins of Kish's horse. "Maybe not." I glanced back at the Raven as we struck out toward the south. "But either way, I expect you'll be dead by sundown anyway, so I wouldn't start celebrating just yet if I were you."

Sarrey was an accomplished rider, much better than I could ever hope to be and, since she knew the area, I allowed her to take the lead. Tako, on the other hand, had never been on a horse before. He sat perched on the animal's back with a look that told me he expected to be thrown off and trampled at any moment. I had selected the gentlest looking of the horses for Tako—a thin black mare with soft, doe-like eyes and a pleasing gate—but that fact seemed lost on the nervous boy as we crossed another small field of lima beans. Tako's horse was nothing but obedient and docile the entire way, but the boy still rode tensely, his good eye round with dread. I'd tried reassuring him that there was nothing to be afraid of, but my words seemed to go in one ear and out the other. Eventually, I just gave up, knowing time would be the only thing that would ultimately soothe Tako's fears.

An hour later, after leaving the farmer's home and beanfields far behind and passing over an open plain of scrub brush, we entered the neck of a narrow, rock-strewn valley surrounded by equally rocky hills. It was here that we hoped to lose our pursuers, for the ground showed little evidence of our passage. The day had begun hot, and now, well past noon, the heat was beyond stifling, but there was little we could do other than try to endure it. There was no wind in the valley to speak of, just dead air and waves of heat shimmering off the rocks. I wiped sweat from my brow and glanced up at the cloudless sky, noticing several turkey vultures with their distinctive wingspan circling overhead. *Don't waste your time*, I thought. *We're not dead yet.*

Sarrey's horse suddenly snorted ahead of me, shying away from the trail as a red snake with black and yellow bands on its head and body slithered across our path ten feet away. The snake was about two feet long, and it paused, curling its body protectively as it lifted its head to stare at us. A dark, forked tongue kept flicking in and out of its mouth, tasting our scent.

"Stay where you are, lord," Sarrey warned, lifting a hand to halt our tiny column. She waited, looking tense, until the snake finally lost interest and slithered away behind some rocks. Sarrey let air out of her lungs. "A Temba coral snake, lord. Very dangerous. Their venom can kill quite quickly."

I nodded. I'd always hated snakes. We progressed a little further into the valley, shadowed part of the way by a curious fox, then stopped for a quick water break, though we were careful to drink sparingly. Kish pleaded for water, but I ignored him. Why waste precious resources on someone who wouldn't be breathing soon anyway? I took the time to examine Tako's eye during the stop, relieved to see that the swelling was slowly coming down. The boy assured me most of the pain was gone now, and though I knew he was being brave and lying, I was pretty sure he would keep the eye.

Five hours later, with the sun sinking in the west, we finally exited the valley, breaking out into heavily forested lands dominated by oak, maple, sycamore, and pine trees. Beyond that lay green-shrouded mountains, and beyond that, Sarrey told me, the sprawling desert known as the Waste of Bones. That's where we planned to join the road that would lead us further inland. The wastelands, I learned, spanned a staggering four million square miles, an area so vast that I could barely wrap my head around it. We'd deliberately avoided using any roads up until this point for obvious reasons, but once we reached the outskirts of the desert, I knew we'd have little choice. I could only pray that the Lions would have given up searching for us by the time we arrived. It was a faint hope at best, but it was all we had to cling to.

We traveled for another half an hour through the trees in the waning light until finally, I signaled that it was enough. We could go no further in the growing darkness and would have to make camp.

"Tako," I said to the boy when we dismounted. "See to the horses. Make sure to stake them out securely." I glanced at Kish, who sat slumped in his saddle, his eyes red-rimmed and filled with suffering. I felt no pity for him whatsoever. I untied his ankles, then his arms. "Get down," I grunted.

The Raven stared at me with blank indifference until I finally snorted in impatience and grabbed the sleeve of his robe, pulling him roughly to the ground. Kish cried out in surprise and landed hard, with the air exploding from his lungs. I dragged him across the forest floor to a modest-sized maple tree, then used more rope to tie him securely to it while he moaned and begged me for water. When I was done, I returned to my horse and unhooked a waterskin. I took a drink, aware that the Raven was watching me enviously.

Sarrey joined me a moment later, her eyes on Kish. "What are we going to do with him?" she asked.

I offered her the waterskin, but she declined. I took another sip. "He's going to answer some questions for me," I said.

"And then?"

I shrugged. "And then I'll send him off to meet his god."

"Do you think that's necessary?" Sarrey asked.

I looked at her in surprise. "That bastard helped murder your family. Have you forgotten?"

Sarrey grimaced and shook her head. "No, lord, I have not." She sighed. "I'm just tired of all the killing, I guess."

I nodded, hefting the waterskin in my hand. "Well, you'd better get used to it, Your Highness," I said. "Because I promise you, there's going to be much more of that before this thing is done." I moved away from the girl then, heading back to our prisoner, who just stared at me with a pathetic look on his sunburnt face. I crouched before him, letting the waterskin dangle by its leather strap between my legs. Kish stared at it in rapt fascination as I began to swing the skin back and forth. I smiled, knowing the battle was already half-won.

"Where is the Eye of God?" I asked.

Kish licked his lips, glancing up at me. "I don't know, lord."

I nodded, having expected that answer. "Who is the Eye of God?"

"I don't know that either, lord. I swear it to be true."

"You've never met him?"

"No, lord."

"You don't know his real name?"

"No, lord."

"You expect me to believe that?"

"Why would I lie, lord?"

I smiled without humor. "Why wouldn't you?"

The Raven glanced down at the waterskin with desire, licking his dry and cracked lips again. "May I have some water, lord?"

"Where is the Eye of God?" I repeated in a calm voice.

"I don't know."

"Who is he?"

"I don't know."

"Is Muwa the Eye of God?"

"No, lord."

"You're sure?"

"I swear it."

"Then who is?"

"I told you, I don't know."

I sighed and uncorked the waterskin, trying not to smile as Kish's eyes lit up with sudden hope. I started to lift the skin to the Raven's lips, and the man moaned in anticipation, then I stopped inches away. "Who is the Eye of God?"

Kish shuddered, his shoulders shaking with disappointment. "I don't know, lord," he whispered.

I drew back the waterskin and took a sip, smacking my lips in satisfaction. I hadn't noticed earlier, but Sarrey and Tako had moved closer so they could hear, standing several feet off to one side of me in the shadows cast by the tree. I glanced at the girl, then back to Kish, deciding it was time to change tact. "Why did your people have Queen Sarrey's family killed?"

The White Raven's eyes widened. "We didn't, lord. Only the king and queen are dead. Princess Magret is alive and well."

I heard Sarrey gasp, and I tried to hide my surprise. I'd just assumed they'd murdered the child as well. "Why didn't you kill her, too?" I grunted.

Kish looked reluctant to answer, shifting his gaze to Sarrey, then quickly away again.

"I asked you a question," I growled.

"She is to be crowned queen-in-waiting, lord," Kish finally said. "A regent will govern until she is old enough."

I nodded, understanding now. "Let me guess. This regent you speak of is Muwa. Am I right?"

Kish looked down. "Yes, lord. He is of royal blood, but as a member of the White Ravens, it is forbidden by the laws of the One True God for him to sit on a throne. This way, the people will accept him."

I laughed sarcastically at that. "So, with the rest of the family supposedly dead, the plan was Muwa would rule Temba in the name of a child that can't even speak yet. That's why you need to find Queen Sarrey so badly, because the whole sorry thing falls apart with her still alive."

"It certainly does put our plans in jeopardy," Kish admitted almost sheepishly. He motioned to the water with his head. "Now, *please*, lord, may I drink?"

"Soon," I said. "Just as long as you keep answering questions." I shifted positions, for my right leg was beginning to ache from an old arrow wound I'd taken many years ago. "What did you bastards put in the Blessed Wine?"

"Lord?"

"Don't play dumb," I said. "I know the madness in the city last night was caused by whatever was in the wine. What was it?"

"I don't know what you mean, lord."

I removed my sword from the back of my belt and laid it on the ground between us. I said nothing, waiting as I stared at Kish. Darkness had settled deeper into the forest, but enough light still filtered through the branches for me to see the Raven's terrified expression.

Kish shifted uncomfortably in the continued silence, looking from me to the sword, then back to me. He cleared his throat nervously. "I really don't know, lord."

"That's too bad," I said. "Because it's starting to look like you don't know anything at all." I smiled and picked up the sword. "Which makes you a liability and essentially useless, now doesn't it?"

I put the blade to the Raven's neck. "Wait!" Kish cried out in desperation. "All right! All right! I'll tell you." I lowered the sword, resting the sharp edge against one of the bound man's outstretched ankles. "We used jimsonweed, lord."

I frowned, having never heard of it. "And what is that?" I asked.

"A plant that grows in the desert, lord," Kish replied. "The leaves and seeds are ground into powder, then mixed with wine."

"And this mixture turns people mad?"

"Not everyone who drinks it, lord," Kish said. "Some people react differently than others. Some go mad, some people just sleep it off, while others just get sick and vomit. There is no way to know how it will affect someone."

"But you knew enough people would be afflicted with the madness to cause bedlam in the city, correct?" I asked. "That was the plan?"

Kish nodded. "Yes, lord. We needed something to distract the troops who were still loyal to the king."

"Looks like it worked," I grunted in disgust. I pushed down with the sword as Kish winced. "Do you know how many lives were destroyed by you and your little birds?" I growled, thinking of Goma and his family.

"It is the One True God's will, lord," Kish said forcefully, suddenly finding his backbone. "Besides, this is all your fault. All you had to do was agree to marry the princess and things would not have gone so far." I heard Sarrey gasp a second time as Kish shook his head. "Muwa tried to warn you, but you were too stupid and stubborn to listen."

"Yes, he did try," I agreed, keeping the blade in place. "So tell me, Kish of the White Ravens. What happens now? Where does all this madness lead?"

Kish blinked. "Lord?"

"Why topple the Royal Family and take control of Temba? For power? Riches? What? What do the White Ravens hope to gain by this?"

Kish looked surprised. "We are God's servants, lord. We seek no power or riches. Our task is to bring awareness to the people, nothing more. Last night was but the first step in that task."

"You're talking about the Enlightenment," I said.

"Yes, lord," Kish agreed, his eyes gleaming with religious fervor. "The One True God has spoken to us, and we, the White Ravens, have heeded His call. We will tear down the lies and false gods and rebuild the world as it was always meant to be. That is our purpose."

"By murdering innocent people?" I asked with a snort.

Kish looked at me with pity. "There are no innocents in this world, lord—only true believers and heretics. The good and just will bathe in the righteous light of the One True God, and those who refuse Him in favor of darkness will be eradicated. It is up to each man, woman, and child now to decide where they stand in the coming war of Enlightenment."

"Uh-huh," I grunted, unimpressed. "And Temba is the first step in this war, is that right?"

"Yes, lord. It is."

"You still haven't answered my question," I said. "What happens next?"

"Why, we keep moving forward, lord," Kish answered. "Spreading our message to the north, east, and the west until all the great kingdoms of this world are united in the light of the One True God."

I rolled my eyes. "You may have succeeded in Temba with a little bit of cunning and some luck, Raven," I said contemptuously. "But once word gets out about what you people are up to, your cause will fizzle out and die like a vine in winter. I'll grant you Temba is a big city, but that's all it is. You have no idea the kind of resources and power the kingdoms to the north can wield. Ganderland alone will crush your kind like ants under our boots if you dare set foot on her soil. I'll see to that."

Kish grinned mockingly. "Is Ganderland not currently besieged by war as we speak, lord?"

"What of it?" I muttered, suddenly feeling uneasy at the triumphant glow in the Raven's eyes.

"And why, exactly, do you suppose that is, lord?" Kish asked. He chuckled and leaned his head forward as much as his bonds would allow. "I'll let you in on a little secret, Lord Hadrack. The war you are fighting with the Cardians and Parnuthians is no accident—and the reason for that is because the White Ravens are already there!"

Chapter 20: Tragedy

I didn't kill Kish that night, deciding after Sarrey had once again voiced her reluctance that the Raven might actually prove useful later. It was a decision that, unfortunately, she and I would very soon come to regret. The revelation that the White Ravens were already in Ganderland and causing mischief like they had in Temba rocked me like a punch to the stomach. My first thought on learning of it had been about First Daughter Gernet and the attempts on her life, convinced that the Ravens must have been behind them. But Kish denied any knowledge of that, even when poked and prodded by my sword, drawing blood. After spending ten long minutes grilling and threatening the man, I reluctantly concluded that he was either a very good liar or was telling me the truth.

Kish also claimed that he didn't know the Ravens' plans for Ganderland. All he knew was that operatives had been sent there some time ago to spread the word about the One True God. These operatives were also tasked with undermining the kingdom's leadership to help weaken it, but Kish swore he didn't know how they hoped to accomplish that. Although, he conceded the ongoing dispute with Cardia and Parnuthia were most likely part of it. The Raven insisted that he was rarely consulted on such matters and was happy just being a simple foot soldier in a holy war. Despite my dislike for the man, I tended to believe him, and as the questioning continued for another hour, it became more and more obvious to me that I would need to find someone higher up the chain of command if I wanted real answers. I knew that person would have to be Muwa—I just had no idea how to get to him.

I slept fitfully on the hard ground that night, as did Sarrey and Tako, with the three of us taking two-hour turns on watch. I'd allowed Kish some water and a few dates after my questioning was over, which seemed to do wonders for the man. I found it ironic that of the four of us, the Raven was the only one who slept soundly, his head slumped forward on his chest while snoring almost as loud as that bastard Chaba had on board *Wandering-Spirit*.

The next morning began with a short but intense burst of rain that left us all wet and shivering, replaced after less than five minutes by a steamy, impenetrable heat that hung beneath the canopy of the forest like fog as the sun steadily rose. Strange birds with bright red heads broken by a band of black at the eyes flitted back and forth above us as our horses fought their way single file through the undergrowth. The birds had dark green feathers and a green mantle, with stark yellow patches on their breasts and flamboyant long green tails that split in two at the end and were tinged yellow at the tips. Our curious companions seemed to be following us, I realized after a while, constantly shifting from one branch to another overhead while turning their heads sideways to watch us pass beneath them. Sarrey told me they were called *lorikeets* and that they usually spent their time feasting on berries and the nectar of flowers.

I'd automatically taken the lead when we first set out, with Sarrey behind me, then Kish, followed by Tako and the two extra horses carrying our meager supplies tied to his saddle. We traveled for six straight hours, stopping only briefly once to eat, stretch our legs, and relieve ourselves. There had been no signs of pursuit so far, and though both Sarrey and Tako had voiced their hopes that we'd lost the Lions, from experience, I knew better. No, they were coming—the only question was when.

I glanced over my shoulder at Sarrey. "How much longer until we reach the mountains, Your Highness?"

"Maybe three more hours," the girl replied, looking uncertain. She shrugged. "It's a guess at best, lord. I've never been this way before. Most travelers take a much easier route to the east."

"But you'll know how to find the trail through them when we get there?"

"I believe so, lord."

I nodded and faced forward again, troubled now by the girl's less than convincing assurances. We'd deliberately headed southwest through the thickest part of the forest on our way to the mountains, avoiding any trails and clearings, aiming to skirt around the small, family-owned farming settlements known as *tachtars* that dotted the land around the vast city. Goma's farm had been one of these.

Less than three hours later, Sarrey's prediction came true, as the trees began to thin and the landscape started to slope upward dramatically. After another hour of steady climbing, we found the entrance to the trail Sarrey had described, which led us to a high, rocky plateau covered in dark lichen, where I reined in the gray. I looked back at the sprawling forest far below and the open fields beyond it as my companions joined me. I could see no signs of riders in pursuit.

"It's beautiful," Sarrey whispered in appreciation. She took a deep breath, filling her lungs with the heady scent of pine that dominated the air. "It's like looking at a painting done by a master."

I nodded in agreement, for the view was indeed a truly magnificent sight from this height. The sky above us was a dazzlingly bright blue, with only a few puffy clouds drifting lazily past, adding to the tranquility of the landscape. I could feel a faint breeze tugging at my clothing, a welcome release after the stifling heat from below. I sighed in appreciation, enjoying the sweat quickly cooling on my skin as Tako guided his horse beside me. The boy rode with more confidence now, and I noticed the swelling around his eye had receded dramatically, though the black and yellow bruising was still very much in evidence.

"How is the eye doing?" I asked him.

"Better, *Hasama*," Tako said with a grin. "I can see again, though it is blurry still."

I smiled. "That's good news."

"Lord Hadrack?" Sarrey said. "Do you think we can stop here for a moment?" She pursed her lips almost shyly, motioning with her eyes to a stand of trees beneath a cliff fifty feet to the north. "I could use a moment of privacy."

"Oh, of course," I said, understanding. "Take whatever time you need, Your Highness. This is a good place to get down and stretch our legs, anyway."

"Thank you, lord," Sarrey said.

I dismounted, handing the reins of the gray to Tako, who also took the reins of Sarrey's horse before she headed away.

"What about me?" Kish asked when I made no move to untie him.

I walked to the plateau's edge, where a gigantic stone shaped like a musician's harp sat, not bothering to look at the Raven as I leaned against it and crossed my arms over my chest. I spat over the side, watching as the glob twisted and turned, winking in the sunlight like a jewel before slapping against a stone below. "What about you?" I grunted.

"I have to piss."

I shrugged. "Then go ahead, Raven. I doubt that nag of yours will care. It must be used to your stink by now."

Kish glared at me, his eyes burning with hatred. "You bastard," he spat. "I've done all you've asked of me. What more do you want?"

I glanced at him and smiled. "You could die and save me the trouble of having to kill you."

The Raven sneered, opening his mouth to respond just as I heard a scream echo from the north. I jumped to my feet in alarm, already tugging at my sword as I started to run. "Watch him!" I shouted over my shoulder as I raced past Tako.

I scrambled over loose rocks and scraggly weeds, losing my footing and cursing just as another scream sounded from the trees, followed by a hissing roar that sent my heart leaping into my throat.

I redoubled my efforts, praying I wouldn't twist an ankle as I hit the treeline and plunged through a wall of dried brambles and tangled vines full of prickly thorns. I ignored the pain as those thorns tore at my face and hands, pushing deeper until I found myself in an open area of exposed rock bordered by tall crags of yellow sandstone. Sarrey stood with her back to a sloping outcrop of rock while a sleek, tan-colored cougar crouched twenty feet away in front of her. A small cub lay on the stone, unmoving between the woman and beast, while a second cub cowered twenty feet above on the ledge of a large butte near a darkened opening.

I reacted without thinking, shouting and waving my sword as I ran right at the cougar. The big cat turned to face this new threat, hissing and spitting with its ears drawn back and gleaming, yellow fangs exposed. I wished I'd had the foresight to bring the bow hooked on my horse's saddle, but I was a poor archer at best anyway, and it probably wouldn't have helped. I paused ten feet from the beast, showing it my teeth and growling myself while I twirled the sword in my hand. I had no idea if that was the right thing to do, but it was all I could think of at the time. So far, I had to admit the cougar looked hugely unimpressed.

I risked a quick glance Sarrey's way, where she remained pressed against the stone. "Are you hurt?" I grunted before focusing back on the big cat.

"No," Sarrey said. She lifted a hand to me. "Lord, you must stop what you're doing right now!"

"What?"

"Don't antagonize her," Sarrey whispered. "I think she only wants her baby."

The mother cougar took a step toward me, hissing in warning and flicking its tail. I stopped growling, though I made sure to maintain eye contact and keep my sword in front of me. The cat studied me suspiciously, still hissing, but when I made no aggressive moves, it finally retreated, heading for its fallen cub. The cougar hesitated over the motionless body, taking a moment to growl at me one more time in warning before she prodded the dead animal with her nose. Blood pooled under the baby's head where it had hit the stone. I waited, holding my breath while the big cat sniffed her offspring, then tentatively licked some of the blood from the cub's fur. Finally, still growling at me, the cougar picked the cub up by the scruff of the neck, then, moving with effortless grace, it sprinted up the side of the bluff to the ledge above before disappearing inside the cave. I caught one last glimpse of a tiny feline face with enormous eyes looking down at me, then the surviving sibling followed after its mother.

I rushed to Sarrey. "Are you all right?" I asked, even more concerned than I'd been when I saw fresh blood on her cheek.

The girl nodded, still looking shaken. "Yes, lord. I think so." I turned her head to examine the wound, which was a long, jagged cut from the corner of her eye to her jawline. "I fell when the cougar appeared and scraped my face on the ground," Sarrey explained when she saw my concern. "It's nothing, lord, really."

I nodded, relieved. "What happened?"

Sarrey looked up at the ledge. "The cub must have heard me moving about and got curious. Part of the rock edge broke off when it looked down and it lost its footing and fell. I went to help the poor thing, but by the time I realized it was dead, the mother was almost on top of me." She took a deep breath, looking calmer now, though her hands were still visibly shaking. "I was certain I was dead, lord. I still can't quite believe that I'm not."

"Can you walk?" I asked sympathetically.

Sarrey nodded. "Of course, lord. I told you, I'm fine. Just a little shaken up, is all."

"Good," I replied. "Then we better get back before that thing decides to return."

I helped Sarrey across the rock and through the trees, using a safer route through the brambles she'd taken earlier, which I'd failed to notice in my haste. We stepped back into the open, and I stopped two feet from the treeline, frozen in disbelief at what I saw.

"No!" I shouted.

I let go of Sarrey, running toward the small, prostrate body lying twisted on the rocks near the harp stone. There was no sign of Kish or our horses anywhere. I dropped to my knees beside Tako, gently rolling him over onto his back, then I cursed. It only took one glance at the boy's bulging, bloodshot eyes and discolored face to know he was gone. I could see mottled discoloration on Tako's thin neck where the Raven had wrapped his hands around it, choking him to death. I moaned in despair and forced myself to my feet on wobbly legs, weeping openly as I stood precariously close to the overhang. I glared down at the lush greenery of the forest below, knowing somewhere in all that Tako's murderer was getting away and there was nothing I could do to stop him.

"I'll kill you, you bastard!" I howled at the trees. "Do you hear me, Kish? I will kill you for what you've done!"

My voice echoed over and over again, while behind me, I heard Sarrey drop to her knees beside Tako. I felt bitterness and anger settle over me as the sounds of her gut-wrenching sobs of grief were interrupted by sharp, mocking laughter rising from somewhere far below. I stared down at all that vastness, feeling nothing but seething hatred and impotent frustration. Finally, I tilted my head back and vented my loss toward the blue sky above me. When I was done and drained of all emotion, I turned back to Sarrey and the boy's motionless body with nothing but cold resolve flowing through my veins. I knew I'd never catch up to Kish now, but someday, hopefully very soon, the White Raven would rue the very day he'd been born. I was going to see to that, I vowed, no matter the cost.

Sarrey and I spent the remainder of that day after we'd buried Tako making our way up the mountain in mostly dejected silence. There was no need for us to talk, for we both fully understood what we were up against now. We had no food or water to speak of and had only one sword between us with many miles to go—all of it on foot. Our situation was beyond bleak, but if that wasn't bad enough, I knew there was a good chance Kish had already joined up with our pursuers, which meant he might even now be leading them after us. I figured we were relatively safe as long as we kept moving since the steepness of the trail we were following would limit the advantage the Lions had with horses. But that would only last so long, and the moment we reached the lowlands, I knew we'd be vulnerable. I had no illusions about what would happen to us then.

"We should get off the trail, lord," Sarrey said after we'd scaled a particularly steep, bottlenecked slope strewn with small, pebble-sized rocks known as scree.

I glanced around and frowned, biting off an angry retort. Didn't she think I would have done that already if it were possible? High cliffs rose to either side of us, as they had almost from the moment we'd set out on foot, with nothing but the odd scraggly bush clinging to the rock that was stained almost white from exposure to the sun. The trail was at best six feet wide where we stood, though, at times earlier in the day, it had been as much as twenty or more. At one point, it had even narrowed down to three feet for a span of about twenty yards, which I prayed would give our pursuers and their horses nothing but grief.

"And just where would you have us go right now, Your Highness?" I asked, keeping my voice even as I wiped sweat from my forehead. It was a wasted effort, I noted sourly as I stared at my wet hand, for the sweat had returned instantly. "You told me this was the only way through this part of the mountains. Were you wrong?"

"No, lord," Sarrey admitted. "Forgive me. I don't know where my mind is at right now."

I studied the girl critically. Her hair was hanging limply in ringlets, looking as wet as if it had just rained. She'd long since stowed away the beggar's robe I'd given her on one of the pack animals, and dark bands of sweat streaked her dress down her chest and under the armpits. Sarrey closed her eyes, leaning forward as she rubbed the back of her neck.

"We should rest here for a while," I said, knowing the girl badly needed it.

Sarrey looked at me, hope in her eyes. "Do you think we can risk it?"

"I don't think we have a choice," I said. "You look like you're ready to fall down." I motioned to the western side of the trail, where an overhang far above us offered a foot or so of shade from the unrelenting sun. "Let's sit down over there. I think we can afford ten minutes or so."

Sarrey didn't argue, which told me all I needed to know. We both sat down gratefully with our backs to the rock, tucking our legs under us to keep our feet out of the sun. The smooth sandstone was surprisingly cool in the shade, and both Sarrey and I sighed with pleasure at the same time. I closed my eyes, trying not to think about how thirsty and tired I was.

"Lord?"

I opened my eyes. "Yes, Your Highness?"

"I'm sorry."

I blinked. "For what?"

"For getting you into this mess."

I waved a hand. "It's not your fault."

"Yes, it is," Sarrey insisted. "If I hadn't jumped from your ship, none of this would have ever happened."

"Well, there is that," I admitted with a weak smile, trying to make light of it. Sarrey's eyes began to instantly fill with water, and I swore, realizing what a fool I'd just been. "It was meant as a joke,

Your Highness," I added hastily, trying to repair the damage. "I promise, I hold nothing against you for what happened. You'd just lost the love of your life, and you weren't thinking. I can understand and relate to that. Truly I can."

Sarrey stared at me searchingly, ignoring the tears cutting small rivers down her dirty and blood-streaked cheeks. "Yes, I remember you telling me that right before I jumped. I'd forgotten. You lost your wife not long ago, is that right?"

I nodded and looked down, unable to meet her eyes. They say that the eyes are the windows to the soul, and if that's true, I didn't want this girl to see that my soul was broken. "I did," I managed to say.

"What was her name?"

"Shana," I answered, still not looking up. "Lady Shana Corwick."

Sarrey paused as she took that in. "It's a fine name, lord. I'm sure she was a wonderful person."

"She was," I said, aware of the crack in my voice.

Sarrey shifted closer, putting a hand on my arm. "I can see the hurt inside you, lord, despite how hard you try to hide it. I think I saw it all along. It is something, sadly, that we have in common now. I only wish it were not so for both our sakes."

I looked up, my eyes meeting hers. I could see nothing but concern and sympathy there. "Thank you, Your Highness. I appreciate that."

Sarrey smiled sadly, squeezing my arm before she sat back again. She rested her head against the cool stone and sighed. "How long do you think we have, lord?"

I hesitated, knowing what she was asking. "Not long," I answered truthfully. "Maybe tomorrow morning—noon at the latest. It will depend on how well they've fared moving the horses up."

"Ah well," Sarrey said with another sigh. She chuckled softly. "It's ironic, lord. After Mondar was murdered, all I wanted was to die so I could be with him again. But now, with my life mere hours away from ending, all I can think about is that I want to live." She looked at me, her fears and fatigue washing away, replaced with a fierceness that took my breath away. "I want to live, lord, so I can take revenge on those bastards who took my city and my beloved from me."

I nodded, understanding exactly how she felt. "Well, Your Highness," I said, standing and smiling down at her. "We're not dead yet, and the Wolf of Corwick still has a few tricks left up his sleeve." I extended a hand to her. "Shall we get moving?"

"Certainly, lord," Sarrey said with a light laugh as she took my hand.

I didn't know why, but suddenly I felt buoyant, as if anything were possible, and I could tell by Sarrey's expression that she felt it too. It was an invigorating and exciting moment as I drew the girl to her feet—one which, sadly, didn't last very long. We took no more than three steps up the trail, arm in arm, when a shout sounded from behind us, followed by a clattering of rocks. Sarrey's eyes went round with dread, and I spun around, looking back down the trail in dismay.

"Damn!" I cursed as men appeared at the base of the slope on foot—men in armor with six-pointed stars on their shields.

The Lions had found us.

Chapter 21: Lions On The Trail

I drew my sword, giving Sarrey a shove up the trail as I headed the other way. "Go, Your Highness! Run! I'll hold them off for as long as I can!"

"I'm not leaving you, lord," Sarrey said in a determined voice. She looked around for a weapon, then seeing nothing close to hand, she selected several fist-sized rocks before joining me at the edge of the slope.

"But—" I started to protest.

"We don't have time to argue, lord!" Sarrey snapped with a fierce expression on her face.

I muttered an oath as her features turned stubborn, knowing that she was right. I planted myself in the center of the trail and looked downward. I dearly wished I had my shield with me, but I'd left it strapped to the gray's saddle. Four men were already halfway up the incline, sweating and cursing as they picked their way cautiously over the scree in a single line. The man in the lead finally looked up and saw me, and he pointed, shouting in excitement to his companions. I could see more men milling around at the base of the slope, though there appeared to be only another four or five of them.

Sarrey hissed in anger much like the mother cougar had hours earlier, before she drew back her arm and tossed one of the rocks. But, despite her good intentions and obvious motivation, the girl was slight and clearly unused to such things. The missile fell well short of the lead man, though it did set off a tiny avalanche when it landed, taking some small stones and rock fragments bouncing along with it down the slope. One of those stones skipped up and struck a Lion on his shin, and he swore loudly, though it didn't hinder his progress any.

The lead soldier looked up at us and laughed contemptuously, shifting his shield in front of him. He was wearing a stained leather helmet and dark cloak over his armor and was beardless, with a fleshy face and small, beady eyes. "Is that all you've got, Wolf?" he shouted. "A girl with some pebbles?"

"Give me that," I growled at Sarrey. She placed the second rock in my hand, and I tossed it in the air several times, taking the measure of it. I'd spent my early childhood chucking an endless amount of stones at birds and marmots or anything else with a pulse, and though it had been many years since then, I still remembered how. I pictured the rock leaving my hand in my mind and striking Beady Eyes, just like I'd done a thousand times when I was a boy—then I threw. "Ha!" I grunted in satisfaction when the stone hit the Lion's shield with a crack exactly where I'd aimed, staggering the man.

The soldier hesitated, not looking as cocky now as our eyes met. I grinned mockingly, and I could see he now understood where this was heading. The soldier shouted in defiance, then began to run awkwardly upward, but the scree and steep slope severely impeded his progress. I looked around for more rocks, knowing I had time.

"Lord!" Sarrey said. She pointed right, where a jumble of jagged stones sat in the shadows against the cliff wall. Some of them were bigger than my head.

I handed the girl my sword before I hurried over to the largest stone. I picked it up, surprised by the weight, then returned to the top of the slope and lifted the rock over my head. Beady Eyes was less than twenty feet from the top now, and I saw those tiny eyes of his go round with fear when he saw what I held. I cried out and flung the stone downward at the man, who was helpless to do anything except lift his shield and pray. As it turned out, neither one did him much good. The rock crashed into the soldier with staggering force, denting his shield and sending the man somersaulting backward in a rush of small stones and dust. The Lion wailed in dismay, and as he tumbled helplessly end over end, he struck those coming behind him, cutting them down like trees in a twisted mass of confused arms and legs. When the dust finally settled, I saw all four of our pursuers lying prone on the ground. Beady Eyes was still, with a second Lion moaning and clutching his right leg. I frowned as the other two groggily regained their feet before retreating in panic behind an outcrop at the bottom of the slope.

"Keep an eye on the bastards, Your Highness," I grunted. "Let me know if they try again."

I spent the next few minutes building a wall of rocks along the top of the slope from one cliff to the other, while below me, the way remained clear of Lions. Sarrey joined in to help me once it became obvious we had time, gathering smaller stones, though we made sure that one of us was always in a position to watch the trail at all times. The man holding his leg had dragged himself away, moaning in agony, and I'd let him go while my initial target, Beady Eyes, remained where he'd fallen, unmoving a third of the way down the trail. I still couldn't see any of the others around the outcrop, but I could hear them arguing, guessing that they were trying to stoke their courage for another try.

Let them come, I thought grimly.

I finally paused in my work to catch my breath once the wall was almost to my waist, with two piles of smaller stones set to either side, close to hand for throwing. I now had the option to use the bigger stones as a barrier or as weapons, depending on what the situation called for. I nodded to Sarrey that it was enough. If those Lions wanted to get up here, then by the gods, I vowed, they'd have to pay a heavy price to do it.

"Now what, lord?" Sarrey asked. "What else do you need me to do?"

I looked at her, impressed. The girl didn't seem afraid at all. In fact, she looked surprisingly calm and relaxed, considering our situation. "Nothing," I said with a shrug. "Now we wait." I glanced up at the sky. The sun had moved off to the west, and the shadows cast by the cliff above were slowly encroaching on where we stood. "It'll be dark in a few hours," I added. "If we can last until then, maybe we can slip away."

Sarrey nodded, looking thoughtful. She leaned her hands on our crude stone wall and peered down the narrow slope. "Why don't they just rush us, lord? They must have enough men down there to do the job." She paused to glance at me. "I imagine they'd lose a few on the way up, of course, but in the end, we're bound to get overwhelmed."

I grinned, liking how the girl wasn't panicking and was instead thinking logically. "I don't think there's actually all that many of them," I said. I motioned to the sloping trail. "I'm guessing they're just an advance party. Those men down there are probably the best trackers the Ravens have and the fittest. Whoever is in charge probably sent them ahead to locate us while the bulk of the force followed with the horses."

"Oh," Sarrey said. She frowned as she thought about that. "Which means the rest will get here eventually."

I sighed. "Unfortunately, true, Your Highness."

"Then I guess we better not be here when they do," Sarrey replied.

I smiled. "Exactly what I was thinking." I took up my sword from where the girl had propped it against our makeshift wall. "But if we can eliminate those trackers before we go—" I added.

Sarrey gave me a wide grin. "Then the bastards will have a hard time finding us when we get off the mountain," she finished for me. Her smile slowly fizzled out. "Just how, exactly, are we going to do that, lord?"

"A damn fine question," I muttered. "One that I wish I had the answer to." I looked further up the trail. "Why don't you go ahead and—" I hesitated as Sarrey's eyes flashed in warning. "I don't mean that, Your Highness. All I want is for you to go and see where this trail leads. If we have to retreat in a hurry, I want to know what's ahead of us."

Sarrey looked at me suspiciously. "You won't do anything foolish while I'm gone?"

"Of course not," I promised, trying my best to look sincere. "I'm going to stay right where I am until you get back."

"You swear to me, lord?" Sarrey said uncertainly.

"May the gods strike me down if I lie," I replied. Sarrey still hesitated, and I turned her around and gave her a gentle push. "Find us a way out of here, Your Highness. Our fate rests in your hands."

I waited several minutes after Sarrey left, then, without a second thought, I hopped over the wall. I did glance up once on the other side, though, the superstitious part of me half expecting a sizzling bolt of lightning to split the skies and fry my bones to ashes. But nothing happened except for the harsh call of a raven sounding from somewhere down the trail. I made my way slowly and cautiously forward, all my senses tuned for any indication that the Lions were aware of what I was doing. There were none, though, for I suppose in their minds, what man in his right mind would even consider doing such a rash and foolish thing?

My boots sank into the scree with each step as I descended, but no matter how careful I was, I couldn't prevent a myriad of small stones from dislodging and rolling downhill every time I lifted a foot. I was surprised the Lions didn't have anyone watching the trail, but I guessed they were confident we had nowhere to go. Whatever the reason, I knew it wouldn't be very long before they heard the noise I was making and realized what it meant. I needed to accomplish my task before they did.

I finally reached Beady Eyes without being discovered and I knelt beside him. The man's neck had snapped at some point during his fall, I saw with satisfaction. I heard a sudden shout just then, and I looked up, my heart in my throat, but it hadn't been a cry of discovery but rather one of intense pain.

"Stop you're whining!" I heard a gruff voice say a moment later from behind the outcrop. "It's just a break, you simpering fool."

"We're wasting time," another voice grunted in impatience. "They're getting away while we stand here with our thumbs up our arses."

"So what," the first man replied. "We caught them before, and we'll catch them again. Besides, do you really want to explain to Captain el Ranta why we left his son alone on this mountain with an untreated broken leg?" I heard a muted reply, then the original voice again. "Good. Now let's get Finagen squared away, and then we can go skin the Wolf and his pretty little bitch."

I took a deep breath and turned to the dead man, knowing I didn't have much time left. First, I took Beady Eyes' sword. Then, grunting with pleasure, I found a knife on him as well as a three-quarter-full wineskin and a pouch with rations in it along with several small coins. I desperately wanted a sip of the wine to ease my parched throat but knew there wasn't time for it now. I set everything aside before I stripped the man of his cloak, which was no small task considering I was trying to be quiet. Beady Eyes hadn't been a big man, and the cloak wouldn't fit me, but I figured Sarrey could wear it to keep her warm at night. I kept glancing up as I worked feverishly, but except for the sounds of pain coming from the wounded man as his leg was set, there were still no signs of our pursuers. I knew that wouldn't last much longer

Finally, when I had the dead man's cloak off, I slung it and the wineskin over my shoulder then stuffed his knife, sword, and pouch in my belt. I stood, looking around until I saw Beady Eyes' dented shield lying half-buried beneath dust and rocks. I stooped and pulled it out, then headed back up the incline, amazed at how well things had turned out so far. I only made it a few steps, however, before I heard a shout behind me that was not given in pain. I glanced back, not surprised to see a group of Lions standing at the base of the grade, pointing up at me in shock.

On a whim, I turned completely around and bowed to them, offering the soldiers a cheeky grin and a salute with my sword. The Lions' reaction was what I'd hoped for, and they began to howl in outrage and curse me and all my ancestors. I smiled when three of them began dashing madly forward up the slope, waving their weapons.

Come on, you bastards, I thought, watching them. *Come on.*

I waited until the furious soldiers were fully committed, their lips pulled back from their teeth from the effort, and their eyes alight with the killing blood—then I turned and started to run. It was tough slogging, sprinting full speed uphill, made a thousand times worse by the scree that fought to hold me back every step of the way. I finally reached the top and my makeshift wall, my chest heaving from the exertion as I started to climb. Though the barrier I'd built had been only to my waist on the other side, this side rose much higher due to the steep slope. The uncertain footing and the extra burden I was carrying didn't help me either as I struggled to get up while the crude wall wobbled precariously beneath me.

A slim hand suddenly appeared over the stone, offering assistance. "Here, lord."

I took the girl's hand in mine, grateful as she helped pull me over. "Thank you, Your Highness," I said once I was on the other side. I'd knocked several rocks off the wall on my way over it, and I hurried to put them back.

"You lied to me!" Sarrey hissed when I was done. Her face was twisted in anger, and she caught me off guard by pounding her tiny fist once against my chest. I was more surprised by her hitting me than hurt by the actual blow itself. "You lied!" Sarrey repeated in an accusing tone.

"I know," I admitted with an apologetic shrug. "I'm sorry, but I saw an opportunity and took it." I glanced down the grade. Though they'd slowed considerably, the three Lions were still coming on, with the remainder waiting at the bottom in indecision, clearly remembering what had happened earlier. I snorted and tossed the cloak and other items aside, retaining the shield as I waved my sword at the hesitant Lions, egging them on. "Come on, you cock swallowers! What are you afraid of? One man and a girl?" I laughed as the soldiers at the bottom continued to curse me, though none were so angry about matters that they chose to follow their fellow Lions up the grade. That suited me just fine. If you were outnumbered, Jebido was always fond of saying, then divide your foes and conquer them a little at a time.

"Look at me when I'm talking to you, lord!" Sarrey snapped. She grabbed my arm, trying to spin me around to face her, but she weighed at best a hundred pounds and might as well have tried moving one of the cliffs towering over us.

I glanced sideways at her in confusion. "What's the matter with you all of a sudden?"

"What do you think?" Sarrey snorted.

I sighed. "Can we please talk about this later, Your Highness?" I motioned to the charging Lions. "Unless it has escaped your notice, we're about to have some company in another minute or so."

Sarrey's eyes flashed. "Don't you ever lie to me like that again—understand!"

There was steel in the girl's fierce expression and in her voice. I pursed my lips and nodded, my respect for her climbing once again. "I understand, Your Highness. It won't happen again. You have my word."

"Good," Sarrey grunted. "See that it doesn't." She bent and picked up some rocks, lining them along the wall. "Then let's get on with this and kill these bastards."

I felt my lips twitch in amusement. "Yes, my queen." She drew her arm back to throw a rock, and I put my hand over hers, stalling her. "Wait until they're closer." I motioned for the girl to move to the end of the wall on my right. "Besides, there's only the three of them, and I could use the exercise."

"Only three?" Sarrey asked incredulously. She was looking at me strangely, though she did scoop up her rocks before moving out of the way as I'd asked.

"Only three," I agreed with a wink. "But be ready to throw those stones of yours just in case."

I waited at the wall, my shield and sword ready as the oncoming Lions slowed when they were about twenty feet away from the top before stopping altogether. Two held swords, the other a glaive. The men formed a shield wall in the narrow passage, talking in whispers while they fought to regain their wind. It was a wise move—one that I couldn't let happen. I wanted them tired and out of breath when they tried to breach my defenses.

"Greetings, traitors," I said with a smile. I set my sword and shield down, then put my hands around one of the stones making up my wall. "I hope you kissed your wives and children this morning before you left home, because you won't be seeing them again in this world." Then I tossed the rock.

I watched in anticipation as the stone hurtled toward the center Lion, but the soldiers had clearly discussed strategy beforehand, and they broke smartly in unison to either side. The rock plunged past the Lions, striking the ground five feet behind them before it began tumbling end over end down the grade while the enemy reformed their wall. I grinned. Despite the failure, I knew these men were caught, with no good options left open to them. They had only two choices—attack a well-defended barrier up a hill or turn tail and run, leaving their backsides vulnerable to my rocks. I was sure the Lions were regretting their haste in coming after me now, though I felt little sympathy for their plight. Below, their companions continued to watch, still reluctant to join the fray. I couldn't really blame them.

I picked up another stone as the enemy all tensed, then glanced at Sarrey and nodded that it was time. The girl instantly threw one of her missiles, which smacked off the soldier's helmet to our right, followed by another that narrowly missed the man's leg. I hurled my rock after that, gratified when the men, distracted by Sarrey, reacted too slowly this time and it caught the edge of the center Lion's shield, almost tearing it from his grasp. That was enough for our opponents, it seemed, for with a united scream, the three men charged toward me. I hastily picked up my shield and sword, balancing on the balls of my feet as I felt the thrill of imminent combat quickly building in my veins.

Sarrey continued throwing her rocks, which did little actual damage, but it forced the Lions to keep their heads down and shields up as they ran through the scree. Finally, the enemy soldiers reached the wall, and on a clearly preplanned signal, they all leaped at the same time, raking their weapons above the stones simultaneously. It was a well-coordinated move and one that would have worked if I hadn't anticipated it. I skipped back three steps, waiting, then, as the Lions' blades all missed, I lunged forward, skewering the man with the glaive in the throat even as I brought the edge of my shield down on the sword hand of the man next to him, pinning it to the stone beneath. That man screamed, bones snapping like dry kindling in a fire, while the man I had stabbed sagged and fell from my sight.

The third man spat curses at me, spittle flying from his mouth as he desperately tore at the wall, trying to collapse it while swinging his sword wildly at me. I easily swatted his blade away, then flung my shield in his face, turning the flesh and bone into a crimson mess before he fell. The Lion had managed to pull down some stones, though, creating a gap, and ever the opportunist, I leaped through it, landing with my feet firmly planted on his already ravaged face. The soldier's muffled screams suddenly ended when I put a foot to his neck, cutting off his wind.

I glared at the last surviving Lion while his companion struggled weakly beneath my boot before he gave one final gag and died. I noted my opponent had reversed his sword and shield due to his broken hand, and he waved the weapon awkwardly at me. I smiled. I'd spent many years training with either hand, but this one clearly had not. "How many more men are coming?" I grunted.

"Enough to bury you ten times over, Wolf," the Lion sneered.

I nodded, hardly surprised by the answer. "How far back are they?"

The Lion licked his lips, dropping his eyes for the briefest of moments. "They'll be here any minute now."

The man was a terrible liar, I thought, shaking my head. The Lion might have been a better fighter than he was a liar before his broken hand, but now I'd never know. I made his death quick and as painless as possible, which I thought was rather good of me, all things considered. After all, it's not much fun taking the life of a cripple, even one bent on killing me. My blood was up now, and after the last Lion fell, I glanced down the slope at the remaining four men, then I began to stalk toward them.

"Lord!" I hesitated and looked over my shoulder at Sarrey, where she leaned over the wall. "What are you doing?" she demanded.

"Finishing this," I grunted.

Sarrey shook her head in amazement. "There are four of them down there, lord, in case you hadn't noticed. They'll kill you."

"I've done pretty good so far," I pointed out. I glared down the slope at the Lions, my hand flexing on the hilt of my sword.

"That's because you've been smart and made them come to you, lord," Sarrey scolded. She motioned toward the Lions. "So don't start being stupid now."

"We need those bastards dead," I replied stubbornly.

"Not if it means you fall to accomplish that," Sarrey said, her voice pleading now. "Listen to me, lord, I beg of you. The rest could be here any time now, and when they arrive, what do you think my fate will be without you to protect me? Do you want to see me raped and murdered?"

I took a deep breath, the killing blood slowly receding as I thought about what she'd said. "No, of course not," I finally admitted.

"Good," Sarrey said with a nod of approval. "Then stop all this foolishness and get back up here, because I think I've found a way off the trail."

Chapter 22: It's A Long Way Down

"You can't be serious?" I grunted. Sarrey and I lay side by side on our bellies on a cliff overlooking a deep gorge. A narrow ledge lay below us, shrouded in shadows and mist. I guessed it was perhaps fifty feet down from where we lay. I glanced at her. "Even if we were foolish enough to climb down there, then what?"

"Follow the shelf with your eyes around that little bend to the north, lord," Sarrey said. She pointed toward a solid wall of granite where the ridge finally ended. "Do you see it? On the crag face right there?"

I frowned. Dusk was settling over the mountain, and I saw nothing but shadows and cold, impersonal stone waiting for us down there—that, and most likely, a highly unpleasant death. "What am I supposed to be looking for?" I finally muttered in exasperation.

"There's a crevasse in the rock face about four feet below the ridge. Can you make it out?"

I snorted and shook my head, then slowly backed away from the lip. "I can't, Your Highness. But even if you're right, so what? We have no idea where it might lead. That could just be a damn hole in the rock going nowhere for all we know."

Sarrey inched away from the edge on her hands and knees, then squatted in front of me. "No, lord," she said. "I saw it earlier in the light of day. I could see inside a little way, and the rock on the floor had green moss on it. The cliff below the crevice was stained dark for as far down as I could see, as well."

I pursed my lips as I thought about that. "Was water coming out of this hole?" I finally asked.

"No, lord. But it hasn't rained much. I'm guessing that fissure is a channel for rainwater, which means it has to lead somewhere, right?"

"Even if it does, it's too risky," I grunted with a shake of my head. "We could get trapped down there."

Sarrey's lips curled into an ironic smile. "And what are we now if not trapped, lord? We both know the Lions probably sent riders around the mountain to cut us off. We can't stay on the trail, and even if we make it through by some miracle without getting caught, those men will likely be waiting for us." She gestured to our left toward a small pile of stones stacked along the cliff's edge. "That's our best route down, lord. I marked it when I was here earlier. There are plenty of good handholds for climbing right there, and I suggest we use them."

I stared at the girl, marveling at her composure and ability to think ahead, not to mention her obvious bravery. Not many people in this world would even consider what she was proposing, and I had to keep reminding myself that Sarrey was only fifteen years old. "So, even if you're right," I said. "Water always travels downhill, which means we would have to climb. We need to get off this mountain, not go up."

"I agree, lord," Sarrey said. "But to do that, we need to stay alive. We're not far ahead of the Lions, and as far as I can see, that crevasse looks like our best chance. But if we're going to do this, we better do it soon before we lose the light entirely."

I took a deep breath as I debated what to do. I'd taken what provisions the Lions I'd killed had on them, and we now had a decent stock of food and four wineskins—three of which contained actual wine, while the other held tepid water. We weren't in danger of starving—at least for now—nor of dying from thirst, and because of that, I knew we could survive on the mountain for some time. But first, we needed to get off the trail so the pursuing Lions wouldn't be able to track us. The cliff where we crouched was nothing but windswept, solid rock, and because of that, I doubted our pursuers would be able to tell where we'd gone, especially if they passed this spot in the dark. Sarrey's crevasse was out of the way and hard to see, and though it would be hugely dangerous, going down there might be the only way we could lose our hunters, as much as I hated to admit it.

"All right," I finally said, coming to a decision. "Let's do it."

Sarrey smiled in satisfaction. "Thank you, lord. You won't regret it."

I held my tongue, experienced enough with reality to be pessimistic about such easily spoken predictions. Regret was something I lived with every day, and I prayed this decision wouldn't be added to the burden I already carried. The shield I'd taken from Beady Eyes had a strap on it, and I slung it over my back so it was secure. I'd offered Sarrey one of the dead Lions' swords, but she'd declined, favoring one of their knives along with a glaive, which also had an attachable strap that I'd found in one of the soldier's pouches.

"I'll go first," I said. I motioned to the double-bladed weapon hooked on Sarrey's shoulder. "I'll take that."

"You can't carry everything, lord," Sarrey protested. "It's too heavy. Besides, I think I should go first."

"You do, huh?" I grunted. "And why is that?"

"Because I know where most of the handholds are, lord, and you don't. When I get down there, it will be almost dark. This way, I can help guide you."

"It's a fair point," I conceded. My hand was still extended toward the girl, and I flexed my fingers open and closed. "But I carry everything, including that toad sticker of yours. Understand?"

Sarrey sighed, realizing there was no arguing with me by my determined look. "Fine, lord. Have it your way." She handed me the glaive, then turned around. "Can you cut the back of my cloak down the middle? Maybe about a foot or so from the bottom?" I did as she asked, and when I was finished, Sarrey tied the two tails around her waist, ensuring nothing could get snagged on the climb down. Satisfied, she made her way to the cliff's edge where she'd left her marker before dropping to her hands and knees. She looked over the precipice as I joined her. "See that bit of outcrop there, lord?

It's got a lot of jagged edges leading all the way to the ledge, almost like a ladder, which should make this an easy climb. I could do it in my sleep."

I frowned. "Don't get cocky," I growled. "You've never done this before, Your Highness and one mistake will be the end of you."

"That's just it, lord," Sarrey said with a knowing smile. "Who said this was my first time?"

I stared at the girl in surprise while Sarrey took my hand before turning and inching her way over the lip. She lowered her body, searching with her feet for support before finally, she nodded that she was ready. "See you below, lord," Sarrey said before she let go of my hand and disappeared.

I leaned over the lip, my heart in my throat as I watched the slight girl make her way slowly down the face of the crag, moving easily and confidently as though she'd been doing it all her life. *Remarkable*, I thought, shaking my head in admiration. *Simply remarkable*.

It took Sarrey about fifteen minutes to make the descent, and I breathed a huge sigh of relief when her feet finally made contact with the rock shelf. I could barely see her now, dressed as she was in her black cloak, with only the faint shimmer of her face allowing me to know where she was.

"There's a narrow shelf about three feet down from the lip, lord," Sarrey called up to me. "Use that to support your feet, then feel around to your right. You'll find a protrusion there."

"I understand," I grunted.

I stood, kicking the stones Sarrey had used for a marker away, then unbuttoned my doublet and used the knife I'd taken from Beady Eyes to cut several lengths from the laces at the neck of my tunic. I hurriedly tied my sword to the haft of the glaive, then rebuttoned my doublet. I hooked the glaive over my neck, letting the weapons dangle at my back, where they rattled against my shield, then carefully eased myself over the lip of the cliff. I immediately felt the ledge Sarrey had told me about beneath my right boot, grateful for the support, then started fumbling around with my right hand for the protrusion. My left arm was still wrapped over the cliff edge, maintaining my balance, and I had to hunch awkwardly.

Finally, I found the protrusion and grabbed hold of the cold stone. Then, saying a quick prayer to The Mother, I let go with my left, letting my body drop below the cliff as I pressed myself against the stone. I started blindly searching for a handhold for my left hand, and once I found one, I began to inch my way downward from one protrusion to another. I wasn't nearly as surefooted as Sarrey, nor was I as confident about my abilities, but I guessed, in the end, it took me about the same amount of time as it had her. Admittedly, though, I couldn't have done it so quickly without her coaching since she could see the handholds and footholds I needed much better than I could from her vantage point.

The ledge was, at best, three feet wide as we made our way along it to the north, with Sarrey in the lead and me following. I had a sudden memory of a similar ledge and another girl from long ago, and I thrust it from my mind. Some things were just not meant to be revisited. We reached the end of the ledge after about ten minutes of careful shuffling, and I was pleased to see that our improvised walkway widened noticeably to almost five feet where it joined up with the opposite cliff.

"The crevasse is just below us, lord," Sarrey said, leaning into me. "Any ideas on how to get down there?"

I frowned. "I thought you'd already figured that out?"

I sensed Sarrey shrug, and then she chuckled, sounding surprisingly relaxed. "No, lord. That's why I brought you along."

"Very funny," I grumbled. I unstrapped my weapons and laid them on the ledge. "Get out of the way so I can take a look." I pressed my back against the rock face, allowing Sarrey to squeeze by in front of me while I supported her. She hesitated in my arms with our noses almost touching, looking up at me with a strange expression. "What?" I finally muttered when the girl made no effort to move. "What's wrong? Are you hurt?"

"No, lord," Sarrey finally said. "It's nothing."

I thought I'd noted a trace of disappointment in her tone but thrust it from my mind. The hardest part of our ordeal was still ahead of us, and that's all I wanted to focus on. I crouched down carefully, supporting my weight on the lip of the ledge as I peered into the depths below. I could see nothing but darkness. I sat back. "Hand me that glaive," I said to the girl. She moved to do so, and I added, "Untie the sword. I don't need it."

Sarrey nodded, and moments later, she pressed the haft of the weapon into my hands. I leaned over the lip again, this time probing carefully with the glaive. The metal blade scraped loudly against the stone until, finally, I felt open space. I explored further until I had a good estimation of the height and width of the crevice.

I fixed that spot in my mind, then turned to the girl. "I'm going to lower you down and swing you into the hole," I told her.

"All right," Sarrey said, sounding uncertain. "But, how do you get in afterward?"

"I'll think of something," I muttered.

"There must be another way," Sarrey said doubtfully.

"There isn't, Your Highness," I said. I set the glaive aside and offered the girl my hand. "Let's go. We're wasting time." Sarrey hesitated a moment longer, and then she put her left hand in mine. "Both of them," I said. "And hold on tight."

I waited until the girl wrapped her hands around me, clutching me tightly, then I slowly lowered her over the edge of the ledge. I held her there, suspended for a moment. "Are you all right, Your Highness?"

"Never better," the girl replied, though I could hear the tension in her voice.

I grunted in acknowledgment, then started to swing her body sideways, gaining momentum. "Let go on three, got it?"

"Got it."

I swung the girl forward. "One," I said when she was at the furthest point away from me. I swung her back and then forward again. "Two." I stared at the spot of the cliff wall that I'd marked in my head, drawing the girl back, then forward one last time. "Three!"

I let go, whispering a prayer as I waited, not daring to breathe. A second later, I heard Sarrey's body land inside the cavity and I sighed in relief. "Are you all right, Your Highness?"

"Yes, lord," came back the echoing reply. "The moss is quite soft in here. I banged my shin a bit on a rock, but otherwise, I'm fine."

"I'm glad to hear it," I said with satisfaction.

"Now what?" the girl asked.

"Now what, indeed," I muttered under my breath. "What's the bottom of the opening like? Is there any way I can jump and get hold of it?"

I heard Sarrey moving around before eventually, she replied, "Doubtful, lord. It's quite slick and smooth."

I nodded in disappointment, afraid of that news. "How wide is the bottom from side to side?"

"Um, hold on." I waited several minutes. "Maybe half as wide as my arms outstretched, lord. No more than that, I'd say."

"Can you set the glaive sideways across the hole so it's secure?"

"Probably," Sarrey called. "Why? What good will that do?"

"If it stays there on its own, you can cut up your cloak and fashion a rope and tie it to it. The glaive should then be able to support my weight."

"Oh," Sarrey said thoughtfully. "That actually might work, lord."

"We'll try it," I said, gaining confidence in the idea. "I'm going to hand the glaive down to you. Be mindful of the blade."

"Yes, lord."

I waited after passing Sarrey the weapon, listening as the blades scraped against stone while she worked to secure it. Finally, I heard her grunt in satisfaction. "That should do it, lord."

"Good, now lay the cloak flat and slice it into long strips, then—"

"I know what to do, lord," Sarrey cut in. "I've seen ropemakers at work many times."

"Yes," I said. "But they were probably using hemp or jute, not cloth."

"Cotton," I heard Sarrey reply in a distracted voice.

I leaned further over the ledge. "What?"

"We mostly make rope out of cotton in Temba, lord." I could hear the sounds of her knife cutting through the fabric echoing up to me. "Which is what this cloak is made from," Sarrey added with an edge to her voice. "So please be quiet and let me concentrate."

I nodded at the reprimand and sat with my back to the stone and my feet close to the precipice. I wanted to mention that the Lions could be upon us at any time and that she should hurry, but doubted Sarrey needed the encouragement. I also wanted to mention that I was a big man and weighed a lot, made worse by the equipment and supplies I carried, but common sense stilled my tongue on that as well. The girl knew that as well as I did, and I'd just have to trust in her ability to get the job done. If the rope failed in the end, well, I guessed I'd have about a minute or so to get over my disappointment before I hit the bottom of the gorge. It was not a very pleasant thought, one which managed to circle the perimeters of my mind like a hungry shark for the better part of half an hour while Sarrey worked.

"There," the girl finally called up to me. "All done, lord."

I moved, suppressing a groan as my stiff muscles protested. I stuck my sword in my belt, then leaned over the ledge again and peered down. I could see nothing below at all. "Tie one end to the haft of the glaive in the center," I said.

"Already done. You should have about five feet or so left."

"You tied it tightly?"

"I triple-knotted it, lord. It's secure."

"It better be," I grunted to myself. I reached down with my hand. "All right, throw the other end up to me."

I waited, my heartbeat increasing. *If this fails*—I thrust the thought from my mind. It would work because it had to work. Besides, I was fairly certain the gods weren't done toying with me just yet. But if I was wrong...

"Get ready," Sarrey called.

I heard something hiss through the air, then felt the end of the rope kiss the back of my hand before falling away. The rope made a sharp slapping sound moments later when it smacked against the rock face below the crevice.

"I missed the damn thing," I said in frustration.

"I know, lord. I'll do it again."

In the end, it took four tries before I was finally able to grab hold of the rope in the dark. I pulled until it was taught, pleased by how tightly braided it was. Sarrey had done a magnificent job.

"Stop, lord!" Sarrey called out in warning. "You're dragging the glaive up the rock. It's too wide there and will fall out!"

"Right," I called down, releasing some of the pressure. I should have realized that would happen. "Can you put it back?"

"Hold on." I heard the girl grunting with effort as I created some slack in the rope for her. "There, lord. All set."

"All right, Your Highness," I called. I wrapped my end of the rope around my right wrist until it was taught, careful not to pull upwards. "Get out of the way now."

"Good luck, lord," Sarrey said, her voice filled with tension. I knew exactly how she felt.

I heard the girl moving deeper into the crevice and I took a deep breath, praying the armourer who'd made the glaive had been competent, then I carefully eased myself off the ledge. I plummeted downward like a stone, coming to an abrupt halt before my momentum swung me forward at speed. I'd anticipated that, however, and I got my feet up to help cushion the impact just in time as I hit the rock face below the opening. I bounced off, then dangled there afterward, swinging back and forth and twisting on the rope. I looked up but could see nothing. So far, both the glaive and the rope were holding.

"Are you all right, lord?" Sarrey called down to me anxiously.

"I'm still breathing," I grunted.

I hurriedly unwound the rope from my wrist, then began pulling myself upward hand over hand while the blades of the glaive scraped loudly against the rocks to either side of the crevasse. I hoped the Lions weren't anywhere close, because if they were, they couldn't help but hear. Finally, my questing hand came in contact with the haft of the weapon, and I wrapped my fingers around it. I let go of the rope with my other hand, then latched onto the glaive, using the power of my arms to pull me up while my feet slipped and slid against the slick rock face. I heard Sarrey grunting with effort as she grabbed hold of my doublet from the back and pulled. With the girl's help, I finally was able to drag myself up and over the glaive, where I fell face forward on the moss-covered rock. We'd made it.

Chapter 23: Trapped

I lay on my back on the cushiony, mossy floor after tossing aside my sword and shield, amazed that my plan had actually worked. Sarrey lay beside me, shivering and trembling as she hugged me—whether from relief after what we'd just been through or from the cold, I wasn't sure. I automatically put an arm around the girl to comfort her, and she rested her head on my shoulder. The enclosure was without question cold and damp, with an earthy, musty smell punctuated by an underlying sharp stench coming from deeper inside the crevasse that I couldn't identify. I could hear nothing but the sounds of our breathing, the wind outside, and water dripping steadily from somewhere in the darkness behind me. There were no shouts of discovery, nor sounds of movement from outside, I noted with relief.

"Let's not do that again any time soon, lord," Sarrey mumbled almost dreamily. She threw an arm over my chest, snuggling into me deeper.

"Agreed," I grunted. I could feel my heart rate finally slowing, and I was starting to breathe more evenly now. I was also keenly aware of how close the girl and I were, which was making me increasingly uncomfortable. "We should get going, Your Highness," I finally said, attempting to sit up.

"Why?" Sarrey asked, not moving. I hesitated when she clung to me almost desperately. "Just a little longer, lord," she pleaded. "I'm so very tired."

I frowned. "The Lions could arrive at any time, Your Highness."

"So what?" Sarrey responded with a snort. "What will they see in the dark? They'll never suspect we're down here."

"Well—" I said uncertainly. I suddenly felt utterly exhausted and fought to keep my eyes open. Finally, I gave a half-shrug in defeat. "I guess it can't hurt to lie here for another minute or two. But that's all."

I closed my eyes, promising myself that it would only be for a moment and no more. I should have known better. I awoke hours later to the sounds of sharp squeaking, grunting, and hissing coming from further inside our refuge. I blinked in confusion, staring up at a jagged and pitted rock ceiling above me, revealed in the weak light. Dawn had arrived, I realized with a jolt of alarm. I glanced down at Sarrey, who still lay against my side with her head resting on my chest. She was snoring softly, with a look of contentment on her pretty face. I saw the scrape down her face from her fall had scabbed over, but for some reason I found it only helped to enhance her beauty.

I shook the girl, annoyed at my thoughts. "Your Highness? Wake up."

Sarrey groaned and her eyelids fluttered before she finally focused on me. "Oh," she said. She rolled onto her back, yawning and stretching before sitting up. The girl's hair was unkempt and frazzled, but it still managed to hang fetchingly over her face. She brushed it back absently around her ears. "It's morning already?" She shivered, wrapping her arms around herself. "How did that happen, lord?"

"I don't know," I grunted, still angry at myself for falling asleep.

Sarrey frowned, glancing into the interior of our refuge. "What's making all that noise?"

"Birds, I think," I answered distractedly. I coughed. My throat felt dry and rough, and I turned my head and spat against the cavern wall. I realized with a shudder that, in our exhaustion, Sarrey and I had lain all night long less than six feet away from the crevice's slick edge. One wrong move in our sleep and we could have rolled out into the abyss. I stood and carefully made my way forward over the moss-covered stone to look outside. A fine mist was drifting ten feet below the opening, and I could hear the excited squawks of hundreds of birds rising from the gorge far below. None sounded like the noises coming from inside the cave, though, I noted. Had the Lions already passed by on the ridge above during the night, searching for us? Or had they set up camp, waiting for the morning? I had no idea.

I felt a thud in my chest when I noticed the glaive still wedged in against the rock walls where we'd left it, with the improvised rope dangling outside against the crag face for all to see. I cursed myself for a fool and quickly drew the weapon and rope back out of sight, grateful that my mistake hadn't led to us being discovered. I untied the rope, rolled it up, and then attached it to my belt. The remnants of Sarrey's cloak wouldn't do much for us, I knew, but the rope she'd made from it was a valuable asset.

Sarrey moved further into the cave, then hitched her dress up to her waist as she squatted with her back against a wall to relieve herself. I averted my eyes, feeling pressure in my own bladder. I turned my back to the girl before I undid my trousers and sent a stream of piss out into the void. I chuckled as I watched the line arc downward, cutting through the mist.

"What's so funny?" Sarrey asked.

I could hear the girl readjusting her dress, and I turned to her after I was done, still chuckling. "I was picturing our White Raven friend riding his horse below and looking up as he enjoyed the gentle, warm rain falling on him."

Sarrey giggled, sounding surprisingly childlike. I stooped, picked up my shield and sword, and then moved to join her before offering her some wine.

"Do you really think Kish is down there?" the girl asked after taking a long sip.

"I have no idea where he is," I admitted with a shrug. Sarrey offered the wineskin back to me and I took a drink, relishing the liquid hitting my dry throat. I grinned at her afterward as I corked the skin. "But I can dream, can't I?" I selected two pieces of dried meat from our rations, handing the girl one as I motioned ahead. "Shall we go see where this thing leads, Your Highness?"

The crevice opening was perhaps eight feet at its widest point in the center, tapering to roughly three feet at the top and bottom. But, as we progressed deeper into the fissure, the space widened dramatically. Sarrey had guessed the crevice was an outlet for rainwater, which seemed likely enough, but neither of us had expected the interior to be this large. After ten minutes of climbing over smooth, rounded stones and through miniature lakes of scum-filled water trapped between the rocks, we reached a large open cavern dominated by a high, sloping ceiling dotted with dark rock that looked eerily like teeth to me. The squeaking and grunting sounds had reached a crescendo by now, and the sharp smell I'd first noticed when I awoke was almost overpowering. Early morning sunlight streamed in from several round openings on one side of the cavern—openings that I saw in alarm were swarming with activity.

I thought I was looking at birds at first, and then I grimaced when I realized the truth. "Bats," I said with distaste.

Sarrey and I both stopped at the same time and looked down as something crunched loudly beneath our boots. I realized the entire floor in the chamber was heaped with bat shit, with cockroaches, centipedes, beetles, and hundreds of other insects I couldn't identify, busily crawling all over it. A narrow channel cut through the shit, leading towards us, and I guessed that was how the rainwater ran off.

"Well, that explains the smell," I muttered. I looked up again. I'd thought the tooth-covered ceiling was made up of rock and nothing more, but now I realized it was moving, with thousands of bats hanging upside down and preening themselves. I glanced at Sarrey. "Are these things going to be a problem for us, Your Highness?"

"No, lord," Sarrey said. "They won't do anything as long as we don't startle them." She looked down at the ground. "But there are things in here that can hurt us. Watch out for spiders, scorpions, and any brightly colored snakes."

"What's a scorpion?"

"It looks like a cross between a crab and a spider," Sarrey explained as we delved further into the cavern. "But it has a stinger on its tail. Most scorpions can't kill us, but their stings hurt, believe me."

"You said *most*," I replied uneasily, scanning the mounds of rock-like shit for anything resembling what the girl had described.

"Yes," Sarrey agreed. "The spitting black-tailed scorpion is the one we most fear in Temba, but there are others equally as deadly."

"It spits?"

"Yes, lord, up to three feet. If you get their venom in your eyes, the chances are good you will go blind." She glanced at me in warning. "Assuming you don't go mad from the pain, first, of course."

I nodded, examining the ground warily as we progressed deeper into the cavernous space. I saw nothing like Sarrey had described, but that didn't stop my imagination from picturing the creatures scrabbling toward us like crabs from every direction. Thankfully, we were able to cross the width of the bat chamber without seeing even one scorpion—dangerous or otherwise. Nor did we disturb the bats, which had begun to settle down to sleep in every nook and cranny above us after a long night of hunting insects.

Sarrey and I paused on the other side of the chamber, faced with two narrow passages—one leading northwest and one southeast. We looked at each other without saying anything, then I shrugged and headed for the southeast passage. As it turned out, my selection proved to be the wrong one, for the tunnel quickly began to narrow until, after less than five minutes of walking, it became so tight that we were forced to turn around and go back.

We entered the northwest passage next, traveling steadily upward for over an hour before we came to another chamber with a large basin of crystal-clear water in the center. A circular hole in the ceiling about ten feet above the water offered us a view of dark blue skies. I cursed under my breath, realizing with dismay that the passageway ended here. There was nowhere left to go.

Sarrey bent at the basin's edge and dipped her fingers in the water. She looked up at me and smiled. "It's cold, lord, but even so, it feels wonderful."

"Uh-huh," I grunted, barely listening. *How were we going to get out of here?*

I turned to ask Sarrey what she thought, then stopped, unable to hide my surprise. Her glaive now lay on the stone near the water's edge, and she'd pulled her dress over her head, dropping it at her feet. Sarrey wore nothing underneath, and I couldn't fail to notice that her breasts were small, yet firm. Her nipples were light brown and quite large, and her stomach was lean and flat, leading to a tuft of thick, dark hair nestled between her legs.

"What's the matter, Lord Hadrack?" Sarrey asked coyly, standing with her hands on her hips. "You're not shy, are you?" I remained where I was, unable to think of a proper response. Sarrey finally chuckled at my silence and pulled off her boots, then turned and dove lithely into the water. She resurfaced moments later with a squeal, pushing her wet hair from her face. "By the gods, that's cold, lord!" The girl treaded water, with just her head and shoulders showing above the surface, though the water was so clear that I could see everything down to her feet and beyond. "Come and join me, lord."

"I don't think so," I grunted, finally finding my voice. "Somebody has to find a way out of here, Your Highness."

Sarrey waved a hand. "We will, lord, just as soon as we bathe. I think we both deserve it after what we've been through. Don't you?"

"Maybe you haven't noticed, Your Highness, but we're trapped in here."

"Nonsense, lord," Sarrey scoffed. "Have faith. We'll think of something once we're clean again."

"Have faith in what?" I muttered.

"Why, in the gods, of course," Sarrey responded. "They clearly favor us."

"Is that right?" I said sarcastically. "You call almost dying countless times in the last two days, *favoring*?"

Sarrey smiled, giving me a pitying look. "Well, we're still here, aren't we, lord?"

"For now," I muttered moodily. I thought of mentioning that both Sumisu and Tako couldn't share in her faith in the gods because they were both dead, but I knew their deaths had hit Sarrey harder than she had let on. Despite our situation, it was good to see the girl happy for a change, and I resolved to do my best not to be such a pessimist all the time. I looked around at our prison instead, my determination to be more optimistic quickly waning as the reality of the predicament we now faced settled in deeper.

Sarrey shook her head in mock wonder. "I have never seen a man scowl as much as you do, lord. With The Mother and The Father's favor, we will triumph over those hairless fools and win back my city. You will see."

"I've been around a lot longer than you have, Your Highness," I said, turning my back to her as she started swimming in circles in the basin. I made my way slowly along the perimeter walls of the chamber, feeling the rock for any hint of air coming in. "And the one thing that I've learned so far is to *never* take the gods' favor for granted."

"I'm not, lord," Sarrey insisted. She glided easily through the water toward me, stopping when her feet came into contact with the gently sloping rock floor of the basin. I watched her out of the corner of my eye as she gathered her wet hair to one side, then began combing it out with her fingers. She hesitated, studying me.

"But why would they have brought us together, then, lord, if not to accomplish their goals?"

I shrugged. "I don't know, Your Highness. I gave up trying to figure out the gods' plans for me years ago."

Sarrey thought about that for a moment before returning to her grooming. I made a complete circuit of the chamber while she worked, searching every inch of the walls, but I found no way out. I cursed when I was done, kicking a protrusion of rock in frustration. I looked up at the hole over the water that represented our freedom. It was so tantalizingly close, but I knew even with the rope we had, it was still too far out of our reach.

"You should come in, lord," Sarrey said sympathetically. "The water is wonderful once you get used to it."

"There's no time for that," I grunted, looking back at her.

"Don't be silly," Sarrey admonished me with a snort. "A few minutes won't make much difference now. Besides, you should see yourself. You look like a beggar from Unwashed Row." The girl wrinkled her nose. "And you smell like one, too."

I sighed. "Your Highness, we need to find a way out of here—*now*."

"Oh, very well," Sarrey said, looking disappointed. She extended her hand. "Then help me up."

I moved closer and leaned over the basin's edge, taking her hand in mine. That's when I realized by the triumphant look on the girl's face that I'd just made a mistake. Sarrey took a firm grip, then grinned mischievously before she yanked backward. Caught off-balance as I was and with her feet planted on the basin floor, it took very little effort for her to pull me into the water. I fell face-first with a shout of surprise, swallowing a lungful of cold water before I could claw my way back to the surface. My sword had slipped out of my belt when I fell, tumbling into the basin, but the weight of my clothing, shield and the provisions I carried were still enough combined to drag me down. I could hear Sarrey's musical laughter of delight as I sputtered and choked, fighting to stay above the water.

"Have you lost your mind, woman!" I screamed at her.

Sarrey laughed musically, swimming lazily around me on her back. I couldn't help but notice her erect nipples jutting out of the water. "When you can't bring the bath to the man," she said with a giggle. "Then you must bring the man to the bath." She finally swam over to me, helping to steady me. "Here, lord, let me help you." Sarrey unhooked my shield and tossed it onto the rock floor of the chamber, then the wineskins and provisions one by one. "There," she said, looking satisfied. "Now, your clothes."

Sarrey started to unbutton my doublet, and I pushed her hands away. "No, Your Highness," I said firmly. "This can't happen."

"What can't happen?" Sarrey asked innocently. "We're bathing, that's all. Nothing more, I swear."

"I don't believe you," I said. I held her eyes. "I can't. Not yet. Maybe never."

Sarrey put her hands on my shoulders as I treaded water. Her eyes were huge and expressive, filled with something I couldn't interpret. "I understand, lord, but that will change. I thought Mondar was the love of my life and that I'd never love another." She bit her lower lip, clearly fighting tears. "And if anyone had told me differently before I met you, I would have called them a liar. But now I—" She hesitated there, unable to meet my eyes. Finally, she looked back at me, resolve evident in her features. "You remember that barn where we hid with Tako and Sumisu on our first night?" I just nodded, sensing the girl needed to get whatever this was about out of her system. "The Mother came to me in a vision there while I slept, lord," Sarrey continued. "She explained my role in all of this and what is required of me. I admit I had trouble accepting what she told me at first, but now I know that it must come to pass if we are to triumph."

I took a deep breath with our faces inches apart. "And what role is that?" I asked, afraid to hear the answer.

Sarrey smiled sadly, and she brushed wet hair from my eyes. "The White Ravens are fools and clearly misguided, lord. But they were right about one thing."

"I doubt that somehow," I grunted.

Sarrey leaned forward and kissed my cheek, then she whispered in my ear. "I know you won't like this, lord, but you and I are destined to marry, just not for the reasons they wanted. Once my city is freed and you are proclaimed my husband, then, as the King of the Temba, you will return to Ganderland with an army of Lions at your back. Together, the Wolf and the Lion will crush our enemies and bring peace back to our world. That is the vision that The Mother gave me, and that is our destiny—but that destiny can only happen if we are united as husband and wife."

Chapter 24: *Maharas*

I should have been shocked, I suppose. Or outraged, or any number of other emotions. But the truth was, I felt nothing but sudden weariness and the desire to go home. I felt completely numb inside—numb to what Sarrey had just said and to the glow in her eyes that hinted at more than just a sense of duty to the gods. I have known many women in my life but have only ever truly loved one. Yet I have seen that look before from both my wife and others, and I knew what it meant. It was obvious that this girl had fallen in love with me, pushed in that direction by a dream, if for no other reason. But had that dream been real? Had The Mother truly visited Sarrey, or had the vision she claimed to have seen been brought on by the girl's fatigue and fear? I didn't know, nor did I expect I ever would for certain. But what I did know was that the Kingdom of Ganderland was in grave peril, besieged on two sides and vastly outnumbered by a relentless enemy bent on its destruction while at the same time being subverted from within by religious zealots. And now this girl—this child with her beautiful face and enormous, expressive eyes, had just offered me the potential to possibly make all that go away—if I dared to take it.

"You're angry with me, lord," Sarrey said, looking hurt, apprehensive, and embarrassed all at once. She drew her hands away from my shoulders, drifting back a few feet in the water. "I shouldn't have told you. I knew it was too soon, but I got carried away."

"I'm not angry, Your Highness," I said. And it was true. I wasn't. I sighed, feeling suddenly saddened by the world we lived in and the hard choices we needed to make to survive in it. "I'm just— I don't know." I looked up at the bright sky above, treading water and wondering what I should say. How could I explain the conflict I was feeling to this beautiful woman when I didn't fully understand it myself? I thought of Shana. What would she say now if she were here? Would she be furious with me for even considering such a union? Hurt at my potential betrayal with someone who was almost half my age? I snorted to myself, knowing that my ever-practical wife would most likely insist that I marry the Temba queen, allowing us to form a powerful alliance. Shana had always been the smarter of the two of us, and the most pragmatic, though that didn't always mean that she had been right all the time.

"I'm sorry, lord," Sarrey said. I could see tears forming in her eyes, and she was shivering now from the cold. "I don't know what I was thinking." She glanced down at herself, her naked body distorted by the water yet still uncomfortably obvious to my eyes. "I just thought if I offered myself to you, here, in this magical place, that together, The Mother and I could make you understand."

"I do understand," I said, keeping my voice soft. "Sort of. But we can talk about it later, once we're free. Now isn't the right time." I motioned her closer. "Come, let's get you dry. You're shivering, and your lips are starting to turn blue." I helped Sarrey out of the water, and she didn't resist, and while she put her dress back on, I sat on the edge of the basin and took off my water-logged boots.

"What are you doing, lord?" Sarrey asked. One corner of her mouth twisted upwards in a wry grin. "Don't tell me you're going swimming after all?"

I chuckled, grateful for her attempt at humor and a return to normalcy between us. "No, Your Highness. It's the last thing I want to do right now." I motioned to the basin. "But my sword is down there somewhere, and something tells me we'll need it before this little adventure is done."

I stood once my boots were off, scanning the water until I spied what looked like the winking of metal on the basin floor. I marked the spot in my mind, then dove. The water didn't feel as cold now as it had the first time, and I swam downward with strong, powerful strokes. I could see the sword where it lay at the bottom of the rounded basin, half-hidden by a thin layer of swirling silt, disturbed by our swimming. The floor was littered with small and larger stones, and I was surprised to see the skeletal remains of a man dressed in green-stained metal armor lying in amongst them as I drew closer. The skeleton's hands were manacled behind its back, I noticed.

I returned my focus to my sword, snatching it up on the first try, then twisted to return to the surface before I hesitated as something along the basin's wall caught my eye. It was a dark, semi-circular opening meeting the floor, which looked like it might be an inlet tunnel. That's all I had time to see, and with my lungs protesting, I kicked upward, breaking the surface moments later as I sucked in great gulps of air.

When I'd caught my breath, I handed the sword to Sarrey. "There's something down there," I said to her. "I'm going back."

The girl's fine eyebrows arched in surprise. "What is it?"

"I'm not sure yet," I grunted. "Maybe a way out of here."

I took a deep breath, then plunged beneath the water again, heading for the tunnel. I reached it moments later, feeling cautiously around the entrance with my hands. The stone was worn and smooth, as if it had been there for hundreds or perhaps even thousands of years. I peered inside but could see little, though I could sense that the opening extended for some distance. Would it lead to safety or a watery grave? I thought of the dead man, wondering what his story was as I turned around, heading back up. I broke the surface, drawing needed air into my lungs.

Sarrey was now crouched on her hands and knees by the basin's edge, and her expression turned from excitement to hope when she saw me. "Well?" she asked eagerly. "What did you find?"

I wiped water from my eyes. "I'm not sure, Your Highness. But it looks like a tunnel of some sort." I pointed south. "It travels that way."

"How far do you think it goes?"

"There's only one way to find out," I replied grimly. I breathed in and out several times, preparing myself for the long dive.

"Lord?" I looked up at Sarrey, a question on my face. "Don't drown, please. I don't want to be left here all alone."

I grinned. "I won't, I promise."

Then I filled my lungs with as much air as possible and dove straight down, kicking my legs. I reached the tunnel entrance and entered it without hesitation. The opening was wide enough to extend my arms outward as I swam, enabling me to move faster. I started ticking off the seconds in my head, wondering how far the tunnel went, just as I saw a faint light appear ahead. I felt a jolt of excitement hit me even as my lungs began to tighten. I ignored the sensation and let out a little air, knowing I was committed now as tiny bubbles swirled around my head. If I didn't find a way out of this tunnel soon, I would end up breaking my promise to Sarrey.

Ten seconds later, the passageway widened and the light grew brighter above my head. I swam toward it in desperation with my chest ready to explode, then broke through the surface moments later. I gasped, sucking in beautiful, life-giving air as I bobbed on the water. I was in another cavern, I saw, though this one was immense, with a ceiling of reddish-white stone towering hundreds of feet over my head. I turned in the water as I drew in great lungfuls of air, then whooped with joy when I saw the source of the light a hundred feet away. It was an arched entrance, and beyond that, bright sunlight, blue skies, and, best of all, tall trees swaying in the breeze. We'd found a way out!

An hour later, Sarrey and I sat on some stones just inside the entrance to the enormous cave, drinking wine and eating. The sun was still low enough in the sky to shine where we sat, and we both enjoyed the warmth as our clothing dried. I'd returned twice through the tunnel to get our supplies and weapons, though I'd been forced to leave my shield behind in the end. There was just no way I could swim fast enough with the drag and weight of it slowing me down. Losing the shield was regrettable, but I felt it was a fair trade-off compared to spending our last days trapped inside the mountain.

    I glanced at Sarrey. I noted that her hair was drying quickly in the sun, though it was slowly twisting into untamed ringlets and tangles as it did, making her look even younger than her fifteen years. I felt a sudden surge of affection for the girl as we sat in companionable silence. Not in a romantic way, mind you, but more like that of an older brother toward a cherished sister. I kept my thoughts about that to myself, though, doubting Sarrey would appreciate it after what she'd told me earlier.

    "What time do you suppose it is, lord?" Sarrey asked.

    I glanced outside, enjoying the fresh air swirling around the entrance, then squinted up at the sun. "By the looks of it, I'd guess early afternoon." I took another long pull from the wineskin I held, draining the last of it. I planned on filling all the skins with water before we left anyway.

    "We're safe now, right, lord?" Sarrey asked.

    I shrugged. "I imagine for the time being. Once we hit the lowlands, that will probably change. The Ravens' entire plans hinge on you being dead, Your Highness, and they won't give up easily."

    Sarrey paused in her eating to give me that steely look that I'd come to know, her youthful innocence gone in the blink of an eye. "Neither will I, lord. Neither will I."

    I chuckled. "That's for damn sure, Your Highness."

    Ten minutes later, with our wineskins now filled with water, Sarrey and I gathered our things before we left the cavern behind for good. The air outside the enclosure was warm, with a strong wind rifling through our hair and clothing. Forests of tall pine trees crowded the mountaintops to the south and west, but the large shelf we stood on was mainly free of them, populated instead by a lush meadow of long grasses and brilliantly colored wildflowers that gave off a sweet aroma. More trees grew below us on the route we needed to take, with the meadow turning into a maze of rocky protrusions and jagged abutments between them and us. I knew the way down through that would be dangerous and take a lot of time and effort.

Sarrey took in a deep breath, sighing in contentment. "It's wonderful here, lord. Like a small slice of paradise made by the gods just for our enjoyment."

"It is pretty," I agreed. *Best enjoy it while you can*, I thought, though I kept that to myself. Black butterflies with white dots on their wings flitted over and around the flowers while the steady drone of hundreds of bees pollinating them filled my ears. A small blue bird with a white belly landed on the stalk of a tall flower six feet away, turning its head to study me before it abruptly flew off. "Come on, Your Highness," I said, heading south. The beauty of the place wasn't lost on me, but now that we were rested and fed, it was time to get moving. "It's high time we got you off this cursed mountain."

We progressed through the meadow less than fifty feet before Sarrey looked behind her and gasped. She grabbed my arm, stopping me. "Lord, wait. Look."

I glanced over my shoulder, not hiding my surprise at the sight that filled my vision. The cliffs surrounding the cavern we'd come from had initially hidden the view to the north from us, but now that we'd moved away, I could see clearly what we'd initially overlooked. I felt sudden wonder and awe as I stared up at the backs of the towering golden statues known as the *Maharas*—the guardians of Temba. The entwined figures were at least a mile away or more, I guessed, but they were so unbelievably large that they seemed like they were almost on top of us. I could see the individual ripples in the sculpted cloaks they wore and even make out the Lion crests on their shoulders. A small, almost invisible black and yellow banner fluttered from the glaive of the male statue.

"We must go there, lord," Sarrey said.

I frowned. "That's a bad idea, Your Highness." I pointed in the direction we'd been heading. "South is that way."

"I know that, lord," Sarrey said. "But getting to the lowlands from here will be treacherous." She gestured north. "The *Maharas* are the answer to our prayers. I should have thought of it sooner."

"Answer, how?" I asked.

"There is a road leading to them, lord. It cuts through the mountains and will take us where we wish to go."

"You're certain?"

"Yes, lord. It was built a hundred years ago to transport workmen and parts for the statues, many of which came from the southern lands. The southern road is still used today by the *Lamada*, the custodians of the *Maharas*, but the northern route rarely is. It will most likely be overgrown in places, but we should be able to pass regardless." I pursed my lips as I thought. "Our pursuers will never think of it, lord," Sarrey insisted, looking worried at my silence. "Few in Temba remember the roads even exist except for the *Lamada*. Trust me."

"How come you know, then?" I asked.

Sarrey lifted her chin. "Because I am the daughter of a Temba king, lord. It is my duty to know everything about my kingdom, even the most obscure."

"All right," I finally said, coming to a decision. "Then we go north, Your Highness. I hope you're right about this."

It took us the rest of the day to reach the duel statues, and by the time we stood at the base of the massive structure, the sun was beginning to set in the west. The *Maharas* were built on top of a giant shelf of black granite, with their boots chiseled out of the stone and the remainder of the bronze bodies attached to them somehow. Sunlight still gleamed on the statue's faces and shoulders, and I was doubly impressed by the workmanship and clear dedication to detail now that I was closer. The man and woman looked incredibly lifelike to me, with their eyes forever searching the horizon for signs of Temba's enemies. *If only they had looked within rather than outward*, I thought bitterly.

Windswept stone surrounded the statue in a diamond pattern, with no signs of rocks, debris, or weeds anywhere. Trees and hardy bushes covered in pink and red flowers rose along the perimeter, but they looked neat and recently trimmed. The road Sarrey had described coming from the city cut through those trees and bushes, but there was no obvious evidence of a similar one heading southward. Sarrey and I stood back a hundred feet from the *Maharas*, both of us remaining silent, moved beyond words as we stared up at the truly inspiring sight.

I didn't even flinch when after long minutes of motionlessness, I felt Sarrey take my hand in hers. "We must not fail them, lord," she said so low that I barely heard her. "The *Maharas* have watched over and protected Temba for almost a hundred years. Now it is our turn to protect them. We must triumph over this evil that has gripped my people."

I squeezed the girl's hand. "We won't fail them," I assured her.

We spent that night housed inside the right boot of the male statue, which was easily bigger than most manor houses. The boot had been cleverly hollowed out, creating a small hall, some living quarters, a workstation, and a small kitchen and pantry, all supported by stone pillars. I'd half expected to find some of the *Lamada* dwelling inside but was relieved to find that the place was abandoned. There were some provisions, though, which Sarrey and I were delighted to discover, as well as several worn cloaks we located in one of the living spaces. The garments were moth-eaten and musty, but neither of us cared all that much.

The hall was situated in the toe of the boot and was perhaps twenty feet long by ten wide. A small stone hearth sat in the hall's center, directly beneath a round hole that looked out to the night sky. A chill had fallen when the sun had finally dipped behind the mountains, leaving us shivering despite our newfound cloaks. But though there was plenty of wood for the hearth and flints close to hand, both Sarrey and I agreed that making a fire was too risky. We sat huddled instead on crude stools and ate hard biscuits I'd found in the pantry, washed down by stale beer I'd discovered in a casket behind a door. Both of us were exhausted and said little while we ate, yet even after we'd finished, neither one of us made a move to go to sleep.

"Do you want to talk about it now, lord?" Sarrey finally asked me in a tentative voice.

"No," I grunted a little more harshly than I'd intended. I knew what she meant, of course, but I still hadn't had time to properly think about what I wanted to do. "How long will it take us to get to the lowlands from here?" I asked instead to change the subject.

Sarrey shrugged, looking disappointed by my response but not surprised. "A day I expect, depending on what the road is like."

I nodded. "And this city you spoke of, Sandhold. How far away is it?"

"Five or six days on foot, lord, if we're lucky."

"Will the people there listen to you?"

Sarrey hesitated. "I hope so," she finally said. "Our relationship with them is very complicated."

"Complicated, how? Who are they?"

Sarrey sighed. She set her mug on the floor, then began running her fingers through her tangled hair, much as she had in the basin. "We call them *Falitari*, lord, which roughly translated means, men of dirt." She looked at me pointedly. "It is not a compliment, at least from our perspective, for they are all the descendants of criminals."

"Criminals?" I said in surprise.

"Yes. Our kingdom was founded five hundred years ago by my ancestor, Anders del Fante. He was said to have been a man with a heart of gold, benevolent to all his subjects, whether wealthy or poor. He saw the best in all people, so the history books say, and refused to accept that some men were just born bad, despite evidence to the contrary. Crimes of all kind were forgiven under his reign, be it theft, rape, adultery, or even murder."

I grimaced. "Let me guess. Things didn't end well because of it."

Sarrey shook her head. "No, lord. One day, a man the king had forgiven three times for three separate murders somehow got into the Royal Chambers. He was quickly caught before he could do any harm, but then Anders called off his guards, insisting that the man was no threat."

I rolled my eyes at the stupidity of it. A wolf would always be a wolf, no matter what anyone tried to tell you, especially if you let him into the henhouse. And if the chickens were too stupid to recognize the beast for what it was, then they deserved to die a painful death. That was the way of the world. It had always been that way, and I knew it always would be. "So," I said. "This man killed the king."

"He did," Sarrey confirmed. "It took three days for him to die, but die, he did. After that, his son, Egon, became king."

"And I assume this Egon took care of the city's crime problem?"

"In a manner of speaking, yes, lord," Sarrey said. "Before Anders died, he had Egon promise that he would not kill the man who'd taken his life, but instead, forgive him."

I snorted and shook my head at the ridiculousness of it. "But Egon killed him afterward anyway, right?"

"Oh no, lord," Sarrey said. "Egon fulfilled his vow and forgave him, just as he'd promised he would."

"I don't understand," I said, confused now. "That makes no sense. How could he let the man who killed his father go free?" I thought of my own father and the lengths that I'd gone to bring his murderers to justice. "Did he not love his father?"

"Very much, lord," Sarrey said. She smiled. "I never said he let him go free, lord. Egon took this man deep into the Waste of

Bones, and that is where he left him. Alive and alone without food or water, but forgiven. If he survived and managed to return to Temba, then Egon promised that he would be welcomed with open arms. But if he did not, well, then justice would be served."

"Did he ever return?"

"No, lord," Sarrey said. "But as Egon's reign progressed, that is how justice became to be meted out in Temba. It still is. Any crime judged severe enough by a panel of judges gets you banished to the Waste of Bones, where the gods decide who is innocent or not."

"What happens to those who commit less severe crimes?" I asked.

Sarrey grimaced. "Prison, lord," she said. "A place called Kenningwood." I nodded thinking of Muwa. "In some ways the desert might be kinder from what I've heard," the girl added. "Anyway, those that somehow managed to survive our *desert justice* in the beginning founded Sandhold, which the Temba have always tolerated—that is, as long as they continue to pay us a healthy sum in goods and gold every year to do so."

"So, they're nothing but a vassal state, then?" I asked.

"In our view, yes," Sarrey says. "Though I doubt they share that viewpoint, somehow."

"And the Bone Warriors? What about them?"

Sarrey picked up her mug and drained it before looking at me. "They are as I said before, wards of the desert."

"If that's all they are," I said. "Why was Sumisu so afraid of them?"

Sarrey grimaced. "Because they consider the desert their own, and resent any Lions or Temba setting foot there. Many skirmishes have been fought in the last few years, with dead occurring on both sides. My father had turned a blind eye to it in the past, but that probably wouldn't have lasted much longer."

"You think a war was imminent?"

Sarrey shrugged. "Who can say for certain, lord? But my feeling is yes, war was coming. I believe that is why Banta went to Sandhold, to negotiate and probably threaten before things got out of hand."

"So, after everything you've told me," I said incredulously. "Why do you think these people will help you?"

Sarrey smiled. "Because I'm not my father, lord."

I shook my head, thinking our chances had gone from almost non-existent down to nothing despite the girl's confidence. I got up and stretched, tired of talking. "I think that's enough for tonight, Your Highness. We better get some sleep. Something tells me that tomorrow will be a long and trying day."

Chapter 25: The Bone Warriors

We awoke the next morning to thunder, gray skies, high winds, and cold, driving rain. It was not the kind of start either of us had been anticipating. We decided to wait out the storm, hoping it would pass quickly—mainly because we didn't have much choice in the matter. Sarrey spent the time repairing her torn dress with sewing implements and yarn that she'd found, and when she was done, she started working on our moth-eaten cloaks. I paced back and forth in the hall like a caged wolf, eager to be off and resenting every minute we were forced to wait.

There were no windows in the hall, but the hole above the hearth was big enough for me to see the sky outside. I'd stop each time in my pacing to glare up at it before turning away with a snort and starting all over again. The roof above our heads was sloped to either side to form the arch of the foot, sluicing most of the water away, but enough was coming in to let me know the rain was still coming down hard outside. A long pole lay on the floor against one wall, used to slide a wooden door closed over the opening, but I didn't bother with it. What did I care if the hearth got wet? Besides, seeing the rain gave me something to focus my anger on.

"You should sit, lord," Sarrey said, not looking up from her work. "By the sounds of things, this storm is here for a while."

"And do what, Your Highness?" I grunted moodily. "Should I take up sewing now?"

"There are worse things, lord," Sarrey said with a shrug. "At least I wouldn't have to listen to you wearing out that stone beneath your feet."

I took a deep breath, biting off a sarcastic reply. I knew the girl was just as eager as I was to get moving; she was just dealing with it differently than me—some would say much better, I suppose. I sighed, then conceded to her wishes by dragging a stool closer to the hearth. I sat, glowering up at the dripping hole in the roof with my arms crossed over my chest. *Drip. Drip. Drip.* I could feel the muscles in my jaws clenching and unclenching as the drops fell into the hearth with maddening repetition. *Drip. Drip. Drip.*

Sarrey studied me with mock wonder, shaking her head. "You should see yourself, lord. You look like a little boy who's just had his favorite toy taken from him. You just need to accept the storm for what it is."

"And what is that, exactly?" I asked. "Good fortune or terrible luck?"

Sarrey shrugged. "Who am I to say, lord? Only the gods know for certain."

"Yes, well," I grumbled. "The last time I looked, the gods rarely let me in on their plans."

"Nor should they, lord," Sarrey said, returning to her sewing. "We are mere mortals, after all, and I expect they have other things more important to contend with these days."

I didn't really have a response to that, so I said nothing. Shana had told me repeatedly over our marriage that when I was stuck in a hole, the best thing to do was stop digging. So that's what I did, knowing the conversation would never swing in my favor anyway. Sarrey was a lot like my wife in that way, I'd come to realize—much to my dismay.

Sarrey and I sat together in silence for a time after that, with nothing but the sounds of the howling wind, driving rain, and the occasional boom of thunder to disturb us. After a while, I stopped glaring up at the hole in the ceiling, leaning forward on the stool with my elbows on my knees while I inspected my hands, which were covered with small cuts and bruises from the past few days. I hadn't noticed that Sarrey had stopped sewing at some point, nor that she was studying me intensely until I glanced up as thunder rumbled outside and the floor trembled.

"What?" I asked at the strange look on the girl's face.

"Am I really so bad, lord? Would marrying me not be the answer to all of our problems?"

I sighed, knowing there was no avoiding the issue any longer. It was time to face it head-on. "Of course you're not bad," I said. "But it's not as simple as that."

"Isn't it?" Sarrey asked, looking annoyed. "What's so complicated about what I'm suggesting? Marriages of convenience are meant to form alliances. They happen in the south all the time, as I'm sure they do in the north."

"Like the one your father set up for you?" I fired back. I was gratified to see her flush at my words. "You remember that one, don't you, Your Highness? The marriage you ran away from because you loved another man?"

"Yes," Sarrey said. I could see hurt in her eyes, and I felt suddenly ashamed of myself for my petty attack on her. Sarrey wasn't my enemy, but right now, because of my own anger and frustration, I was treating her as if she were. That needed to stop. "I loved Mondar more than life itself, lord," Sarrey continued, putting a hand over her heart. "You, of all people, know that. But my beloved is dead and I am not, much as I wished for a time that I was. But now my kingdom needs me, as yours does you, and whatever insignificant wants you and I harbor for ourselves pale compared to that."

"I have no wish to be a king," I muttered weakly, fumbling for words that would make Sarrey understand. I felt a sudden lurch of sadness in my chest, remembering the look of love and pride on Shana's face when King Tyden had named me the Lord of Corwick. It seemed so very long ago now. I hadn't wanted that title, either, but still, it had come to me regardless.

"You poor, poor man," Sarrey said. I was shocked to see tears threatening in her eyes. "The pain inside you is as obvious to me as those terrible scars on your face." Sarrey looked down at the cloak in her lap. "I, too, know what that pain is like, lord. I have felt the kind of love that makes your insides soar, knowing that anything in this world is possible when you're with that person you cherish, only to have it taken cruelly away. I have felt love, lived love, and bathed in love with more joy than I can properly express, and I know more than you think what agreeing to this union would cost you." Sarrey looked up at me, her face set with determination. "But agree you must, lord, if our kingdoms are to survive. We can't let our feelings for those who are gone stand in the way of that, no matter how we wish otherwise. We have to fight our enemies together, here, in the world of the living, and the best way to do that is by uniting."

"I—" I hesitated, searching again for the right words to express my doubts. But truthfully, I've never been much good at it, more suited to swinging a sword than talking about inner turmoil.

"It's not a betrayal of them, lord," Sarrey said softly, reading my thoughts as plainly as a book. "No matter what you think, I know Mondar and Lady Shana would agree with me if they were here right now. They would understand."

"But it is betrayal," I whispered, crushed inside because I knew Sarrey was right and for the sake of others, I would have to give in. *Forgive me, my love*, I thought. I lowered my head, hiding the misery I felt inside. "I will marry you, Sarrey del Fante," I said through gritted teeth. "For the sakes of our kingdoms, I will do it. You have my word." I stood abruptly then, heading for the doorway without looking at the girl, for I suddenly needed to be alone.

"Lord?"

I hesitated at the entrance and looked back reluctantly.

"I am sorry, lord," Sarrey said in a cracking voice. "I truly am. I hope someday, when this is all over, you will be able to look at me differently than you do right now."

The storm lasted for another few hours, and I spent that time in one of the small living quarters off the workroom, brooding and reliving memories of Shana. Sarrey was wise enough to leave me alone until the storm finally petered out; then, finally, she came to see me. She stood in the entrance tentatively, not saying anything as I sat on the framework of a wooden cot stripped of bedding, staring at the floor without actually seeing it.

Finally, Sarrey cleared her throat almost reluctantly. "The storm has ended, lord, and the sun is shining."

I looked up and gave her a wan smile, trying to hide what I was feeling inside. I could tell by Sarrey's expression that I hadn't fooled her. "That's good news," I said. "I guess we better get going, then."

"Are you all right, lord?" Sarrey asked, sounding worried.

I brushed past her into the workroom. "Of course I am, Your Highness," I said over my shoulder in a flat voice. "Why wouldn't I be? It's not every day a man gets betrothed to a queen."

The road leading from the *Maharas* to the south was really nothing more than a barely seen trail filled with wet, twisted vines, energetic saplings all fighting for space, and prickly hawthorn shrubs. The thorny plants seemed intent on impeding our progress while inflicting as many wounds on us as possible. Sarrey and I spent most of our time and energy hacking at them with sword and glaive to cut a path, sending their plump berries sailing in all directions like little drops of red rain. The only benefit to all that work, I suppose, was that the plentiful berries were ripe, edible, and quite delicious.

Sarrey had guessed that it would take us a day to reach the lowlands, but by evening we were still trapped high up in the mountains and forced to camp among the plants and trees. The next morning began clear and cool, and with renewed vigor, we set out again, though the heat quickly returned. Neither of us spoke again about what had been agreed upon in the hall of the *Maharas*, though I'm sure it was on her mind as much as it was mine. We finally reached the lowlands by mid-afternoon, using small woodlands and forests dotting the countryside for cover as much as possible until, eventually, they gave way to open land dominated by small hills of brown scrub grass and yellow sandstone.

"We're getting close, lord," Sarrey said when the terrain abruptly turned flat. The ground here was covered by a thick layer of yellowish dirt, with only the odd, stubborn patch of weeds or dry, brittle grass growing.

"Is this the Waste of Bones?" I asked Sarrey.

The girl snorted. "No, lord. This place will seem like paradise compared to that. We call it the Outer Ring. Consider this a warning of what's to come if we go much further."

I nodded, about to ask where the road was in all of this flatness when I saw it for myself, mostly hidden by dust almost a hundred yards ahead. I'd been expecting something a little more dramatic, but in reality, Sarrey's Bone Road was nothing more than a worn, windswept path of wheel ruts and faded hoof prints.

"You want us to travel along that?" I muttered uneasily.

"Yes, lord," Sarrey said. "Why? What's wrong?"

I looked around, able to see for miles in all directions. "There's nowhere to hide out here, Your Highness. If the Lions come along, we'll be easy prey for them."

"Then we better hope they don't," Sarrey said, moving forward with determination. "Besides, the trail in the mountain where we left them is miles to the west. That's where they expect to find us, so why would they think to look here? And by the time they do, we'll be long gone." She smiled. "It's all part of my plan, lord."

"If you say so, Your Highness," I grumbled as I followed. I didn't bother trying to explain to her that plans rarely worked out the way we expect. Hopefully, she wouldn't learn that lesson the hard way.

We reached the Bone Road and headed southeast, with the sun overhead burning down on us with unrelenting ferocity, causing our sweat-soaked clothing to cling to our bodies. I took off my cloak, intent on throwing it aside, but Sarrey stopped me.

"No, lord. The nights here get cold. Very cold. You will need it."

I grunted in acknowledgment, carrying the garment under my arm instead. "You said five or six days to get to Sandhold?" I asked.

"Yes, lord."

I nodded, thinking of the four waterskins I carried. I knew we would need every last drop to survive, and I was grateful that I'd refilled them in a mountain stream earlier that morning. "Do these Bone Warriors live in the desert, Your Highness, or Sandhold?" I asked to pass the time.

"Both, lord. Many of the more powerful *Rhana* have their own strongholds in the Waste of Bones." She saw my curious look and added, "*Rhana* means tribal chief."

I nodded in understanding. "What's Sandhold like? Is it big?"

"Not really, lord," Sarrey answered. "Only several thousand people live there." She motioned ahead. "The Bone Road mainly follows the coast around the desert all the way to city."

I perked up with interest at that. "Do they have a port? Ships?"

"Yes, lord. The port is small but serviceable for bringing in some goods. But most of the city's trading is done through the desert by caravans, traveling to cities such as Cordova, Brudburn, Braton, and Manderia. The *Falitari* tend to frown on trading with us, as you can well imagine."

"I can," I said, hardly blaming them. I glanced to my right, alarmed to see a cloud of dust rising from the desert coming our way. I grabbed Sarrey's arm, already looking around for somewhere to hide. I saw nothing but a few nondescript rocks, none of which were bigger than a small dog. "We have to get off the road," I said urgently.

"And go where?" Sarrey replied tensely. "You said yourself there's nowhere to hide out here."

I drew my sword, now able to make out at least twenty men on horseback. The riders were dressed in bronze chest armor that gleamed in the sunlight, supported by leather straps over their shoulders. Each man wore a white tunic underneath his armor, with a matching white turban on his head that wrapped around the face, leaving only the eyes visible. They carried bronze-coated shields shaped like elongated teardrops punctuated by a half-moon-shaped opening at the bottom. I assumed this allowed the riders to balance them easily on their thighs. Each man wore open sandals and carried a sword in a golden sheath. All had several throwing spears tied to their saddles. The rapidly approaching riders were flying a black banner depicting a white skeleton holding a flaming sword above its head in triumph. Bone Warriors, I guessed with a sinking feeling swirling in my gut.

Sarrey groaned when she saw the banner. "Sheath your weapon, lord," she said out of the side of her mouth as the riders drew closer. I hesitated, waving away the clouds of dust drifting over us as the mounted men broke apart, then encircled us before halting their horses. "Do it, lord!" Sarrey hissed urgently. "These are not men you want to anger, believe me."

I sighed, then did as she asked while the dust slowly drifted away. None of the Bone Warriors said anything, with only the occasional stamp of a horse's hoof or the jingle of bits breaking the silence while the mounted men studied us with unfriendly eyes.

"Peace and goodwill, friends," Sarrey said. "May the desert winds always blow in your favor, and may the gods always watch over your houses."

No one acknowledged Sarrey's words, which I assumed was some form of formal greeting. She glanced at me in despair, looking small and frightened now, with her earlier bravado gone.

I stepped forward a pace. "My name is Lord Hadrack of Corwick, and I would ask that you help us."

A tall man sitting astride a shiny brown stallion slowly unwound his turban, revealing a face sculpted of stone. He was beardless, with a great mustache that hung down both sides of his mouth well past his chin. "I have heard this name," the man grunted. His eyes were dark and piercing like a hawk's as he studied me. "They call you Wolf, yes?"

I inclined my head. "Some do." I motioned to the speaker. "And what might I call you?"

"I am known as Telman," the man simply said.

I waited for more, but Telman just sat his horse, staring at me steadily. I glanced sideways at Sarrey, not sure where to go from here.

"Your name is well known in Temba, *Rhana* Telman," Sarrey said. I could see the color had drained from her face. Whoever this man was, I guessed that he was no friend. "Never has there been a more fierce or noble warrior than you."

"This is true," Telman agreed in a flat, emotionless voice. He flicked his cold eyes from the girl back to me. "And what would a wolf and a lion princess be doing out here all alone and unprotected, one wonders?"

I saw Sarrey start in surprise. It was clear that the Bone Warriors somehow knew who she was, despite her frazzled looks and dirty clothing. "There has been some trouble lately in Temba," Sarrey replied carefully.

"This is known to the Bone Warriors," Telman replied. "What is not known is the answer to my question."

"Traitors have overrun the palace and brought madness to the city," Sarrey responded. She gestured to me. "Lord Hadrack saved my life and helped me to escape, but our pursuers are close. We need your help."

Several riders muttered something unintelligible at that, but Telman said nothing, sitting like a statue on his equally motionless horse.

"The White Ravens have gained control of the throne," I added, deciding there was nothing to lose now by telling the truth. "We need your help to get it back." This time I heard distinctive laughter coming from behind the heavy cloth turbans hiding the warriors' faces.

"You speak of the hairless ones?" Telman asked.

I nodded. "I do."

Telman shrugged. "Perhaps they will rule Temba better than the feckless Lions, then. What happens in the City of Shame means nothing to the Bone Warriors. It can burn to the ground for all we care."

"You're wrong," I retorted. "It will mean something because the Ravens won't stop there. They will come for you too, eventually."

Telman smiled for the first time, revealing sparkling white teeth. "Then let them come, Wolf. It has been a while since we last feasted on lions' meat." I saw the man look past me then, and he frowned. "Perhaps that is about to change."

I turned. Another dust cloud was fast approaching from the northwest along the road, with at least thirty riders all bunched tightly together. There were two men in the lead, I saw, both with gleaming bald heads and dressed in white robes that flapped behind them like the wings of gulls. Behind the Ravens rode several soldiers bearing the distinctive black and yellow Lion banners streaming from their glaives. The Raven to my right was Kish, I saw as they drew closer, and it took me a moment to recognize the second man, who looked hugely different without his beard, hair, and eyebrows.

I cursed in disgust, for the White Raven was Rorian.

Chapter 26: An Uneasy Alliance

The riders came to a halt twenty feet away from Sarrey and me. I glanced over my shoulder at the Bone Warriors, a few of whom had drawn their swords, though most now held spears in their right hands, poised for throwing. This was going to get bloody in a hurry, I knew. I drew my own sword once again, pressing Sarrey behind me as I faced the Lions. The Bone Warriors clearly weren't our friends, but if I had to choose the lesser of the two evils, then at the moment, they were it. I just hoped we wouldn't get trampled when the inevitable charge happened.

"Get ready," I told Sarrey. I motioned with my head to the south. "When I give the word, you run that way into the desert as fast as you can. Understand?"

"Yes, lord," Sarrey said in a frightened voice. "But what about you?"

"Just worry about yourself," I grunted. "Whatever you do, keep running no matter what happens."

"I'm not leaving you behind."

"Then you risk dying here and letting the Ravens rule Temba forever," I grunted. "Besides, Your Highness, this won't be my first battle. I'll be fine."

Sarrey didn't respond to that, whether not believing me or just too overwhelmed at the moment, I wasn't sure. I focused on Rorian, about to shout obscenities at him. But then, something about his expression stalled me. The bald scholar shook his head slightly in obvious warning when our eyes met, and I felt my anger toward him deflate somewhat, replaced by sudden confusion and hope. *What was the sly bastard up to now?*

"Lord Hadrack," Kish said smugly once the dust had settled. A small black snake chose that moment to slither out from a rock in front of his horse, and the animal skittered sideways, rolling its eyes. The snake seemed oblivious to the troubles of men and kept going, leaving a thin trail in the sand in its wake. It took Kish a moment to regain control of his horse once the snake was gone, and when he had, he cleared his throat and smiled at me. I remembered that smile from when we'd first met—like a starving predator eyeing wounded prey. It was clear that Sarrey and I were the prey. "How wonderful to see you again, lord," Kish continued. He flicked his eyes to the girl. "And you as well, Princess."

"You'll burn at the feet of The Father for murdering that poor boy!" Sarrey snapped.

Kish smirked. "Sadly, it seems that you live in the past, Princess. Haven't you heard? There is no Father, nor is there a Mother. There is only the One True God." Kish shrugged. "Besides, what's the life of some wretched little slave boy when compared to our God's needs?"

"One god, One heart, One mind," Rorian chanted dutifully.

"Indeed, brother," Kish said, glancing at the scholar with approval. He turned his attention to the Bone Warriors, ignoring us completely now. "I want to thank you, my desert friends, for finding these fugitives for us. Queen Magret will naturally reward you quite handsomely for it."

"She's just a baby and can't even speak yet," I growled. "Besides, she's not the queen. Sarrey is."

Kish smiled condescendingly at me. "You are incorrect, as usual, Lord Hadrack. Queen Magret is the rightful heir to the throne, though I concede that she is still quite young." He flicked his eyes back to Telman. "Muwa del Fante, a relative, has graciously, though reluctantly, accepted the role of Regent until Queen Magret comes of age. He will be the one rewarding you for your service, in the queen's name, of course."

I turned to look at Telman. "This bastard is lying to you. The Ravens have no intention of giving you anything other than a slit throat. Don't trust him or them."

"Of course this foul creature is lying, Wolf," Telman said. "Are his lips not moving?"

The thin Raven's expression hardened at Telman's words, while on some unseen signal, the Lions began spreading out across the road in a two-line formation.

"There is no reason for bloodshed to happen between us," Kish said, clearly fighting to keep the anger from his voice. "All we want is Lord Hadrack and the girl, nothing more."

"Perhaps they do not wish the same," Telman responded flatly, looking unimpressed.

Kish shook his head in irritation. "Be reasonable, friend. We outnumber you by at least ten men."

"This is fact, Raven," Telman readily agreed. He flashed his teeth in a wide grin, though his eyes remained hard as flint. "Shall we wait, then, until more of your men arrive so that the odds are more even? Or shall we just kill you all now and offer up your bones to the gods?"

Kish flushed at the man's words, but he managed to maintain his composure. "There is only one god," he said between gritted teeth.

"There are many gods, Raven," Telman countered. "Your self-righteous hubris just makes you blind to seeing them."

Kish blew air out of his nostrils in frustration. "Will you withdraw your men and leave these two to face the justice they deserve in Temba or not?"

"Not," Telman responded bluntly.

"Why? What can they possibly mean to you?"

"Nothing," Telman grunted. He shifted in his saddle. "But you, funny little man, annoy me greatly."

Kish's mouth dropped open comically. "That's your reason for shedding blood?" he spluttered in disbelief. "Because I annoy you?"

"It's as good a reason as any," Telman said. "Besides, I like a good fight."

The thin Raven's lips pressed together in a thin line of anger until he finally sighed in resignation. "Very well. If that is your wish." Kish waved a hand in the air. "Come, brother," he said to Rorian before pulling his horse around. "What comes next is not for men of God like us."

"Hiding in the back as usual, eh Kish?" I taunted.

The Raven shot me a look filled with loathing, but he didn't bother replying as he and Rorian guided their horses behind the massed Lions. Kish's place was taken by an older soldier with a beardless, firm jaw and a no-nonsense air about him. I turned to Sarrey, knowing there wasn't much time. "Go now," I whispered, pushing her toward the sprawling desert. "Get out of here before it's too late."

Sarrey hesitated, her huge eyes filled with worry. "Be careful, lord. We still have much to do together."

I nodded but said nothing, watching tensely until Sarrey had moved far enough off the road that I knew she was safe from being trampled in the initial charge. She stopped there, though, standing with her glaive held in both her hands and a stubborn look on her face. I groaned, praying that the girl wouldn't be foolish enough to try joining the fray when it happened.

I focused back on the Lion leader. "That woman is the true Queen of Temba," I said, pointing. "Sarrey del Fante, eldest daughter of Alba del Fante. Did you not swear allegiance to her house—to her bloodline?" I let my eyes roam over the silent soldiers. "Did all of you not bend the knee to her father and pledge to serve his family even if it meant the loss of your life?" Several soldiers reacted to my words by dropping their eyes, which I took as a good sign. I hurried to continue, "Whatever these White Ravens have said or done to buy your loyalty, it isn't worth selling your soul. Nor your honor. These conniving creatures care nothing for you or your families. All they want is power. I implore you not to let them have it."

"A pretty speech, Lord Hadrack," Kish called out in amusement from the back. "Quite inspiring, actually, though sadly misguided. These men are now soldiers of God, and their allegiance is to Him and no other. The One True God has shown them the path they must take to reach the Realm Beyond. Your flowery words are wasted on them."

I glanced over my shoulder at Telman, who nodded grimly at me. We both knew instinctively that the time for talk had ended. Now was the time for action. "Then so be it," I whispered as I focused back on the enemy.

The Bone Warriors moved without warning, drawing back their spears before flinging them in a wall of death toward the Lions. I heard the whistling as the iron-tipped spears arced over me like hungry hawks, and then I started to run. Behind me, thunder rose from the hooves of the Bone Warriors' horses as they charged forward while their riders emitted bloodcurdling battle cries. I imagine most men would have immediately headed for the side of the road and safety in my situation, caught as I was between two opposing mounted forces—at least the sane ones would have, anyway. But my blood was up by now, the anger I'd felt about losing Sumisu and Tako, not to mention my pending betrayal of Shana, coming to the fore. And so, throwing all caution aside, I charged straight at the line of armored Lions with blackness in my heart and death in my intent.

Men and horses screamed in pain moments later when the Bone Warriors' spears arrived, and I saw several soldiers in the front line tumble from their saddles. Many of the spears clattered against the Lions' ready shields, however, or flew past them, doing little harm. I knew the volley of spears was only meant to distract the enemy rather than decimate them, giving the Bone Warriors precious time to close with the enemy. If some of the Lions died in the process, well, that was just good fortune. I caught a glimpse of Kish ducking low over his horse as a spear sailed over his head, and I laughed at the look of terror on his sickly white face. I lost sight of the bastard moments later in the swirling dust cloud kicked up by the hooves of the combatants' horses.

A Lion suddenly loomed over me, and I instinctively parried the downward stroke of his glaive, then latched onto his arm and twisted in a crouch, yanking him from the saddle. The soldier cried out in surprise as he sailed over my head, landing with a crunch and grunt of pain in the sand on his back. The man struggled to rise with the wind knocked from him and blood on his lips. I scurried over to him and stabbed downward into his chest, crunching through heavy leather armor, muscle and cartilage even as I tried to snatch at the reins of the downed man's horse. But the terrified beast was having none of it, and it ran off, disappearing into the dust as Bone Warriors and Lions clashed all around me in a wild melee of clanging metal and screams.

I stood, hesitating for a moment—which in a pitched battle is never a good thing—and a heartbeat later, the shoulder of a horse struck me from behind, sending me reeling forward. If not for the rear end of a Bone Warrior's mare breaking my fall, I would have tumbled to the ground and been at the mercy of the battling fighters' churning hooves. It's rare a man can claim that his life was saved by a mare's ass, but mine was that day, sending me bouncing off to the side, where I somehow managed to stay on my feet only to find myself staring at a confused black stallion with haunted eyes. The horse stood stock still while a wounded Lion hung suspended awkwardly from its stirrups. The man was struggling feebly, with blood running in a river from beneath his armor, where it pooled at his neck beneath his bushy beard. The soldier's mouth moved when he saw me, and he reached out a hand in gratitude as I dashed toward him. I slapped aside the Lion's hand, quick to snatch up the reins of the horse this time before the beast could run away.

"Help me!" the Lion croaked in a pitiful voice.

The man's lower leg was twisted almost completely around, clearly broken, and I fought to extricate his boot while he screamed and howled in agony. I didn't bother saying anything to him, for his pain meant nothing to me. Finally, once I'd freed the now whimpering Lion, I let him drop to the ground and the death that awaited him there beneath the milling horses' hooves. Then, with a whoop of renewed energy, I leaped into the saddle. I had a horse now to go along with my sword and pent-up rage, and I intended to use all three to wreak devastation on the enemy.

"Kill them!" I screamed. "Kill the Lions!"

I kicked the stallion into motion, sending him charging into the thick of battle. A soldier turned in his saddle to look back at me, and I lashed out with my sword at him as I swept past, hacking deep into the man's forearm even as I hauled on the stallion's reins to turn around and try again. My opponent howled in pain, with his cry silenced a moment later when a Bone Warrior smashed him across the face with his golden shield, sending him somersaulting backward over his horse's rump. The Bone Warrior paused to smile at me, his unwound turban hanging down his chest, revealing a young, handsome face marred by a scar on his cheek. I smiled back, then we both broke apart—he deflecting an attack by a Lion with a glaive, me to look for a new enemy to kill.

My search didn't take long, for moments later I reached a small knot of battling riders circling each other as great plumes of dust swirled around them. I saw Kish and Rorian behind the combatants, and I nudged the stallion into a run with my feet, one hand on the reins, the other holding my sword low by my side. An opening appeared in the melee, and the well-trained stallion barrelled into it while I lay about me with my sword at any Lion I saw. Within minutes, we'd eliminated half the remaining Lions, pushing them back until they formed a collapsing barrier around the two Ravens. The Bone Warriors pressed onward from the front and sides, showing no mercy to their foes as they cut them down relentlessly until, finally, only one remained.

That man sat his horse wearily, watching bitterly as we surrounded him and the two Ravens. I glanced at Rorian, but the scholar appeared calm and composed. I could not say the same for Kish, who, without any eyebrows, looked like a frightened owl as he searched frantically for a way out.

"You fought well, Lion," Telman said to the last surviving soldier. The Bone Warrior leader looked like he'd just risen from a pleasant night's sleep rather than having just participated in a vicious battle. Telman's shield was dented from a blow, and his turban was splattered with drops of blood, but other than that, he looked unscathed.

The Lion said nothing, his chest rising and falling as he sucked in air while he waited for inevitable death. A Bone Warrior obliged him a moment later by pulling a spear from the sand and flinging it into the air before he caught it on the way down and then threw it with deadly accuracy at the Lion, catching him in the stomach. The man groaned and tipped sideways in the saddle, then fell with a clatter to the ground, leaving only Kish and Rorian to stand against us. Behind me, I heard the telltale sounds of warriors moving among the wounded and dying Lions, silencing them.

"What would you have me do with these sheep, Wolf?" Telman grunted at me.

I pointed my sword at Rorian. "Let that Raven be," I said. I fixed my eyes on Kish, who was trembling uncontrollably as he looked around at the Bone Warriors. "The other one is mine."

Telman shrugged. "Very well." He gestured to several of his men. "Get the girl." I looked at the man in alarm. "Do not worry, Wolf. None here will harm her. There are others who will decide what to do with all of you when we return to Sandhold."

We locked eyes, two hard men measuring each other until finally, I took a deep breath and nodded my acceptance. For really, what choice did I have? I wondered if things had just gotten better for us now or worse. I dismounted, patting the stallion's sweat-streaked shoulder in gratitude before I made my way toward Kish and Rorian. The scholar was holding the bridle of Kish's horse, though the skinny Raven seemed unaware of it as he watched me approach fearfully. I doubted that even if Kish had tried to get away, he would have gotten very far with the Bone Warriors hot on his trail. I stopped in front of the two men, nodding briefly to Rorian before focusing on Kish. The scholar and I would have words soon enough about all of this, but for now, that could wait. I had something much more important to do at the moment.

"Get down," I growled at Kish.

"Now, Lord Hadrack," the thin Raven began in a shaky voice. "Let's not be too hasty. Surely we can work something out?"

"I believe the man told you to get off your horse," Rorian said.

Kish looked at the scholar in surprise, frowning when he saw Rorian's hand on his horse's bridle. "Brother, what is the meaning of this?"

Rorian smiled. I was still having a difficult time getting used to his new look. "Just because a man has no hair does not make him a Raven. Now get down." Kish just gaped at him, and finally, Rorian sighed, then pushed the thin man out of his saddle without warning.

Kish landed with a surprised squawk in the sand, sending up a small cloud of dust. Rorian barely glanced at him as he kicked his heels into his mount's sides, leading Kish's horse past me. "We'll talk after you're done," the scholar grunted.

"That we will," I agreed.

I turned and watched him go, marveling at the man's nerves of steel as he made his way past the silent, watching Bone Warriors without even glancing their way. I returned my gaze to Kish, who was sitting up now and staring at me with fear-filled eyes. I smiled, which for some reason seemed to terrify the man even more. The skinny Raven began to scramble backward across the sand, shaking his head and making a high-pitched keening sound while I stalked toward him. He didn't get very far. I grabbed the Raven by the scruff of his filthy robe, then hauled him unceremoniously into the air as he sobbed like a newborn babe. I set the man on his feet, then placed the point of my sword against his thudding heart.

"Any last words?" I growled.

"Please, don't," Kish whimpered. "I beg of you, lord, don't kill me!"

"Is that what Tako said just before you choked the life from him?" I hissed.

Kish sagged in my grip at my words, and he started to cry harder. I looked down with contempt as drops of piss stained the sand between his legs. I snorted, then pushed the hooked blade as deep as I could into the bastard's heart. I waited as warm blood began to mix with the dying man's piss on the ground, and then, as the light started to fade from his eyes, I leaned closer. "You only know half of the truth, Kish," I whispered. "Someone has been lying to you. The One True God you follow is known as the Master, and his children are The Mother and The Father. I know this because I have read the real codex. The Father really does exist, as you will find out shortly." I smiled at the look of confusion and sudden doubt on the Raven's face. "Enjoy the heat, you ugly bastard."

I twisted the blade to the side, destroying what was left of the man's heart, then tore it out with a quick snap of my wrist in an explosion of blood and gore. I turned and walked away, not bothering to look around as I heard Kish's body collapse. I headed for Rorian, who had dismounted and now stood beside Sarrey within a circle of Bone Warriors. The man with the scar I remembered from the battle approached me and held out his hand, and I passed him my blood-stained shotel without slowing or saying anything.

Sarrey threw her arms around me after I'd pushed through the crowd of Bone Warriors guarding her. "Are you all right, lord?"

I glanced back at Kish's corpse as the desert winds toyed with the dead man's white robe. "I am now," I said. I fixed my gaze on Rorian's hairless features and snorted. "You look ridiculous."

The scholar grimaced. "I am aware of that, Lord Hadrack. Thank you."

"You did that to yourself just so you could find Sarrey and me?"

"Of course not," Rorian scoffed. "I barely know her, and I don't even like *you*."

I shook my head, unable to keep the smile from my lips. "Then why did you do it?"

"I could think of no better way to find the Eye of God than to become one of these creatures," the scholar replied. "I found the message you left for me and located the secret passage, but lost track of you in Unwashed Row. That's when I decided my best chance was to become a Raven and infiltrate them. It was only afterward, once I'd learned the Eye of God's location, that word came you and the queen were being hunted in the mountains. I decided, after some internal debate, that it wouldn't sit well with me later if you were captured and killed and I'd done nothing to help—so here I am."

I nodded, remembering how Rorian had posed as a Pathfinder many years ago to locate the codex in the Ascension Grounds of the Piths. No other man could have done that. "And?" I asked curiously. "Where is this Eye of God?"

"Some distance away, lord," Rorian replied gravely. "Which means we are going to need a ship so we can go kill the bastard. A big one. Luckily, I know just where we can find one."

Chapter 27: The Ship In The Harbor

"You're certain that it's *Sea-Wolf*?" I demanded.

Rorian sighed in a long-suffering way. He adjusted his posture in the saddle, not looking at me as sunlight gleamed off his bald head like a lantern beam in the dead of night. Sarrey rode on my other side while the Bone Warriors rode in front and behind us as we headed deeper into the desert, having left the carnage and dead bodies of the enemy far behind. A long train of riderless horses captured in the battle brought up the rear, tied together by ropes and carrying the dead Lions' confiscated weapons and shields that would be sold later. Only four of the Bone Warriors had been killed during the fighting, which I thought with admiration was nothing short of remarkable. I'd been surprised and slightly appalled when those men were stripped of anything of value and then left forgotten in the sand where they'd fallen, joining the Lions as food for the desert scavengers. The overwhelming victory over the superiorly numbered enemy had shocked me. Yet, none of the warriors seemed even remotely surprised by it, exuding a quiet, competent confidence that reminded me greatly of the Piths.

The afternoon sun hung high in the sky above our long procession, blazing hot and impossible to ignore, with the intense heat shimmering off the sand, hurting my eyes and giving me a headache. Rivers of sweat ran down my back and along my temples into my beard as I stared at Rorian pointedly while waving away buzzing flies that were determined to land in the corners of my eyes. I rolled with the motion of my horse, trying to ignore my fatigue as I waited for the scholar to answer. I'd long since grown bored of the flat, featureless landscape filled with nothing but wind-swept dunes of brown-gray sand and the occasional butte of reddish stone. At least talking helped to pass the time.

"I already told you everything, lord," the scholar insisted in exasperation. I continued riding beside him in silence until he eventually shrugged in weary resignation. "Fine. Have it your way. All I know is a large ship full of northerners came to Temba looking for you recently. Their leaders were described as a fiery, silver-haired older man, a small young man dressed completely in black with fierce eyes, and a constantly smiling lord who tried and failed to keep the other two in check."

I felt my lips twitch in amusement as I pictured their faces in my mind, knowing without question that it had been Jebido, Baine, and Fitz. My heart soared at the thought, for it seemed like a lifetime since I'd last seen them. I couldn't wait for us to be reunited again, and once we were, I knew no Raven or Lion could stop us.

"What happened?" Sarrey asked, though, like me, she already knew. We'd been traveling across the hot sand for over an hour already, and I'd grilled Rorian about what he knew the entire time. There probably wasn't anything left to learn about what had occurred, but just talking about my men warmed my belly and brought my spirits up.

"They were told Lord Hadrack had been executed a week ago, Your Highness," Rorian answered, leaning forward to look past me at the girl. Sweat rolled down his nose in a glistening rivulet to drop on his horse's neck, though the plodding beast didn't seem to notice. "Which did not go over very well with these men, as you can well imagine." He almost smiled as he glanced sideways at me. "Having met many of Lord Hadrack's friends and sworn men, I can't say that I am surprised. Our young lord here seems to have a peculiar knack for gaining fierce loyalty from those who serve him."

"That's because he's an honest man and a natural leader," Sarrey responded proudly.

Rorian glanced from the girl to me, his eyes turning thoughtful. *Nothing ever slips past that bastard*, I thought. "Tell us the rest of it," I said hurriedly before Rorian could ask any uncomfortable questions about my relationship with Sarrey.

"Your friends demanded answers from the regent, lord," Rorian said. "They—quite rightly, as it turns out—did not believe him when he insisted you were dead. I understand you have met Muwa, so you know he can be charming and convincing yet firm in his convictions. Your men left the palace frustrated and angry, and on the way back to their ship, they ran into some soldiers and an argument broke out. A Lion was killed—I don't know by who—which led to a pitched battle in the streets. Your men eventually managed to escape and sail away, although I understand the ship was damaged in the process. They were last sighted heading south along the coast, which logically should lead them to Sandhold eventually, where I expect they will dock for repairs." Rorian nodded his head toward Telman. "Exactly where that fellow says we are going right now." He slicked the sweat from his shining scalp, glanced at his shimmering hand, and then smiled at me. "It would seem that the gods and good fortune have not abandoned us completely, lord."

I took a deep breath and nodded my gratitude to Rorian, who fell silent. I wondered how badly damaged *Sea-Wolf* was, praying it wasn't too serious. I'd spent all my gold on the forged codex only to lose it in the end, and I knew there was little money left to pay for extensive repairs. I turned to Sarrey. "So, what happens when we get to the city, Your Highness?"

The girl shrugged. "I can't say for certain, lord."

"Do they have a king or ruler we'll need to bargain with?"

"Not really, no. There are many tribal leaders, such as Telman, but most of the day-to-day decisions in Sandhold are made by a council known as the Circle of Life. My father and Banta deal with them almost exclusively."

"Ah," Rorian said, joining back in the conversation. "I have heard talk of this council, Your Highness. It is made up of three women, correct?"

"That's right," Sarrey agreed. "Each year, a respected grandmother, a widowed matron, and a virgin daughter are selected from within the city to form council."

"Why only women?" I asked curiously.

Sarrey shrugged. "All human life begins inside a woman, lord, as we all know. When our life cycle ends, each of us hopes that Judgment Day is kind and sends us to The Mother in the Realm Above. Hence, the Circle of Life is daughter, matron, grandmother, and lastly, The Mother herself."

I glanced ahead at Telman, finding it hard to imagine a man like that taking orders from anyone, let alone women such as Sarrey had just mentioned. I motioned to the Bone Warrior leader. "Will this council be more sympathetic to us than he is?"

Sarrey followed my eyes. "It's possible, lord. It will depend greatly on the disposition of the women who sit there this year. Sometimes the members of the Circle of Life are less inclined to hate the Temba, which means our relationship with them improves. Other times it is the exact opposite, and all communication ceases. The fact that Banta went there at all is a hopeful sign, though."

I turned to Rorian. "You mentioned you met Muwa earlier," I said. "Didn't he suspect you weren't who you said you were? He must know all the Ravens in Temba."

The scholar chuckled. "I told him I was from Cordova." Rorian smiled modestly at my look of surprise. "I am impeccably well-informed about all aspects of the jobs I undertake, lord. Nothing is left to chance. You, of all people, should know this."

I let Rorian's boastful words wash over me without reacting. I'd seen and heard it all from the man many times before. "And it was Muwa who told you where the Eye of God can be found?" I asked, surprised he would offer up such valuable information.

"No," Rorian admitted. "Another Raven that I befriended. I got him drunk on Cordovian wine, which can do wonders for tight lips."

I mulled that over. The Eye of God was supposedly living on an island even further to the south than The Iron Cay and Temba—a place known as the Edge of the World—where storms, hidden shoals, and treacherous seas abounded. I understood now why Rorian needed *Sea-Wolf* and, with it, my help. The scholar hadn't come into the mountains and risked everything to save Sarrey and me out of conscience as he'd claimed, which I should have realized from the beginning. No, he'd done it, as usual, for his own ulterior motives—which, in this case, was to kill the Eye of God. My ship and men were clearly the key to that happening for him, though I saw no reason not to let the man get his wish. After all, we both shared the same goal in the end. But before Rorian and I went after the Eye of God, I needed to take back Temba for Sarrey, not to mention negotiate somehow with the *Falitari* for our release.

I glanced around me at the silent warriors whose faces were protected from the wind, sand, and sun by turbans. I envied them as that sun beat down on us mercilessly, understanding now why they wore them. The warriors were a dangerous-looking lot, I conceded, and after what I'd seen in the recent battle, I knew they would make powerful allies. *Or enemies,* part of my mind whispered. I tried not to think about that, focusing inward instead as silence fell over the three of us.

We were roughly three days out from Sandhold as the crow flies, Telman had told me, which meant there were still many miles to go over rough, inhospitable terrain before I would get a chance to see my ship and friends again. Our procession slowly plodded past the skeletal remains of an ox, which stared back at me with empty and resentful eye sockets long since bleached by the sun. I looked up at the cloudless sky and sighed as a lone buzzard circled hopefully overhead. It was going to be a long three days.

Our journey to Sandhold proved mainly uneventful, although we did lose one of the Bone Warriors who'd been injured in the battle with the Lions. The man's wounds had become infected after the second day, and we'd spent most of that night listening to his fever-induced babbling until abruptly it ceased near dawn—blissfully ended by a sharp knife across the throat from Telman. The nights in the desert were shockingly cold, just as Sarrey had warned me. But though the Bone Warriors gave us some food and water and didn't mistreat us, we three were forced to sleep on the ground without blankets, under guard and shivering far from the warmth of the fires the others made.

The terrain began to change the morning of our third day, with more rocky outcroppings appearing surrounded by hardy clusters of plants with white flowers that Sarrey informed me were called lovegrass. We also started to see clumps of towering date palm trees mixed with various shrubs like desert thyme, *tamarisk*, and *ephedra alata*. We entered a dry wash buttressed on both sides by four-foot-tall plants sporting whitish-green flowers and tiny grape-like berries that the Bone Warriors picked at as we rode past. Sarrey said the plants were known as nitre bush or *nitraria billardierei*. I thought the fruit tasted a great deal like grapes, though they were much saltier. I stopped eating them after only a few, for I found they made me thirsty and the Bone Warriors were quite stingy with their water supply.

We finally reached the coast by late afternoon, turning southeast as our long procession followed a series of flat, rocky plateaus that towered above a narrow strip of sandy beach before giving way to the open water. The land here was barren of trees and just as inhospitable as the desert we'd left behind, yet, even so, I breathed in the smell of the ocean with gratitude, enjoying the cooling breeze coming off the water. An hour later, I could just make out the tops of buildings on the horizon, with all but the golden domes of the structures hidden by a swath of hill-covered forest. We stopped at a meandering, lively stream fifty feet inside the forest line to let the horses drink, then followed a well-worn trail through the trees for another hour.

Finally, we reached a clearing on a hilltop overlooking the city of Sandhold, where Telman paused, giving our horses a breather. The settlement from what I could see was small compared to many of the Gander cities I knew, and it was positively dwarfed by Temba. I stood up in my stirrups eagerly, but I couldn't see the port nor *Sea-Wolf* over the heads of the many horsemen in front of me. Telman eventually whistled sharply through his teeth, then started down the hill along the trail while I waited impatiently with Sarrey and Rorian for our turn.

"There, lord," Rorian said in satisfaction as he pointed. "Just as I told you."

I saw a towering mast in the distance, and as the riders in front of me dwindled, I could see more of the great ship's body nestled in a small harbor, framed by the setting sun dropping behind her. I shielded my eyes from the glare until, finally, I reached the crest of the hill and saw the features of my ship more clearly. I started to curse violently, shaking with anger as I studied the huge vessel's sleek lines.

"What, lord?" Rorian asked in obvious surprise. "What's wrong?"

I glanced at Sarrey, whose look of despair mirrored my own. "You tell him, Your Highness," I growled, unable to say anything more as I felt crushing defeat settle over me.

Sarrey shook her head, the color gone from her face as she turned to the scholar. "That's not *Sea-Wolf*. That black ship down there is called *Spearfish*, and it's owned by Lord Boudin of Cardia."

Chapter 28: The Circle Of Life

Sandhold was easily the cleanest city that I'd ever seen. The streets were neatly laid out in straight lines, with virtually no refuse to speak of anywhere that I saw. I didn't even notice any horse shit in evidence, which I thought was nothing short of remarkable. Vendors of fruits, vegetables, wine, and various raw and cooked meats lined the roads to either side, just like they did in the north, but they were surprisingly polite to passersby and rarely raised their voices. I compared that to Gandertown or Halhaven, where the noise of so many merchants shouting at once could hurt ears and make eyes water as aggressive sellers competed with one another for attention.

I saw no beggars, either, which was just as astounding as the absence of shit. Unarmed soldiers with white capes and gold-painted helmets walked alone through the crowd on every street, laughing and joking with people in a friendly way. The soldiers looked relaxed and comfortable among the common folk, which was another stark contrast to the north, where from habit, both sides tended to view the other with suspicion and distrust.

"The city watch," Telman explained when he saw my curious eyes on the soldiers. "They keep the peace, though there is rarely a need. Their function is more traditional than anything else now. Despite the inglorious history of our early ancestors, Wolf, we have very little crime here and our dungeon cells are usually empty." He glanced at me, amusement playing on his lips. "Well, most of the time, anyway."

I wondered what he meant by that as I rode beside the Bone Warrior while he led our procession through the city like a king. Many in the crowd called out to him, waving cheerfully as our horses plodded past with their hooves clopping loudly against the cobblestone streets beneath us. Telman would acknowledge each person by name, flashing his dazzling smile, though he remained all business and never stopped to exchange pleasantries. It was clear to me that the man was a popular figure here, and though he and I had mutual respect, if not liking for each other, I knew that inside, he harbored a great deal of resentment toward Sarrey. Telman had refused to talk to the girl during our journey, and I'd seen him looking at her more than once with an expression of naked loathing when his turban was unwound.

I worried greatly for Sarrey because of those looks—more so now that I understood the popularity and power the man clearly wielded in Sandhold. Human nature was the same everywhere, I knew, despite some obvious differences here in the south. And although I wasn't sure exactly how things were done in this city yet, I guessed that just like elsewhere in the world, a man such as Telman would have many political allies who would likely side with him. All I had standing in the way of that were three women who might or might not share Telman's views about the del Fantes. If their thinking did fall in line with Telman's, then I knew Sarrey, Rorian, and I were in a great deal of trouble. It was not a very comforting thought.

I looked over my shoulder at Sarrey, who rode alongside Rorian directly behind Telman and me. She gave me a wan smile, looking noticeably worried, which I could hardly blame her for. The girl was smart, and I knew she was having the same thoughts and doubts as I was. Sarrey and the scholar were followed by the rest of our much-reduced procession, since the captured horses, along with half of our original force, had broken off to the east long before we reached the city gates. Now we were left with seven men to guard us, all flying fluttering black skeleton banners from the tips of their spears.

I'd queried Telman several times on whether or not we were on our way to meet the Circle of Life, but the Bone Warrior just played coy with me and gave cryptic answers that did nothing to satisfy me. I'd also asked him what he knew about my friends or the big Cardian cog sitting in the harbor, but all I got were noncommittal shrugs. There was nothing I could do or say to that except grind my teeth in frustration and worry about my men, while my stomach churned with angry impotence. I could tell by the look on Telman's face that he was greatly enjoying my obvious discomfort—the bastard.

We finally reached a square laid out with dark gray flagstones, dominated in the center by a statue depicting three women kneeling at the feet of The Mother as they reached up to her. One of the kneeling women was very old and bent, while another held a babe to her naked breast. The last was a young girl with long flowing hair and an innocent face marred by tears on her cheeks—the Circle of Life, I guessed.

Telman led us past the statue toward a large rectangular structure built on a platform of three steps. The building was open to the air above and to the sides, surrounded by rounded sandstone columns that were wide at the base and fluted in the center before expanding outward once more at the top. Horizontal lintels that I estimated were easily ten feet thick ran across the top of the columns, and a smaller beam of marble sat nestled atop those, decorated with depictions of various trades such as carpentry, tanning, smithing, and many more carved into the surfaces.

The square was not overly crowded, with perhaps fifty people turning to watch us ride past, although I did see a small group of people hovering around the steps of the building we were quickly approaching. Some were sitting quietly, while others paced back and forth, looking anxious. Two men off to one side were arguing, but that disagreement ended abruptly when a soldier in a white cape appeared and yelled at them to be quiet.

"Petitioners," Telman said, motioning to the men, women, and children on the stairs. "That building is the Hall of Justice, and they seek an audience with the council to air out whatever grievances they have between each other."

I nodded in understanding, for as a lord, I'd mitigated disputes between my people in Corwick countless times. It was a job I never looked forward to or enjoyed, for there were always two sides to every story and finding the truth within them was not always easy.

"Are we to become petitioners, then?" I asked. Telman just grunted, which I couldn't interpret as a yes or no. "Is the council's ruling always final?" I added, trying to gain as much information as possible.

"It is," Telman muttered grudgingly.

"So, *Rhanas* like yourself don't have any sway if you don't like the outcome?"

Telman glanced at me, studying me carefully before finally, he snorted. "The Wolf is no fool, it would seem." He halted his horse near the steps leading to the Hall of Justice and indicated we should dismount. After our horses were led away, Telman guided us up the stone stairs, which were more like individual platforms, each of which was at least twelve feet deep. He turned to me at the top. "Listen well, Wolf, for I shall not repeat it. The petitioner speaks first, airing their grievance against the accused, who will then attempt to refute that charge. After both have spoken, witnesses are brought forward by each party to present evidence for or against them. After that, any may speak their piece in a bid to help sway the council before they render their final decision."

"And I imagine we are the accused, and you will be the petitioner speaking against us?" I challenged.

"Not against you, no," Telman said. "The Circle of Life will decide what to do with you and your mysterious White Raven friend without my interference. I have grown to respect you, Wolf, as one fighting man to another, and I have no wish to speak ill of you." He flicked his gaze to Sarrey, his dark brown eyes now hard and cold. "I cannot say the same for that one."

"What about the right of appeal should the Circle of Life choose against me?" Sarrey demanded, not flinching under the

Bone Warrior's gaze. She lifted her chin in challenge. "Will I be given that at least, or is this all a forgone conclusion and just for show?"

Telman took a deep breath and didn't answer, looking annoyed.

"Well?" Sarrey snapped.

The Bone Warrior focused on me, ignoring the girl. "The accused will be allowed an appeal once the ruling has been given. But be warned, this is done rarely and cannot be taken lightly."

"And why is that?" Rorian asked. The scholar's hair and beard were starting to grow back, but his face and scalp were burnt bright red from the desert sun and peeling. I'm sure I looked no different than he did.

"Because if the accused loses," Telman grunted, looking as though he relished the thought. "Then her life is automatically forfeit."

"Oh," Rorian said soberly in response.

The scholar glanced at me, both of us sharing a silent message. I didn't know what charges would be brought against Sarrey and possibly us in that building. But getting the Circle of Life to understand what the Ravens were and the threat they posed was paramount, which I knew would not be easy considering their ingrown distrust and even hatred for the del Fante family.

I locked eyes with Telman. "I ask you, man to man, to set aside your differences with this girl and speak on her behalf. She is not her father and should not be treated as if she were. Sarrey del Fante will make a good queen, and I promise you whatever problems exist between the Kingdom of Temba and the *Falitari* can be fixed."

Telman's eyes widened before he started shaking his head in admiration. "I will say this about you, Wolf. You have a bigger ball-sack hanging between your legs than you do a brain rattling around in your head." Telman turned away from me, chuckling and still shaking his head as he crooked a finger without looking back.

"Follow me, and keep your mouths shut unless you are spoken to. Do that, and you might actually survive this."

The Hall of Justice was bigger on the inside than it looked, with a raised platform in the center surrounded by stone benches on three sides. Canvas awnings suspended by ropes hung above the platform, rolling and flapping softly in the light breeze as they threw shade over three women who sat side-by-side beneath them on carved wooden chairs. At least a hundred people sat among the benches, with soldiers in white capes flanking the platform to either side.

Two men stood at the platform's base several sword lengths apart, each in a large circle of painted red brick. The rest of the floor was faded yellow sandstone, making the rings stand out dramatically. Telman led us through the rows of benches while those seated began whispering to each other at our appearance. I caught more than one unfriendly eye fixated on Sarrey.

"Sit," Telman ordered us after he'd shooed away a man and his wife and two children sitting on the front bench facing the platform. The father gave the Bone Warrior a black look, though he didn't say anything as he hustled his family to another bench in the back.

Sarrey, Rorian, and I sat on the stone warmed by the sun and the previous occupants while Telman sat some distance away from us. The rest of his men took their places on the benches behind. I focused my attention on the platform and the women sitting there. The oldest of the three sat to my left and was clearly the Grandmother. Her skin was wrinkled, and her nose was long and pointed, accenting her sunken cheeks and weak chin. The Grandmother's hair was thin, gray, and hung to her waist in untidy strings. She sat hunched forward in her chair, balancing herself on a cane as the man in the circle to my right pleaded his case. The old woman kept her head turned sideways as if to hear better, and when she smiled at something the man said, she revealed nothing but toothless gums.

I guessed that the woman in the middle chair was in her thirties, wearing a worn green dress that showed its age. This would be the Matron. Her dark hair was cut short like a young boy's, which, combined with her round cheeks and pert nose sprinkled with freckles, gave her a youthful, mischievous look. The woman's eyes were kind and filled with sympathy as she listened to how the speaker's beloved dog had been trampled by the horse of the man standing in the circle to my left during a drunken race through the city streets. *This woman will be the key*, I thought instinctively. *Get her on our side right away and we could win this.*

The third woman, the Virgin, was no woman at all, I saw, but in fact, a child just on the cusp of adulthood. She was twelve or thirteen years old, dressed in a simple white cotton tunic and a green, full-length skirt. Her hair was light brown and braided into loops on either side of her head, and she wore a silver pendant around her neck. I felt my heart sink when I saw her eyes—which were cold with dislike—fixated not on the speaker, but on Sarrey del Fante. I knew by that look that we were in big trouble.

After the man who'd lost his dog had spoken, the accused spent several bumbling minutes trying to explain what had happened. All he did, though, was further cement in everyone's minds that he was an arrogant fool that blamed all those around him for his own faults. No witnesses or anyone else wished to speak after the man was mercifully done rambling, thank the gods, and after less than a minute of conferring, the council ruled in favor of the petitioner. Telman stood once the two men had stepped out of the circles and made his way to the left ring, stopping in the center.

"You have a grievance to bring to the council, *Rhana* Telman?" the Virgin asked. Her eyes were glowing with eagerness and anticipation, and I shared a worried look with Rorian.

"I do, Honored One," Telman said gravely. He turned and pointed at Sarrey. "With the full weight of history behind my words, I, *Rhana* Telman ar Hadeda of Dune's Peak, accuse Sarrey del Fante and all those who bear her name of murder and attempted genocide."

I heard gasps, followed moments later by enthusiastic clapping and cheering from the onlookers. The Matron frowned when it continued, and finally, losing patience, she signaled one of the soldiers to call for silence. Once the clamor had faded, the Matron cleared her throat. "This is very unorthodox, *Rhana*. Never has a member of the Royal Family stood in judgment before council."

"Then I think it's high time one did, Honored One," Telman replied with a bow.

"There are repercussions to consider here," the Grandmother interrupted in a voice cracking with age. She banged her cane against the floor for emphasis. "Repercussions that supersede simple revenge for past wrongs done young man. Temba has let us live in peace for many years, and this truth must be weighed carefully by sober thinking, not by sword rattling. For never forget that we are nothing but an irritating pimple on the asses of the Temba, no matter what we wish to believe—pimples that can be popped at their whim." She pointed at Sarrey, her thin arm shaking. "If we put this child on trial as you suggest, *Rhana*, then I think it is fair to say that the truth of our existence will change dramatically and for the worse." She glanced at her fellow council members. "Temba can march thousands of Lions this way at a moment's notice. More if they call for an assembly of the people. They can also assault our waters with an armada of ships we couldn't hope to hold back. Which means the scales of risk and reward can fall only one way in this, as any fool with eyes can see. For this reason, I believe this young man's petition should not be granted, and that the child should be returned unharmed before this gets any worse."

The old woman slumped back in her chair, clearly exhausted from her impassioned speech.

"Thank you, Grandmother," the Matron said thoughtfully. "As always, your words of wisdom cut through all else."

"Do they?" the Virgin responded angrily. She didn't bother to look at the old woman. "Words of caution said by someone with one foot in the grave." The young Virgin's eyes flashed. "A woman who has lived a long life and never felt the pain of a loved one being sent to the desert." The Virgin focused on Sarrey, and her upper lip curled in contempt. "I was born in Temba under the cruel, iron rule of the del Fantes, so I know more than anyone here what they are like. My mother and father were poor, and they occasionally had to take food without paying for it so our family could eat. One day my mother was caught stealing a pear in the market, and for this *terrible crime*, she was sentenced to the Waste of Bones."

I saw Sarrey lower her head in dismay out of the corner of my eye, and I reached over and took hold of her hand in support, squeezing it.

"My father was devastated by the unjust ruling," the Virgin continued. "And rather than let my mother go alone to face the unknown by herself, he chose to stay by her side, abandoning his family." The Virgin wiped at her eyes. "Neither of them were ever seen again. My older brother was so enraged that he began spending his days in King's Square beneath the Yellow Palace, shouting his hatred up at its mighty walls. That lasted a week, until one day, he was charged with mischief and sentenced to the desert. I never saw him again, either. I was young and alone, filled with despair, so one night, I slipped through the side gates and ran out into the desert to be with them all." The girl's thin shoulders shook with emotion as tears rolled down her cheeks.

I thought of the statue outside and the crying young virgin there, wondering if it was an omen somehow.

"But the desert sands chose not to take me as I'd hoped," the Virgin sniffed through her tears. "And two days later, I was found by the Bone Warriors and brought here. I didn't understand why at the time I was allowed to live, but now I do." She pointed at

Sarrey. "And that is to ensure this woman pays for the crimes of her bloodline."

Sarrey stood then, and without asking for permission, she stepped boldly into the right circle. "I am sorry for your loss, Honored One," she said. "I know what it means to lose the ones you love, and I grieve for you and everyone who has lost people to the desert sands." Sarrey lifted her chin defiantly. "But sometimes hard choices needed to be made—choices that seemed right at the moment, but when examined through the wisdom of time, do not now. I am not responsible for the laws that caused these deaths, but I am in a position to see that they end. So, I stand before you and give you my word that the old ways will not continue. No longer will people be sent to the desert to die, and no longer will the Temba and *Falitari* be at odds over it."

"And that makes everything better?" the Virgin asked with a sneer. "All you do is speak big words that bear no fruit." She looked at her fellow council members. "This woman tells us what we wish to hear, but I guarantee the moment she returns to Temba, her father will renege on whatever she promises. The del Fantes always do. They cannot be trusted."

I blinked in surprise at the young girl's hate-filled words, realizing that the council still didn't know what had happened in Temba. I glanced at Telman, who was smiling to himself. The Bone Warrior was well aware of what had occurred and was clearly biding his time to use that news to its greatest effect.

"You would start a war over this foolishness, child?" the Grandmother asked wearily.

"This war has been coming for hundreds of years," the Virgin shot back. "You've just been asleep and haven't been paying attention. But now, for the first time since this city was founded, we have the upper hand over the Temba because of this girl. I say we use it."

"And then what?" a voice shouted from behind us. People turned as a tall, distinguished man with an elegant gray beard wearing a rich black cape over a brown tunic and black trousers approached. "What will you do then, Honored Ones, once you try this child? Will you storm Temba with your paltry army afterward, or will you cower behind your walls waiting for the inevitable retribution?"

"Your presence was not requested here, Vizier Banta," the Virgin said sternly, looking annoyed now.

The tall man strode toward Sarrey, putting his arm around her as the girl sagged against him in relief. "And now I see why, Honored One." He let his angry gaze drift from one council member to the next. "What you are proposing here is outrageous. The king will be infuriated when he hears of it. Is that truly what you want?"

"Your king is dead," Telman spat. I could tell he and Banta had little liking for each other. More gasps arose from the onlookers while the councilors all registered their surprise.

"Utter nonsense," Banta snorted. He glanced down at Sarrey, who was looking up at him. I saw a silent message pass between them before the tall man grimaced, understanding setting in.

"Honored Ones," Telman said. "A new dawn has broken, for Alba del Fante is dead just as I claim, murdered along with his wife by members of a sect known as the White Ravens." The Bone Warrior pointed to Rorian. "Men like that one." Many eyes turned to Rorian then, examining his white robe with curiosity. "These Ravens have taken control of the city," Telman continued. "A del Fante child still sits on the throne, but she is nothing more than a toddler and, in truth, is but a convenient figurehead. The real power in Temba lies with a man named Muwa, who has been designated regent."

The Virgin's eyes turned shrewd at that news. She gestured to Sarrey. "But this one is the eldest daughter and by rights should be queen. Is that not true, *Rhana*?"

"Yes, Honored One," Telman agreed. "We intercepted her trying to escape from the Lions. It is my understanding that they were quite eager to remove her head from her shoulders. I thought the girl's value could not be overstated under the current circumstances, so I returned here with her so that you, in your wisdom, can decide what must be done."

"I applaud you for your rational thinking, *Rhana*," the Virgin said in approval. "Your loyalty will not be forgotten."

"And what of this other man, then, lord?" the Matron asked, fixing her eyes on me. "Who is he in all of this confusion?"

"Lord Hadrack of Corwick, Honored One," the Bone Warrior answered. Telman turned to smile at me. "The very leader of those men from Ganderland that the council imprisoned in the city dungeons just last week."

Chapter 29: By Land And Sea

I was on my feet in an instant, ignoring the Bone Warriors behind me, who rose with a clatter of armor and drew their swords. I felt the sharp kiss of cold steel on both sides of my neck moments later, but I ignored it, fighting to contain my growing anger. "Where are they?" I demanded. "Where are my men? What have you done with them?"

The Matron studied me with interest before finally she waved off the Bone Warriors. I felt the weight of their blades recede as the Matron gestured to the circle where Banta and Sarrey stood. "Please, lord, step forward and be recognized."

I did as the woman asked, fighting to control my emotions. I realized that screaming and yelling at these people would do little good and would certainly not help my men. I needed to be smarter about things and try to understand what had happened to them. I smoothed my features and walked into the ring, giving Sarrey a whisper of thanks when she squeezed my forearm in support.

"My apologies, Honored One," I said, inclining my head to the Matron. I nodded to the Grandmother as well, who regarded me steadily, then to the Virgin, who stared down her nose at me with wary suspicion. "My apologies to all of you. I hadn't known the fate of my men until just now, and I lost my head for a moment hearing that they were so near. I meant no disrespect by my outburst, and I assure you it won't happen again."

"I understand," the Matron said kindly. "Your affection and genuine concern for those under your command are as obvious as it is admirable, lord. We are all human, and no harm has been done by demonstrating that fact."

"Thank you," I said gratefully. I cleared my throat. "May I ask why my men have been incarcerated, Honored One?"

"That is something of a rather delicate matter, Lord Hadrack," the Grandmother answered for the Matron. She leaned forward on her cane, an expression of disapproval evident on her weathered face. "Quite delicate, actually."

"I don't understand," I said, for truly I didn't.

The Grandmother sighed. "Your men arrived in Sandhold recently on that hulking black vessel out in the harbor, which we were told was damaged in a battle with the Lions. Our shipwrights, in good faith, agreed to facilitate repairs to said ship—for a fair price, of course."

I took a deep breath as I tried to puzzle through what that meant. "Do you mean to say that my men sailed here in *Spearfish*, not *Sea-Wolf*?"

The Grandmother blinked at me. "I do not know what a Seawolf is, lord," she finally said. "But yes, your men arrived here in the vessel known as *Spearfish*."

"Were there Cardians aboard her?"

The old woman frowned, then leaned toward the Matron and whispered something to her. She sat back in her chair after receiving a reply, apparently satisfied. "There were not, lord."

I nodded, trying to comprehend, though in hindsight, I suppose it should have been obvious to me by then—yet it wasn't. "So," I said, thinking incorrectly that I understood the gist of the problem. "Once the repairs were completed, my men couldn't pay. Is that the issue? If so, I assure you, Honored Ones, that once I return—"

"Payment was not the issue," the Virgin snapped. "They had gold aplenty, which for the time being has been confiscated, as has that ship."

I pursed my lips as I thought about what that meant. Where had the gold come from? Lord Boudin? I discarded that idea immediately since the last I'd heard, the Cardian had used up all his coin to pay The Fisherman for the forged codex. But if the gold had not come from him, then who? And more to the point, why had my men sailed here on *Spearfish* and not *Sea-Wolf*? Where was my ship? I shook my head at the mystery, desperate for more information.

"I am confused, Honored Ones," I said. "If my men could pay for the repairs, why are they now in prison?"

"Because there was an incident of grave indecency committed by one among them that could not be ignored," the Grandmother continued, once again giving me a disapproving look. "We have yet to rule on this man's fate, but until then, we felt it appropriate to have all of your crew locked up where they can do no more harm."

"What happened?" I asked, almost afraid to know.

The Grandmother gestured for the Matron to answer, and the younger woman fixed her kind eyes on me. "The daughter of one of our most distinguished *Rhanas* was accosted in a tavern by one of your men." I groaned at that, knowing instinctively that she was talking about Baine. The little bastard could never resist a nice pair of tits. "This daughter was betrothed to another," the Matron continued, "with the clear understanding that her maidenhood would remain unbroken until her wedding night. That, unfortunately, is no longer the case, which has caused a rather vigorous disagreement between the two parties. One insists that the marriage continue regardless, while the other rejects that notion, describing the girl as *damaged goods*. Both fathers have vowed revenge against the perpetrator, and thusly, council decided it would be wise to remove him and his companions from sight until judgment and proper compensation can be determined."

I rubbed my hands over my eyes wearily, silently cursing Baine and his wandering cock. It wasn't the first time that I'd done so, and I was pretty sure it wouldn't be the last, either. "May I see them, Honored Ones?"

"Perhaps in time," the Grandmother conceded. "But first, there are other matters to attend to." She fixed her eyes on Sarrey. "We still have not decided on a course of action for this one."

"*Rhana* Telman," the Virgin said, turning to the Bone Warrior.

"Yes, Honored One?"

"If we were to contact this Regent Muwa and offer to return the Princess for a substantial ransom, would—"

"Queen," Sarrey cut in defiantly. "I am the rightful Queen of Temba, which is something that you'd best remember."

The two girls locked eyes with mutual dislike, neither backing down, until finally, the Matron cleared her throat, breaking the stalemate. "Your claim to the Temba throne is not in question here, Your Majesty. That is a matter between you and others. What is in question is whether or not the petition brought to council regarding your family's crimes against the *Falitari* has merit."

"You are playing with fire, Honored Ones," Banta growled. He stabbed a finger at the platform. "If this council insists on going through with this farce, then I assure you your people will suffer the consequences."

"We are here to do what is right, regardless of threats, Vizier Banta," the Matron said, though I detected reluctance in her voice. "That is what we were chosen to do, and that is what we will always strive to do."

I sensed that the Matron truly wanted no part of this and would side with us, though she was doing her best to appear neutral. The Virgin was a forgone conclusion the opposite way, and I knew any attempt to convince her otherwise would be a waste of time, leaving the Grandmother as the deciding vote. The old woman had argued against trying Sarrey right up until she'd learned of the coup in Temba. Now though, I felt she was sitting precariously on the fence, waiting to be swayed one way or the other. I needed to push her our way. "May I speak, Honored One?" I asked, focusing specifically on the old woman.

The Grandmother nodded, leaning forward on her cane and turning her head sideways. "You may."

"Whatever grievances your people have against the Temba, justified or not, must be set aside if you wish your city to survive. The White Ravens may not seem like a threat to you now, but I assure you they are. The only hope this city has is helping Queen Sarrey regain her throne so that together, we can eradicate them like the disease they are. If you do not help, I promise the Ravens will eventually use the might of Temba to crush you and bend your people to their will."

The Virgin laughed shrilly. "What nonsense is this? The del Fantes have always been our biggest threat. Not some silly bald men in white robes preaching foolishness that no one believes."

I ignored the girl, keeping my eyes on the wrinkled old woman. "You have seen much in your life, Grandmother," I said respectfully. I felt encouraged when the woman nodded while a shadow of past pains flickered in her eyes. "But nothing you or any of us has seen can compare to what the White Ravens plan for our world."

"And what exactly is that, lord?" the Matron asked softly.

"They call it the Enlightenment," I said.

"That hardly sounds menacing," the Virgin cut in with an impatient snort. "Maybe we could all use some enlightenment."

The Grandmother banged her cane against the floor in irritation. "Let the man speak, child," she rasped. "Better to be silent and thought a fool than to open your mouth and remove all doubt." The Virgin glared at the old woman with her eyes flashing outrage, but she said nothing more.

I nodded my appreciation to the Grandmother. "The White Ravens have sent agents to all the major kingdoms in the north, intending to infiltrate them and spread their lies just as they did in Temba."

"But they're not here in Sandhold, now are they?" the Virgin pointed out, ignoring the Grandmother's obvious annoyance. "So why should we care?"

"They're not here because they didn't need to be—until now," I responded.

Sarrey had told me Temba was the biggest and most powerful of the many city-states on the southern continent. But it was nothing compared to the vast kingdoms of the north like Ganderland, Cardia, and Parnuthia. I knew that's why the Ravens had targeted the city first, using it as a testing ground to see how their strategy worked before trying to take on much bigger prey. Now I just had to convince the Circle of Life of that. I spent the next ten minutes explaining my thoughts to the council while the Matron and Grandmother listened attentively to my every word. The Virgin just toyed with her fingernails, looking bored.

When I was done, the Matron took a deep breath as she sat back in her chair. "The picture you paint is not pretty, Lord Hadrack."

"No, it's not," I agreed.

"There is something that I find quite curious in all this, lord," the Grandmother said. She flicked her eyes to Rorian, who remained on the bench, watched by the Bone Warriors. "Where, exactly, did this silly notion of a singular god come from? We all know there are two supreme gods, The Mother, and The Father, so why has such an obvious fabrication been embraced so readily by so many?"

"Some people are easily swayed, Honored One," I said evasively.

The old woman chuckled, the sound coming out dry and raspy. "There is truth in that, lord," she said. "My father told me long ago that for every wise man the world produces, it spits out a thousand idiots and fools." The Grandmother tapped a bent finger on her cane as she studied me. Finally, she nodded to herself. "There is something you aren't telling us, lord. I can sense it."

"I have been completely honest with you," I said carefully.

"Perhaps," the old woman muttered. "But you don't have to lie to not tell the truth. When you speak of this One True God, your words lack conviction, as if something troubles you there. Tell me why?"

I paused, caught off guard by the woman's uncanny insight. Only Rorian and I, of all of us here, knew there was actually some truth to the White Ravens' claims, and I silently cursed myself for somehow giving that away. I struggled to think of something to say that might repair the damage done.

"Lord Hadrack?" the Matron said. She was studying me intently. "You ask much from us, and it disturbs me to think that you might be actively deceiving us somehow."

I nodded, knowing by the look in her eyes that I was quickly losing her support. I couldn't allow that to happen. I glanced over my shoulder at Rorian, who shrugged. A big help he was. "There is something else I have not mentioned yet, Honored Ones," I finally admitted reluctantly. "But it will take some time to tell of it."

"How much time?" the Virgin grunted in obvious irritation. "This has already gone on far longer than it should have. We are here to validate a petition put forth by *Rhana* Telman and nothing more."

I spread my arms, committed now. "What is time compared to the truth, Honored One?"

The three women conferred quietly, then sat back in their chairs. The Virgin's features were twisted in anger, but she held her tongue.

"You may proceed, Lord Hadrack," the Matron said. "We will listen and judge if what you say has merit to the problem at hand."

I bowed my head. "Thank you. I would humbly request, though, that what I am about to tell you be for the ears of the council and no one else."

The Matron thought about that, then she nodded. "Very well." She motioned to a soldier. "Clear the gallery and have your men wait outside on the steps."

"But, Honored One—" the soldier began to protest.

"That was an order, Captain," the Matron said firmly. "*Rhana* Telman will stay, so we are in no danger of being murdered." She turned her eyes to me. "Are we, Lord Hadrack?"

"No, Honored One," I said. "Most certainly not."

Ten minutes later, only Telman, Rorian, Vizier Banta, Sarrey, the three councilors, and I remained inside the Hall of Justice. I spent the next several hours telling them everything about the original codex with its missing pages and how it had begun a civil war in Ganderland. I knew the council were aware of that already, for who wasn't? But I wanted the sequence of events to be clear in their minds. Next, I told them about how we'd learned of a second, intact copy of the codex and my search for it on Mount Halas. This they clearly had not known. I told them about Waldin's cave and how I'd found his journal there but not the codex—though I didn't mention Sabina at all. There was no need to go into all of that. I described in detail how a man named Rorian—the same man who now sat with us dressed as a White Raven—had finally located the codex in the land of the Piths and had brought it to me on the banks of the White Rock near Land's Edge, ending the war with the savage warriors.

"You mean he's not really a White Raven?" the Matron asked in surprise at that point, gesturing to Rorian.

"No, Honored One. He came south on his own to find the Eye of God, who had his family murdered months ago. Rorian only posed as a Raven to learn where that man is located, intending to exact revenge on him. That's why he was with the Lions when *Rhana* Telman found us."

"Oh my," the Grandmother whispered, looking suddenly small and frail. "This is all quite irregular."

"And where is this Eye of God, lord?" the Matron asked, staying focused.

"The Edge of the World, Honored One," I answered. "That's why I need my ship—" I paused. "That's why I need that ship in your harbor and my crew, so Rorian and I can go kill the bastard and end this. But first, we need your help to get Temba back."

"There is one thing you seem to have left out in all this fantasy of yours, lord," the Virgin said. I noted that her tone was slightly more civil now, though I could still see anger and resentment in her eyes.

"Which is, Honored One?"

"What exactly this codex said that you claim has caused so much trouble to so many."

I took a deep breath, having expected that question sooner or later. I glanced over my shoulder at Rorian, who sat with his arms crossed, a frown on his face. He shook his head slightly when he saw my eyes on him. I looked away, forgetting about him as I formed my thoughts. I'd told the Circle of Life the truth about everything that had happened so far, but now that was about to change.

I cleared my throat. "The codex revealed that the White Ravens are right about their god," I said bluntly. I lifted a hand as gasps of amazement arose from the three women on the platform. Sarrey grabbed my other wrist and shook me vigorously, demanding to know what I meant, but I dared not look at her, afraid by doing so that I'd be unable to go through with the lie. "They are right and wrong at the same time, Honored Ones," I added.

"Explain," the Grandmother said with a frown.

"The White Ravens have twisted the words written in the codex to their own ends," I said.

"Twisted, how?" the Matron asked.

"They claim that the One True God is the only god and that The Mother and The Father are fabrications, but that is untrue. Having read the codex from end to end, I can tell you that all three do exist."

"Three gods, not two or one?" the Grandmother asked, looking baffled.

"Yes, Honored One," I answered. "The Mother and The Father, as well as a third being known by many different names. The Piths call him the Master, which I suppose is as good a name as any for us to use." I glanced at Sarrey's horrified face, then at Vizier Banta, who was staring at me with a mixture of shock and suspicion. I focused back on the Circle of Life, the completion of the lie ready on my lips. I had no idea at that moment that my words spoken in haste and need would forever reshape how we viewed religion in our world. I just wanted Sarrey to survive the day and for my friends and men to be freed. This seemed like the best way to make that happen. "Each god is equal in all things, Honored Ones," I continued. I pictured Rorian stiffening behind me at my words, for he knew as I did that the Master was the father of the First Pair and stood above them. I forged ahead anyway, undaunted. "There are also three realms, not two as we've always believed—Above, Below, and Beyond." On inspiration, I added. "These places are known as the Unified Realms, Honored Ones."

Silence filled the room for several minutes until, finally, the Grandmother cleared her throat. I never got a chance to hear what she had to say, though, because just then, a soldier appeared, holding his sheathed sword down so it wouldn't slap against his legs as he hurried toward the platform.

"Forgive me, Honored Ones," the man said, out of breath. I recognized him as the Captain from earlier.

"Yes, what is it, Brader?" the Matron asked, still looking stunned from what she'd just heard.

"A fleet of Temba ships has just been sighted off Syme's Reach. They'll be here tomorrow by midmorning at the latest."

The three women on the platform shared worried looks. "How many ships, Captain?" the Grandmother asked.

"At least forty, Honored One," the soldier responded. "Maybe more." He hesitated. "There is something else, I'm afraid. Our scouts have also detected a large force heading this way through the desert. I have yet to receive verification, but it can only be the Lions. It would seem, Honored Ones, that the city is about to come under attack from both land and sea.

Chapter 30: The King Of Temba

"It's to be war and death, then," the Grandmother said dismally, breaking the appalled silence. She focused on me, her old eyes moist with emotion. "You were right all along, Lord Hadrack."

"I wish I were not, Honored One," I said humbly. "But now that we know the Lions are coming, I would ask that you release my men immediately."

"And why would we do that?" the Virgin demanded hotly. "They will stay right where they are." She lifted her chin, her nostrils flaring. "For all we know, you orchestrated this entire thing—you and that conniving del Fante bitch!"

"That will be enough, Annamay," the Matron snapped, losing her temper for the first time by using the child's name, which I gathered was frowned upon. The Matron turned to me. "Forgive her, lord. We are all just overwhelmed by this distressing news."

I stepped forward several paces, stopping only when Telman and the soldier put hands to sword hilts in an obvious warning. I looked at the Bone Warrior, shook my head that he'd think me so foolish, and then focused on the Matron. I pointed in the direction of the harbor. "Give me my men and that Cardian vessel out there, and I promise you I will deal with those ships before they ever get close to the city."

The Matron frowned. "How, lord?"

"I don't know yet, Honored One," I answered truthfully. "But I have some of the keenest military minds and experienced sailors among my crew. Together, we will find a way."

"You mean you would fight for us, lord?" the Grandmother asked in surprise. "Not sail away?"

"I would," I said firmly. "The Ravens are my enemies just as much as yours."

"Why even consider it?" the Virgin asked, her voice filled with scorn and suspicion. "You know we are hopelessly outnumbered."

"I have been outnumbered many times before, Honored One," I answered with a shrug. "Yet, here I am." I motioned to Sarrey. "Besides, I know that's what the queen would want me to do."

A soldier abruptly appeared from outside, looking nervous as he motioned for Captain Brader to join him. "If you will excuse me, Honored Ones," the captain said with a bow before heading away. He conferred with the soldier for several long minutes while we waited, then returned, looking bemused. "There has been an odd development, Honored Ones. It seems we have two separate groups attempting to cross the desert, not one. The first has a lead of twenty or so miles, while a much larger force follows behind in their wake."

"Could this first group be an advance party?" I asked. I was already thinking of defensive options as I reviewed what little I'd seen of the city and the terrain outside of it.

Captain Brader hesitated at my abrupt question, then at a nod from the Matron, answered me. "It would seem not, lord. My scouts say the group is made up of men, both old and young, as well as many women and children."

"Are there Lions among them?"

"Yes, lord. The scouts saw their armor and shields."

"What about horses?"

"Some, not a lot."

"How many people are we talking about?"

Captain Brader shrugged. "Anywhere between a thousand to two thousand, lord."

"And the ones following?"

"Early estimates put them at five to seven thousand—all fighting men."

I pursed my lips at that formidable number. "Horses?"

"Perhaps five hundred, no more."

"And you said they were about twenty miles behind the first group?"

"Yes, lord."

"Are they gaining ground on them?" Captain Brader simply nodded as I stroked my beard, thinking. "Do you believe these people are the hare and the soldiers behind are the fox?" I finally asked.

Captain Brader grimaced. "That would be my guess, lord, yes."

"But why flee into the desert at all?" I asked. "Why not take the road around where the going is easier and safer?"

"I imagine they knew they would be quickly caught that way and hoped their pursuers would not follow them, lord."

"That makes sense," I said, impressed by the man's efficient manner and sharp mind. "When will the first group arrive at the city?"

"Tomorrow morning around first light if they march the rest of today and all night, lord."

"Do you see that happening?"

The captain shook his head. "Highly unlikely, lord. These people have already spent many days in the desert to have gotten this far, which is no easy task. There are women, children, and the elderly among them. The Waste of Bones can be unforgiving to the strongest of men, let alone the weak and infirm. Even if the survivors have sufficient food and water, which I doubt, they will be exhausted and slowed by stragglers. I predict most, if not all, will become easy prey for those coming from behind."

"So you believe they will be caught long before they can reach us?"

"With the information I have at present, I think it's a virtual guarantee, lord."

I turned to the council. "We need to send horses and wagons out right now so we can bring those people inside our walls," I said.

"Why?" the Virgin snorted. "Let them face the desert sands like so many of us have had to do because of del Fante laws. Why should we care about their fate?"

The Grandmother sighed as she leaned forward on her cane to stare at the Virgin. "You are a cold-hearted child," she said, shaking her head sadly. The old woman turned her head and focused back on me. "But even so, she's not wrong, lord. Bringing Lions into Sandhold will not sit well with the people and could cause a mutiny. It's not worth the risk."

I rolled my eyes in frustration. "The real enemy could be inside your walls soon enough," I grunted. "And once they are, they will sack this city, raping and killing everything in sight. Is that what you want?" I pointed north toward the Waste of Bones. "There are people out there who can help us fight. Hundreds and hundreds that can take up swords to defend your walls."

"Old men, women, and children," the Virgin said scornfully. "What good will they be? All they'll do is drain our resources and cause nothing but trouble. Better the desert takes them."

"Every sword will count in this fight, Honored One, believe me," I replied, trying to control my temper. The hatred inside this little bitch went deep, and trying to get past it seemed an impossible task. "Besides," I added in a calm tone. "There are Lions loyal to the queen among them by the sounds of things. These men can fight, and we could use their experience."

"Bone Warriors will not fight side by side with Lions," Telman rumbled. "We have spent our entire lives trying to kill them, not befriend them."

"Then you are all fools, and your city will fall because of it," I responded bluntly. "Now is not the time to worry about old grudges, now is the time to unite into something better before it's too late. Queen Sarrey has already indicated her willingness to do that, so what are you waiting for?"

The three women shifted in their chairs uncomfortably until, finally, the Grandmother cleared her throat. "Even if we were willing to go along with this, lord, I told you that the people will not react well. There will be rebellion within our walls if we let in these Lions. The loathing the *Falitari* feel for the del Fantes runs deep, and I fear even with our blessing, it will go badly. It would be best, I think, if those people remain outside our walls as suggested. I do not relish it, lord, but I see no other—"

"What if I abdicate, then?" Sarrey suddenly said, surprising us all. I could only stare at her in astonishment as she continued, "You state that the issue between our peoples is the name del Fante, so let's remove that obstacle. If the Circle of Life will swear here and now that you will save those people in the desert and let them in, then I will renounce my claim to the throne in favor of another."

I opened my mouth to protest, then clamped it shut at a sharp look of warning from Sarrey. I knew what she was doing and hated the thought of it, though I had to admit the logic behind it was brilliant. By abdicating her right to rule, Sarrey would undermine the only argument against allying with us in one fell swoop. It was an incredibly brave and selfless thing to do, and I felt nothing but admiration and respect for the girl.

"I think this idea is extremely rash, Your Highness," Banta said. "There are other ways that—"

"There are no other ways," Sarrey snapped. "The sins of my family have finally come home to roost, Vizier, and now is the time to take responsibility for them. That is what I intend to do if allowed by this council."

I studied the three women intently as the full import of what Sarrey was suggesting began to sink in. The Grandmother was sitting back in her chair, mulling over Sarrey's words with her lips twisted in a slight smile. The Matron looked surprised, yet thoughtful, while the Virgin was leaning forward, her eyes fixated intently on Sarrey as if afraid she'd misheard her.

"Can this actually be done?" the Virgin finally asked. "By the laws of Temba?"

"It's not without precedent," Sarrey replied. "My great uncle Hortan del Fante abdicated in favor of his younger brother, Felian del Fante."

"Hortan del Fante was an eighteen-year-old halfwit who didn't know his ass from a hole in the ground," the Grandmother snorted. "Hardly a prime example, Your Highness. Besides, the lad still abdicated for another del Fante, your great grandfather, ensuring the bloodline continued."

"Which I'm not intending to do," Sarrey responded in a firm voice. "Agree with my proposal, and you have my word that there will be a new name and bloodline on the throne in Temba from hereafter. One that will work in harmony with the *Falitari*."

The Matron pursed her lips as she thought. "And what do you say to this, *Rhana* Telman?" she finally asked.

The Bone Warrior fixed his hawkish gaze on Sarrey as he clasped and unclasped his big hand on the hilt of his sword. "It seems like a fair bargain, Honored Ones," he said grudgingly. "One that I believe the people would approve of. But if we intend to do this thing, it must be now. We are wasting time, and much needs to be done to prepare for the coming attack."

The Matron turned to the Grandmother. "What say you?"

"I think the merit of this idea cannot be ignored, so I say yes," the Grandmother answered with a nod. "And may the gods watch over us all."

The Matron turned next to the Virgin. "And you, child?"

The Virgin hesitated, playing with her fingers as she thought before finally, her eyes hardened with suspicion. "I say, nay. Something smells about this, and I don't trust her."

"I see," the Matron said, not looking surprised. "So, the decision falls to me, then." She sighed and placed her hands in her lap, then finally smiled at Sarrey. I knew by the kind and hopeful look in her eyes that we'd just won—at least for now. "We, the Circle of Life, accept your terms, Your Highness."

"Thank you, Honored One," Sarrey said, lowering her head humbly.

"Now that the decision has been made, child," the Grandmother said, sounding amused. "Who, exactly, will you be naming as your successor?" I felt the old woman's eyes settle on me, the amusement on her withered features even more evident now. She knew what Sarrey intended to do, I realized.

"I name Lord Hadrack of Corwick as the new King of Temba," Sarrey stated without any hesitation. "Long may he reign!"

An hour later, the entire city of Sandhold was abuzz with activity, with hoarse shouts competing with the constant ringing of hammers, anvils, and the ripping of saws that echoed off the walls as people prepared for the expected siege to come. Riders on fast horses were already on their way to the many Bone Warrior holdings sprinkled throughout the desert, recalling them to aid in defense of the city. Every available wagon had been sent north into the desert to bring the fleeing Temba back safely. Carpenters and their apprentices worked frantically to shore up walls and fortifications the best they could, while butchers slaughtered cattle and sheep by the droves to drape their hides over vulnerable wooden roofs. The terrified bleating and cries of the doomed creatures only helped to further the atmosphere of apprehension that had settled over the city.

Women and children weren't idle during this time, either, I saw, with all but cripples, babes, or the infirm busy hustling livestock that had escaped the axe into shelters, filling water buckets, fletching arrows, or a thousand other tasks that sent them scurrying in all directions like busy bees. The frantic activity reminded me greatly of the siege of Gasterny Garrison—the first one—and I dearly hoped the result would not end up the same as it had then. I followed Captain Brader and an honor guard of three through those crowded streets, heading for a squat stone building where my men were being held. My heart was racing at the prospect of seeing my friends again, though it was tainted by the knowledge that I was now a king—albeit a very reluctant one.

I'd taken Sarrey aside where no one could overhear us after the official abdication, and I thought again about our brief conversation before I'd left with Captain Brader.

"Are you sure this is the right thing to do?" I'd asked the girl, still shocked by my sudden and unexpected rise in station.

Sarrey looked up at me with a coy smile, amusement in her eyes. "Why wouldn't I be, Your Highness?"

I frowned at that, hugely uncomfortable with the title. "You know I don't want this," I whispered.

Sarrey laughed, looking relaxed as she shook her head in mock sympathy. "I do know that. So who better to hold the throne than you, Your Highness? For truly, has there ever been a man more respected worldwide for both his fighting prowess and intellect than you? The Bone Warriors and Lions will follow you to the ends of the world once they get to know you as I have, Your Highness. Mark my words."

"Call me Your Highness one more time," I growled, "and I swear I'll put you over my knee right here."

Sarrey smiled infuriatingly. "Well, I have to call you something, don't I?"

"Lord will still suffice," I muttered. "Or better yet, just call me Hadrack."

"Then lord it is, lord," Sarrey said with a giggle.

I sighed. "You're taking this rather well," I said, starting to feel suspicious. "Why is that? It's not every day one loses a throne."

Captain Brader and his men approached us then, and I turned to join them just as Sarrey put her hand on my arm, stalling me. "Who says I lost the throne, lord?" she whispered with that coy smile back once again. I stared at her in confusion for a moment before she added, "I promised the Circle of Life that anyone bearing the name del Fante would never rule Temba again, and I meant that." She grinned widely. "But I don't recall promising not to marry a king named Corwick once this is all over with, now did I?"

I shook my head at the memory as I followed Captain Brader up the stone stairs of the prison, torn between my feelings of admiration for the girl and anger at her assumption that our union would still happen. Now that I was King of the Temba by her hand, it meant that I didn't need Sarrey anymore to gain command of the city's powerful armies and rich treasury, which perhaps the girl had overlooked in all her clever maneuvering. But could I do that to her? Could I spurn Sarrey so callously after all we'd been through together?

I thought suddenly of Sabina, remembering how badly my rejection had hurt her, though I still believed that it was justified to this day. Was I soon to do the same thing to another young girl—one who had done me no harm and had been nothing but kind to me? Things had moved so quickly that I wasn't sure of my intent just yet, but I had to admit I was tempted to renounce our agreement, which on one level, horrified me, and another, delighted me.

If only Jebido could see me now, plotting like some craven Cardian bureaucrat, I thought bleakly.

I'd given Sarrey my word that we would marry to form an alliance together, but that pact had been for mutually beneficial reasons—at least, it had been from my end, at any rate. Now, though, I'd just been handed a way out of the agreement, one which would permit me to remain faithful to Shana's memory and allow the besieged Kingdom of Ganderland to benefit—if I chose to take it. But that meant rejecting Sarrey, though I knew doing so would crush her and end our friendship, which was something that I greatly valued. I'd never been a political animal, more suited to swinging a sword in open battle than sparring with twisted words in court, and I was in a foul mood by the time I'd climbed the stairs with my escorts.

"This way, Your Highness," Captain Brader said, cutting into my thoughts as he ushered me through a doorway guarded by two soldiers.

I nodded, trying to shake off the blackness I felt inside as we entered a small room where two men sat around a square table playing dice. The men jumped to their feet at our appearance, looking surprised. I noticed a stone staircase off to one side leading down into semi-darkness, lit by a weak torch on the wall halfway down. I could also hear the sounds of someone singing rising from the depths, and despite my mood, I couldn't help but smile, recognizing Putt's distinctive deep voice.

"Your men are in the cells below, Your Highness," Captain Brader added. "Shall I lead the way?"

"No," I grunted. I decided I wanted to see my men on my own. "Where are the keys?"

Captain Brader snapped his fingers, and with a metallic jingle, one of the men at the table unhooked a set of iron keys from a belt around his waist and offered them to me.

"I'll take it from here," I said, accepting the keys. "You can go, Captain. Thank you."

"As you wish, Your Highness," Captain Brader said, inclining his head. He motioned to the men at the table. "Elres and Finny will be here if you require assistance."

"Understood," I muttered as I headed down the stairs.

I paused to take up the torch from its wall sconce, then continued, finally stopping at the base of the stairs as I looked around. I wrinkled my nose at the smell of piss, shit, and sweat. A narrow corridor rose in front of me, dark and foreboding, and from somewhere ahead, I heard water dripping between the pauses the singer took. I hefted the torch, then started walking, focusing on Putt's voice. The darkness was absolute, my feeble torch seemingly about to be swallowed up by it at any moment. Weak firelight surrounded me like a halo, flitting across the stone walls and high ceiling above me as I progressed. My footsteps rang out loudly against the floor, and as I neared the end of the corridor, the singing abruptly stopped.

"Well, it's about time, you heartless bastards!" I heard somebody grumble from ahead. I grinned, for it was Jebido. "We haven't eaten anything since yesterday."

"The last time I saw you, old man," I said. "You could have stood to miss a meal or two."

"By the gods!" Jebido gasped as voices I recognized called out in sudden hope. "Hadrack, is that really you I hear over there?"

"In the flesh," I said with a chuckle as I moved into a large room, revealing several small pens lined with steel bars crammed with men to either side of me.

Cheers erupted then as the men pressed themselves against the bars, thrusting their hands out to me. I saw Tyris and Putt, Berwin, Fitz, Baine, and Jebido, and I laughed with delight as I hurried forward to grasp Jebido's outreached hand.

"I knew you were alive!" Jebido cried out, pounding his other fist on the bars. "I just knew it!"

"You never give up on me, old friend," I said, choking back emotion.

I could see tears running down Jebido's weathered cheeks, and I felt wetness in my own eyes as I squeezed his hand. Finally, I let him go, almost spun around as my men crowded to get to me, those that could slapping my shoulders and back in welcome. I met Baine's eyes where he stood next to Fitz, and he grinned at me sheepishly, lifting his hands to his sides. I knew it was his way of apologizing, and I could only smile back, my anger about what he'd done gone, replaced with relief that all those I cared so deeply for were alive and well.

"How are you all?" I called, having to shout to be heard.

"Better now, my lord!" Tyris cried. I noticed his left eye was covered by a dirty cloth wrapped around his head, and I frowned, examining my men closer. I saw many of them were sporting wounds, though none seemed serious enough for real concern, thank the gods.

"Are you here to free us, my lord?" Berwin called out. "Or have you just come down here for the sights?"

"Actually, you bastard," I said with a laugh. "I thought this was a brothel. And I have to say I'm disappointed, because you lot are the ugliest whores I've ever seen." Men laughed and hooted as I lifted the keys I held and let them dangle musically. "But, since I'm here anyway, I guess I might as well let you dogs out." I grinned. "Besides, lads, we've got some fighting to do today!"

Chapter 31: Spearfish

"She's a fine ship, my lord," Putt said. "The Cardians can't fight worth a damn, but by the gods, they sure do know how to build themselves a proper boat."

I nodded in agreement as the former outlaw and I finally finished our tour of *Spearfish*. The ship was indeed impressive, just as Putt had claimed, and I was glad of it, for I would need everything she had to give me very soon. Now, done with the inspection, I leaned against the portside gunwale on the lower deck and crossed my arms over my chest while the crew bustled around me as we prepared to set sail. I took a deep breath of satisfaction, enjoying the late afternoon breeze as I let my eyes wander over the Cardian vessel, dominated by the new, sparkling white mast overhead. Wolf's Head hung on my hip where it belonged, and my brother's Pair Stone hung around my neck once again. Because of that, I felt suddenly buoyant and filled with confidence. My plan was going to work. I was convinced of it.

Spearfish was shorter than *Sea-Wolf* from stem to stern and not as wide, but though I wasn't much of a sailor, even I could appreciate her sleek lines that promised great speed and power. The fore and aftercastles were not as large as those on my cogs, with only enough room for perhaps ten of my Wolf's Teeth to shoot effectively with their longer bows. I'd brought fifteen of the archers with me when we'd first set out from Ganderland, but now there were only eleven left. I knew I would need every one of them to be at their best if we were to succeed. The ship was steered by specially designed oars on either side of the stern rather than a rudder in the center like *Sea-Wolf*. I'd thought that might be problematic, but Putt didn't seem bothered by it. It seemed like a waste of an extra man to me, with the potential for miscommunication during a battle a real concern.

"So, do you think she's ready for this?" I asked Putt.

"I do, my lord," the former outlaw confirmed with a grin. "The repairs went well, all things considered. We have a new mast, sail, yardarm, and both sides of the keel have been reinforced with lapstrake planking. The fire damage on the starboard hull has been fixed, and the leaks in the hold plugged. All in all, I'd say it's better than we could have hoped for in such a short amount of time."

"Good," I muttered. Despite Putt's optimism and assurances about *Spearfish's* abilities, I dearly wished I had *Sea-Wolf* for what I planned. I knew intimately what that ship was capable of, whereas *Spearfish* was a relative unknown. Unknowns heading into a battle could get you killed. "What about fashioning a ram like I asked? How feasible is it?"

Putt's face fell. "That, unfortunately, is a task no one here is qualified to do, my lord. Especially in the time we have. We'd need Hanley for that, and I'm not sure even *he* could design and build it in time. The hull on *Spearfish* is strong, my lord, and will do the job if needed. Trust me."

I nodded doubtfully as I thought about *Sea-Wolf* and her magnificent ram, feeling my good mood dissolving at the discouraging news.

"I'm sure *Sea-Wolf* is still out there waiting for us, my lord," Putt added, looking pained. I knew how much he loved that ship, and I'm sure her fate still bothered him as much as it did me. "The old girl was hung up on that rock pretty good," Putt continued. He shrugged. "We tried to pry her loose afterward with *Spearfish*, of course, but she wouldn't budge an inch. We'll get her back, though. You mark my words."

"The tides could have washed her away by now," I pointed out pessimistically.

Putt grimaced and dropped his eyes. "Perhaps, my lord. But I think she was up high enough." He shrugged. "I guess there's only one way to find out."

"We don't have time for that right now," I grunted.

I closed my eyes, picturing the desperate scene that had led to *Sea-Wolf* running aground on an outcrop of an island, described to me by Jebido, Baine, and Fitz after I'd freed them from prison.

Fitz had begun the story, with Jebido and Baine adding to it when needed. "We saw the Cardians' sails early in the morning about three days after you and Sarrey were taken," my friend told me. "We ran into a storm that first night, and Putt was forced to run with the wind away from The Iron Cay or risk capsizing."

I nodded. That would have been the night I'd escaped my cell through the hole in the roof caused by the storm, only to be recaptured later by The Fisherman.

"We lost our bearings in the storm, and it took several more days to find the island again," Fitz continued. "But once we did, we started circling it about fifty miles out, trying to decide the best way to get past that damn chain barrier so we could get you back."

"I was already gone by then on my way to Temba," I said. "So it would have been a waste of time, anyway."

"Yes, but we didn't know that Hadrack," Jebido added bitterly. He cursed. "If only we'd seen the Temba ships leaving, none of this would have happened. But we didn't."

"Yet, Lord Boudin managed to see you," I pointed out.

"He did," Baine agreed. "The bastard came after us with both his ships, so we decided to draw them away from the island, hoping to separate them enough to make a move on one or the other."

"The smaller cog was named *Windrunner*," Fitz said, taking up the story. "She wasn't nearly as fast as *Spearfish*, so she fell behind quite quickly, just like we'd hoped. We decided to keep going further south under full sail, anticipating that Lord Boudin would stay on our stern while *Windrunner* fell further and further back. It worked. We did that for a day and a half until we eventually lost sight of *Windrunner's* sail. We never did see that little ship again."

"That was good thinking," I grunted. "You evened the odds without having to fight."

"It was Fitz's idea," Baine said.

I glanced at my friend, who looked pleased with the praise. "It was more of a group decision, Hadrack," he said modestly.

"Anyway," Jebido continued. "We reached a group of small islands and—"

"It's called an archipelago," Fitz cut in.

Jebido hesitated, giving the lord an annoyed look. "Anyway," he finally continued. "We started navigating through this *archipelago*, but then another storm hit us out of nowhere."

"I'd never seen such big waves, Hadrack," Baine said. "Not even that time I went overboard. It was so dark that we couldn't see a damn thing, and we spent several hours sailing like blind men and praying to the gods that we'd make it through." Baine shook his head sadly. "But the gods weren't listening to us, and finally, a wave came that tossed us sideways like a cork, right onto the top of an outcrop."

"The rock was formed almost like a saddle," Fitz added, using his hands for emphasis. "But it was sharp and jagged in places. One of the points punched a hole in *Sea-Wolf's* bow large enough for a horse to ride through. The hold flooded with water after that, but once the storm eased, most of it drained off."

"We didn't know how bad the hole was at the time, though," Baine pointed out.

"That's true," Fitz conceded. "Not until the storm broke. We were still trying to figure out how to fix it and float *Sea-Wolf* off the rocks when Lord Boudin showed up. That bastard's ship looked untouched by the storm."

"He ordered us to surrender, of course," Jebido said, chuckling as he replayed the scene in his head. He glanced at me. "I imagine you know what we told him, Hadrack?"

"I have a fair idea," I replied with a grim smile.

"Lord Boudin offered us a deal," Baine said. "Give him the codex, and he'd sail away and leave us alone." All three men laughed at the same time before Baine added, "We told the bastard if he wanted the damn thing, then he'd have to come and take it from our dead hands."

"I take it he tried?" I said.

"The fool did just that, Your Highness," Jebido confirmed. He grinned when I gave him a dark look. I'd forbidden any of my men from calling me that, but it seemed Jebido couldn't resist teasing me. He thought my being named a king was one of the funniest things he'd ever heard. I couldn't for the life of me understand why. "It was a fine battle, Hadrack," Jebido said with obvious relish. "The lads were magnificent. It's a shame you missed it."

"You killed all the Cardians?" I asked, although I'd already guessed the answer. I was disappointed that I hadn't gotten the chance to deal with Lord Boudin on my own, but his death would be welcome news just the same.

My friends exchanged glances of anticipation before Baine cleared his throat. "All but one, Hadrack, and he's not going anywhere. We left him for you."

I felt my eyebrows lift in surprise as I realized what I was being told. "Where is he? You didn't leave him on *Sea-Wolf*, I hope?"

"Of course not," Jebido snorted. "That ship's too good for the likes of him. No, we marooned him on the smallest island we could find with enough food and water to last him several months if he's careful."

I thought of the seven rings etched on my sword—one for each man I'd vowed to kill—relieved to hear my revenge against Lord Boudin might yet be taken. "He could have found a way off since then," I suggested, trying to temper my hopes. "The man may be a filthy Cardian, but he's a damn resourceful bastard just the same."

Jebido grinned, his eyes dancing. "There's nothing on that island, Hadrack. Just a few thin trees, some rocks and sand, flocks of seabirds, and lots of crabs surrounded by water filled with hungry sharks just hoping to taste Cardian meat. No, that ugly turd-sucker isn't going anywhere until you're ready to carve him up." He snorted. "We left him there bare-arsed, with nothing but his sword to keep him company."

"Well then," I said, satisfied. "I guess we'll just have to pay our castaway a visit once things here are settled." I smiled. "And after that pleasant business is over, we'll go have a talk with that bastard Fisherman."

My friends shared another knowing look. "No need for that, Hadrack," Baine said. "After we dropped Lord Boudin off at his castle of sand, we sailed back to The Iron Cay in *Spearfish* looking for you." He chuckled. "They thought we were Cardians and never even blinked when we anchored in the harbor."

"Is The Fisherman dead, then?" I growled, guessing that was the case by the looks on my friends' faces.

"We strung him up across the entrance to the harbor from a rope," Fitz confirmed. "As a warning to anyone else that tried to cross you. But not before he told us what had happened to you." He motioned to Baine. "This one can be quite insistent with his knives."

"The Fisherman was also good enough to hand over a fair amount of his gold before he left this world for the Realm Below," Jebido added with a chuckle. "That's how we were able to pay for the repairs to *Spearfish*." My friend glanced at Baine, the laugh dying, replaced by a frown. "Everything was going fairly well after we left The Iron Cay, despite that unfortunate altercation in Temba. That is until Baine and his cock decided to ruin things for us here."

"It wasn't my fault this time," Baine insisted. "The girl just wouldn't leave me be. It's like she'd never seen a man before or something. All I wanted was some beer and pie and to eat in peace. That's it. Was that too much to ask?"

"Sure it wasn't your fault," Jebido snorted. He rolled his eyes. "Of all the women in this city, you had to pick that one to rut with."

"I'm telling you, this time—"

I'd stopped listening at that point as Jebido and Baine began to quarrel. It seemed some things never changed. What had happened hardly mattered anymore, anyway. All that mattered was that we were together again and ready to fight.

"My lord?"

"What?" I grunted, brought back to the present by Putt.

The former outlaw motioned to the water behind me. "That Bone Warrior is coming, my lord."

I turned, bracing my elbows on the railing as I watched Telman approaching the ship in a sleek outrigger that cut through the water toward us from the shore. A black-painted catamaran followed him, towing four more outriggers behind it, all of which were also freshly painted black. The outriggers were filled with bundles of kindling and dried reeds, and I knew beneath them lay vats of highly flammable pine resin.

"You're sure this will work, my lord?" Putt asked doubtfully as he leaned beside me.

"It will," I grunted. "As long as the Lions do what I expect them to."

"And if they don't, my lord?"

I clapped the former outlaw on the back and grinned. "Then we improvise, Putt. We improvise."

I'd ordered several of the crew to set up barrels covered by planks underneath the aftercastle as a kind of solar for me, and I waited there with Baine, Jebido, Fitz, and Tyris for Telman to come aboard and join us. Tyris wore a black patch over his left eye, which he'd lost during the escape from Temba. I'd worried the blond archer's skill with a bow would be diminished because of the loss of half his vision, but after watching his practice sessions earlier that day, those fears were quickly put to rest. Even with one eye, the man was a better shot than almost anyone I knew—Baine and some of the Piths being the exception, of course.

"Your Highness," Telman said by way of greeting as he stepped into the enclosure. He held a rolled-up parchment in his right hand, and a second, much older man with rounded shoulders, a bulbous nose streaked with purple veins, and a frazzled white beard entered behind him. Several stone-faced Bone Warriors had also accompanied Telman onto the ship, but they waited outside in the open, watched suspiciously by my crew.

"Is that it?" I grunted, motioning to the parchment.

"Yes, Your Highness." If Telman felt any animosity or resentment toward me because of my new title, he gave no sign of it. In fact, the man seemed quite accepting and even pleased that I was now the King of the Temba, which had surprised me immensely. Sarrey had been right all along. The Bone Warrior motioned toward the improvised table, and I nodded assent. He rolled out the parchment, revealing a detailed map of Sandhold and the surrounding coastline and landscape. He then gestured to his companion. "This is Rewalt Tane. He knows the waters around here like no other."

I nodded to the older man. "Go on."

Tane pointed to an outcrop along the coast. "This is Syme's Reach, here, Your Highness, where I'm told the Lions' fleet was first sighted."

My men leaned forward to look, with Baine, Telman, and Tyris holding the ends of the map to keep it flat. "Are they still expected to arrive here by midday tomorrow?" I asked.

"They are, Your Highness," Telman confirmed. "I sent out a few Bone Warriors to follow their progress along the coast several hours ago. They will, as per your instructions, ensure they are seen as much as possible."

"Good," I muttered. My biggest fear was the Lions would decide to spend the night on land in a fortified camp. I wanted them out on the water where they'd feel more secure and would likely be less alert. The sight of the Bone Warriors shadowing the Temba along the coast should make that happen, making them fearful of an ambush should they try to make landfall. "And there's no chance they will keep sailing during the night?" I asked the old sailor.

"Highly unlikely, Your Highness," Tane said. "I doubt they know these waters well enough to attempt it. There are too many hidden rocks and shoals along the coastline to take that chance in the dark. No, they will stop."

"Couldn't they just go further out to sea and keep going?" Baine asked.

Tane paused to think about that, then he shrugged. "I suppose they could, yes. But we're in the thick of hurricane season now, and they risk getting caught out there. A good blow can throw all those ships back this way and against the rocks quicker than you can fart."

"Besides," Telman added. "My guess is the Lions want to arrive around the same time as the land force."

"Speaking of that," I said. "Any news about our fleeing hares?"

"No, Your Highness," Telman said with a quick shake of his head. "No word yet, though I expect they should be returning any time now."

"All right," I said, focusing back on Tane. "What's your best guess as to where they'll anchor?"

Tane put his finger on Syme's Reach, then began moving it along the coast toward Sandhold. He stopped three-quarters of the way to the city, pausing to look up at me with a gap-toothed smile of satisfaction. "Here, Your Highness." He tapped a point in the water. "The Giant's Knees."

"What's that?" Jebido asked.

"Two very large, round cliffs jutting out of the water side by side. Legend says a giant fell asleep there a thousand years ago, and the ocean eventually covered him up. Now all you see are his knees. Youths from the city go there all the time to dive from the top of the left knee. Many are never seen again."

"By the gods, why would they do that?' Jebido asked, sounding baffled.

"For bragging rights, of course," Tane answered with a chuckle. "They call it Dead Man's Leap, you see. It's a treacherous thing to attempt, but those that make the dive successively gain great notoriety and prestige."

I shared a look with Fitz, pretty sure I knew what was going through his mind. "Why do you think the Lions will anchor there?" I asked the old sailor.

"Because the Knees are a natural water and wind brake, Your Highness," Tane explained. "The spot is well-known for its calm, almost non-existent tides, with deep pools between the rocks and the coast teeming with all manner of fish. The divers climb from the windward side up a series of foot and handholds chiselled into the face, then jump into those pools on the other side." The old sailor grimaced. "It's the climb that's the most hazardous, so I'm told." He shrugged. "Anyway, the Lions can lay offshore protected from the wind by the Knees while still being far enough from land that arrows can't reach them. They'll also be close enough to the city to strike at us come mid-morning. If it were me, that's where I'd stop for the night as sure as I'm standing here."

"Do the people from Temba know about Dead Man's Leap?"

"I doubt it, Your Highness. They tend to show little interest in our ways."

I stroked my beard as I thought, encouraged by what I was hearing. "Do you think we can sail to the far side of those cliffs and anchor there without being seen?"

"It might be tricky at night, Your Highness," Tane said cautiously. "Nobody has ever tried that. The surf breaks pretty hard against those rocks, and the winds can swirl unpredictably."

"But can it be done?" I pressed him.

Tane grimaced. "As long as the seas remain reasonably calm, Your Highness, there is a good chance, yes."

"And can we get archers up on the rocks using this path you spoke of?" I asked. If the answer was no, then the plan that was forming in my mind wouldn't work.

Tane gave me that gap-toothed grin of his again as he began to understand. "I expect you could get a few, Your Highness, and I know just the person who can help with that, too."

"Good," I grunted. "How high are the cliffs? Will they be able to see our mast from their side?"

"Probably not," Tane said. "But I suggest you paint it black just to be safe. The Knees are around eighty feet high each, but there's a gap between them and that white mast of yours will stick out like a sore thumb, especially if there's any moonlight."

"Duly noted," I said. "How long will it take for us to get there?"

Tane shrugged. "Three, four hours, maybe, depending on the winds. If you have to use the oars, well, you know."

I glanced past the supports holding up the aftercastle. A noticeable shadow had already begun to fall over our little gathering, though outside the sun was still trying gamely to shine. I knew that wouldn't last much longer and we probably wouldn't get there ahead of the Lions before dark, which suited me just fine. I wanted them settled in anyway.

I nodded to myself, focusing on Tane's dirty finger where it remained poised on the map. "All right, then," I said, the decision made. "We're off to the Giant's Knees. Let's go kill us some Lions!"

Chapter 32: The Giant's Knees

The Giant's Knees were exactly what Rewalt Tane had claimed they would be—two wide, massive dark cliffs jutting out of the water side by side, rounded by centuries of exposure to the elements. Weak light from a half-moon in the sky behind *Spearfish* gleamed off the surface of the water and wet rock, and though we were still at least half a mile away from our target, I could hear the roar of the surf already as it broke against the base of the cliffs. Tane had warned me this would likely be the case, but despite the danger that surf represented, I could feel myself smiling. I knew if we could hear that noise from this far away, then the Lions, who I hoped were already anchored on the other side of the Knees, should be all but deafened to anything else.

"Maybe they should have called those things the Giantess' Tits," I overheard Baine say in a low voice. He grinned and nudged Jebido, who stood beside him leaning on the forecastle railing. "I met this baker's daughter in Lestwick last year," Baine continued. He sucked in air through his teeth as he pointed ahead. "I swear to the gods, Jebido, that girl's tits looked just like those right there." I saw my friend's teeth flash in the weak moonlight. "Only much bigger, of course."

Jebido snorted and shook his head, well-used to Baine's preoccupation and obsession with the fairer sex's upper anatomy. We were all aware, unfortunately. I still blamed Einhard for Baine's fixation after he'd introduced my friend to debauchery at an early, impressionable age when the Pith chieftain had rescued us from the mines of Father's Arse. Thankfully, I'd been slightly older than Baine, and the turn of a pretty face didn't affect me as much as it did him—or at least, I liked to tell myself that, anyway.

I stood behind my friends, my legs spread as I rolled with the ship's motion while the stay lines above my head and planking beneath my feet stretched, creaked, and moaned. We'd circled around the Giant's Knees and were coming in from the south toward the coast at a crawl, following Tane, who commanded the black catamaran ahead of us that had been renamed *Silent Victory* in anticipation of tonight's assault. Telman had offered to come with us, but I'd declined, thinking it would be better to have him and his men defending the city if an attack came sooner than expected. The Bone Warriors were savage fighters, but they were ultimately desert dwellers and unsuited for this kind of task, so I'd brought mostly seasoned soldiers and experienced seamen from the city to augment my own men.

The catamaran's sail was lashed firmly against her mast like ours was, and her crew were using oars wrapped in sailcloth to creep across the water, as were my men coming behind them in *Spearfish*. The four outriggers and their deadly cargo tied to *Silent Victory* followed obediently like submissive dogs on chains, virtually unseen by the naked eye except for telltale streaks of foaming surf bubbling in their wake. There were also two more black-painted outriggers in the water lashed tightly to the stern of *Silent Victory's* double hull, one to either side. These would be crucial to my plans once my archers were in place.

The half-moon that I dearly wished would go away continued to shine down on us with frustrating resolve, undaunted by the wishes and machinations of men far below it. I'd prayed for clouds to blow in during our journey from Sandhold but had been gifted with nothing but clear skies and mischievously twinkling stars that seemed amused at our plight. I was doubly grateful now that I'd taken the old sailor's advice and had *Spearfish's* mast and anything else that might stand out on the ship painted black. Granted, it had been a trying task for my crew to do while under sail, what with the boat rocking and rolling with the waves as it had, but I'd thought they'd done an admirable job considering the circumstances.

Our hull had already been painted black by the Cardians, thank the gods, and thus needed little attention, and each man wore a dark cloak cinched tightly around them so no glint of armor or weapons would show. Now, as *Spearfish* skimmed over the water toward our destination like a silent, shadowy ghost ship of death, I prayed we'd remain invisible to our quarry against the dark horizon and sea beneath us. I estimated the armada of Lions we would soon be engaging numbered at least a thousand men, while I only had one hundred and fifty to draw on. I hadn't wanted to bring any more fighting men than that, for every sword sailing with me was one less available to defend the city. I could only hope the element of surprise, coupled with my fireships and archers, would help to balance things out.

I knew my plan would either succeed spectacularly from the start or quickly turn into a disaster, for in truth, there would be no middle ground this night. I thought of Muwa and his damn coin—one action with two possible results then thrust it from my mind. We would win because we had to win. It was as simple as that. I stiffened as a lantern suddenly flared from the catamaran where a sailor stood behind a wooden barrier at the stern, with the harsh light extinguished a heartbeat later. I turned to alert Putt that the signal had come, but the former outlaw and his keen eyes had already seen it.

"Back up on those oars, lads!" Putt hissed in a low voice. "Nice and gentle now. Don't make any noise. We need to stay away from that swell."

I felt *Spearfish* shudder and slow beneath my feet, fighting the wind and current as the rowers labored to keep her from drifting further inland and possibly hitting the rocks that lined the base of the cliffs. I moved to stand beside Baine and Jebido, searching the darkness for any evidence that the Lions were anywhere around. I thought I could see the tips of the Giant's Knees towering above us like disembodied heads, but below them, there was nothing but featureless blackness meshing with the coast behind.

Waves continued to crash against the Knees in a crescendo of sound, sending spray washing into the air forty or fifty feet high before falling back with wet slaps against the planking of the ship's deck, soaking us all to the bone. I clung to the railing as *Spearfish* pitched and rolled beneath my feet while she fought gamely against the unpredictable swells. I could hear the oarsmen cursing under their breath as they strained to keep the cog steady, and I wondered how Tane and his catamaran were faring in their smaller craft if we were having such difficulties.

Jebido pressed his lips to my ear. "We're too close!" he hissed. "That bastard Rewalt brought us in too far." I thought my friend sounded nervous, which didn't surprise me. Despite having spent so much time on board ships, Jebido despised the water and had an open fear of drowning. I could hardly blame him for that, for who in their right mind would relish it?

"No, he didn't," I said, hoping it was true as I protected my face from the stinging spray that stubbornly sought out my eyes. "We're still at least fifty yards out," I added, though it was nothing more than a guess. "Maybe even as much as a hundred, so don't worry. We've got plenty of space between us and those rocks."

"Then why hasn't that old bastard signaled to drop anchor?"

I was glad Jebido couldn't see my smile in the gloom. It seemed ironic having him call someone else *old*. My friend was probably only a few years younger than Tane, though I couldn't be sure of that. Jebido had refused to tell Baine and me how old he was, no matter how many times we'd begged him. "I don't know why he hasn't signaled yet," I admitted.

As if in answer to Jebido's question, lantern light suddenly appeared from *Silent Victory*, disappearing briefly as someone used their hand to cover the flame before removing it again. The bright glare abruptly went out for good moments later.

"Drop the anchor!" I heard Putt call out softly at the signal. "Lower the boat."

I nodded in satisfaction. The first flash of light had been to tell us that we were in prime position, the second that the Lions were where we'd hoped they'd be and had done what I'd prayed they would—lashed all their ships together in the Temba tradition. I grinned in the darkness. The Lions had essentially formed themselves into a giant shield wall on the water, secure in the knowledge that with their overwhelming numbers, they were safe from any conventional attack. But they hadn't given any thought to an assault by fireships, which I hoped my men and I would soon make them come to regret.

I heard the stone anchor being tossed overboard moments later, waiting from experience with my hands on the railing as the faint splash came, followed by the cog trembling from the sudden jolt. Next came the squeak of a pulley and the sounds of men grunting with effort as they fought to lower an outrigger I'd brought on board over the side.

"You better get going," I grunted to Baine. My friend nodded and turned to leave just as I put a hand on his arm. "Remember, target the ships closest to the shore. I don't want any of those bastards looking our way."

"I will."

"And be careful getting up there. Those rocks are bound to be slippery."

"It'll be fine, Hadrack," Baine said with a resigned smile. He was well used to me hovering over him like a mother hen. "I've climbed worse."

"That you have," I agreed, smiling back weakly as I let my friend go. I was doing my best not to show how worried I was for him and, judging by his expression and Jebido's, failing miserably.

"Make damn sure you keep your mind on the task at hand, boy," Jebido added with a growl. "And whatever you do, don't start suckling on those rocks. They really aren't tits, you know."

Baine laughed and slipped away into the darkness with his bow hung over his shoulder. He, Tyris, and three of my Wolf's Teeth would be scaling the left cliff, guided by a seventeen-year-old boy named Giree Flan, who Tane promised me knew the route going up better than anyone.

"What was that?" Jebido grunted moments later as something that sounded like a scream rang out during a rare break in the raging swell.

The water crashed against the rocks again moments later, obscuring anything else, and I strained my ears to hear more. I was on edge as I waited and listened, my hands on the railing aching from the pressure where I held it tightly. Had it really been a scream or just some trick of the wind? I blinked as spray filled my vision. "Do you see anything?" I finally whispered.

"Nothing," Jebido replied. He wicked water off his dripping beard. "It's blacker than a whore's heart out here."

Moments later, I heard the sound again and I slowly relaxed, realizing with relief that it had just been a burst of high-pitched laughter echoing from the far side of the cliffs. I glanced upward through the falling sea spray, certain I could make out a faint orange glow silhouetting the tips of the Knees. Was that coming from fires on the catamarans? I certainly hoped so.

"Somebody's having a good time over there," I muttered with satisfaction.

"It does sound like it," Jebido agreed. He grinned at me. "Damn fools should have placed sentry boats to the east and west just in case, but they're too busy drinking and doing who knows what else."

"That's good for us," I said. I clapped my friend on the back. "I love a negligent enemy. It just makes our job that much easier."

Jebido moved along the railing, pointing off *Spearfish's* starboard bow. "There they go, Hadrack."

I joined him, watching as a dark shadow glided silently through the water toward the Giant's Knees. My archers were on their way, and all that was left for us to do now was wait.

Almost an hour later, a small flame flared along the top of the left cliff and then went out a moment later. "They made it," I whispered to Jebido in relief. I turned, made my way to the opposite railing, and looked down into the darkness that enveloped the lower deck. I could smell the men packed together below like cows in a stall, waiting for the word to fight. "All good, Lord Fitzery?" I hissed. I couldn't see Rorian, but I knew he was down there with the rest, armored and eager. I was glad of it, too. The bastard had a way of getting under my skin, and the less I saw of him, the better.

"All good, Lord Hadrack," came back the hushed reply. "The men are ready for fresh meat whenever you are."

I nodded as a low rumble of anticipation arose from below. My Wolf Pack were indeed ready, just as I knew they would be. I still didn't know for sure how much we'd be needed in the coming minutes, but just the same, it was best to be prepared. "Be ready on the anchor and oars, Putt," I called softly across the length of the ship. "We might have to move fast with little warning."

"I have men standing by, my lord. We'll be ready."

I returned to Jebido, picturing in my mind what was happening in front of us, since I still could see very little. Tane would have had his men in the two outriggers long ago, and now with the signal to move, each outrigger would begin towing two of the fireships behind them—with one outrigger going around the Giant's Knees to the west and one to the east. Once they were in calmer waters, swimmers would go overboard and begin pushing the fireships toward the massed Temba flotilla. From my experience as a captive on *Wandering-Spirit*, I knew the Temba soldiers and sailors would likely be sitting around metal braziers, drinking, laughing, and telling lies. Those men would also most likely be looking into the flames as well, which would ruin their night vision, allowing my fireships to get well within striking distance. Or at least, that's what I dearly hoped and prayed would happen.

Once the fireships started closing in on the moored flotilla, Baine and his archers would start dropping arrows on the enemy vessels closest to the shore, causing confusion and further distracting the Temba from the true threat approaching on their flanks. Then, as the swimmers gave one final shove before breaking away, it would be up to Baine and Tyris to send fire arrows into the kindling, which would eventually ignite the vats of resin that lined the floors from stem to stern. It was a bold plan, and one that needed a lot of things to go right for it to work. I unconsciously grasped the Pair Stone around my neck and said a prayer to The Mother as I waited with Jebido, barely daring to breathe while the minutes went slowly by. Finally, after what seemed an incredibly long time, I heard faint shouts of confusion rising from behind the rocks, followed by cries of pain. I showed my teeth in a fierce grin just like my namesake, the wolf, feeling the lust of battle rising in me. It had begun.

"There!" Jebido shouted, pointing upward as a torch burst into flames on the peak of the left Knee.

I could see the silhouettes of my archers clustered together on a flat section of the clifftop, with two men standing apart from the others—Baine slight and deadly and Tyris tall and measured. Both men moved with relaxed, easy precision as they used the torch to light the resin-soaked rags wrapped around the base of their arrow shafts. Tyris turned to face westward while Baine faced east. Both men drew at the same time, then released, repeating the process while the rest of the Wolf's Teeth continued to rain arrows down on the Lions. Suddenly, a sound like a thousand bellows all blowing at once erupted from the west, followed instantly by searing orange flames cascading into the sky amid terrified screams and shouts of confusion. Another whoosh of air moments later came from the east as a fireball arched into the sky, followed by the second fireship exploding and adding its flames to the sudden inferno.

"Putt!" I roared. I lifted Wolf's Head—which had somehow found its way into my hand without my knowledge. "Raise the anchor and give us some speed! Let's go kill the bastards!"

My men below roared with approval, tossing aside drenched cloaks that were no longer needed and banging weapons against shields and armor. The time for stealth and secrecy was now mercifully over. Now was the time to shed blood.

Jebido turned to face me as the anchor rose and the oars bit eagerly into a churning sea that was now stained bright red and orange from the reflection of the flames. I'd never seen anything so beautiful in my life. "I've missed you, you bastard," my friend said with a laugh as he hurried to shed his cloak. Underneath, he was dressed in plate armor that gleamed in the eerie glow that lit the sky, rocks, and coast as if day had come. "Life was damn boring while you were off romancing your queen, Your Highness."

I tossed aside my own cloak. "I didn't know Sarrey was a princess or a queen when I met her," I said, not hiding my irritation. "Any more than you did. Besides, I haven't *romanced* her or anything else, so get that foolish thought out of your head."

"Hard to!" Putt's voice rose from the aftercastle. "Get us around that damn rock, or we'll be nothing but a wet stain and a pile of splinters!"

I glanced ahead in alarm, concerned we might crash, but the cog was already turning away from the threat of the Giant's Knees with plenty of room to spare. Putt was just being Putt.

"You haven't?" Jebido grunted, looking surprised. "After all that time you two spent alone together in the mountains?" he shook his head. "Are you sure? Because by the way that lass looks at you, I'd—"

"Leave it alone, Jebido," I growled in warning. I turned away from him, glancing to starboard as we swept past *Silent Victory*, where she lay anchored a hundred feet out from the rocks. Men on the deck were waving us onward and cheering, and I could see Tane standing at the stern, his arms crossed over his chest. I cupped my hands around my mouth. "Rewalt, fall back! We'll take it from here!"

Tane waved in acknowledgment before the catamaran was left behind as we swept around the left flank of the Giant's Knees, powering through the swirling waves into calmer waters. I felt my mouth drop open in disbelief at the sight that awaited us there while Putt shouted at the rowers to cease their efforts behind me. *Spearfish* started to drift slowly forward as a solemn silence quickly filled the ranks of my men, who moments before had been waving weapons and shouting with bloodlust. Now, like me, all they could do was lean over the railings and stare ahead in wonder at the destruction we had wrought on the enemy. Fire raged across the entire breadth of the water where the flotilla of catamarans had been moored together. I watched spellbound as giant flames leaped from one ship to the next, feeding hungrily on ropes, netting, crates, and reefed sails or crackling along mast and spars, encouraged by a steady breeze sweeping along the coastline.

"By the gods," Jebido finally whispered in awe from beside me. "This must be what the fire pits in the Realm Below look like."

I said nothing, silently agreeing with my friend. More than a third of the Temba armada was already burning, mostly around the borders, with voluminous clouds of choking smoke twisting and writhing as it rose toward a nighttime sky that was now transformed into a glowing pink, red, and orange sunset of death. I thought the speed at which the enraged fire was moving was nothing short of stunning, having never seen anything like it before. Horrible screams echoed across the water as men flailed and swatted at their bodies, hair, and beards, trying in vain to extinguish the relentless flames consuming them that refused to go out. Even those who'd managed to dive into the water remained burning for a time before the fire searing their flesh was finally extinguished. I noted that few of those men were moving by the time it did go out, leaving the charred bodies to float facedown on the current as wisps of smoke rose from tattered and blackened clothing.

"What in the name of The Mother is happening?" Jebido asked in bewilderment.

"It's the burning pitch," I answered with dawning realization. "The explosions must have sent it shooting into the air, only to have it fall back on the Lions like rain."

I unconsciously shuddered as I watched men whimpering and calling out to their mothers as they died horribly. I'd seen men perish in every conceivable way in my lifetime and had gladly sent many of them to their deaths myself. But this—this just seemed wrong somehow. Already I could smell the telltale scent of charred flesh, the sickly-sweet odor bringing back memories of Corwick and those who had died there, burnt alive by the nine men who had killed my father and sister. I sighed and sheathed Wolf's Head, my bloodlust gone now as I watched the carnage, knowing the weapon would not be needed this night after all.

From what I could see, a fair amount of the Lions had been assembled in the center of the flotilla when we'd attacked, perhaps gathered there to hear a rousing speech of victory from their leader. I didn't know. But whatever the reason, it had spelled doom for many as the flames spread quickly, trapping them. I could hear the panicked cries as men looked for a way out, calling for someone to save them from the horror of the flames. I shook my head at the waste, knowing there would be no savior for those men this night.

"There wasn't any choice, Hadrack," Jebido said, picking up on my mood as usual. "The only chance the city had was ensuring these men never got there. You've accomplished that and then some without losing a single man. You should be proud."

"Proud?" I said with a snort. I turned my back on the flames, feeling the heat prickling the skin on the back of my neck as I regarded my friend. "Most of those poor bastards over there probably didn't even know what they were fighting for. Muwa and his damn Ravens have fed them nothing but lies. Once this is over, Jebido, I'm going to need allies." I hooked a thumb over my shoulder. "Do you think any survivors of that are going to forgive me and bend the knee after this?"

Now it was Jebido's turn to sigh in exasperation. "What did you think was going to happen, Hadrack?"

"That's just it, Jebido," I said. I turned toward the flames, determined not to look away again from what I'd wrought. "This is *exactly* what I wanted and hoped would happen. That doesn't mean I have to feel good about it."

Jebido put his hand on my shoulder. "That's what makes you special, Hadrack," he said. "It's easy to be a good warrior. It's much harder to be a good man. You are both."

"My lord?"

I glanced sideways as Berwin climbed up to the forecastle. "There are men in the water, my lord," he said. "Survivors. Lots of them. They're swimming for the shore. Shall I tell Putt to intercept them?"

I glanced at Jebido, who just shrugged, not committing himself. "No," I finally said wearily. "Their fleet is destroyed. That's enough. Let them be. I doubt any will be eager to keep fighting after this, but if they decide to, we'll deal with them then. There's been enough death for one night."

"Yes, my lord," Berwin said, sounding disappointed.

"Signal Baine and Tyris to come down," I added. "We're going back to the city. That's where the real fight is going to be."

Chapter 33: Reaction To Their Action

We arrived back in Sandhold just before dawn broke, yet despite the early hour, the city was still bustling with frantic activity. The news of our victory over the Lions had traveled almost as quickly as the resin-fuelled fire had raced across the hulls of our enemies' doomed catamarans. Before I'd even left the harbor and *Spearfish* behind—accompanied by Jebido, Baine, and Fitz on horseback—everyone knew of the armada's demise from one end of the city to the other. Rorian and the rest of my men had remained on board the ship, but Rewalt Tane followed after our mounts on foot, leading a rowdy mix of Sandhold's triumphant sailors and soldiers who had sailed into battle with us.

Every one of those men was now being hailed as a hero, with the city's inhabitants taking a moment from their labors to cheer them as we passed. Jubilant women threw red and pink flower petals over the heads of the men while they marched through the streets, led by Tane and a half-drunken, flute-playing sailor who never seemed to get winded. Some of the women in the crowd began dragging the heroes out of line, begging them for a kiss, which was something I'd wager many of these hardened, mostly ugly men had never experienced before without handing over hard-earned coin. There was a palpable sense of excitement in the air, a festive mood bordering on giddiness now that the threat from the sea had been eliminated. Every living soul within Sandhold's walls knew well that the very streets they were gathered on might be awash in blood soon. But for now, the news of our unprecedented victory was clearly a welcome relief from the fear hanging over the city.

"Wolf King! Wolf King!" the people began to roar as we came to a small market square. "The savior of Sandhold! Wolf King!"

I frowned at that. I hadn't saved anyone from anything—I'd just evened the odds a little. I knew the one-sided victory we'd had over the Lions was not likely to occur again, and despite the joy and relief everyone was feeling at the moment, things still looked grim for us. An army of anywhere between eight and ten thousand men was even now marching across the desert toward the city. At best, Sandhold could only counter them with about three thousand defenders—half of which I suspected would have little to no experience in warfare. We would have the ferocity of the Bone Warriors to count on, of course. But at only a thousand strong, would they be enough?

No matter how I looked at things, I could see nothing ahead for us but a long and protracted siege, and to that end, I reviewed what I knew about Sandhold. The city was situated on a slight rise overlooking the harbor to the west, about fifty miles from where the drifting sands of the Waste of Bones finally ended. There was nothing but open scrubland after that, stretching from the desert to the city on both the southern and eastern approaches.

That was the good news, especially since our western flank was now safe from an attack by sea. The bad news was the entire approach from the north was covered by vast forests of ironwood trees, mesquite, acacia, and desert willow, which I knew would be a problem. Only about thirty yards of open land lay between the forest and the outer walls, a fact that those responsible for planning the city's defenses should be ashamed of. Those trees would offer any attackers coming from that direction ideal cover. So, on my recommendation, the Circle of Life had sent out woodcutters to cut back the trees, leaving some where they fell to form a barrier that would be difficult to cross. It would help, I knew, but even if we'd had twice the amount of men with axes that we did, they still wouldn't be able to make much of a dent during the limited time we had left before the Lions arrived.

My biggest concern by far was the city's stone walls, which were not nearly high enough in my view and were in sorry disrepair in several key places. Stonemasons were working frantically to shore up the weak points, but even so, I knew a determined foe could easily scale the low walls. A wooden palisade with a ditch was being built from some of the larger felled trees to protect the harbor, but it remained to be seen if the fortifications would be finished in time. I thought of Gasterny Garrison and the weak walls there that had failed to hold back the tide of invaders, praying I would not bear witness to a repeat of that horrible defeat. The front gate facing south was one of the bright spots, I conceded, stout and formidable with a well-designed barbican, but there were two smaller gates to the north and east, both of which were vulnerable. If it were me, that's where I would attack.

I sighed, falling deeper into blackness as we progressed, ignoring the revelers around me. Nothing about our situation seemed worth celebrating to me, and so I rode with my head down and shoulders hunched, staring at my horse's ears and trying to drown out the sounds of merriment.

"Would you stop acting so damn glum, Hadrack," Jebido finally grunted at me. "You'll frighten children with that look on your face." My friend swept an arm around at the cheering crowds as we headed for the square's exit. "At least acknowledge these poor people, so they don't think you're an arrogant bastard with his nose planted firmly up his own arse."

I glanced at Jebido in annoyance but eventually did as he asked, lifting a hand reluctantly in salute. I immediately regretted it, for moments later, the cheering became twice as deafening as before. People began rushing forward then, standing four of five deep as they reached up to me, clasping and unclasping their hands for my touch as if somehow it would make some difference to their lives. I thought it strange and irrational behavior, but then again, who was I to judge what was normal or not in these trying times?

Young women and girls took my salute as leave to run perilously close to our horses once the main crowd was left behind, giggling up at us and waving long, brightly colored cloths overhead.

A large group of men and boys sawing logs at the end of the square stopped to watch us pass. They doffed their hats and placed them over their hearts, then began chanting, "Wolf King! Wolf King! Wolf King!" I found the entire display hugely embarrassing and was glad when we finally trotted out onto another street, leaving them behind.

One fetching girl with long red hair stubbornly stayed with us, running behind our mounts and waving a bouquet of yellow flowers. Baine eventually turned and saw her, his face breaking out in a wide grin before he stopped his horse with a cluck of his tongue. My friend waited for the out-of-breath girl, accepting the flowers from her before he leaned down for a long and enthusiastic kiss. Afterward, he glanced back wistfully at her once we'd continued onward a few paces, his expression changing from obvious infatuation to that of a child who'd just been caught stealing a sweet when I gave him a dark look. The randy bastard just never seemed to learn.

We finally reached the courtyard where the Circle of Life statue stood, and there we were greeted by more wildly cheering citizens. It was a much different scene from the first time I'd arrived here with Sarrey and Rorian not that long ago. Rewalt Tane and his men had left us several streets back—presumably to find taverns where the drinks flowed freely and the whores would most likely be grateful, warm, and accommodating.

Telman was waiting for us as my friends and I dismounted near the steps to the Hall of Justice. "Your Highness," he said with a smile. "I understand your expedition was a success?"

"You understand correctly," I said, forcing a grin. "What's the news from the desert?"

"All the Temba have successively been recovered," Telman said. "Those that survived, anyway. There were more Lions than we expected among them—almost half." He fell in beside me as we climbed the stairs. I was still dressed in my armor, and I removed my helmet, tucking it under my arm. "They are led by the famous swordsman Alfaheed al Anta," Telman added, sounding impressed. "He claims that he knows you."

I glanced at the Bone Warrior in surprise. "Alfaheed, here?" I turned to Jebido. "Was he not at The Iron Cay when you returned in *Spearfish*?"

"No," Jebido grunted. "We never saw him. The truth is, Hadrack, I'd forgotten all about that bastard."

We reached the top of the steps, and Telman paused on the stone. "He is meeting with council now, and I think it best if you hear what he has to say directly from him. Not all things are as they would appear, it seems. Also, my scouts reported a baggage train left Temba along the Bone Road not long after their army entered the desert. It seems they, too, anticipate a siege."

I mulled over everything I'd just learned as we entered the Hall and made our way through the benches. The Circle of Life were sitting where I'd seen them last, with a small group of city soldiers standing nearby. I thought the two women and the girl looked exhausted, with the Grandmother appearing especially drawn and weak. Alfaheed stood before the platform facing the council with his hands clasped behind his back. He turned as our heavy boots scraped loudly against the stone floor, our eyes meeting across the distance. The last time I'd seen the Temba was just before he'd struck me unconscious while I'd been stranded in the water with Sarrey. *Perhaps very soon, I'll get to return the favor,* I thought, giving the man a hard look.

Sarrey sat with Banta on one of the benches to my right, and she jumped up when she saw us approaching. "Lord!" she cried, catching me off-guard by rushing into my arms. "I'm so glad you're back! Are you all right?"

All eyes were on us, I saw as I pushed the girl away self-consciously. "I'm fine," I growled a little more harshly than I'd intended. I softened my tone. "What's going on?"

"Your Highness," the Grandmother said in a strained, cracking voice before Sarrey could answer. "On behalf of this grateful council, I would like to congratulate you on your stunning victory. You promised results this night, and you delivered them better than any of us could have hoped for. It's clear now that your stellar reputation as a master of war was not overstated and that we made the right choice by letting you lead the expedition."

"Thank you, Honored One," I said with a slight bow. "But I couldn't have done it without the men of Sandhold. They are the ones who risked all and deserve your praise, not me." I shifted my gaze to Alfaheed, who stared back at me calmly, looking relaxed. "May I ask, Honored Ones, why this man is here? He is no friend of mine."

"So we understand," the Matron said. She took a deep breath. "*Hasama* Alfaheed was quite clear about why that is, Your Highness. Although, to be fair, he does not share the same animosity toward you as you obviously do for him. Quite the opposite, it would seem."

My eyebrows rose. *Hasama*? Alfaheed was a lord? I waited, knowing there were bound to be more surprises to come.

"If I may, Honored One?" Alfaheed said. The Matron nodded, and the Temba turned to me. "I don't suppose apologizing for hitting you would help?"

"Probably not," I grunted. "But it's a damn good start."

"Very well, then," Alfaheed said with a disarming smile. "I apologize for hitting you, Lord Hadrack. I had little choice at the time, I'm afraid. It was either one of The Fisherman's men or me, and their touch might not have been as...er...restrained."

"Your Highness," Sarrey interrupted in a warning tone. "This man is now your king by right of abdication, so show him the respect he deserves."

"Ah," Alfaheed said with a nod. "You are, of course, correct, Lady del Fante." He inclined his head to me. "Forgive me, Your Highness."

"What do you want?" I asked, the suspicion in my voice evident to all.

Alfaheed shrugged. "The same as you, Your Highness. Peace for both Temba and Sandhold."

I snorted. "And why should anyone believe you? You sold your soul to The Fisherman the last time I looked."

Alfaheed's expression darkened. "No, Your Highness, in this, you are mistaken. My father sold my soul to The Fisherman over a gambling debt. I honored that debt to the best of my abilities, but now that he's dead—" Alfaheed gestured to my friends— "thanks to your companions here, my obligation is ended and I am free to resume the life I once had." Alfaheed frowned. "Or at least, I would have been if not for the Ravens. So you see, your enemies are also my enemies."

I pursed my lips as I thought, feeling my anger toward the man dissipating somewhat. I still had a small, permanent dent on the back of my skull where he'd struck me, however, which could not be easily forgotten or forgiven. I decided that restitution was still in order for that, be it now or later. "Were you on the island when my men attacked?" I asked.

"I was not there, Your Highness," Alfaheed replied with a smile. The smile quickly faded, replaced by a confident hardness. "If I had been, the results would have been far different and The Fisherman would still be alive. So, it would seem the gods favored us all by my being away."

I felt Jebido stir angrily beside me, and I gave him a look before he could say anything. "Where were you, then?" I asked Alfaheed, not taking the bait by allowing my men or myself to get into a pissing match with the Temba. All fighting men boasted about their prowess, for it was as natural to them as breathing or eating. But something told me Alfaheed wasn't doing that here but rather was just stating the obvious—at least from how he saw things, anyway.

"The Fisherman sent me to the Isle of Grinoldi to collect on an overdue debt. By the time I returned, your men were long gone, with only the scavenged remains of The Fisherman's body to welcome me home."

The Grandmother cleared her throat. "While I understand your need to explain yourself, *Hasama* Alfaheed, I think we should move on to the matter at hand. We are, unfortunately, constrained for time."

"Of course, Honored One," Alfaheed said to her with a bow. He focused back on me. "Judging by your reaction to Lord Boudin, I gather you have dealt with Cardians before, Your Highness?"

"I have," I confirmed, not hiding my distaste. "Many times. The lot of them are nothing but cowards and greedy scum."

"That is undisputedly true," Alfaheed agreed.

"What do those bastards have to do with anything?"

Alfaheed smiled. "That is who marches on Sandhold, Your Highness. Or at least, a good portion of them are Cardians, anyway. I understand there are some Cordovians among them as well, while the rest are just sheep and misguided fools from Temba who do what they're told." I shared a glance with Fitz as Alfaheed continued, "The Ravens planned things well, Your Highness. They knew most of the Temba senior officers would never abandon the king for a made-up god, so they eliminated them on the night of the riots and brought in mercenaries to take their places. The assassinations were meticulously plotted, targeting not only soldiers but men holding high positions at court and within the city's administration—my father and brother were two of these. They even killed the Sons and Daughters and had mercenaries posing as rioters burn down most of the Holy Houses. Now they're coming for Sandhold."

"And you just happen to know all this how?" Jebido grunted suspiciously.

"I know all this," Alfaheed retorted, "because I have ears, and I have eyes. Even a halfwit could have figured out what was going on in Temba after only spending a few hours there. I was once a member of the King's Guard, and the moment I realized the extent of what had happened, I started reaching out to men I knew, trying to assess the level of loyalty remaining in the city. Many of my previous acquaintances were dead, though, and those that weren't were keeping their heads down and doing whatever they were told to for fear of repercussions. The madness of those riots quickly receded in Temba after the first night, but they were replaced by something much, much worse."

"Worse, how?" I asked, trying to imagine anything being as bad as what I'd witnessed.

"The mercenaries were given total control of the city by the White Ravens, allowed to do whatever they wanted to whomever they wanted. Every man, woman, and child was forced to publicly repent the First Pair and acknowledge the One True God. Those that did not were charged with harboring *unacceptable views* and were murdered in cold blood, including their families. If a mercenary saw a woman he fancied, married or not, he would take her, sometimes in public places without any repercussions. Supposedly all men are considered equal under the White Ravens' laws, but those are just empty words not worth the price of the parchment they're written on. The reality is the new regime takes whatever they want from the people, enriching themselves and telling them that it's for their own good while insisting that the One True God loves them—they just need to believe. It's a farce, of course, nothing but robbery and rape disguised as faith, but unfortunately, in Temba right now, there is no escape from it."

"But you got away," I pointed out.

"Yes, Your Highness. I worked covertly with some I knew, and when an opportunity presented itself, we gathered those unwilling to live under such tyranny any longer and we fled. The Ravens sent their trained dogs after us, of course, but every last one of us was willing to die rather than stay, so we had little to lose. That's why we headed into the desert despite the danger, thinking they wouldn't dare follow. But in that, we were wrong. The White Ravens had originally planned to attack Sandhold in a month from now, but with our escape, it seems they decided to kill two birds with one stone and march on the city now."

"Will the men who left with you fight?" I asked.

Alfaheed grinned. "With extreme prejudice, Your Highness. Every one of them has seen friends and family raped or murdered in recent days. They will fight to the death."

I glanced at Telman. "Tell me more about this baggage train. How many wagons? How many men are guarding it?"

Telman shrugged. "A hundred or so wagons and carts with perhaps five hundred soldiers, all on horseback."

"Why didn't they just transport the supplies by ship?" Baine asked. "Wouldn't it be safer?"

"That would have been a sounder choice," Telman agreed. He shrugged. "Maybe whoever leads them isn't all that smart."

"Are the wagons and carts pulled by horses or oxen?" I asked.

The Bone Warrior frowned. "Why does that matter?"

"Because horses travel faster than any ox can," I explained. "The calvary will have to move at the baggage train's speed."

"Ah, I see," Telman grunted. "My understanding is they are pulled by oxen."

I nodded, processing that. "And do your scouts have a guess as to whether they will arrive before or after the main army?"

"That is still too hard to say, Your Highness," Telman said. "But I'm told a desert storm, known as a *Janumai*, has forced the army to a crawl. They won't arrive now until this evening at best."

"Good," I said, pleased. "That buys us some more time." I glanced briefly at Sarrey before focusing again on the Bone Warrior. "I understand the Bone Road travels along the coast?"

"Mostly it does, yes, Your Highness. But a ridge of impassable mountains separates the two. There are several gaps, though, if you know where to look for them."

"Even better," I muttered as my mind raced. The idea that was growing in my mind had been tempered by fear that the survivors from the armada would link up with the baggage train and tell them what had happened. Now that seemed unlikely.

"They will have scouts out, Your Highness," Telman warned.

"Of course they will," I said. "I would expect no less."

I glanced at Jebido, who grinned with approval, clearly understanding what I was thinking. "But they'll be looking ahead to the road or watching the desert, not the mountains," my friend said.

"Exactly," I agreed. "Right now, that baggage train out there has no idea their fleet sits at the bottom of the sea. As far as they're concerned, their left flank is protected. We need to take advantage of that fact. The key to stopping every invading army since the beginning of time is to cut off their supplies. Horses need fodder and men don't like to fight on an empty stomach, especially when they're far from home in a strange land."

Telman scratched at his beard. "You'll need a sizable force to accomplish that," he said. "We'd be leaving the city vulnerable."

"I think it's worth the risk," I replied firmly. I turned to the three women on the platform. "Honored Ones, the army coming our way is bound to be exhausted and short on supplies when they get here. They won't be able to forage for food, water, or fodder in the desert, so will be depending heavily on that baggage train to keep them fed. If we destroy it, those men will quickly starve. It takes an awful lot of food to feed ten thousand men."

"It is something to consider, Your Highness," the Grandmother said cautiously. "But—"

"Forgive me, Honored One," Fitz said, cutting the old woman off. He glanced at me, motioning with his head to the side. "Can I talk to you for a moment, Hadrack?"

I frowned in annoyance, but I'd seen that look in Fitz's eyes before and knew better than to discount it. My friend had something important he wanted to tell me. "What is it?" I asked once we were out of earshot of the others.

"My father was a hard man, Hadrack," Fitz said.

I sighed, not relishing listening to one of Fitz's cryptic lectures. "You brought me over here to tell me that?"

"No," my friend said with a chuckle. "Obviously, there's more. My father was a hard man but also a fair one. Most lords are cruel and care very little for the common folk, but he wasn't like that at all. In fact, he was beloved by them because he always listened to their side of the story without bias." I glowered at Fitz as he hurried to continue, "I asked my father once why he cared at all, and he told me because he believed that all our lives are dictated by our actions. For every action we take, good or bad, there is an opposite reaction, though sometimes it's not always obvious."

I rolled my eyes. "This is not the time for philosophy, Fitz."

"For instance," the lord continued as if I hadn't spoken. "Suppose you kicked a cat out of your way in the morning, then happened to stub your toe painfully in the afternoon. Was it a coincidence or a reaction to your earlier action? Or better yet, suppose you beat your wife for not having dinner ready in time, then get the runs from the food and spend all night shitting. Again, every action has a reaction, which, for want of a more elegant phrase, we'll call payback. Do you see?"

"What I see is a man losing his mind right in front of me," I grunted sarcastically. "Do you have a point, Fitz?"

"I do," my friend said with a smile. "You told me the White Ravens put some kind of desert plant in the wine that turned the people in Temba mad, yes?" I nodded, my eyes narrowing. "So," Fitz said, clearly relishing himself now. "Would it not be a fair and just reaction to their action if we were to return the favor?" I gaped at Fitz as I realized what he was saying. "We have Bone Warriors who know the desert well and can no doubt find this plant," Fitz added. "And we have a source from which we can distribute it, assuming we don't do anything hasty and foolish, such as destroy it."

"The baggage train," I whispered in wonder, feeling my heart thudding against my chest. "We use it against the Ravens just like they used the people of Temba against the king."

"Exactly," Fitz agreed triumphantly. "Then, once the plants have done their work, we go kill the bastards and end this thing once and for all!"

Chapter 34: The Baggage Train

    The mountain range—known as the Clinboro Line—was pretty much what Telman had described now that I could see its jagged peaks clearly in the daylight. I thought the chain of mountains looked vaguely like the jutting spine of some monstrous, undulating snake-like creature from where I stood on *Spearfish's* lower deck. The individual summits were not nearly as high as I'd expected, though, with the tallest topping out at what I guessed was just over a thousand feet. The peaks were mainly covered by barren, scaly rock and glistening silver shale, adding greatly to the serpentine illusion. Stunted, crooked trees bare of foliage grew at the base of the range, eventually giving way to a thicker pelt of green forest above that looked virtually impenetrable from my vantage point. I wouldn't have relished trying to move any sizable force through those mountains at the best of times, just as the Bone Warrior had told me. Which meant for my needs, they were more than ideal.

    We'd been forced to use the oars when we first set out from Sandhold around mid-morning, but in the past hour, the lethargic wind at our backs had strengthened, propelling us southward at speed, giving the men a much-needed respite. I leaned over the railing on the lower deck as the dark water gushed below me along the cog's portside hull, gurgling and frothing and leaving small whirlpools in our wake while the ship swept along the coast. I'd been mingling with the men for the past few minutes, enjoying the warm sun and easy camaraderie dominated by vulgar jokes and crass insults. It was the kind of atmosphere that only fighting men who have repeatedly faced death can fully understand or appreciate, and, truth be told, it had been a welcome relief from all the trappings of being a so-called king.

Spearfish was as packed with men as the ship could safely be, with fifty of our best fighters and a hundred archers augmented by my Wolf's Teeth moving about on her decks. More men were below in the hold where there was no wind, working at preparing the jimsonweed the Bone Warriors had gathered from the Waste of Bones. I was told that the desert people had been using the plant for generations, but only cautiously in small doses as a pain suppressant. Which meant no one knew for sure how much we would need for what we planned, or for that matter, if anything else other than the plant needed to be added to the concoction.

Fitz had taken charge of the entire process, and I thought again about our conversation from earlier this morning when I'd checked in on his progress.

"It's called improvising," Fitz insisted with a shrug and grin when I'd queried him—not for the first time—on whether or not he knew what he was doing. My friend had workers using three millstones to crush plant seeds while he experimented with the finished result, measuring and combining them with ale that a very reluctant volunteer was sampling. That volunteer was Berwin, who, like most of my men, was always eager to drink beer but was understandably more than a little leery about what Fitz was putting into it.

The milling had met with mixed success, for it turned out the plants needed to be dried first, which we'd learned the hard way. But since we didn't have time for that, Fitz had settled on working with the seeds alone, although it was painstaking to separate them from the main body of the plant. Luckily, the Bone Warriors had found more than enough jimsonweed to satisfy our needs.

I examined Berwin with a critical eye where he sat on a stool after drinking a full tankard, with the lad staring at me accusingly. I suppose I could hardly fault him for that, since his volunteering had been my idea, not his. "How do you feel?" I asked over the incessant grating noises of the millstones turning.

"Not bad, lord," Berwin admitted grudgingly. He glanced up at the two burly men standing over him, both ready at a moment's notice to pounce if he showed any signs of madness. "That damn knee that's been bothering me this past year is feeling much better, which is kind of nice."

"That's good," Fitz said enthusiastically. He jotted something down on a piece of parchment, then leaned forward and pulled Berwin's left eyelid up, peering into the eye.

"What are you doing?" I asked.

"I saw old Haverty do this once with a fellow that got kicked in the head by a mule. He said you could tell if the man's brains inside were mush or not by the way his eyes looked."

"Ah," I grunted. "And?"

"And nothing," Fitz said with a disappointed sigh. "I don't know if what I'm seeing is normal or not. Maybe Berwin's brain was already mucked up before I started."

"Ha, lord!" Berwin snorted with a lopsided grin. "That's funny."

I shared a look with Fitz. "Give him some more," I said. "A lot more."

"Maybe we should wait a bit, Hadrack," Fitz replied cautiously. He motioned to an upright wine casket where a set of scales sat with the bronze cup on one arm half-filled with a fine brown, flour-like substance. "I've already given him more than I expected. There's no telling how long it takes for the jimsonweed to work and—"

Berwin suddenly spasmed on his stool then, his eyes widening before he growled and leaped at me without warning. "I'll kill you, Father! I'll kill you!" the thin warrior cried.

Berwin's strong hands were around my neck a heartbeat later, and his red-rimmed eyes only inches away from mine were filled with hatred. The thin warrior's lips were pulled back in a snarl, with his yellow teeth gnashing at me before moments later, he fell sideways with a groan as one of the guards cracked him over the head with the rounded pommel of his sword.

"Well," Fitz said after a moment as he looked down at the prone man. I could see Berwin's chest rising and falling, guessing he'd have a nasty headache when he awoke. "It would appear the damn stuff works after all."

That had been several hours ago, and Berwin remained in the hold, conscious now but trussed up for his own safety while screaming words at the top of his lungs that made no sense. I truly hoped Fitz's experiment hadn't damaged the lad, for he was a good man and a faithful servant.

"Care for some company?"

I turned and nodded as Jebido moved beside me, bracing his hands on the railing. He breathed in deeply while the wind rustled his silver hair and beard. "A fine day for an adventure, eh, Hadrack?"

"That it is," I agreed. I paused to look back at the stern, where Baine was entertaining some of the men by juggling five knives in the air at once. I'd seen him do it many times before, but the display of skill and speed never failed to amaze me. I gestured toward my juggler friend with my chin. "Somebody seems to be in good form today."

Jebido glanced back. "Yes, let's just hope there aren't any pretty women with this baggage train. Who knows what trouble the little bastard will get us into if there are."

I chuckled. "You're still mad at him?"

"Damn right, I am," Jebido grunted.

I shrugged. "You might as well get mad at a rabbit for digging a burrow or a truffle hog for rooting beneath a stand of hazelnut trees. That's Baine's nature, and we just have to accept it."

Jebido shook his head. "Well, look at you, Hadrack, all noble and wise now. Will wonders never cease? I guess being a mighty king suits you."

He'd said that last bit in a teasing voice, which annoyed me instantly, as I'm sure my friend knew it would. "Do you always have to be such an ass?" I snorted.

"Of course I do," Jebido said with a chuckle. "That's *my* nature, Hadrack."

I opened my mouth to reply but hesitated at a cry from the lookout far above us. I peered upward, shading my eyes.

"The Giant's Knees dead ahead, my lord!"

I leaned out over the railing to peer past the bow. The rounded tips of the Knees were indeed visible now on the horizon. "Putt!" I shouted to the former outlaw. "Take us around them. I don't want to get hung up on any wrecks!"

"Yes, my lord," Putt shouted back.

"I see smoke," Jebido muttered a few minutes later.

What little remained of the defeated Lion armada had washed up on the shore, I saw as we bore down on the Knees, lying half-submerged in the tall reed grass that danced and whipped about in the wind. Whisps of gray smoke trailed into the sky from some of the blackened hulls, with the smell of charred wood hanging heavy in the air despite the breeze at our backs. I couldn't detect any bodies in the water, though, guessing they were either hidden by the reeds, had been dragged to the bottom by their armor, or had washed out to sea.

Jebido stiffened, and he pointed inland. "Men on the shore, Hadrack. There."

I followed his finger, watching as a group of figures appeared beneath some trees on a knoll overlooking the water about a hundred yards east of the cliffs. They stared back at us silently, and I could almost feel their sullen resentment. "How many do you make out?" I asked.

Jebido shrugged. "Maybe thirty or so. It's hard to tell with all the shadows."

I nodded. Others could still be hiding further back in the trees, but that number seemed about right to me. "Putt," I called out again.

"My lord?"

"Get us in closer to those men and hold us there."

"Hold us, my lord?"

"Yes," I called. "I want to talk to them."

"As you wish, my lord."

Jebido looked at me skeptically. "And what, pray tell, do you expect to accomplish by doing that?"

I shrugged. "I have no idea. Sometimes you just have to go with your instinct."

I hurried up the ladder to the forecastle as the sail was trimmed and men began working the oars, turning us back toward the coast. We crawled across the water carefully while a sailor using a weighted hemp rope took soundings, with the ship finally coming to a halt fifty yards out from the shoreline. It was more than enough for my purpose.

I cupped my hands around my mouth. "Who speaks for you men?"

The group on the knoll had increased now, numbering almost fifty, though many of the new arrivals appeared wounded. A tall soldier with a thatch of grey hair and a square-cut beard stepped out from the trees and made his way to the edge of the knoll. "I am Fander al Mata. What do you want, *Klespa*?"

I heard some of the men from Sandhold grumbling below me on the lower deck. *Klespa* was a Temba word that roughly translated meant, *desert rat*.

I pointed north over the mountains toward the Waste of Bones. "By this time tomorrow, the plague that is the White Ravens, along with their mercenaries, will be destroyed, and the Kingdom of Temba will finally be free of them, as will Sandhold."

Laughter echoed over the water from the knoll at that. "Is that right, *Klespa*?" Fander shouted, sounding amused. "And who are you to make such a statement? The One True God Himself?"

"I am Hadrack Corwick of Ganderland, the Wolf of Corwick Castle," I replied harshly. "Hero of the Pair War, killer of The Nine, commander of the forces that defeated the Piths at the battle of Lands End and then the Cardians during the battle of Silver Valley, and now elected Warlord of the city of Sandhold. That is who I am!" A hush fell over the knoll at my bold words, and I nodded in satisfaction. No one was laughing now. "Yesterday, I was named the King of Temba by Sarrey del Fante, the rightful heir who abdicated the throne to me." I could hear gasps of surprise coming from across the water. "And I am the one who sank your fleet last night without losing a single man. So, mark my words. I intend to destroy that army in the desert just like I did your ships."

I paused then to let that sink in. "But you men do not need to die out here. The Father chose to wash away your sins with fire and let you live, and because of that, I offer you one chance at further redemption. Bend the knee to me and say your words, and I swear you will be welcomed back into the fold without prejudice. Do not, and I will sail on and leave you behind. But be warned, for without your vow, I will consider you my enemies and make it my life's work to hunt down every last one of you. And if you doubt my resolve, then think of the nine men who killed my family that are even now burning at The Father's feet. They doubted my resolve once, too, yet all are dead." I spread my hands out to my sides. "The choice is yours. Is it to be brothers in arms, or is it to be blood enemies?"

I held my breath then, the entire ship's compliment waiting in silent anticipation for the men on the shore to seal their fate one way or the other. Finally, Fander al Mata drew his sword, then reversed it point down in the ground before he dropped to one knee. One after another, men came out from beneath the trees and did the same, lining the ridge of the knoll as they began to say the words that would bind them to me for life.

"That was something to behold," Baine said out of the corner of his mouth as he came to stand beside me. "A true inspiration, Hadrack." He glanced sideways at me. "But why bother wasting time with these men? Half of them are wounded, not to mention we don't have room for them on board the ship."

"I know that," I said as the Lions on the knoll continued to recite their vows. "But I'm trying to build an alliance here, Baine. One that we can use to crush Cardia and Parnuthia when we get back to Ganderland." I nodded toward the kneeling Lions. "And this is how it starts, with mercy."

"Uh-huh," Baine said doubtfully. "And what about them?" he asked, indicating a group of eight men standing defiantly off to one side of the kneeling Lions. "Are they part of this *alliance* you're forging, too?"

I grimaced. The men wore red capes and high, black pointed boots. Cardians. "No, they're not," I grunted. I waited until the kneeling men had finished pledging their swords to me, indicating with a hand that they should stand. "Fander al Mata," I called out once they were all on their feet.

"Your Highness?"

"What is your rank?"

"Sergeant, Third Mark, Your Highness."

"From this day forth, you will be a captain."

"Yes, Your Highness," the Lion said, lowering his head in gratitude. "Thank you."

"You will make your way back to Temba as best you can, Captain," I ordered, feeling my heart hardening, knowing the next part had to be done. I had been merciful with these men, but sometimes a king's mercy can be interpreted as weakness if it goes too far. Now was the time to send a message that all here could understand. "But before you leave, Captain," I said, focusing on the mercenaries. "There are those among you who did not kneel. A price must be paid for that failure."

Fander al Mata glanced over his shoulder at the Cardians, and even from this far away, I thought I detected a hardness in his eyes. The Temba lifted his sword to me in salute. "I understand, Your Highness. It shall be done."

I sat propped up against an alder tree hours later, sweating from the intense heat and dozing while mosquitos, gnats, and the occasional black fly buzzed hungrily around me. *Spearfish* lay anchored in a small inlet some twelve miles to the southwest, watched over by Putt, several sailors, and a sheepish and bleary-eyed Berwin while the bulk of my men and I had trekked inland, looking for the pass through the mountains that Telman had told me about. That pass had turned out to be more of a barely seen notch than anything else, proving to be narrow and treacherous, dominated by uneven shelves of slick rock and loose shale that left my men cursing and grumbling as we fought our way through. Now though, after the long, exhausting journey, we lay hidden fifty feet back from the treeline of a forest that bordered the Bone Road, waiting for any signs of the baggage train's approach. So far, there had been none.

Dusk was still several hours away, but the shadows beneath the canopy were already increasing much faster than I would have liked. I prayed the baggage train arrived before night set in, not relishing having to fight in the dark, which would effectively neutralize the advantage my archers gave us. But, regardless of when that baggage train eventually did appear, the attack would have to go ahead as planned, for there really wasn't much of a choice. I grumbled and slapped in annoyance at a mosquito that had landed on my right earlobe, then cracked open my eyes. Jebido lay nearby with his head propped up on a fallen log and his helmet pulled down over his eyes. I could hear him snoring lightly, and I smiled. The old bastard had always been able to sleep anywhere, no matter what the situation might be.

A twig snapped to my left moments later, followed by Rorian appearing around a copse of trees. He nodded to me cordially enough, but his eyes were hard and unfriendly as he walked past me without saying anything, which was fine by me. I guessed he was going to take a piss or shit somewhere out of sight, but I honestly didn't really care all that much what he did. My relationship with Rorian was usually strained at the best of times, and it was damn obvious the bastard was unhappy with me right now. He and I had argued not long after we'd arrived at our destination, with him adamant that we needed to go after the Eye of God above all else before he had a chance to get away. But, as much as I relished finding and killing that man, it wasn't as much of a priority for me as it was for Rorian. I'd explained to the scholar in no uncertain terms that I was the one in charge here, not him, and that he could either follow my orders or leave. I didn't care which. Rorian was not the kind of man who took being dependant on another easily, and the truth was he needed me, my men, and *Spearfish* to reach the Edge of the World—and we both knew it.

I stiffened as the familiar, harsh cruck-cruck of a raven suddenly sounded three times from the direction of the Bone Road. It was Baine, signaling that someone was approaching—thank the gods! I stood, kicking Jebido's left boot to wake him before I headed north through the trees. I spotted Baine moments later, crouched behind some boxwood shrubs. He glanced back as he heard me coming, then motioned to his eyes, then the east. I squatted beside my friend, but from my vantage point, I couldn't see anything except an empty road.

"Listen," Baine whispered as I looked at him quizzically. I tilted my head, just able to make out the faint sounds of what might be hooves and possibly the squeaking and rattling of wagon wheels. "Maybe a mile away, still," Baine added. "We've got time."

"Scouts?" I asked.

Baine smirked, hooking a thumb behind him toward a pair of dark leather boots that I'd failed to notice sticking out from another boxwood bush. "Only one that I've seen. The dumb bastard rode right up to me, Hadrack. I almost felt bad killing him."

"Where's his horse?"

"In a small clearing to the south. A fine mare. Young Giree is watching over her."

"Good," I grunted. Giree was the lad who'd led Baine and the others up the side of the Giant's Knees. The boy was quick, agile, and smart, and he'd begged me to allow him to come along with us. After his bravery the night before, I hadn't the heart to deny him. "Any signs of the others yet?"

Baine shook his head. "Not a hair, Hadrack. But they're out there, somewhere. I can feel it."

"All right," I said. "I'll stay here and keep watch. Go get the men into position." Baine nodded and started to head away. "And make sure they stay put until I give the signal," I added, lifting the polished antelope horn that hung around my neck. "We've only got one chance at this."

Baine grinned and gave an exaggerated bow. "As you will, Your Highness."

I shook my head at my friend's back as he glided away through the trees like a cat. Would I ever live down being named a king with him and Jebido? I looked to the east again, now able to discern a distinctive dust cloud hovering on the horizon. They were coming. Behind me, archers flitted through the trees, with Baine leading a contingent away to my left and Tyris to my right. I winced whenever a bow got caught in brambles or a man cursed under his breath as he tripped over a log or hidden obstruction.

I compared that to my Wolf Pack—all veterans of a hundred battles—who had moved into position to my rear as silently as a

Holy House mouse during morning prayers. Each man was armed with a sword and a heavy Gander shield and carried a ten-foot-long pike that would stop a charging warhorse in its tracks. But despite the quiet approach by my men, the constant sounds of rustling leaves, twigs cracking and whispered words and curses continued to fill the forest as the archers from Sandhold clumsily took their places. I snorted softly, imagining what Wiflem Prest, the captain of my guards, would do to them if he were here. The man was as tough a taskmaster as they came, and every one of my Wolf Pack and Wolf's Teeth had felt the lash of his tongue and weight of his scarred fists at one time or another during their training under him.

I looked up as Jebido and Rorian joined me. Both wore shields on their arms and held naked blades in their right hands. Neither carried pikes. I nodded to them, with none of us feeling the need to speak. We'd all done this sort of thing many times before. We waited then as the mosquitoes droned happily around us in clouds, with the rumble of the approaching cavalry growing louder in our ears, merging now with a hundred other sounds that betrayed the nature of our quarry. I could hear the crack of the lash now, accompanied by the bellowing of oxen, braying of mules, and metallic clanking of tin pots as the wagons and carts rolled, bounced, and rumbled over the road behind the mounted men.

Jebido touched my arm moments later, pointing northwest, where I could see another dust cloud quickly approaching. I nodded, pleased. Everything was going according to plan so far. That dust cloud would be Alfaheed, who, accompanied by one hundred and fifty Lions, had positioned himself perfectly to intercept the baggage train precisely where we lay hidden within the trees. I knew it would only be another minute or so before the enemy cavalry detected them, and when they did, I expected those riders to react the same way that I and probably anyone else would have in their position, which was to stop the baggage train and face the threat directly while bringing up the mounted reserves from the rear. What the enemy Lions couldn't know, though, was that my force lay hidden in the trees on their left flank, nor that Telman and his Bone Warriors had circled around through the desert to meet up with the Bone Road several miles behind the baggage train, effectively boxing them in from three sides. It was a neat little ambush and one that I hoped would pay dividends by giving us a quick, decisive win.

Jebido leaned close to me. "There's still time to change your mind about this, Hadrack. After your success this morning, maybe it's worth trying to talk to them first."

I took a deep breath. I'd initially considered giving the enemy a chance to surrender before we attacked, but the danger there was I didn't know how many actual Lions were among the protective force. If there were mainly mercenaries guarding the baggage train and they refused to drop their swords, then the element of surprise would be lost to us, which meant I'd inevitably lose more men. I also needed that train to remain undamaged as much as possible, and a long, drawn-out battle was something that I could ill afford. I knew the moment the blood started to flow the drivers would panic and scatter, running their wagons and carts back toward Temba or out into the desert to escape us. And while it was true most were pulled by oxen and probably wouldn't get that far, locating them after the battle was won would use up precious time—time that I just couldn't afford to lose.

"No," I finally replied grimly. "We stick with the plan." I gestured toward the road and the approaching riders. "Those men out there knew the risk when they belted on their swords today. We all know. No, we hit them hard and fast before we lose the light, then we sort the rest out afterward."

The lead enemy horsemen were almost even with our position now, and suddenly I heard shouts of alarm rising from them as they finally saw Alfaheed and his men. A strident horn sounded from the front of the baggage train moments later, with the men on foot leading the oxen cursing as they fought to get them to stop. The carts and wagons were stretched out in a ragged line for almost half a mile to the east, and they began to slow one by one amid confused shouts as clouds of dust rose around them like fog, helping to add to the uncertainty of the moment.

I grinned when I saw the first of the rearguard appear as they spurred their horses forward exactly as I'd hoped, streaming in and out of view through the heavy dust along both sides of the train. I looked to the northwest again, where Alfaheed and his men had massed their horses to block the road two hundred yards away from the head of the milling enemy riders. The sun hung low and dark orange over the mountains behind the horsemen, silhouetting each body and the nine-foot-long ash spear they held in a brilliant, fiery aura. I fingered the horn at my neck, waiting for the optimum moment to use it. That moment came a heartbeat later when three faint but sharp blasts from a horn identical to mine sounded from the south, signaling that the Bone Warriors had engaged whatever Lion rearguard remained.

I lifted the antelope horn without hesitation and blew three notes of my own. Then, with Jebido, Rorian, and the Wolf Pack at my back, we burst out from the forest line. Baine and Tyris' archers were already appearing to my left and right all along the line with their bows ready. I nodded to Jebido, who, together with Rorian, broke away to the right, followed by half our men. The other half remained with me as we raced to the left, forming into a tight shield wall of bristling pikes in front of Baine and his archers. If any of the enemy were foolish enough to try to run them down, then they'd have to break through our line first to do it.

"Archers, nock!" Baine cried from behind me. "Draw! Loose!"

Fifty-one bows sang as one, hurtling a mass of dark shafts at the confused Lions, who were still milling about on their horses at the head of the baggage train, clearly surprised by the turn of events and undecided about which enemy to face. Moments later, the wave of arrows landed in amongst them like angry wasps, their heavy iron tips clattering against hastily raised shields or slicing through leather armor into vulnerable flesh. Men tumbled from the saddle by the twos and threes from the devastating barrage, with the sounds of their agonized screams mixing with those of the wounded horses, adding further to the mayhem and carnage.

"Again, you beautiful bastards!" Baine cried happily. "Nock! Draw! Loose!"

To my right, I could hear Tyris' commanding voice as his archers targeted the rearguard, who were trying valiantly to get to the front. The road was a mass of confusion now, with terrified drivers frantically trying to turn their carts and wagons around to flee, just as I'd predicted. I had nothing against any of the civilians in the baggage train, though, and had expressly forbidden my men from hurting them if possible. But those terrified people didn't know that, which meant I needed to end this now before things got out of hand. I placed the horn to my lips again, blowing two short notes—the signal for Alfaheed to charge.

The Temba lord heeded my call, yellow and black pennants streaming in the wind from the hafts of their lowered spears as the Lions bore down on the enemy, who ironically were also flying identical Lion banners. I could feel the ground trembling beneath my boots from the shod hooves of the charging horses as the blood in my veins began to sing with the lust for battle. But, despite the almost overwhelming desire to join in the fray, I kept my men in place, for the Wolf Pack and I were here only for defense this day, not offense.

I held my breath, watching as moments later, Alfaheed's force collided with the enemy in a deafening screech of metal, splintering wood, shouted oaths, and horrific screams that I imagined could be heard easily for miles around.

"My lord!" the soldier to my left suddenly called out. "We've got cavalry approaching."

I cursed myself under my breath, so focused on the main battle that I hadn't noticed a knot of riders bearing down on us to our right in a desperate bid to take down our archers—the fools. "Right flank shift, double line," I ordered calmly.

My well-trained men moved in perfect step with each other, half maintaining the front wall as we turned to face the threat while an equal amount of men formed behind us. A small stand of pine trees rose to my left, which protected our flank there, but our right side was vulnerable, so my men automatically curved protectively around the archers on that side. I stood in the center of the first row, waiting with sword drawn as my men braced the butts of their pikes on the ground. They then turned their bodies sideways while using their extended left leg to support the shafts, which were now pointing outward past their shields at a forty-five-degree angle. Meanwhile, the second row had balanced their pikes on the tops of their shields, with the pole weapons rising a foot or so over the heads of our first line, creating two rows of deadly iron points. I was hoping our crisp discipline and obvious training would deter our attackers, but they showed no signs of slowing, riding low in the saddle as arrows whizzed over their heads from Tyris' archers to our right.

"Don't let those bastards get behind us!" I shouted to my men, knowing that in this, we were vulnerable. Each of the attackers rode a horse that was easily a thousand pounds or more, and they would make short work of our archers if allowed to get past our wall. I glanced behind me. "Baine! Care to lend a hand here?"

My friend glanced at the approaching riders, and he grinned. He turned his slight form toward the enemy and an arrow appeared in his hand before he nocked, drew, and shot all in one smooth motion. The lead rider's horse screamed a heartbeat later when the shaft thudded into its neck with a meaty smack. The beast faltered and stumbled twice, yet somehow kept its feet before finally turning and running off while the rider on its back cursed and fought for control. Baine calmly shot again, sending a Lion somersaulting off the back of his mount to land unmoving on the ground.

    Now, with less than thirty yards left before the enemy were on top of us, we braced for the impact of heavy horses just as more bowstrings began to thrum from behind me, decimating the front ranks of the charging cavalry. Yet, even so, the ones behind came on stubbornly regardless, seemingly undaunted by the deaths of their comrades. I suppose they really should have known better, but sometimes the rage of battle makes men do reckless and inexplicable things. I, of all people, understood that well enough.

    Only six riders managed to survive the barrage of arrows by the time they reached our wall of pikes, but horses can be smarter than men more often than not, and they quite rightly balked from our deadly points, turning aside or rearing back on two legs. Several soldiers tumbled from their saddles, landing hard, while the rest fell moments later to our spears or arrows. Some of my men in the front rank dropped their pikes to pounce on the stunned Lions lying on the ground, quickly dispatching them with their swords.

    I looked to the northwest as sudden cheering arose from the road. Alfaheed and his Lions had now been joined by Telman and his Bone Warriors, all of them clapping each other on the back and waving weapons in the air like the best of friends.

    And just like that, the Battle of the Bone Road was over and the baggage train was ours.

Chapter 35: A Night To Remember

"Well, it's a good night for this," Jebido commented from beside me as his breath rose in a fine mist around him. "Let's just hope this concoction of Lord Fitzery's works the way he says it will, or we're going to be in big trouble, Hadrack."

I nodded in agreement, saying nothing while I chewed on a hunk of Cordovian cheese that had the texture of a slug and the smell of a five-day-old gangrenous wound. Despite the feel and the aroma, though, the cheese was surprisingly good and I was enjoying it immensely. I glanced at the full white moon that hung over our heads, the gleam illuminating the constantly shifting sands of the Waste of Bones to our right.

We were finally on our way to Sandhold with our captured baggage train nearly three hours after the battle for control for it had ended. I sat with Jebido on a padded bench at the front of the lead wagon, which was drawn by two identical-looking oxen with heavily muscled necks and dull eyes. There were no reins to guide the beasts, though, so Putt walked beside the animals with a switch in one hand to keep them focused and a torch in the other. Jebido and I wore worn cloaks—as did all the men who'd come with me from *Spearfish*—with our armor and weapons except for a knife on each of our hips stashed in the backs of the wagons and carts we'd confiscated. For all intents and purposes, we were just simple tradesmen and nothing more, or so I hoped it appeared.

Most armies depended mainly on foraging when campaigning, but the Ravens were smart enough to know they'd find very little on the way to Sandhold and so had sent everything they needed to feed their army with the baggage train, at least for the short term, anyway. I guessed that they, like us, were expecting a lengthy siege, although I'm sure the Ravens were hoping the people of Sandhold would capitulate quickly when they saw the scope and breadth of the force at their gates and the ships amassed in the harbor. There would be no thoughts of surrender from anyone in Sandhold, of course, but if I had my way, our soon-to-be night's work would make the Raven threat obsolete.

Though substantial enough at first glance, I guessed the supplies we'd captured would probably only last the invading army a week at best, and then only if they were used sparingly. Ten thousand fighting men can eat and drink a lot per day, even if the food is carefully rationed. The hardest part about conducting a successful siege has always been the logistics behind it, for often times a campaign can take months, even years, especially when dealing with heavily fortified towns. Without a constant source of food and other necessities, an army made up mostly of conscripts will slowly whither and die on the vine, eaten away from the inside by sickness, low morale, and desertion.

But in the case of Sandhold, once the Ravens had the lands around the city completely under their control, they'd then be free to move whatever additional supplies and fresh troops were needed from Temba to the encircled city at will without fear of attack. And though our scouts had seen no evidence of siege engines as of yet, that didn't mean the enemy wouldn't use them later on if they were needed. I figured the Ravens were waiting to see if the city surrendered first. If it didn't, then I knew it would be a fairly easy affair to use the Bone Road to bring those engines from Temba.

My men had done a hasty inventory before we'd set out, finding everything from wine, ale, dried meats such as goat, mutton, and beef, rice, grain for making porridge, salted fish, honey, olive oil, spices, and barley for the horses, to canvas tents, bundles of arrows and extra shields, swords, and glaives. The baggage train had also included a herd of two hundred head of beef for slaughter, but I didn't want to be bothered with them, so I had ordered they be set loose in the desert. If the cattle managed to survive the sands and heat, then the Bone Warriors could round them up later. Fitz had spent the ensuing hours during our preparations moving from wagon to wagon, adding carefully measured amounts of jimsonweed powder to the wine and ale caskets and the water vats—though not before I'd let all the men sample a well-earned drink of ale or wine first.

I glanced ahead, picking out Alfaheed's dark form in the moonlight, where he rode at the head of his mounted Lions. Telman was bringing up the rear more than a mile behind the sprawling baggage train, with his Bone Warriors now flying the hated black and yellow Lion banner and dressed in the armor of their vanquished foe. Few among the warriors were happy about wearing Lion attire. But despite their grumbling and unease, all understood the necessity of it if we were to maintain the illusion that all was well when we reached Sandhold.

The wagon Jebido and I rode in was much bigger and more luxurious than most of the other freight wagons, carts, and water wagons in the lengthy procession, most of which had no benches at all. My men were either forced to walk alongside their draft animals to keep them moving like Putt or, in the case of the smaller carts drawn by mules, ride on their backs. I'd initially thought about refusing to ride in the wagon and walking instead as an example to my men, but Jebido had convinced me it would be an error.

"If you want men to respect you as a king, then you must act like one," my friend had admonished me. "All kings ride, Hadrack. They do not walk like a commoner."

And so I had given in to his wisdom, knowing that, as usual, my friend was probably right. The wagon and three more just like it behind me had all belonged to a plump, wealthy Cordovian trader who clearly liked his comforts, such as padded seats. I'd left the fat man and everyone else involved with the baggage train behind on the road, guarded against marauding animals by the surviving Lions who'd surrendered to us. Those men had been offered the same deal as I'd given the soldiers near the Giant's Knees, with most bending the knee to me. And though I felt fairly certain I could trust them after they'd pledged their swords, I was not willing to risk being betrayed by one or more of them on this night of all nights. Too much was at stake for that.

    None of the defeated Lions had been given their horses back because of my distrust, and so I'd left them on foot with just a sword or glaive and nothing else, with orders to return with their charges to Temba. As for the confiscated horses, I'd kept enough of them for my men to ride once our business with the Ravens was completed, and made a gift of the rest to Telman. Those extra horses—some two hundred and fifty strong—were even now being driven to the northeast to Dune's Peak, Telman's stronghold in the desert. I knew those horses would net the Bone Warrior leader a tidy sum at auction once this war was over, which was fine with me. I suppose some might say the gesture was nothing more than a bribe for the man's continued loyalty. And if that's what they wanted to call it, then so be it—since, truthfully, that's exactly what it was.

    As for the Cordovian and Cardian mercenaries among the baggage train and the few Lions who'd refused my offer, we'd stripped them naked and sent them out into the desert with the cattle, prodded in the ass by the tips of the Bone Warrior's spears. If those men lived somehow by the grace of the gods, then good for them. If they died out there, well, I considered it good riddance.

    Hundreds of people were involved in maintaining the baggage train, each with a needed skillset, such as drivers, drovers, millwrights, bakers, blacksmiths, fletchers, cooks, cobblers, butchers, and a hundred other thankless jobs that were needed to keep an army fed and on its feet. I'd been pleased to find no whores among them, though, which was unusual, as most armies were almost always followed by camp followers looking to make some easy coin off lonesome soldiers. I guessed the Ravens, with their pious attitudes, either frowned upon that sort of thing or had promised the men they could sample the spoils in Sandhold all they wanted once the city fell.

A rider appeared on the road ahead four hours after we'd first set out. He stopped to talk to Alfaheed, who, upon listening for a moment, wheeled his horse around and trotted back down the line of his men toward us.

Alfaheed swung his horse alongside our wagon, nodding his head to me. "We're about ten miles from Sandhold, Your Highness."

"Good," I grunted. "And the enemy?"

The Temba smiled. "Encamped a quarter mile outside the walls in the southern fields, just as you predicted."

I nodded, not surprised. The land there was wide and flat, with a natural windbreak of hills and trees to the west where the sea lay and good sightlines to the city. It was a logical spot to settle that many men. "Any signs of aggression from them?" I asked. I doubted the Ravens would be foolish enough to attack right away, but you never knew for sure. The invading army had just finished a difficult march and would be tired, so throwing them against the walls immediately would be reckless and almost guaranteed to fail, especially in the dark. I didn't know who was in charge of the Raven army, but if it was Muwa as I suspected, then he would likely wait until the morning before making any moves. The White Raven was an evil, misguided bastard in my estimation, but he was also smart, measured, and not the kind of man to make rash decisions. At least, I hoped so for the sake of our mission.

"Not that our scouts could see, Your Highness," Alfaheed responded. "They're busy digging ramparts around the campsite."

"Sentries?"

"Yes, numerous. But I doubt they'll even bat an eye at us when we arrive."

"Where would you suggest we make camp?" I asked.

"There's another field about a half mile south of the army's position, Your Highness. It's close enough to move the wine and ale in by carts but far enough away that it's unlikely any strays will wander over and get suspicious when they don't recognize any of us."

"All right," I said. "Then I think we're set. Let's go give the Ravens a party they won't soon forget."

It took more than an hour for all our wagons to make it to the southern field Alfaheed had described. But even before the last cart trundled to a stop, I had my men working at unloading and stacking all the supplies on the ground except for the tainted wine and ale caskets, which were transferred to open carts. While that was going on, others began going through the motions of making camp by lighting cooking fires and busying themselves setting up tents. If anyone from the Raven encampment were watching us, they'd see exactly what they would expect a baggage train like ours to be doing once it reached its destination. My only concern was if a high-ranking officer became curious about why we'd made camp so far away and rode over to investigate.

I grunted with effort as Jebido and I rolled a casket of ale along the bumpy ground toward the back of a half-filled cart. Jebido had initially frowned when I'd joined in the work, but after giving him a warning look, he'd just shrugged without making any comments. I might be a king in name, but by the gods, I had no intentions of standing idly by when there was hard work to be done. With help from Baine and Putt, the four of us rolled the casket up a plank and into the cart, and after we got it settled into place, Jebido and I jumped back down to the ground.

"Are you all right?" I asked my friend, worried when I saw a flash of pain cross his features after he'd landed awkwardly.

"I'm fine," Jebido replied, waving it off. "This old back of mine isn't as strong as it used to be, is all."

"That's because you don't rut anymore," Baine said bluntly from where he stood above us in the cart. A pole torch flickered ten feet away, lighting up my friend's handsome features. "Trust me, Jebido, there's nothing better for your back than sliding into the saddle between a woman's legs and humping away like a mad dog." I tried to keep a straight face, knowing what was coming, while beside Baine, Putt chuckled. "That back of yours is feeling neglected, my friend, and that is why it hurts so much."

"Neglected, huh?" Jebido grunted, shaking his head in mock wonder. "And you're telling me rutting can fix that?"

"Of course it can," Baine insisted as if it were obvious. "Think of your back as a bow, Jebido, made from the finest wood, all supple and well-oiled. It's wonderful when new, but like everything else, that bow needs more attention as it ages. Leave it sitting in a corner day after day and year after year, and eventually, it will stiffen and lose flexibility. That old bow needs constant upkeep now to get the most out of the aged wood, you see. And the best way to do that is by using it as much as possible." Baine bowed dramatically. "No need to thank me."

"My back's like a bow, eh?" Jebido muttered sarcastically. He glanced at me and rolled his eyes. "You sure about that?"

"Have I ever lied to you?" Baine asked with an infectious grin as he jumped to the ground.

"Every damn day since you were an annoying brat with snot rolling down your nose," Jebido replied with a snort. "Every damn day."

"Ha!" Baine laughed. He clapped the older man on the shoulder. "When we get back to Corwick, I'm going to take you to Halhaven to get that old bow of yours working properly again. There's this brothel on Silverkeep Street that you have to see to believe. The whores there do things with their tongues that make even *me* blush. They'll get you shooting your arrows straight again in no time, mark my words."

"There's nothing wrong with my *arrows*," Jebido growled, his eyes narrowing. "Say that again, and I swear you'll wish that you hadn't."

Baine lifted his hands, palms up. "Of course there isn't, Jebido. No need to get mad." He glanced at me mischievously before focusing back on his target. "But just the same, maybe you should do some target practice on your own first. Those whores can be downright demanding, and like you said, you're not a young man anymore."

Jebido turned to me, dropping his hand to his knife. "Hadrack, I think you'd best say your goodbyes to Baine, because he's just said one word too many."

"All right," I grunted, having had enough of the back and forth. "Let's get back to work, you two." I motioned to Jebido. "You can carve him up later all you want, but for now, save it for the Ravens."

Jebido pointed a finger at Baine, who was smirking openly. "This isn't over."

"I'd be disappointed if it was," Baine shot back before he turned, gesturing to Putt to follow him to get another casket.

"That boy needs to be brought down a peg or two," Jebido grumbled as he watched them leave.

I shook my head. "Why do you let him get to you like that?"

"Wait until you get a little older, Hadrack. Then you'll understand," Jebido answered testily.

My friend put his hand on my arm a moment later, motioning behind us. I turned, nodding to Alfaheed as he approached, leading his horse behind him by the reins.

"We're ready, Your Highness," Alfaheed said. "*Rhana* Telman's men have arrived and are waiting for me to the west. Your horses are picketed the south of the camp as you asked, saddled and ready."

"Good," I grunted. The western coast was hidden from our view by some low hills peppered with thick woodlands, but I knew from talking with some of the Lions from the baggage train that the Ravens planned on having men waiting along the shore to update the fleet on what was happening. I'd tasked Alfaheed and Telman to eliminate those men just in case they returned with the news the ships were nowhere to be seen before our job was done. After that, the two lords were to remain hidden in the trees, waiting for the right moment to strike the camp. But that moment could only happen as long as we got the wine and ale loaded and on its way.

Less than an hour later, we were on the move with forty carts filled with caskets, and as the first of those carts entered through a gap in the earthen ramparts of the campsite, the Raven army that mostly lay sprawled around hundreds of fires began to stand and cheer us wildly. I could hardly blame them for their eagerness after the long, grueling march through the unforgiving desert with only water to sustain them.

I'd relinquished the lead of the procession to Fitz, who was unknown to the Ravens. I walked instead in the middle of our convoy, holding the bridle of a mean-spirited mule that continuously rolled its eyes at me and tended to just stop without warning, causing confusion behind us. I carried a switch, of course, which I'd used enthusiastically on the mule's ass, but that only seemed to make matters worse. I'd tried pulling on the beast's bridle as well with mixed success until, by blind luck, my grip slipped one time and I'd ended up grabbing a handful of one of its ears instead. The mule did not like that at all, and after a few more solid tugs, I'd found the beast to be much more cooperative regarding the task at hand.

Once inside the ramparts, we began to spread out, each cart heading for different sections of the huge camp while cheering soldiers ran alongside, clapping us on the back and shaking our hands. I smiled and nodded to them beneath the hood of my cloak, mumbling nonsensical words and being careful to keep my eyes lowered. Finally, I stopped the mule in an open area and waited, holding the animal's bridle as eager men pressed in around the back of the cart. I could hear Jebido calling out to the happy soldiers, trading jibes and good-natured jokes with them as he used a ladle to fill the metal tankers each man always carried on them with either ale or wine. I knew the same scene was being played out everywhere around the campsite, and I smiled. The madness was only a few hours away.

I felt that smile disappear a moment later, though, when I saw two men with gleaming bald pates and white robes hurrying past the crowd around my cart, with neither man glancing at it or showing the slightest interest in what was inside. One of the Ravens was Theny, who'd brought me food that first night in Temba, and the other was Muwa. I watched them with hooded eyes as they made their way around campfires, tents, and racks of weapons and shields to pause before a large square tent with blue, six-pointed stars painted on the outer canvas walls. Muwa said something to his companion, then pushed the tent flap out of the way and disappeared inside while Theny walked away with his hands thrust inside the sleeves of his robe.

I glanced around, but no one was paying the slightest bit of attention to me, focused as they were on the wine and ale. A weapon rack stood nearby, and I dropped the mule's reins and moved to it, selecting a glaive. I thrust one of the blades deeply into the ground near the mule, and then when satisfied it was secure enough, I tied the reins to the shaft. "You be good," I whispered to the beast, who chose that moment to wiggle its ears as if mocking me. I headed to the back of the cart, fighting my way through the crowd of jubilant soldiers until I could see Jebido. I waved until I finally caught his eye. "I'll be right back," I called out to him.

Jebido frowned and said something in reply, but his words were lost to me in all the commotion and noise. I waved again, then turned, pausing as a grinning soldier pressed a full tankard of wine into my hands. I took it, accepting his enthusiastic pat on the back as I headed away, moving toward Muwa's tent with my head down. I almost threw away the tankard once I was clear of the crowd, but then changed my mind. I hadn't known what I'd planned to do when I'd first set out, but now I did. I reached Muwa's tent, pausing to look around cautiously before scratching on the canvas opening.

"Yes?" I heard from inside.

I lowered my voice. "Wine for you, lord?"

"That swill?" I heard Muwa snort. "Thank you, but no. I have plenty of my own."

I frowned, then took a deep breath before I swept aside the tent flap and stepped inside. The interior was lit by several candles giving off enough smoke and smell to identify them as tallow, most likely sheep's fat. Muwa sat with his profile facing me on a narrow wooden bench with high rounded sidearms and no back. He was reading from a thick book balanced on his lap, with one hand holding a candle above the pages. The Raven's concentration on the words was so fierce that he seemed completely unaware that I'd entered.

I waited for a count of ten, then finally cleared my throat, with my hood still hiding most of my face. "Wine for you, *Galata*?"

Muwa looked around sharply at the Temba insult, the creases in his forehead exaggerated by the shadows cast by the candle. His face was calm, yet his eyes were hard with anger as they fixated on me. "What did you just say?"

I stepped further into the room without answering, pausing to set the tankard of wine down on a small table made from a stump of oak.

Muwa closed the book he'd been reading with a snap and stood to face me. "I asked you a question," the Raven said.

I spread my arms to my sides. "I believe I called you, *Galata*," I answered. "It means white slug if I'm not mistaken? I hope I pronounced it correctly?" I slowly lowered my hood to reveal my face. "Because I'm not from around these parts, as you likely recall."

Muwa's eyes widened when he recognized me, his round face looking almost comical without eyebrows. "Lord Hadrack?"

"In the flesh," I said. The Raven glanced past me to the entrance. "No, don't worry," I added. "There's no one else, just you and me."

"I see," Muwa said thoughtfully. The bastard had gotten over his surprise quickly and now, once again, looked calm and at ease. I couldn't help but admire him for that. "May I ask, Lord Hadrack, what it is you want from me?"

"Oh, I thought we could talk," I said.

Muwa inclined his head. "A splendid idea, lord." He motioned to a bench identical to the one he'd been using. "Would you care to sit down?"

"I'd prefer to stand, thank you."

"Ah, of course," Muwa said, not looking surprised. He put his hands behind his back, still holding the book. "And what would you care to discuss, lord?"

"How about you breaking camp and leaving, for starters?" I suggested.

Muwa pursed his lips. "Why would I want to do that?"

"Because if you don't, I intend to destroy your army."

"Oh my," Muwa said, looking genuinely amused. "That is something to consider, lord. May I enquire as to how you expect to do such a thing? I have ten thousand men at my disposal, while you only have, what, a paltry two or three thousand?"

"Yes, but they're inside city walls," I pointed out.

"Which are old and weak," Muwa countered.

"Are they?" I said with a chuckle. "Maybe we have a few surprises in store for you yet."

The Raven's eyes hardened with suspicion. "What are you up to, Lord Hadrack? Why did you really come here?"

"I came here to give you an ultimatum," I said. "Surrender to me now, while there's still time to stop the bloodshed, and as the legitimate King of Temba, I swear I will be merciful to those men out there."

Muwa couldn't hide his surprise at that. "King? What nonsense is that?"

I grinned. "Sarrey del Fante abdicated to me yesterday, Muwa. Hadn't you heard?" I extended my hand arrogantly. "I wish I had a crown or fancy ring, but since I don't, you may kneel and kiss my hand instead."

I was gratified to see anger flicker across the Raven's features briefly. "I don't know what game you are playing, lord, but it's clearly a foolish one. I need only shout, and there will be a hundred armed soldiers here moments later."

"But where's the fun in that?" I said, my voice now a growl. I took off my cloak and threw it aside. "Maybe the best way to settle this once and for all is staring us right in the face, Muwa."

"You can't be serious?" the Raven said. "You would dare fight me? Here?"

"I would," I said. I knew I was taking a risk, but I was pretty sure I had the measure of a man like Muwa. The Raven was supremely confident in his abilities, but so was I, and I knew he would fight me if I pushed him far enough. "The question is, will you cower behind other men's swords," I taunted. "Or will you prove once and for all you deserve that throne you so obviously crave?"

Muwa sighed. "You are a fool, Lord Hadrack."

"King Hadrack," I corrected. "And as my first order of business as king, I hereby relieve you of your position as Regent. I will allow you to work digging cesspits in the city, however, since I feel I owe you for rescuing me from King Alba's justice, even though you had ulterior motives." I took the knife from my belt and held it up. "And since you do not use weapons, it's only fitting that I don't as well." I moved to the entrance and tossed the knife outside, then returned. "And once my business here is finished and your army is destroyed, I intend to sail to the Edge of the World and separate the Eye of God's ugly bald head from his shoulders."

"Oh, you have been busy, lord," Muwa said. He shook his head in mock sorrow. "It would seem that I have badly underestimated you, despite being warned repeatedly not to do so."

"Warned by who?"

Muwa shrugged. "Get past me, and maybe you'll find out, lord."

"Fair enough," I grunted. "Shall we keep talking or get on with it?"

"Getting on with it suits me just fine, lord," Muwa said.

The Raven moved then, tossing the book he held at my face before he dashed forward, already sweeping a leg to knock my feet out from under me. It was done with breathtaking speed and power, but after seeing Muwa dismantle two Lions barehanded not long ago, I was expecting such a move and was prepared for it. I ducked, letting the book arc over my head, pages flapping like bird wings before striking the canvas behind me while I latched onto Muwa's extended leg at the ankle. I stood then, using the power in my legs to launch the Raven into the air, where he soared backward, arms windmilling for balance before he landed on the bench, collapsing it as a whoosh of air was expelled from his lungs.

But Muwa was far from done, and he spun aside just as I stamped my right boot where his face had been before kicking me in the back of my left knee. I dropped instantly, that knee going numb as the Raven snatched up a broken plank from the bench and lashed out backhanded, catching me on the left cheek. My head snapped back from the blow, blood spraying onto the canvas walls as I staggered and almost fell. I took two wobbly steps away from my opponent, wincing at the sharp pinching in my knee as Muwa stood and arrogantly brushed himself off with one hand. He still held the piece of wood from the bench like a club in the other.

"I thought you didn't use weapons," I said, wiping blood from my face.

"Correction, lord," the Raven replied, breathing easily. The bastard looked no worse for wear from his fall as far as I could tell. "I told you I don't *carry* weapons. I never said I wouldn't use them if the situation warranted it."

"Ah," I muttered. I turned my head sideways and spat blood. "You might have mentioned that little bit of information before I tossed my knife away."

"An oversight, lord. I assure you it won't happen again." Muwa slowly removed the chain holding the six-pointed star from around his neck, then his robe, revealing cotton trousers and a brown tunic underneath, which he pulled over his head and tossed aside. The Raven's torso was heavily muscled and scarred, much like my own, and I noticed he had a blue star tattooed over his heart. "Have you ever been imprisoned, lord?" Muwa asked. "Felt the bars closing in on you and the despair chewing away at your insides like rats feasting on a carcass? Can you imagine what it must take to survive such a thing?"

I thought of Father's Arse from so long ago. "I can," I growled. "I was a slave for nine years of my life."

"I see," Muwa said, looking a little taken aback by my answer. "I didn't know that." He shrugged. "Then you know from experience that only the strongest of the strong come out alive from those places."

"I do know that," I agreed. I flexed my knee, gratified that the feeling was coming back. It still hurt something fierce, but at least I could put decent weight on it now. I grinned at my opponent. "That's why you're about to die, and I'll be giving your regards to the Eye of God when I see him."

Then I charged.

Chapter 36: Ravens And Poetry

An hour later, I sat on the unbroken bench in Muwa's tent, enjoying some Cordovian wine from his private stock while I read the book of poetry he'd thrown at my head earlier. Poetry had never interested me much in the past, but I had to admit that some of what I was reading was really quite good. The author—Lascar dal Vineci—had been the son of a Temba lord more than a hundred years ago, and his prose was filled not only with humorous satire and witty insights, but also with fantastical ideas for inventions that left me shaking my head in wonder. I'd laughed out loud or gasped in amazement numerous times while I drank and read, which Muwa—who lay on the floor on his side facing me with his feet trussed and hands tied behind his back—did not seem to appreciate.

I glanced down at the Raven, who I saw was having some difficulty breathing through his shattered nose. I imagine the three broken ribs weren't helping him much, either. "Listen to this, Muwa," I said enthusiastically. "Lord Vineci hypothesized that men could actually fly just like the birds do by using this winged wooden contraption that he designed. Can you imagine such a thing? I wonder if he actually managed to do it?"

I turned the book so the Raven could see the detailed illustration that I was looking at, though I guessed it was a little difficult for him, what with his blackened right eye being swollen shut as it was. The man mumbled something unintelligible around the gag in his mouth, and I paused, examining him closely, but there were no signs of madness yet that I could see.

I shrugged, returning to my book only to look up moments later when three distinctive scratches sounded at the entrance, the signal letting me know it was Jebido. My friend stepped inside a moment later.

"The carts are on the way back to our camp, Hadrack," Jebido said.

"You unloaded all the caskets?"

"Yes. At least half of them are already empty, and the rest are going fast."

"That's good," I said with a satisfied nod. "Is anything happening out there yet?"

"A few fights so far resulting in one death, but nothing out of the ordinary for an army of this size," Jebido replied. He glanced down at Muwa. "What about him?"

"No reaction so far," I said. Muwa had been barely conscious when I'd forced the tankard of tainted wine down his throat, and I'm sure he didn't even remember me doing it. I still hadn't told him what was going on yet, though I could tell by the dismayed look in his eye that the Raven was starting to suspect.

"Well, you can't stay in here much longer, Hadrack," Jebido said. "One of those White Raven bastards was heading this way, so Baine had to cut his throat. There could be more coming for all I know. We need to move before things get out of hand."

"Agreed," I said. "You, Baine, and Putt better head back. I'll be right behind you."

"That's a bad idea, Hadrack," Jebido said, his face clouding. "If Lord Fitzery is right, then once this thing starts, it's going to move faster than a brush fire. That's not something you want to get caught up in."

"I've got time," I insisted. I gestured to Muwa, who was glaring up at me. "This shouldn't take too much longer."

Jebido snorted. "You stubborn fool. Why do you always have to do things the hard way? Why not just kill him and be done with it?"

"Because then he gets off easy, Jebido. No, I want Muwa to understand what he did to all those people before he dies. And the best way to do that is for him to experience it firsthand." The Raven started shaking his head then, trying to make himself understood through the gag. I just smiled down at him mockingly. "Now you're starting to see, aren't you?" I dropped to my knees beside the man, putting a hand to each of his temples as I lifted his bald head and stared into the eye that still worked. "I destroyed your fleet last night, Muwa," I said. "And today, I took your baggage train." I pointed toward the entrance. "My men have been giving your army wine and ale laced with jimsonweed for over an hour now. You remember jimsonweed, don't you?"

I waited, enjoying the moment as Muwa's eye bulged and his skin turned red while he fought to speak. Finally, I untied the gag, then put the point of my knife I'd recovered earlier to the Raven's throat. I slowly drew the blade lightly back and forth across his vulnerable skin. "Speak louder than a whisper, you bastard, and I'll give you a nice gaping red smile right here, understand?"

"I do, Lord Hadrack," Muwa rasped out, his voice sounding high and reedy from his broken nose. He licked his swollen, battered lips and glanced sideways up at Jebido's stern face, then back to me. "I don't suppose asking for mercy would help?"

"Of course it would," I said agreeably. I saw hope rising in the man's features and added, "I'll give you the same kind of mercy you gave all those people in Temba. Doesn't that sound fair?"

Muwa deflated noticeably. "What I did, I did in the name of the One True God, lord, and I stand by it," he said stubbornly. "If only we could talk about this in depth, you would come to understand that sacrifices must be made for the good of us all. My actions were justified, and I—"

I snorted and jammed the gag down the Raven's throat without warning, having heard more than enough. The last thing I felt like listening to right now was a sermon from a pious hypocrite like Muwa. Outside, a sudden scream sounded, followed by hoarse shouts and the clanging of weapons. It had begun.

"That's it," Jebido grunted. He brushed aside the tent flap, pausing in the opening to wiggle his fingers at me urgently. "Come on, Hadrack. We have to leave right now!"

I stood, wincing as my left knee protested. Muwa suddenly spasmed and started squirming like a fish on a hook, shaking his head and moaning. At first, I thought he was just trying to get my attention again, but when I looked down and saw his twisted features, I realized with relief that the madness had finally come for him.

I slashed with my knife, cutting the bonds around Muwa's feet, which he instantly kicked wildly. "None of that now," I grunted as I struck the man in the face with my balled fist. More blood exploded from Muwa's shattered nose, and he sagged, whimpering while he fought to breathe. I pulled the gag out of his mouth and tossed it aside, having no intentions of letting the bastard die from something as simple as lack of air. No, his fate required something more appropriate. I looked up at Jebido. "Help me get him on his feet."

Jebido and I lifted Muwa by the armpits while he struggled weakly in our grip, and we dragged him to the entrance and stepped outside, where Baine and Putt were waiting. Both men looked relieved to see us. I paused then as a thought struck me. "Hold him," I told Jebido before I turned and ran back into the tent, hurrying to snatch up Lord Vineci's book. The drawings and concepts inside were almost all beyond my ability to comprehend, but I knew Hanley back home in Corwick would relish a chance to study them. "All right," I said upon my return. "Let's go."

"Which way?" Jebido grunted.

The madness I remembered well from Temba had already started in earnest, with half the tents in our vicinity lit up like torches while men fought, screamed, and died among them. A soldier scrambled past us on all fours like a monkey, shrieking as he looked behind him in terror. Another to our left was hacking and slashing at nothing with his glaive until finally, he tripped and fell into a campfire, where he lay unmoving in the flames. Moments later, the nauseating smell of burning flesh rolled over us.

"Take a good look, Muwa," I whispered into the Raven's ear, holding on tightly to the man's bare arm. "This is what your god brings to the world—nothing but madness, suffering, and death. Is it worth it?"

Muwa twisted his shining bald head to look at me, and for a moment, I thought I saw something in his expression, some sign of understanding, before he suddenly hissed and snapped at me like a dog. I flinched backward just as his teeth clicked shut, narrowly missing the tip of my nose before Jebido had a chance to haul him back. I glanced past the Raven to my friend. "Let him go," I said. "It's time this White Raven met The Father."

"Gladly," Jebido grunted with distaste.

We released Muwa at the same time, shoving him several paces away from us. The Raven stumbled, unbalanced as he was with his hands tied behind his back. He finally steadied, sniffing the smoke on the wind for a moment before he tilted his head back and howled at the full moon. A moment later, Muwa was lost from my view, heading at a run around a burning tent. I never saw the bastard again.

It took the four of us nearly half an hour to get free of the encampment, and much like in Temba, the things we witnessed during that time would stay with me forever. I'd told my companions all about the horror of that night in Temba, of course, but describing something after the fact and seeing it firsthand for yourself are two very different things. Needless to say, we were a solemn bunch when we finally got back to the baggage train, where we found most of my men standing on a slight rise, watching the events unfolding in fascination. I should have been angry that the horses weren't drawn up and ready to go, I suppose, but in truth, there was nothing to fear from the Raven army right now, and it didn't really matter. I doubted there would be much left of it come morning, anyway.

"My lord," Tyris said, hurrying up to us. "Thank the gods. Someone told me you'd returned some time ago, but I couldn't find you anywhere. Had I known you were still in—"

"That's fine, Tyris," I said wearily, cutting off the blond archer. "No harm done. I stopped to say hello to an old friend and got held up." Tyris' eyebrows rose, but the man had known me and my ways for many years, and he said nothing further. "Any casualties?" I asked.

"Only two, my lord," Tyris answered. "One of the carts was flipped over by a mob on the way back, and the men and the mule were slaughtered."

I nodded, knowing it could have been far, far worse. "Very good. Get the horses. It's time to get away from here and join up with the others."

"Yes, my lord."

We spent the next five hours waiting and watching from beneath the trees in the hills, with the ocean at our backs and the flatlands spread out in front of us. The fields below our position were lit up starkly from the flames, allowing me a good view of the Raven encampment—or rather, what little remained of it. Occasionally, a soldier would appear on foot coming our way, his eyes wide and crazed while he babbled nonsense and wobbled unsteadily on his feet. If the man had the distinctive flat features of a Temba or even a Cordovian, we subdued him and tied him up to wait for the madness to pass. If, on the other hand, he was dressed in a red cape and wore pointed black boots, then all we had to offer him was a quick and painless death. It was more than any of those bastards deserved, in my view.

I watched the carnage below for the better part of an hour, then, growing bored of it, I retreated deeper into the trees to sleep for a while with orders that I was to be woken at dawn or if anything interesting happened. As it turned out, they both occurred simultaneously when I felt a rough hand on my shoulder hours later, shaking me. I groaned and sat up, my body stiff and sore, with my left knee where Muwa had kicked me protesting the loudest. "What is it?" I asked Baine, who squatted beside me.

"The sun's rising," my friend replied. "And we've got some activity below."

"What kind of activity?" I asked with my breath rising around me. Despite the cloak I wore, I shivered in the cool desert air while I rubbed my arms vigorously to warm them.

"The White Raven kind," Baine said. He turned his head and spat. "Looks like the bastards have organized themselves. Maybe the jimsonweed is wearing off. I don't know. Either way, something's up. I counted close to twenty of them running around and shouting orders. They're hard to miss in those robes."

I stood, stamping my feet and hobbling around on my bad leg for a few steps before the blood began to flow and the knee started working properly again. I paused near a tall oak, undid my trousers, and then relieved myself against the tree as I glanced back at Baine. "Organized how?"

"Looks like they're getting ready to go somewhere, Hadrack. There must be at least seven or eight hundred soldiers formed up already, with more joining them all the time."

"Go where? Back to Temba?"

"That would be my guess," Baine agreed. "The Ravens don't have enough men to take Sandhold now, and they know it. They're probably just hoping to hold on to what they already have so they can regroup and try again later."

I frowned as I laced up my trousers. Baine was probably right about the White Ravens' plans. Despite clipping their wings last night, more of the enemy had survived than I'd hoped. Certainly enough to do more damage and cause added mischief later on if I allowed them to leave now. "Horses?"

"Maybe fifty at most," Baine said. He stood smoothly and grinned. "They're still disorganized and look ripe for a charge to me, Hadrack. We won't get a better chance than this."

I nodded. "What do *Hasama* Alfaheed and *Rhana* Telman say?"

Baine shrugged. "They wanted to attack right away without waking you." My friend grimaced. "Lord Fitzery talked them out of it, insisting that it was your decision to make, not theirs. The last I looked, that Bone Warrior was ready to skewer Lord Fitzery."

"Well, we can't let that happen," I grunted. I stooped and picked up Wolf's Head, sliding the weapon into its sheath. "Let's go talk with them before someone ends up dead."

I headed for the treeline with Baine, where I found almost four hundred Bone Warriors and Lions armed and mounted, waiting for the word to move out. Telman and Alfaheed were sitting their horses' side by side beneath a towering aspen, deep in conversation. The two had become fast friends, which despite the many years of animosity between their peoples, hadn't surprised me in the least. Both were tough, competent fighting men with keen minds and similar philosophies. Fitz sat his horse some distance away, one hand on his sword as he glared at the two men. I saw his hard features relax with relief when he saw me approaching.

Fitz inclined his head to me as I made my way toward the lords while Baine went to fetch his horse. I paused a moment later as the lad, Giree, appeared through the trees leading a black mare with soft eyes that I'd ridden earlier from the baggage train to the hills. I nodded to the youth in gratitude as I swung up into the saddle. Giree had had the foresight to strap one of the round Lion shields on the mare in anticipation of an attack, I noted with approval.

"Good morning," I said in greeting as I guided the mare next to Alfaheed and Telman. "I understand the enemy is not done quite yet."

"So it would appear," Alfaheed agreed, nodding toward the encampment and the soldiers gathering there. I noticed most of them wore red capes and shiny black boots.

"These dogs would all be dead by now if not for him," Telman grunted, motioning to Fitz. "That one would rather we sit here all day with our fingers up our arses while they prepare."

I said nothing as I glanced out at the open field, which was now being kissed by orange, red, and yellow rays as the sun rose slowly in the east. The destruction of the Raven campsite was staggering, seen in daylight, with hundreds and hundreds of corpses lying twisted in the scorched grass. Not a single tent was left standing that I could see, with giant plumes of black smoke billowing skyward from every corner within the earthen ramparts. Cardian soldiers were picking through the rubble and bodies while others were gathering to the south where a white-robed Raven stood on an upended casket, waving his arms passionately. I couldn't hear what the bastard was saying from this far away, though I could imagine.

"And exactly how would you have done that?" I finally asked Telman. "Taken care of it, I mean? From what I can see, the enemy outnumber us by a wide margin."

"By running the bastards down with a quick charge, Your Highness," Telman grunted. "Men on foot make easy prey for cavalry."

"Like my archers were during the Battle of the Bone Road?" I asked. I sensed Fitz grinning to my left but chose not to look at him.

"That's different," Telman said.

"How so?"

"The enemy were confused, and you had good defensive position."

I pointed to the encampment, which was encircled by a wide ditch and eight-foot-high earthen ramparts. "And what is that down there if not a good defensive position?" I asked. The Bone Warrior frowned as I raised a pair of fingers. "There are only two entrances.

One to the north, and one to the south. Both are no wider than three horses abreast. Block those with shield walls and pikes, and then what becomes of your cavalry charge?"

"We go over the embankments," Alfaheed suggested.

I shook my head. "Cardians are generally cowards, but they aren't necessarily stupid ones. The ditch will be too wide for a horse to jump. They will have made certain of that. But, even if you managed to get over it somehow, the climb would be difficult. I imagine they also have archers down there, which would add to your problems."

"Then we go through their shields, Your Highness," Telman growled, looking annoyed.

I nodded. "Yes, you could certainly do that—eventually. But at what cost?" This time I did glance at Fitz, who was indeed smiling. He'd known all along what the right course of action should be.

Telman shrugged. "Men die in battle all the time, Your Highness. Victory and glory are all that matter."

I shook my head and grinned. "Are you sure you're not a Pith, *Rhana*?" The Bone Warrior grimaced, and I guessed by his expression that he wasn't sure what a Pith was. "Anyway," I said. "Lord Fitzery was right to insist you wait."

"Why?" Alfaheed asked. "The longer we sit here, the more time they have to recover their strength."

"Quite true," I conceded. "But sooner or later, the Ravens will have to leave that encampment for the open fields. And when they do, they'll be vulnerable. That's when we strike them the same way we did the baggage train."

I looked in the direction of the city while Telman and Alfaheed digested that. I could just make out the solidness of Sandhold's outer curtainwall a half mile away, almost hidden by the haze of smoke drifting past. I had little doubt the ramparts would be crammed to overflowing with anxious inhabitants wondering what was happening.

"*Rhana* Telman, how many horsemen do we have inside the walls of the city?"

"Roughly a thousand, I believe, Your Highness," the Bone Warrior answered grudgingly.

"Good," I said, pleased. "Send a messenger to them now. I want those men in the saddle ready to ride within half an hour. Nobody moves until they hear my signal, and when they do, they are to attack the head of the column." I smiled. "And make sure to tell them to sharpen their spears while they're waiting."

"Yes, Your Highness," Telman said, his eyes gleaming now with appreciation for the plan.

An hour later, the Cardians—led by a procession of Ravens—began to head out the southern opening of the encampment as the sun rose higher in the sky and the land warmed. I guessed they were heading for the baggage train, planning to salvage what supplies they could before the long trek back to Temba. They were about to be disappointed.

I waited until the last of the marchers were well out in the open, the column stretching in a ragged line of men two abreast. "*Hasama* Alfaheed," I said, nodding to the man. "I do believe the moment has come."

The Temba grinned, then lifted a horn and blew three sharp blasts, signaling the horsemen in Sandhold to attack. I raised a hand to hold our men in line, though all within the trees had long ago been briefed on their role and knew now was not the time to move. I heard the unmistakable sound of the city gates creaking open, then the thunderous pounding of hooves before a mass of horses and men with banners flying and armor and weapons twinkling in the sun appeared. The horsemen streamed southeast at a gallop, angling around the marchers to strike at their front. Predictably, confusion ensued among the Cardians when they saw the riders on their flank, with small groups hastily forming into shield walls all along the ragged line.

"Now!" I shouted, swinging my hand forward.

We burst from the trees, racing headlong down the grade, then skirted our horses around the smoking ruins of the Raven encampment. Shouts of dismay sounded from the enemy's rearguard when they turned and saw us, and I smiled, enjoying that special moment of excitement and anticipation just before the battle was joined and blood began to flow. I lifted Wolf's Head in the air, shouting along with the others as we bore down on the doomed Cardians, who were clumsily trying to adjust to this new threat. A quarter of a mile ahead of us, I saw the cavalry from Sandhold wheel about and launch themselves at the front of the column, followed by a crash of splintering wood and ringing of iron as they collided with the hastily forming Cardian shield wall.

Mercenaries screamed and died beneath that first charge in droves, hacked down by swords or run through by the riders' heavy spears. The cavalry pressed onward through the confused ranks of Cardians, with some of the defenders shifting to form a protective square around the White Ravens. I could hear the cries of delight from the horsemen echoing across the field as they ignored that square, focusing on easier prey and slaughtering any man who dared to stand in their way. Then, with the enemy either dead or scattered before them, the riders swung about, lances lowering for a second, devastating charge—this time at the square itself. I laughed out loud as many of the Cardians in the ranks broke and ran, tossing aside their weapons and abandoning the gaggle of white-robed Ravens who cowered in their center.

Then we hit the massed rearguard, and I had no further time to think about anything but the task at hand—killing Cardians.

Chapter 37: The Edge Of The World

One week later, the city of Temba was in a festive mood, for it was execution day, and a holiday had been declared. Forty-seven Ravens and a hundred and three collaborators were set to be beheaded for high treason, with the sentences to begin at midday. These were to be the first official executions the city had seen since the days of Egon del Fante's reign hundreds of years ago. I'd wanted no part in watching it, of course, but as king, my presence was not only necessary but expected—especially since I'd been the one to pass judgment on the accused.

Some from the upper echelons of Temba society had suggested mercy for the Ravens and their ilk, allowing them the opportunity to repent and once again pledge allegiance to the throne, or if not that, then a chance to be judged by the gods in the Waste of Bones. But I'd made it quite clear that banishing criminals to the desert would no longer be Temba policy, which had left court officials scrambling to come up with alternatives that did not include the horrors of Kenningwood. The lawmakers had repeatedly implored me to rethink my decision, but I'd given my word to the Circle of Life that the practice would end in return for their cooperation, and I had no intentions of breaking that promise. The people of Temba would just have to adapt the best that they could.

As for letting the Ravens repent, I knew that would be a mistake. These men were fanatics, and no amount of bending the knee to me or anyone else would ever change that fact. No, the White Ravens and their skewed ideas needed to be eradicated from the city once and for all, and after that, from the rest of the world, even if it had to be done by rooting them out one by one and killing them.

I stood on the upper balcony outside the king's private rooms in the Yellow Palace with my hands braced on the stone railing as I looked down at King's Square—which was a massive, enclosed courtyard far below me where the executions were to take place. It was the same location where I was to have been flayed alive only a few short weeks ago. *Oh, how things have changed,* I thought, shaking my head. The courtyard walls were decorated with garish yellow and gold banners, with several thousand curious onlookers all facing a long raised platform at the north end set at an angle to the outer walls. Five wooden blocks stood in a line down the length of the platform, each with a shaped curvature in the center where the victims' necks would rest.

Seeing the chopping blocks suddenly reminded me of Calban Castle and how close I'd come to losing my beloved Shana to an executioner's axe there once. That axe had belonged to my father, stolen from me by Quant Ranes, one of the nine men who had destroyed my village. I'd later fought and killed him in the tunnels beneath the castle and taken back my axe, which I still had to this day, hanging over the mantle in my rooms in Corwick Castle. It seemed a lifetime ago now that I'd rescued Shana from the clutches of her then-husband, Lord Demay, and I felt a heaviness wash over me as happy memories of the times spent with my wife filled my mind.

I was so engrossed in my thoughts that I didn't notice someone had come to stand with me at the railing until I felt a light touch on my arm. "You look so sad, lord," Sarrey said when I turned in surprise.

The girl was dressed in an elegant burgundy satin gown in honor of the momentous occasion. A wide strip of gold braid ran down the center of her dress, with the collar around her neck made from a soft white fur that I guessed might be ermine. More fur encircled the cuffs at the end of her flared sleeves and along the hem of her skirt, which brushed the ground. She looked very exotic and beautiful, I thought. I was dressed in my regular armor, forgoing the usual kingly attire for familiar comfort, though I had conceded to wearing a black and yellow cape that I detested to appease both Sarrey and Vizier Banta. I steadfastly had refused the gem-studded crown I was offered, though, determined never to put the damn thing on my head.

"Would you care to talk about it?" Sarrey added in a kind voice.

I sighed, trying to shake off my melancholy. "It's nothing," I said. I gestured to the crowded square, deflecting away from my true thoughts. "It's just that I've killed a great many men in my lifetime, but never in this way."

"Are you regretting your ruling, lord?"

I snorted. "Hardly. Those men deserve their fate, and we'll all be better off with them gone from this world. I guess I'm just feeling like a pompous fool way up here, watching while other men swing the blades of my justice."

"Have you executed men before then, lord?" Sarrey asked curiously. "By your own hand, I mean?"

"I have," I grunted. "That's the role each lord in Ganderland must assume as wardens of the King's Law." I gestured again to the platform. "It's easy to decide a man's fate when you don't have to worry about getting your hands dirty. But when you're the one looking into his eyes just before you swing the blade, it humbles you. We are all fallible, even lords and kings, and every time I've taken a life that way, I've prayed to the gods that I've made the right decision."

"Surely you aren't considering going down there and chopping the heads off all those traitors by yourself, are you, Your Highness?" Vizier Banta asked from behind me.

I turned, realizing the man had been standing in the open doorway to my rooms this entire time. "Of course not, Vizier." I motioned him forward. "Come and join us."

"Sadly, Your Highness, I cannot just yet," Banta said with a slight bow. "I am needed elsewhere in the Palace. I just stopped by to pass on a message from Lord Fitzery. It seems the ship your men had been seeking has just now been towed into the harbor."

"*Sea-Wolf*?" I said in surprise, feeling excitement shoot through me. "They actually found her?"

"Indeed they did, Your Highness," Banta said. "My understanding is the damage was quite extensive, but they managed to repair the ship well enough to get her here."

"Thank the gods for that," I said in relief. I'd wanted to go with Baine, Jebido, and the others to search for and hopefully recover *Sea-Wolf*, but my endless duties as the new King of Temba had kept me from it. A symphony of horns suddenly sounded from below, and I frowned as brightly-garbed dignitaries flanked by Lions in full battle armor entered the square, while the onlooking crowd cheered. The executions were about to start, and I hissed with impatience. I wanted to go to the harbor and see my ship and friends, not stand on this cursed balcony in the hot sun all day, watching men lose their heads. I glanced at Banta. "Any estimation on how soon *Sea-Wolf* can be made ready to sail?"

"No, Your Highness," Banta said regretfully. "But Lord Fitzery did state that it did not look good, so if I were you, I would temper my expectations."

I nodded, disappointed yet hardly surprised. I was set to leave in the morning on an excursion to the End of the World to find the Eye of God, and a foolish part of me had hoped that I could take *Sea-Wolf* along. "Thank you, Vizier," I said. "Is there anything else?"

"One small matter, Your Highness. A *Rhana* from Sandhold named Dachmar has requested an audience at your earliest convenience. He claims that one of your men impregnated his daughter and is demanding restitution for her dishonor."

I groaned, knowing the Vizier could only mean Baine. "What kind of restitution?"

"The kind that involves blood I believe, Your Highness," Banta said with a blank face.

I sighed. "Tell *Rhana* Dachmar that I will speak with him after the executions and we will come to some equitable arrangement then."

"Very good, Your Highness," Banta said. He bowed and turned to leave.

"Oh, and Vizier?"

"Your Highness?"

"Make sure someone tells Baine to stay on *Spearfish* until further notice. I don't need any more pregnant daughters right now, nor do I need a dead *Rhana* if he's foolish enough to make a move against Baine before we talk."

"It will be done, Your Highness."

I shook my head at my friend's endless follies as the Vizier left, listening to his boots clicking on the polished marble floor of my lavish accommodations. I still felt like a fraud every time I went into those rooms.

"You can't really blame the poor thing," Sarrey said.

"Who, the *Rhana*?"

Sarrey chuckled. "No, silly. His daughter. Baine is very handsome and dashing. He's hard to resist."

"Is that right?" I said, annoyed for some reason.

"Oh yes," Sarrey said. She looked up at me with her eyes half-closed. "At least for some women, I suppose."

"But not you?" I grunted.

"No, lord," Sarrey said. She put her hand on my arm again. "I have my sights set on someone else." She smiled mischievously. "Someone much taller who has promised to marry me."

Sarrey began rubbing my arm much the way Shana used to, and I unconsciously pulled it away, aware of the hurt look on the girl's face. "I'll be setting out at first light tomorrow morning," I said, just for something to break the awkward silence. Below, jeers and hissing erupted as a line of shackled bald men appeared through an archway to the south. Their feet were bare, and they were dressed in simple gray tunics that hung to their knees, not even afforded the last wish of dying in their white robes. That had been my doing. It was vindictive, I know, but it made me feel good just the same. The crowd made way for the doomed men, though many began throwing rotten vegetables and horse dung at them as they passed. The helpless Ravens could do little but lower their chins to their chests and accept the abuse being heaped on them, as soldiers prodded them along with glaives. I glanced at Sarrey. "I'm told the journey can take weeks, so I don't know when I'll be back."

Sarrey's eyes flashed with sudden anger. "What are you saying? That you're going back on your word. Because if you—"

"I'm not going back on my word, Sarrey," I said, cutting the girl off. "I said I would marry you, and I will. All I'm telling you is I'll be gone a while, that's it. We can talk about the wedding when I get back."

"Why can't we discuss it now?" Sarrey demanded. "There are a thousand things that need planning and I need your input."

I sighed. "No, you don't, and we both know it. Just do whatever you think is best."

More cheers sounded from below as five men wearing black hoods holding massive axes climbed onto the platform. They were followed moments later by an equal amount of Ravens, herded like sheep to the slaughter up a wide flight of wooden steps by Lions and then forced to kneel with their heads on the blocks. One of them was Theny, who we'd captured after the battle at the Raven encampment, which had been an almost embarrassingly one-sided affair. The executioners slowly moved into position, axes raised as a hush of anticipation fell over the courtyard. Every eye turned upward then, looking to the balcony where I stood with Sarrey.

"What are they waiting for?" I whispered out of the side of my mouth.

"For you, lord," Sarrey said, her tone more amiable now. "You must signal the executioners to strike. They will not move until you do."

I nodded, lifting my right hand briefly as the cheers below began again before I dropped it back to my side. Five blades instantly flashed in the sunlight, and even from our lofty height, I heard the meaty thunks as cold steel cleaved through skin, muscle, and bone. Moments later, workers scurried onto the platform, picking up the severed heads or carrying away the limp, headless corpses while women with rags tried vainly to soak up some of the blood.

It was going to be a very, very long afternoon.

The skies were black and threatening when we first set eyes on the Edge of the World nearly three weeks later. The island was, in fact, a dormant volcano, shaped much like the curved blades of the shotels the Temba favored. I guessed the landmass measured at most ten miles in length and maybe five in width, with the conical peak of the volcano with its tell-tale crater dominating the tip of the island's southern portion. A second mountain rose along the thicker northern coast, though it was much smaller than the one to the south and had no crater that I could see. Could an island this small house two volcanos? I didn't know. Hills covered by shards of volcanic rock and rich fauna intersected the two mounts, joining them together in a ragged chain broken by forest-covered valleys. The Edge of the World was ringed almost entirely by fringe coral and shifting sandbars, with a long, narrow lagoon running along the inside curve of the island that was protected by a double wall of slick barrier reefs jutting ten feet or more out of the water. A natural inlet led into the lagoon from the north, and from my vantage point on *Spearfish's* forecastle, I could see several small ships moored close to a sandy beach at the southern end.

"Well, that's that," Jebido grunted. He gestured to a score of figures running across the sand toward the west, where a round stone hillfort rose on a high promontory overlooking the beach. "So much for the element of surprise."

"It won't matter," I said grimly. "We've got more than enough men to get the job done." I glanced over my shoulder at the flotilla of ten catamarans spread out behind *Spearfish*, each with a colorful yellow and black Lion sigil displayed proudly on their sails and carrying a compliment of a hundred soldiers. I thought I could hear a bell tolling across the water from the shore, but I knew it might just be the wind playing tricks on me. I glanced up at the cloudy skies, praying the approaching storm would blow over before I focused back on our prize, studying the fortress with an experienced eye. "It looks like they've got earth ramparts around the base of the walls," I said as we drew closer. "Maybe eight feet high." The hillfort was relatively modest from what I could see, with a keep and no more than twenty buildings inside. A ramp of dirt and stone rose from the beach to a narrow wooden bridge spanning a ditch, which led to a squat gatehouse buttressed by two formidable square turrets. Long tapered pennants flew above the turrets, but I couldn't make them out from this distance. I had little doubt they depicted a six-pointed star.

"And I'd wager that ditch runs all the way around," Fitz commented.

"A moat, you mean?" Baine asked.

I shook my head. "Not unless there's a mountain stream feeding it from somewhere, which I don't see. They've picked a good location for the fort, but at that elevation, it would be next to impossible to get enough water up there to make a difference." I glanced at Alfaheed, who stood close by with his hands crossed behind his back. "Do they get a lot of rain here?"

The Temba shrugged. "Who can say for certain, Your Highness?" He smiled wryly. "They don't call it the End of the World for nothing, after all."

"Why haven't they started destroying the bridge yet?" Baine asked.

"A damn fine question," I muttered. I shrugged. "I guess we'll find out soon enough." I could feel the wind tugging at my cloak, and I glanced at the skies again. The clouds were rolling and undulating wildly over our heads, but so far, there was no rain to speak of, nor thunder or lightning. I knew the wise course of action would be to wait, but in truth, I was sick and tired of the Southlands and just wanted to return home. The Eye of God was the only thing left standing in my way of that.

"We should wait for this to pass before we make landfall, Hadrack," Jebido grunted—my friend, as always, reading my thoughts correctly. He motioned to the island. "Those bastards aren't going anywhere."

"Agreed," Fitz said.

"The beaches are free from defenders at the moment," Alfaheed responded when I looked his way. "I say we capture them before that changes."

"A good point," I replied. I glanced at Rorian, who stood some distance away from us. His face was etched in serious concentration as he glared toward the shoreline with his arms crossed over his chest. "And you?" I said. "What do you think we should do?"

The scholar turned to me, his eyes dark, hard, and filled with suppressed violence. His eyebrows had mostly grown back, giving his features an even darker cast. "Need you ask, lord?" he growled.

"No, I suppose not," I said. Revenge can eat away at a man, dominating his every thought, as I well knew, and I recognized the resolve to do whatever it took in the scholar's eyes, for I carried that resolve as well. We were so close now that Rorian could smell the blood pumping in the Eye of God's veins—blood he desperately wanted to spill. I had no intention of cheating him of that. "Very well," I said, coming to a decision. "We go in now and capture the beach as *Hasama* Alfaheed suggests. Then we take it from there."

"And if that storm hits while we're about it?" Jebido asked.

"Just pray the gods are watching and it doesn't," I said, hoping I was making the right decision.

I sent the catamarans into the lagoon first, simply because they were more maneuverable and had much smaller hulls than *Spearfish*. Because of that fact, I reasoned the ships should be able to get close enough to the beach to allow my men to get ashore quickly on their own. I watched anxiously as, one by one, the double-hulled Temba boats powered by their oars slowed in the water and came to a shuddering halt when their hulls struck the soft loam near the shoreline. Soldiers immediately jumped into the surf and waded onto the beach, then quickly and efficiently took up defensive positions facing the hillfort. Yet, as the numbers of my force continued to grow on the sand, I saw no evidence of movement from the enemy fortress at all.

I frowned, feeling a deep sense of unease rising in my gut as I studied the closed gates suspiciously. What was going on here? I could see no defenders lined along the ramparts ready to pepper us with arrows, nor were there the usual shouts and clamor of panic that you'd logically expect to hear coming from a fortress about to undergo an assault. Even the bell that I'd thought I'd heard earlier was no longer tolling. The only sounds coming from the shore were the shouted commands of my men and the snapping of the Lion and Wolf banners they held.

"Well, this is new," Fitz muttered as *Spearfish* slowly sailed along the lagoon, propelled by her oars. He took off his helmet and scratched his scalp vigorously. "I've never seen this before, Hadrack."

"Do you think it's a trap?" I asked.

"I don't know," Fitz said with a shrug. "What other explanation can there be?"

I studied the empty bridge, but for my life, I could see no obvious danger there. I wondered briefly if they'd cut through the supports underneath, hoping many of us would die when it collapsed, but then discarded the idea as unlikely. I'd seen no activity there at all, but even if they had somehow been warned we were coming and had weakened the bridge beforehand, I wasn't stupid enough to send my entire force across without checking first.

"Maybe they don't have as many defenders as we were led to believe," Jebido suggested. "If not, they might have all retreated to the keep to make a stand there."

I nodded, thinking Jebido's idea made some sense. We'd gotten a lot of useful information about the island's defenses from a young Raven named Flisp, who'd preferred talking to us rather than being subjected to Baine's blades. That talkative Raven had told us the fortress was usually manned by as many as three hundred Ravens, not to mention new recruits that were constantly coming and going. I'd still had Flisp beheaded after he'd told us everything he knew, of course, but at least his death had not been as painful as it might have been otherwise. I'd believed what he'd told me at the time, but now, in hindsight, I was beginning to wonder if the youth had lied after all about the fort's strength.

I waited, tapping my fingers on the gunwale with restless energy while Putt guided *Spearfish* as close to the shore as he dared before lowering the anchor, leaving us still a good two hundred yards out. The two enemy vessels to the south were both single-masted longships much like the Cardians used, I noted, though they seemed somewhat wider to me and shorter in length. I could see no activity on either one and, in fact, thought they looked long abandoned, which logically meant they were no threat to us. I turned my attention back to the beach, where Temba sailors worked to lower outriggers into the water from the catamarans. Those boats would be used to transfer my men to the shore.

"We're ready for you, my lord!" I heard Tyris call from the lower deck.

"All right," I grunted to my companions. "Let's go."

I'd had the skiff from *Sea-Wolf* moved to *Spearfish*, and it was now in the water below us, rocking gently on the slight tide beside the cog's portside bow. I let Alfaheed, Baine, Jebido, Fitz, and Rorian precede me before I lowered myself down a heavily knotted rope, joining them on the benches as a brawny sailor took up the oars. He pushed us away from *Spearfish's* hull, then began rowing us toward the shoreline with powerful, measured strokes. No one said anything, though all eyes remained steadfastly fixated on the beach, searching for any signs of threats. There were none.

Rorian was the first to jump out when we hit the shore, the scholar striding toward the hillfort without looking back as he drew his sword. Jebido was next, followed by the others, then me. My boots immediately sunk into the wet sand, with my nostrils filled with the musty scent of the soil, mixing with the aroma of rotting vegetation and decaying marine life washed up on the beaches. A small sand crab hesitated as I moved past it, rearing back with its claws extended defensively.

"Don't worry, little one," I whispered as I drew Wolf's Head. "I have bigger prey to hunt this day than you, trust me." I passed the formations of Lions waiting patiently in the sand, stopping ten feet in front of them to inspect the hillfort again. Rorian had halted near the edge of the beach where it met the ramp, but I could tell by his stance that he was ready to charge at any moment. There were still no signs of life to be seen from the fortress. "*Hasama Alfaheed*," I finally called out.

"Yes, Your Highness?" the Temba said.

"Send two men to inspect the bridge underneath and report back. Also, send scouts around that hillfort to look for any surprises that might be waiting. There could be men hiding in the ditch."

"Right away, Your Highness."

As it turned out, the bridge was intact and had not been tampered with, nor were there any forces waiting in ambush. The wind had died down considerably while we waited for the scouts to return, and the cloudy skies were now much clearer, revealing a dazzling blue sky.

"So, what do you think?" I asked my companions after the last of the scouts had reported their findings. Some may think me overly cautious for waiting, but in truth, I felt it justified. I'd been involved in enough battles and sieges to know that something didn't add up with what I was seeing. I just couldn't figure out what it was.

"Enough of this!" Rorian shouted. He gestured to a battering ram made from a solid oak log and capped with iron that the Temba had unloaded from one of the catamarans. "Give the order to break down the gates, Hadrack."

"*Lord* Hadrack," Baine growled, taking two steps forward and lowering his hand to the knife at his belt.

I put my hand on Baine's arm, letting him know I wanted no trouble here. We were all on edge—Rorian more so than most of us—and allowances needed to be made for that. I glanced around. "Any reason not to do as our impatient friend suggests?"

"I can think of a thousand," Jebido grunted pessimistically. "But I'm not getting any younger standing here, Hadrack, so let's just get this over with and go home."

"Agreed," Fitz said grimly.

Baine relaxed then, and he nodded to me, though not before giving Rorian a look of disdain. The scholar didn't seem to notice, his attention already back on the hillfort.

"You agree, *Hasama* Alfaheed?" I asked the Temba.

"I do, Your Highness."

"Then give the order," I said.

Alfaheed gave a slight bow, then strode away to face the massed soldiers. He pointed up at the hillfort. "Lions, there is a gate over there that is stopping us from killing Ravens! So what are we going to do about it?"

A thousand throats cried out then, rattling weapons in reply as twenty burly soldiers picked up the ram and began moving toward the bridge at a trot. I followed behind them, with Rorian to my right and Baine to my left. Tyris and my Wolf's Teeth followed with their bows nocked and ready to shoot at the first sign of the enemy while the rest of my army brought up the rear, led by

Alfaheed, Jebido, and Fitz. The ram-bearers reached the bridge, their boots pounding against the planks as their pace increased. I glanced up at the ramparts, but there were still no signs of the enemy. Despite that, I kept my shield raised just in case, still suspecting some form of ambush.

The ram-bearers were now twenty feet from the gates, shouting as they raced forward, until finally, with a crash, the iron-plated head hit the wooden obstruction. I'd seen rams used in siege warfare many times, and in every incidence, it took multiple attempts to break through even the flimsiest of gates—but not this time. The hillfort's double gates burst open on the first try, surprising everyone as they crashed inward without splintering. Incredibly, they hadn't been barred! The ram-bearers hesitated, backing off while my men streamed around them and charged into the small courtyard inside, screaming war cries and waving weapons only to stop dead in their tracks in astonishment at what they saw. I shook my head in disbelief as I entered the fort, slowly lowering my sword.

"Well damn," Jebido whispered in wonder beside me.

The courtyard was filled with white-robed bald men—but every last one of them was dead.

Chapter 38: The Eye Of God

"Well?" I asked Fitz. My friend was kneeling beside the twisted corpse of a White Raven lying in the fetal position near a wagon filled with hay.

Fitz stood up with a sigh to face me. "Near as I can figure, Hadrack, they all died from some kind of poison."

I nodded, having expected that answer. I studied the White Raven, who was thin, short, and disfigured by a clubbed foot. I guessed he was maybe eighteen years old at the most. The boy's white robe was stained with yellow vomit down the front, with clumps of food and white slime smearing his purple lips. His tongue was the color of coal, hanging out the side of his mouth grotesquely. A blue, six-pointed star with a chip out of it lay in the dirt near his right hand, which I assumed the boy had been holding to give him courage while the poison took hold.

Shouts echoed back and forth throughout the hillfort as Lions searched the buildings and grounds for threats, but so far, they had found nothing but more dead Ravens. I'd decided to leave searching the keep until the end, my instinct telling me that if anyone was still alive in the fortress, it would be there. That decision had not gone over well with Rorian, of course, and I'd been forced to have some of my men restrain him until the other buildings were secure. When we went into the keep, it would be cautiously and in force, not led by a man bent solely on revenge—a revenge that was starting to look like it might have been stolen from him anyway.

"Why aren't there any women and children here, Your Highness?" Alfaheed asked me.

"The Ravens are sworn to celibacy," I explained, having learned that from Flisp. "By putting on the white robe and shaving their bodies, they accept service to the One True God and nothing else. Even their families are abandoned, never to be seen or talked to again."

Alfaheed grimaced in understanding and walked away while I glanced up at the walls. I'd placed archers on the ramparts to keep an eye on things, with half my men waiting outside the fortress on the beach and the other half inside searching buildings. I was still leery of an ambush, but that fear was subsiding minute by minute as more reports of dead Ravens continued to arrive. Finally, when I was satisfied the entire compound had been searched, I glanced at Rorian, who was glaring at me with suppressed fury. I decided there was no point in keeping him back any longer and nodded to the men holding him that they could let him go. The moment he was free, Rorian raced up the wooden stairwell that led to the first floor of the square, four-story keep. A narrow forebuilding of stone buttressed the stairs on the right, but again I saw no sign of defenders at the loopholes. If there were any hiding there, the scholar was a dead man.

I followed after Rorian at a more leisurely pace, leading my Wolf Pack. If there was fighting to do inside in the close confines of that building, I wanted men I knew well and could trust to get the job done right. I doubted there was a need to hurry now anyway, for the arched oak doorway at the top of the staircase was bound to be barred shut and would need to be broken down with axes first before anyone could get inside. But, as with the gates earlier, I was wrong about that.

Rorian reached the door safely and lifted the latch, then flung it open before he darted inside, disappearing into the shadows. I cursed under my breath, hurrying up the staircase now with Wolf's Head in my hand and my men trotting behind me. I passed through the doorway into a great hall, where I saw several Ravens slumped over one of the wooden tables in pools of their own vomit. A raised platform stood at the end of the hall, with several blue star banners dangling from the ceiling. A long table covered in blue cloth sat on the platform, with several high-backed chairs behind it. No one—dead or alive—was sitting in them. The hall's ceiling was low, with massive dark wood beams spanning its twenty-foot width.

An arched entranceway across the room led to a staircase, and I instinctively headed that way, knowing that's where Rorian must have gone. The narrow steps led both up and down in a spiral with a central support pillar running from top to bottom. The stairs were cunningly designed, giving right-handed defenders the advantage over those coming up, since the narrowness of the steps, coupled with the support pillar, would greatly impede the attackers' sword arms.

I glanced behind me at Jebido. "Take half the men and go down to the ground floor. The rest of us will go up."

Jebido nodded his understanding as I began to climb with my shield held defensively in front of me. I reached the next floor, which turned out to be separated into guest rooms. I found nothing within those rooms but dead Ravens, most lying in their beds covered in vomit. I headed for the top floor, which was easily as large as the Great Hall below. The ceiling was made of vaulted stone and towered twenty feet above my head. I could see what I thought might be the faded paint outlines of a Blazing Sun and Rock of Life at the peak of the wall at the far end of the room, separated by a shuttered window. I guessed the space had once been used as a Holy House but now was clearly serving a similar yet at the same time very different purpose for the Ravens.

The familiar six-pointed star banners hung on both sides of the walls, with a massive star made of blue crystal suspended from a chain in the center of the room. A White Raven with his head down and face hidden by a hood sat in an ornately carved chair directly beneath the crystal. The stone floor around the chair was painted in the form of a star, with six dead Ravens lying on their backs at the end of each point. The hands of the dead men were crossed over their chests, and all had blissful looks of contentment on their faces despite their black tongues and the ever-present stench of vomit that filled the room. Rorian stood ten feet away with his back to me, facing the man in the chair.

The scholar glanced over his shoulder at us, and he grimaced in disappointment as I made space for my men to enter. My Wolf's Pack began to spread out around the room with a clanking of armor and weapons as I gestured toward the Raven. "Is he—?"

"Dead, Lord Hadrack?" the Raven asked with a chuckle. He lifted his head, revealing only the lower portion of his face. "Sorry to disappoint you, but my time has not yet come." He chuckled again and shifted on the chair, motioning toward Rorian. "Though I dare say that will change if this one gets his wish."

I frowned, certain I recognized the man's voice. "Are you the Eye of God?" I asked.

"I am," the Raven agreed. He didn't react as Rorian growled, stalking forward with his sword ready to strike.

"Wait!" I called out.

Rorian hesitated and looked back at me, his body quivering with tension. "Don't you even think of trying to take this from me, Lord Hadrack."

"I would never consider it," I said, meaning it. "I just want to ask him some questions. That's all. You can do whatever you like with the bastard after that."

Rorian relaxed somewhat at that. I stepped over the dead body of a Raven, moving closer. "Do I know you?" I said to the seated man.

"You might say that," came back the reply. "I certainly know you."

"Remove your hood."

The White Raven made no move to comply, and finally, Rorian put the tip of his sword to the man's chest. "Lord Hadrack asked you to remove your hood, vermin."

The Eye of God sighed in resignation, then slowly did as he was told, revealing a handsome face devoid of beard and hair. I frowned, not recognizing him in the slightest.

"Your Highness!"

I turned as Alfaheed strode urgently toward me. He pointed. "I've seen this man before, Your Highness. The night The Fisherman offered you the codex. He was there, remember?"

I nodded, recalling a man who'd sat quietly in the shadows and said nothing. I'd heard him speaking outside the house where I'd been held captive. That's why I'd found his voice familiar. I turned my gaze back to the Eye of God. "Where did The Fisherman get the codex? From you?"

"Naturally," the Raven stated.

"You knew it was a forgery?"

"Of course I did," the man said, sounding amused.

"What did you hope to accomplish by selling it through The Fisherman?"

"Blessed anarchy," the Eye of God said without hesitation. He smiled at me condescendingly. "We humans are such foolish creatures, Lord Hadrack. Easily manipulated if you know how. The falsified codex was designed to cause dissent in the north, allowing my operatives greater leeway to fulfill their assigned goals."

"You're talking about the Enlightenment?"

"Indeed."

I hesitated, thinking. "Did you try to have the First Daughter killed?" I finally prodded, returning to the beginning where all of this had started.

"Certainly," the Eye of God responded without blinking an eye.

"Why?"

"Because she poses a threat to the One True God's plans, of course," the White Raven said. "First Daughter Gernet is a very shrewd and cunning woman with a network of spies who could cause us endless grief if given half the chance. By eliminating her for someone...shall we say, more amenable to our cause, it would—"

"You're talking about one of your operatives?" I grunted in surprise, cutting him off. "Inside the Holy House itself?"

"Correct, lord."

I frowned, feeling suddenly uneasy. "Why are you telling me all this?" I gestured to Rorian. "You know you're going to die at this man's hands very soon, so why not just lie about everything?"

"Who says I'm not lying, lord?" the Eye of God said straight-faced. "Perhaps all that I'm telling you is nothing but misdirection? Then again, perhaps it isn't. Either way, it falls upon you, lord, to determine in which direction the truth lies, not me." He smiled, looking pleased with himself. "Bear in mind, though, that one can certainly disperse a lot of wasted energy chasing one's own tail endlessly doing that. Just food for thought."

"Maybe I should let my friend take out some of his aggression on you right now," I said in annoyance. "Perhaps that will get us to the truth a little quicker."

"If you wish," the Raven said with a disinterested shrug. He glanced at Rorian, studying him thoughtfully. "But before he does, may I ask why this man is so clearly antagonistic toward me, lord? More so than most here, it seems."

"You don't know?" I asked suspiciously.

"Should I?"

"You sent your hired swords to Afrenia to have me killed," Rorian spat out. "But they failed, killing my family instead."

"Oh, I see," the Eye of God said, looking unfazed. "You would be Rorian of Afrenia, then. How silly of me not to have realized. Truthfully, though, I'd actually forgotten all about you and your family." The scholar ground his teeth, clearly not trusting himself to speak. I could see the knuckles of his right hand wrapped around his sword hilt turning white with anger. "Anyway, Rorian of Afrenia," the Raven continued. "I do apologize for the hardships you've undoubtedly experienced at my behest. Eliminating those few who knew the truth about the Halas Codex was part of the overall plan. There were certainly no hard feelings from my end." He glanced at me, then Fitz and Baine. "Unfortunately, not every part of the plan went as expected, as it turned out."

"Hadrack!"

I turned to see Jebido hurrying up the stairs, his face flush from the long climb. He flicked his eyes around the room in surprise, pausing briefly on the seated Raven before coming back to me. "There are prisoners in the basement, Hadrack. Quite a few of them."

I frowned. "This is not exactly the right time, Jebido. We can deal with them later."

"Yes," Jebido said, holding up a hand. "But I thought you should know that one of them is Malo."

I blinked in surprise, turning suddenly when Rorian cursed. The Eye of God had begun twitching in his chair with his eyes turned up in his head and white foam bubbling at the corners of his mouth.

"No!" Rorian cried out. "You're not getting off that easily, you bastard!" The scholar rushed forward, stabbing his sword into the Eye of God's chest. The Raven's eyes bulged in surprise, and he cried out, revealing a rapidly swelling black tongue. Moments later, bile and food particles spewed out from the Eye of God's mouth, covering Rorian with slop before the White Raven sagged and died, filling the room with the stink of his emptied bowels.

Malo looked terrible. I suppose I shouldn't have been surprised, but seeing him shackled in chains, naked and shivering where he lay on filthy straw was not what I'd expected. The dungeons were dark and damp, with each cell no longer than the length of a man lying down and half again as wide. Almost every one of the cells was occupied, and I set my men to freeing the prisoners and helping them get outside into fresher air. All were shaved bald, wearing threadbare clothing if they were lucky, or like Malo, nothing at all. More than half needed to be carried, with many unable to speak, staring at us with wild eyes.

"What in the name of the gods have they done to these poor bastards?" Jebido whispered.

I shook my head. "I don't know." I knelt beside Malo, who was staring at me with no recognition whatsoever. He'd curled himself up into a ball in a corner, whimpering softly with his shackled hands covering his chest. A long purple scar that hadn't been there the last time I'd seen him ran along his right cheek from the corner of his eye to the corner of his mouth, giving him a ghoulish look. I reached out to touch the man's arm, which immediately sent him into a fit of hysterics. "It's all right," I said soothingly, retracting my hand. "No one wants to hurt you, Malo. It's me, Hadrack. We're going to get you out of here." I glanced at Rorian, who was fiddling with a set of iron keys, trying to unlock the shackles on Malo's ankles. "What's taking so long?"

"I don't know," the scholar said. "None of these seem to work."

"They worked for the other prisoners," I grunted.

"I am aware of that, lord," Rorian said grimly. I could tell the scholar was still on edge, his long-awaited revenge clearly not everything he'd hoped it would be.

I stood, knowing by the crazed look in Malo's eyes that nothing I said right now would be able to get through to him. Hopefully, later, once he'd had time to recover, that would change. I glanced at Baine standing with Jebido in the doorway. "You stay here with Rorian. If he can't get those shackles off, try to pry them free with one of your knives."

"All right, Hadrack," my friend said, though not with much enthusiasm. Baine had never cared much for Malo.

I exited the tiny cell, and with Jebido and some of my men, we worked at ferrying the remaining prisoners from the basement to the ground floor, then to the first floor and outside, where food and water were being supplied. Most of the prisoners were barely functioning, hiding their eyes from the harsh sunlight or simply lying down in the dirt and weeping. One man, though, caught my eye, standing stark naked as he doused a casket of water over himself. The man was big and heavily muscled, a far cry from the skinny wretches we'd brought up from the dungeons.

I strode over to him. "What's your name, friend?"

The man eyed me critically, then perhaps realizing he was being rude, he shrugged. "Grom Langer."

"I'm Lord Hadrack of Ganderland," I said.

Grom's eyes widened. "Forgive me, lord. I didn't know."

I waved off his apology as Fitz came to join us. "Think nothing of it." I gestured toward the other prisoners. "After your ordeal, I'm surprised you can even stand."

"I haven't been here that long, lord," Grom explained. He signaled for another casket of water, this time taking a long gulp before wiping the back of his mouth. "No more than a week or so, I think."

"Where are you from?"

"Cordova, lord."

"The Ravens took you prisoner?" Fitz asked.

Grom glanced down at the ground, looking suddenly embarrassed. "No, I came to this place voluntarily. I foolishly wanted to become a White Raven."

I couldn't hide my surprise. "Then why did you end up in a cell?"

"All recruits do, lord," Grom said. He shook his head. "I didn't know that until I arrived."

"Why cells?" I asked, perplexed.

"They call it Rebirth, lord."

"Rebirth?" Fitz said.

Grom grimaced. "Yes. They use a process of beatings and rewards to break our will, constantly feeding us with lies about the One True God. I'm told some of the stronger ones resist, but eventually, all succumb. When you're finally free to walk out of those cells, you're not the same man that went in. Hence the Rebirth."

I thought of Malo. Clearly, not all had given in to the Ravens' cruelty. "Are you saying every Raven has had to go through this process before they can join?"

"Yes, lord. I believe so."

"Even the Eye of God?" Fitz asked.

Grom's face turned hard. "I don't know about him. All I know is he's the worst of them. Always whispering empty words in your ears. You can't imagine how many times I've dreamt of bashing in that pious bastard's scarred face."

I stiffened. The man who Rorian had killed had no scars on his face. I felt my heart thudding in my chest in horror as dawning realization set in. I grabbed Grom's arm and shook him, praying I was wrong. "Tell me about the scar on his face! What does it look like?"

Grom stared at me in confusion. "Uh, purplish, lord." He slowly traced a line from his right eye down to his mouth. "Runs like this."

"Mother help us!" I whispered, already turning and running back for the keep.

Malo was the Eye of God!

Chapter 39: Castaway

Malo was gone by the time I got back to the cell. So was Rorian. But Baine remained, lying unmoving face-down on the floor with bright red blood staining the straw beneath him. Blood was also smeared on the stone wall above his head. "No!" I shouted in dismay, dropping to my knees by my friend's still form. I gently rolled him over as Fitz and Jebido looked anxiously over my shoulder. Moments later, I felt an incredible rush of relief when Baine groaned. His face was covered in straw, sticking to the blood, and I was certain his nose was broken, but thank the gods, he was alive. I shook him gently. "Baine? Baine, can you hear me?"

Baine groaned again before his eyes flickered and then opened. He focused on me, looking confused. "Hadrack?"

"It's all right," I said, cradling my friend's head in one arm like an infant. I used my free hand to search Baine's body, but thankfully I could find no other wounds. I began working then to pull the bits of straw from his face. "Take a moment," I said gently as Baine struggled to sit up.

"What happened?" my friend asked weakly. He glanced past me to Jebido, who was leaning on my shoulder anxiously.

"Maybe you can tell us, lad," Jebido said, the worry evident in his voice.

Baine winced, trying to sit up again. This time I helped him, biting my lip as my friend wobbled unsteadily in my grip. "I'm not sure, Jebido. The keys wouldn't work on Malo's shackles, so I did what Hadrack suggested and used my knife on the locks. Rorian was talking to Malo, trying to get through to him, I think, but I really wasn't paying much attention." Baine hocked loudly, then turned his head and spat out a clump of blood. He closed his eyes, and I was glad I still held him, for I was sure he would have fallen sideways otherwise. "I remember Rorian said something about his wife, Thera, to Malo, which got a reaction. I know Malo started talking about something after that, but I can't remember for my life what it was." Baine glanced at me, pointing to his head. "Everything is kind of foggy up here right now, Hadrack. Anyway, I got the last shackle off just as Rorian started yelling. Then everything went dark." Baine shrugged. "I'm sorry, but that's all I remember."

"You did good, my friend," I said, patting him on the arm fondly. "Real good. Rest now. Tyris and Putt will help you out of here when you're ready." I removed my hands, watching Baine critically for signs he might fall, but except for a slight tremor in his right arm, he seemed to be regaining his strength quickly. I stood. "I've got to go, but I'll check on you later."

"I'm fine," Baine said, waving me away. "Just go find that bastard, Hadrack."

I leaned down to squeeze my friend's shoulder, then turned to Fitz and Jebido. "Nobody gets out of the keep without my say-so, understood?" Both men nodded, their faces set and serious. "I want men searching every floor. If there's a dried-up mouse turd hiding somewhere in here, I want to know about it."

"We'll find the bastard, Hadrack," Jebido growled.

I brushed past Jebido and Fitz into the narrow corridor filled with curious onlookers. I pointed at Putt and Tyris. "You two stay here with Baine. If Malo is stupid enough to come back here to try and finish the job, then feel free to gut the bastard."

"With pleasure, my lord," Putt grunted.

"The rest of you get moving," I snapped. "Find him! And find Rorian while you're at it!"

It didn't take long to find both Malo and Rorian, as it turned out. Though when I arrived, one was already dead, and the other was close to it. It had been Giree of all people who had found them, having followed a faint trail of blood to a small room off the dungeons that no one had noticed. That room housed some grain stores and a circular well of stone, I saw as I strode through the doorway, sword in hand. Rorian lay on his side with his back pressed against the well, clearly dead. One arm was stretched out as if pointing toward Malo in accusation, where he sat propped up against a wall, staring at me with hooded eyes as he clutched at a gaping wound in his naked belly.

The former House Agent chuckled when he saw me. "It's been a long time, Lord Hadrack. You're looking well."

I nodded, stepping closer. A blood-stained sword lay on the dirt floor halfway between Rorian's corpse and the former House Agent. I kicked it away, then crouched six feet from the wounded man, taking no chances. Malo might be injured, perhaps fatally, but I remembered well how fast he could move. I saw a six-pointed star tattooed over his heart, half-hidden by thick hair. I shook my head in disgust, recalling how Malo had been careful to keep his hands over it in the cell. I should have looked closer. "You certainly had me fooled," I finally said grudgingly. "Pretending to be a prisoner was smart. I only realized the truth once I got outside."

"What gave me away?"

I pointed to his face. "Your scar. One of the men in the cells described it. That's how I knew."

"Ah," Malo grunted in acknowledgment. "I originally planned on killing them all, but we were running out of time by then. Besides, it would surely have led to questions if they were all dead and I wasn't." He winced as dark blood seeped from around his fingers, then chuckled. "The best-laid plans, eh, Hadrack?"

I grimaced. "What happened in the cell with you and Baine and Rorian?"

Malo motioned weakly toward the corpse with a bloody hand. "I'd forgotten how smart that bastard was." He lifted an eyebrow. "How is Baine, by the way? I smashed his face against that wall pretty hard."

"Fine," I said. "You broke his nose, but he'll live."

"That's a shame," Malo grunted. "I never liked that little weasel."

"The feeling is mutual, believe me," I replied, doing my best to control my anger. I rubbed my face wearily, still trying to understand. "Dammit, Malo. Why? Why did you do this? You were the most loyal man I'd ever met. There was a time when you would have gladly fallen on your sword if you thought it would help the House. What happened?"

Malo coughed and winced. "Do you really need to ask, Hadrack? The codex you gave me is what happened."

"You forced me to give it to you," I said. "Remember?"

"True," Malo conceded.

I sighed. "How could you let that damn thing corrupt you?" I said, not hiding my disdain. "I thought you were better than that."

"The codex didn't corrupt me," Malo replied firmly. "All it did was help enlighten me about the injustices in our world."

"Oh please!" I scoffed, having heard the same tripe from Muwa's lips. "That's utter nonsense, and we both know it. This whole thing was about obtaining power for you and nothing else. Admit it."

Malo shrugged. "Think whatever you wish, Hadrack. I will go to the One True God knowing that I did everything that He asked of me. That's all that matters."

"Is that right?" I said sarcastically. "So, your god wanted you to fail, is that it?"

Malo laughed painfully. "What makes you think I failed?"

"Look around you, Malo," I said, waving a hand. "The White Ravens are finished. Your religious movement, or whatever you want to call it, is over."

"Ah, Hadrack," Malo said, chuckling again. "I remember how young and naïve you were when we first met. Do you recall? In that cage in the forest when I saved you?" The former House Agent shook his head as he regarded me. "You're not so young anymore, I admit, but you certainly are still naïve."

I glanced over my shoulder, where Fitz and Jebido stood at the entrance, listening. Jebido rolled his eyes at me before I turned back to the wounded man. "I know about your operatives in the north, Malo. I know about the Seven Rings, too, and I also know what you tried to do with the forged codex. This thing is over, whether you want to believe it or not."

"And what will that knowledge do for you, Hadrack?" Malo asked scornfully. "Will it change anything? No, I think not. The die is cast and the Enlightenment will happen with or without me. You've won the battle today, I freely admit that. But so what? I'm just one insignificant foot soldier in a war that you can't win. Change is coming for this world like a Temba storm, whether you and those like you wish for it or not."

Malo hesitated then, his eyelids fluttering as his chin lowered to his naked chest and his breathing grew even more ragged. The loss of blood was clearly taking its toll, and I knew he'd probably be dead in another minute or two unless the flow was stopped. I took a chance and moved closer, shaking him. "Where is Waldin's codex, Malo? Is it here in the keep?"

The former House Agent smiled through blood-tainted lips and weakly shook his head. "Not on the island," he whispered hoarsely.

"Then where is it?"

"Where you'll never think to look," Malo muttered without opening his eyes.

"Why not tell me?" I demanded, frustrated. "What does it matter now?" With the codex still out there somewhere, I knew everything could still be lost. I needed to find it and keep it hidden until the war was over and the White Ravens were all eradicated like the vermin they were. After that, well, we'd see.

Malo lifted his head, opening his eyes. I could see the familiar hardness and stubbornness in those eyes that I remembered well. "Because the very fact that you want it so badly is why you'll never learn its location from my lips," the former House Agent said so softly that I barely heard. He closed his eyes again, leaning his head back against the wall, and this time no amount of shaking could awaken him.

I slowly stood, feeling impotent anger as I motioned Lord Fitzery closer. I put my hand on my friend's forearm. "You're the closest thing we have to a healer, Fitz. Don't let this bastard die. I don't care if it takes a hundred years, he's going to tell me what I want to know one way or another."

Nearly two months later, I stood on *Sea-Wolf's* forecastle, breathing in the salt-tainted air coming off the waters of the Tides of Mansware. *Sea-Wolf's* new hull chopped easily through the waves with an almost joyous energy, while behind the cog, *Spearfish* and seventy-five colorful catamarans carrying more than eight thousand troops followed as we headed northeast. Every sail was filled, billowing and snapping in the strong breeze, with the stark white canvases on the ships contrasting strongly with my new sigil of two black heads joined at the base of the skull—one a wolf, the other a lion. I still felt deep uneasiness whenever I saw that sigil, created in celebration of the union between Sarrey and me that had occurred almost a month ago.

"Are you ever going to tell us?" Baine asked from beside me. My friend was balancing a wooden bowl on the tip of one of his knives, making it spin in a dizzying way—no small feat considering the rolling swells beneath *Sea-Wolf's* hull.

"What's the matter?" Jebido grunted. "Are you looking for pointers on how to do it right?"

"Ha!" Baine said with a snort. "Your jokes are almost as old as you are, Jebido. You really need to do better. Lord Fitzery is much funnier than you are, you know."

Jebido's mocking grin instantly turned to a frown at the mention of Fitz's name, and I couldn't help but laugh. It was always a competition between Jebido and Fitz, no matter what the reason, though I couldn't fathom why that might be. Baine's broken nose had healed well, though now there was a noticeable bump on the bridge. If anything, I thought it made him look even more dashing and mysterious than before—the smug little bastard.

"Well?" Baine said, prodding me with one hand while somehow managing to keep the bowl spinning.

"Well, what?" I grunted.

"How was it? Did she make a lot of noise? Was there any—?"

"How about you mind your own business?" I snapped. "What goes on between my wife and me in the bedroom is no concern of yours."

"But, Hadrack," Baine continued.

I grabbed the spinning bowl and tossed it more forcefully than intended to the deck. "I said mind your business, and I meant it," I growled.

Baine frowned, then stooped to pick up the bowl. "Fine, be that way," he said sulkily before stalking off toward the ladder. He looked back over his shoulder at me. "I was just trying to make conversation, that's all."

"It's a wonder someone hasn't cut that boy's tongue out yet," Jebido said with a sigh after Baine had gone. "Or cut off something else just as annoying. The gods' know he deserves it sometimes."

"Baine's still young," I muttered. "So it might happen yet." I thought of *Rhana* Dachmar from Sandhold, who I'd essentially had to pay a king's ransom to so he'd drop his claim against Baine. I didn't know what had become of that man's pregnant daughter, nor did I want to, though I had seen Baine with a young girl more than once before we left Temba. Had it been her or some other female easily swayed by charm and good looks? Honestly, I hadn't wanted to find out.

Jebido regarded me critically. "What's eating at you, Hadrack? You've been moody ever since we left Temba."

I sighed. "Do you want the full list of problems we still face?"

Jebido shook his head. "Nope. Just the real reason you've got that black look all the time. Is it Malo?"

"I don't waste much time thinking about that bastard," I grunted. That was a lie, of course. The former House Agent had survived his wound, thanks mostly to Fitz's skill. I'd questioned him every day since then about the location of Waldin's codex, but he'd refused to answer every time. We'd searched the entire island and come up empty, so it had now come down to a contest of wills—one which, by the gods, I intended to win. Malo was even now chained in *Sea-Wolf's* hold, where he would remain until I figured out what to do with him.

"Then what is it?" Jebido prodded. "Is it the girl?" I stiffened unconsciously and my friend nodded, his suspicions clearly confirmed. "That's what I thought. Are you still feeling guilty after everything that's happened these last few months?" I closed my eyes, tempted to answer but determined not to. Jebido moved closer to me, leaning on the railing as he nudged me gently with his elbow. "If you can't talk to me, lad, then who else in this world can you talk to?"

I felt sudden emotion welling up in my chest and fought against it. "Shana," I finally whispered hoarsely. "I could always talk to her about anything."

Jebido sighed sadly. "Well, I hate to break it to you, lad, but as much as I wish it weren't true, that wonderful woman is gone now. You need to come to terms with that, and the sooner you do the better, before it wrecks you."

"I'm already wrecked, Jebido," I said softly, feeling bitterness in my mouth. "The walls might still stand, but nothing is left inside. You just haven't noticed."

"Oh, you know what I've noticed?" Jebido said, sounding angry now. He didn't wait for me to answer. "I've noticed that, as usual, you're being a selfish ass, Hadrack." My friend was using that scolding tone I'd been hearing ever since I was a boy of eight. I sighed, knowing a lecture was coming. "Queen Sarrey isn't Lady Shana. That's a fact we can all agree on, but she's a damn fine lass just the same and deserves better from you." He pointed a finger at me. "You're the one who agreed to marry her, Hadrack, unless you've forgotten."

"But I only did that—" I started to protest.

"I don't give a damn about the *why*, Hadrack," Jebido interrupted. His face above his silver beard was very quickly turning a bright red. "The fact is, you're the one who stood up in the Yellow Palace before the gods and spoke the words of union. No one forced you to do anything." He lifted a finger in anticipation. "And don't go giving me that—*I did it for Ganderland nonsense*."

"It's not nonsense," I growled, getting angry myself now. I swept my hand behind me toward the ships following. "What do you think that is, Jebido? Would they be here if I hadn't married her?"

Jebido shook his head in disgust. "We both know they would have, Hadrack. So stop playing this game. You are the King of Temba. These men will go wherever you tell them whether you are married to Sarrey or not." He hesitated there, putting both hands on the railing and looking out to sea. "So, my question to you is this," Jebido continued. "Why did you marry her if it's causing you so much pain?" He looked sideways at me. "The truth now."

I hesitated. The question was one I'd been asking myself for weeks now, ever since the wedding. I'd convinced myself that I'd gone through with the marriage to Sarrey because I'd given her my word I would. That was, on the face of it, true. I'd also told myself that our union made both Temba and Ganderland stronger, which we would need in the coming months and years. Also true. But, the real answer lay deep down in the dark recesses of my mind where only shadowy thoughts lurked. It was a place I rarely liked to visit, for the undeniable truth was I'd been horribly lonely since Shana died. I had my friends to count on to be sure. No man could ask for better, but, even so, they could not replace that special closeness shared between a man and a woman who were in love. The last three weeks in Temba had been some of the best days of my life since Shana had died, and all of that was due to Sarrey del Fante. It was an admission that always sent daggers of guilt into my heart, for I'd firmly believed that I could never love again. Part of me still wanted to believe that.

I turned to Jebido, forcing the words out before I lost my nerve. "I think Sarrey might be pregnant."

My friend's bushy eyebrows rose in astonishment, which quickly turned to an expression of delight. But before he could say anything, we were interrupted by a shout from above. I glanced up at the lookout. "The island, my lord!" the man cried out, pointing off our starboard side.

I focused that way, able to discern a white sail on the horizon, though I couldn't see any evidence of land yet. I felt excitement surge through my veins. This moment was something that I'd been looking forward to for a long time, and right now, I was in the perfect mood for it.

I headed for the ladder, pausing when Jebido grabbed my arm. "Do you want to talk about it?"

"What's there to talk about?" I grunted. "Sarrey is back in Temba, and I don't know when I'll see her again. She's pregnant, or she's not. Either way, I expect I'll find out sooner or later." I shook off his hand and motioned toward the distant sail. "Besides, I've got more important things to think about right now."

The islet was circular, with a diameter of perhaps fifty feet. Most of it was covered with white sand and rock, with a small stand of palm trees at the northern end. I could see a crude hut formed out of fronds and driftwood beneath the trees, but I could see no signs of the inhabitant. I assumed he was inside the shelter, watching the great armada of ships approaching. I prayed his belly was rolling and twisting with fear as I glanced at the catamaran anchored two hundred feet away from the islet. That ship had been stationed there for several months now, ensuring Lord Boudin remained well-fed and healthy until I was ready for him. There's no sport in killing a man weakened by hunger and disease.

More islands dotted the horizon around us, but none were close enough to the islet for a man to swim to, and even if they had been, I'd already seen more than one shark fin knifing through the green waters around the ship. Jebido had chosen Lord Boudin's prison well, just as he'd assured me.

I felt a nudge on my arm. "There, Hadrack," Fitz said, pointing toward the tiny island.

I shaded my eyes as a figure appeared from beneath the trees and walked to the shore's edge. He was tall and naked, his skin the color of bronze and his hair and beard shaggy and long. He carried a sword in his right hand that reflected the sunlight back to me. I took a deep breath in relief. I'd feared the bastard might have died from some ailment during his long captivity, despite the food and water he'd been given. I dropped my hand to Wolf's Head, thinking of the seven rings inscribed by the gods on her blade. "Soon," I whispered. "Very soon."

"We're ready for you, my lord," Tyris said moments later, gesturing over the gunwale.

I nodded and unbuckled my sword, handing it to Jebido. I stripped off all my clothing, accepting Wolf's Head back after I was naked before hooking the weapon over my shoulder.

"You be careful over there," Jebido muttered. "Don't take any unnecessary risks. Kill him quick and be done with it so we can go home."

I grinned as I flipped one leg over the gunwale. "Now, where would the fun be in that, Jebido?" I laughed at the dark look on my friend's face, then lowered myself into the skiff where Berwin awaited me, holding the craft tight against *Sea-Wolf's* hull. "Where is it?" I asked.

Berwin pointed to a small cloth bundle in the bow. "There, my lord." He hesitated as I settled myself onto the bench by the oars. "Are you sure you don't want me to go with you, my lord?"

I shook my head and motioned to the dangling rope. "No, get going."

Berwin took a deep breath and nodded, then jumped, pulling himself easily up the knotted rope. I was on my own now, and I pushed off from the big cog, then started to row toward the islet. Lord Boudin had been told I'd be coming sooner or later, and I could only imagine what it must have been like for him, waiting day after day, wondering when I would finally show up. I smiled. Well, that day had finally come.

The water around the islet for at least fifty feet was shallow, with the bulk of the landmass hiding beneath the waves. If the ocean had been lower by several feet, I guessed the tiny island would probably have been ten times as big as it was. I could hear the waves lapping against the exposed shoreline as I drew closer and could feel Lord Boudin's eyes burning into my naked back while I rowed. I didn't bother looking over my shoulder, knowing with certainty that he would wait and make no move against me. The man was a Cardian and a bastard, but he was also a lord and had some semblance of honor. Besides, the deal he'd been offered was simple; win against me in a fair fight, and he'd be free to take the skiff and sail away unmolested.

I felt the bottom of the boat scrape against rock, and finally, I turned, tossing a rope attached to the bow onto the shore. "Pull me up," I ordered.

Lord Boudin hesitated, then stuck his sword in the sand before doing as I asked. Once the skiff was safely ashore, I stood, drawing Wolf's Head with a ring of steel before letting the sheath drop to the bottom of the boat. I stepped onto the sand while Lord Boudin retreated to retrieve his weapon.

"When you said it would be a fair fight, lord," the Cardian said, looking calm and amused. He gestured to my nakedness. "I didn't think that you meant it literally."

"I always keep my word."

"As do I," Lord Boudin replied. He motioned to his own naked body. "I made a skirt of leaves initially, but it itched horribly. I actually prefer it this way."

I studied the other man critically. He appeared fit and healthy, with his legs and arms rippling with muscle. The massive shoulders that I remembered on the man seemed even larger now, too. "You look well, lord," I said amiably. "I'm glad of it. This southern climate seems to be agreeing with you."

"It's been surprisingly relaxing here, Lord Hadrack," Lord Boudin said. "I've had nothing to do all day but train or sleep." His voice sounded rough, clearly not having been used for some time. The Cardian swished his sword by his side. "Though I must say, I'm glad it's finally over. I've been greatly looking forward to this."

"As have I," I said. "My apologies for not coming to kill you sooner, but unfortunately, I encountered some delays."

"Painful ones, I hope?" Lord Boudin replied.

I smiled. "Only for my enemies."

The Cardian's face darkened. "You can't imagine how many ways I've dreamed of killing you these last few months, lord."

I chuckled. "I'm glad I could keep your mind occupied, lord. I'm sure a man could go mad out here all alone without some goal to hang onto, even if it is nothing but fantasy."

Lord Boudin smirked. "We'll see, lord."

I stretched, loosening my muscles as I breathed in the salty air. "I'd like to express my gratitude to you, Lord Boudin," I said. I motioned with Wolf's Head to the black ship anchored in the distance not far away from *Sea-Wolf*. "*Spearfish* is a fine ship, and as things turned out, she was instrumental in my success. I'm delighted that I've been able to add her to my fleet." Lord Boudin's eyes flashed at that, but he held his temper. "Now, before we get on to business, lord," I continued. "I wonder if you might answer a question or two for me?"

"Such as, lord?"

"Did you know the codex The Fisherman was selling was a forgery?"

Lord Boudin blinked in surprise at that, and unless he was a spectacular actor, I guessed that he hadn't known. "A forgery?"

"Indeed," I said. 'I'd actually read the real codex years ago, so I knew the moment I saw it."

"Then why did you bother bidding on it?" the Cardian asked, looking perplexed.

I shrugged. "That hardly matters now, lord." I pursed my lips as I thought. "What happened to that mealy-mouthed Son that was with you?"

"I don't know, lord," Lord Boudin grunted. "Nor do I much care."

"You didn't like him?" I asked.

The Cardian grimaced. "You've met him. What do you think?"

"Good point," I conceded. "By the way, the Eye of God is dead. I thought you might like to know that."

"Who is that?" Lord Boudin asked in confusion, confirming what I'd begun to suspect. For whatever reason, this man had not been privy to the White Raven plot. I found that interesting, though it didn't stop me from hating him any less. Nor would it affect what happened next.

"Any more questions, lord?" the Cardian asked. "Because if not, I'd like to kill you now so I can get off this cursed island."

"It's an islet," I said with a condescending smile. Lord Boudin frowned. "An island this small is usually called an *islet*," I explained. My smile fell away, replaced with cold resolve. "I do have one last question before we get to things, though." Lord Boudin indicated with his sword that I should continue. "Who decided to take Lady Shana Corwick hostage? You and your fellow Rings or the Overseer?"

"I think you already know the answer to that, lord," Lord Boudin said. He lowered his eyes for the briefest of moments. "If it helps any, our intent was never to see her harmed. I was truly distressed when I learned of her death."

"It doesn't help," I growled.

Lord Boudin merely nodded, not looking surprised. I waited then, knowing the time for talk had ended. We were two naked men armed only with swords and a deep hatred for each other. There really was only one way for this to go. The Cardian was the first to move, darting forward as he slashed sideways at my midriff. I parried, flicking his blade aside with a clang of steel. His move was undeniably quick but flawed, and I'd considered disarming him right then and there. But that would have been too easy. Behind me, I could hear faint cheering coming from the ships. I stayed focused, stalking forward on the balls of my feet, ignoring the hot sand searing the tender skin of my soles. Lord Boudin retreated beneath my advance, watching me warily. Perhaps he'd sensed that I'd gone easy on him.

"You know Ganderland has probably fallen by now," the Cardian said with a sneer. If he was hoping to make me angry, thinking it might make me do something rash, then he needn't have bothered. I was already burning as hot as one of The Father's pits—I just had it contained on a tight leash. "Parnuthians attacking from the east and Cardia from the west," the Cardian continued. "That doesn't bode well for your side, lord."

"Says you," I grunted.

I feinted for his right armpit, and when the Cardian hastily twisted aside, I lashed out with my left fist, catching him a glancing blow on the cheek just above the line of his beard. The deeply tanned skin instantly split open like an overripe melon as I danced back across the sand while Lord Boudin swatted at the empty air in frustration with his sword. Blood flowed freely from the cut on the Cardian's cheek, and he paused to rub at it, staring at the red smear on his palm in annoyance.

"You hit like a girl, lord," Lord Boudin finally said contemptuously. He wiped his hand on the dark hairs of his chest indifferently and smiled. "I was planning on toying with you, but after that dirty business, I've changed my mind."

"I don't blame you, lord," I said. "The mind you were born with wasn't much good, anyway."

Lord Boudin frowned at that, and he growled low in his chest like a dog who's suffered one too many beatings. I was almost thirty years old the day we fought on that islet, and by then, I'd crossed swords with more men than I cared to remember. Each and every one of those men had approached the battle differently. Some were fast and slippery, some clever, while others were big and strong, depending almost entirely on brute strength. Some men fought with maniacal ferocity and some with measured caution, but every one of them would ultimately show a flaw, sometimes a barely perceptible one, that would make the difference between victory and defeat. I'd already learned Lord Boudin's weakness and knew I could beat him. It would just take time to wear him down—or at least, it should have.

To this day, I don't know why my childish needling got to the Cardian, for as warriors, we both had heard every insult known to man at one point or another during a fight. But Lord Boudin suddenly became unhinged at my words, rushing at me recklessly while screaming and hacking with his sword. Perhaps it was all those days of solitude in the sun and heat; I don't know. Now it was my turn to retreat, but not out of fear, for the swings were long loopy things and incredibly clumsy. I could have killed the bastard a half dozen times during the time it took him to reach me. But I didn't. No, the fact is, I was fascinated by the man's almost suicidal rush—that, and I wanted to prolong the fight as much as possible.

I let Lord Boudin close on me. His eyes were red with anger, and spittle was flying from his mouth. I dodged another wild swing, twisting away and using the flat of my sword to smack his bare ass as he swept past. The Cardian's momentum carried him to the shoreline, and he roared in anger, turning with his sword raised. I rushed forward and grabbed his wrist, holding his arm up with the blade held at an angle above my head. I was much taller and stronger than my opponent despite his great muscles, and I smiled down at him, letting him see how effortless it was for me to keep him there. The Cardian lashed out with his left fist, screaming his hatred at me. I shifted my head at the last moment, letting his punch sail past my ear, then I brought my right knee up hard into his manhood. Lord Boudin screamed, buckling while I held him suspended for a heartbeat before I twisted his wrist savagely until I heard a snap, followed by a second, louder scream. The Cardian's sword dropped, bouncing off my back and taking some skin with it. I barely noticed. Lord Boudin fell to one knee, crying out as I twisted his arm back as far as it would go without breaking.

The man's wrist was already shattered, which I knew must be excruciatingly painful. I decided to give him something else to think about. I applied pressure, using the strength in my arm and back, until I heard something pop near his right shoulder blade. The Cardian howled in agony and I let him go, watching dispassionately as he flopped to the sand facedown, sobbing. I stooped and picked up his sword, then tossed it as far into the ocean as I could while cheers from the ships filled my ears. I thought suddenly of the three whores from Hillsfort, Flora, Aenor, and Margot. Flora and Aenor were both long dead now, but Margot lived in Camwick, happily married to a candlemaker. I'd met the whores when I'd gone to find Hape, one of The Nine, and after the stories they'd told me, I'd allowed them to beat the bastard to death in the name of all those who had died in Corwick. It had seemed a fitting end for him.

I looked down at Lord Boudin, tempted to do the same to him. But then I changed my mind. I used my bare foot to flip the man on his back.

"Please, Lord Hadrack, I beg of you," the Cardian sobbed. He lifted his left hand imploringly to me—a hand that bore a red ruby ring.

I growled, grabbing the man's hand and ignoring his cry of pain as I worked to get the ring off. It was on there tightly, and I'm pretty sure the finger snapped at some point while I worked, but that was the least of the bastard's worries. I had no idea what I would do with the ruby ring, I just knew Lord Boudin wouldn't be needing it any longer. The Cardian was still pleading with me as I finally removed the ring and held it up, admiring the gleaming gemstone in the sunlight. Annoyed at the man's constant wailing, I kicked him in the stomach to shut him up, then turned and retreated up the beach. I found a flat stone and placed the ring on it, then stabbed Wolf's Head into the ground beside it.

Then I returned to Lord Boudin and went to work. The apothecary, Haverty, had told me once that there were over two hundred bones in the human body. That seemed like an awful lot to me, but I was hugely motivated that day to find out if the man spoke true. Now, in all fairness, I can't be absolutely certain I broke every bone the Cardian possessed, but by the gods, I gave it a damn fine try. When I was finished more than an hour later, I retrieved my sword and the ring, placing them in the boat before I picked up the cloth bundle. I unwrapped it, revealing the forged codex, then returned to Lord Boudin's shattered body, where he lay spread-eagled in the sand on his back. I was pleased to see the man was still alive somehow with his eyes half open, though whether he could see me or not remained a valid question.

I smiled down at him anyway and lifted the codex. "I thought you might want this, lord," I said. "Since you came all this way for it." I tossed the book on the Cardian's caved-in chest that was struggling to rise and fall. "At least you'll have something to read while you wait to die."

I turned then, not looking back as I pushed the skiff into the water, jumped in, and began to row back to *Sea-Wolf*. I could hear and see my men on the ships, all of them waving weapons over their heads in celebration, and I smiled, feeling an almost overwhelming sense of fellowship with them. I knew there were still so many questions left to answer, so many things left undone, but those could all wait for another day. Today, at this moment, I felt nothing but contentment. I glanced up at the sun overhead, certain I could feel Shana's presence smiling down on me, and with it, surprisingly, I felt the guilt I'd been carrying about Sarrey del Fante slowly fade away.

    It was time to go home.

EPILOGUE

"You look tired, lord," Malo said. He gestured to a stool off to one side of his cot. "Would you care to sit?"

"I would," I grunted. I shuffled to the stool and lowered myself onto it, unable to suppress a sigh of relief. "It's been a long night. I've just spent most of it hunting down three rapists. A nasty business, that."

"Ah," Malo muttered. He smoothed the long hairs of his white beard. "It seems the more things change, the more they stay the same."

"Sadly true when it comes to this," I agreed. I adjusted Wolf's Head so the hilt couldn't jab me in the side.

"You were never fond of rapists, as I recall," Malo said.

I could feel his eyes on me, searching curiously as if trying to locate the man he'd known hidden somewhere in my shrivelled bones and wrinkled skin. I was doing the same to him. It was clear that neither one of us was particularly impressed with what we saw. There is no dignity in getting old, no matter what some might tell you. I cleared my throat. "My steward tells me you're ready to do the world a favor and finally die," I muttered.

Malo made a wheezing noise—his form of laughter—pausing moments later to cough repeatedly. I waited for the fit to end, in no hurry now. The former House Agent reached for a wooden cup on a small table near his cot with a shaking hand, gulping the contents greedily. He finally set the cup down, ignoring the liquid he'd spilled down his beard as he smiled. I noticed he had few teeth left. "It appears that you haven't changed much, lord." Malo paused to look me up and down. "In temperament, at any rate."

I folded my arms over my chest, regarding the other man with hard eyes. "What are you dying from?"

"Being old, Hadrack," Malo said with a weak chuckle. "Nothing except being old and worn out." The former House Agent shivered and he pulled his blanket closer around his thin frame. "How long have I been down here now?"

"Almost forty years, I think," I said. I wasn't entirely sure, but that seemed about right.

"Forty years," Malo repeated in wonder. He shook his head. "That's almost as old as I was before—" He trailed off then, looking suddenly confused and frail. He stared at me after a moment, blinking watery eyes. "What was I saying?" I just sat there, not answering until finally, Malo shrugged. "Ah well, what does any of it matter now, anyway?"

"You have something you want to tell me?" I grunted, getting impatient now. Malo was unquestionably in a sorry state, the man he'd been before long gone now, leaving nothing but a withered husk behind. But even so, I felt no pity for him, nor any remorse for having put him here. The only regret I had, I suppose, was that he hadn't told me sooner what I wanted to know, allowing me to cut his throat and be done with him.

"Do I?" Malo muttered. He looked down at his hands. The nails were long and yellow, and he picked at something black under one of them.

I leaned forward. "Where is the codex, Malo? Tell me, and I'll end your suffering. You have my word."

"The codex?" Malo whispered. I saw something in his eyes then, a light of clarity reappearing. "You want to know where it is?"

I blew air out of my nostrils. "Stop playing games with me, Malo. Just tell me. It doesn't matter anymore, anyway. The world has moved on."

"If the codex doesn't matter, then why do you want to know where it is?"

I sighed and sat back. "Because it's the only piece of the puzzle left before I die. That's why."

"And I own that piece," Malo said, chuckling again. "Which gives me power over you, no? The roles of the jailer and the jailed reversed?"

I frowned in disgust and half-stood. Even at the end of his life, Malo was still a hateful bastard. "Are you going to tell me, or should I just leave you here to rot and die?"

Malo waved a conciliatory hand. "Sit, lord, please. I'm just teasing you, is all." I sat back down, trying to control my anger. "I will tell you, I promise. But before I do, I have a question for you."

"Which is what?" I growled, still suspicious the man was toying with me.

"Why did you stop coming to see me?" Malo asked. "At first, it was every day, then every week, then every month, until finally, nothing. Why?"

I leaned forward again, smiling. "I'm glad you asked that, Malo. I stopped coming here because, over time, what you knew and the threat it posed no longer mattered to the world outside these walls." I pointed to the closed door. "Out there, we have nothing but peace and prosperity now. There are no wars anymore, with the Unified Kingdom of Ganderland living in harmony with all other nations under the guidance of the Three Gods. The world today is very different from the one that you tried to destroy."

"I didn't try to destroy it," Malo protested.

I ignored him. "You once told me that you hadn't failed, do you remember? That day in the keep at the Edge of the World? You promised me nothing could stop what you'd set into motion and that the Enlightenment would happen. But it didn't. You were wrong."

Malo wheezed laughter again, sounding genuinely amused. "Was I, lord? Think about what you just told me. Think about this wonderful world outside that you just described. Is this not exactly what I promised you would happen?"

I frowned, uneasy now. "What are you talking about?"

"What is the one constant in everything that has occurred since the original Halas Codex was found?" Malo prodded.

"War?" I grunted immediately. "Nothing but war, misery, death, and destruction."

Malo nodded in acceptance. "Yes, I suppose that's true. But that's not what I meant. Think of the history of those years—all the moments that transpired that led to the radical changes you have described. What one item, if removed from the equation of any of the key events, would have stopped those changes from happening?"

I shook my head, at a loss. I was tired, oh so tired, and my brain felt leaden. "I don't know," I finally admitted.

Malo pointed a shaking finger at me. "You are that constant, Lord Hadrack. You are the Enlightenment, or rather, the key needed to make it happen."

I gaped at the former House Agent in astonishment. Finally, I snorted. "You've lost your mind. What nonsense is this?"

"Have I?" Malo grunted. "Think about what I'm telling you. Would this wonderous new world you are so proud of still exist if my White Ravens and I hadn't been there to push you? Would the Cardians and Parnuthians have attacked Ganderland without our meddling? Would the Temba have become your allies? Would the Houses have been at each others' throats if not for us? The answer to all of those questions is a resounding no."

I rolled my eyes. "So, you're claiming what you did was a ruse all along just to get me involved? Do you know how ridiculous that sounds, Malo?"

"That's not what I'm saying, lord," Malo said. "I didn't know any of this back then, either. I was only doing what I thought was right." He waved a hand around the cell. "But I've had many years to think about it and to understand. I was as much an instrument of the gods as you were—a foil, as it were, to provoke and to motivate you."

I felt my eyes narrow. "You said, *gods*. What happened to your One True God? You don't believe in that anymore?"

Malo shrugged. "One god, three gods, what does it matter now if the end result is what was desired? The power all comes from the same lifeforce, anyway."

I leaned forward and wearily rubbed my hands down the length of my face, feeling the raised scars earned from a lifetime of fighting. What Malo was saying was clearly insane, yet a part of me couldn't help but acknowledge it. I'd always felt from the moment those nine bastards had ridden into my village that the gods were watching over me, pushing me in the direction they wanted me to go. Hearing Malo validate that feeling in a most unusual way only added to my confusion. More so because a part of me knew he might be right.

I looked up then as Malo gasped, clutching at his chest. He fell back on the cot, his eyes round as he tried to speak. I jumped to my feet, leaning over him.

"It's time," the former House Agent managed to say in a strangled voice. He clutched at my arm feebly. "Forgive me for what I've done, Hadrack. I truly wished you no ill."

I hesitated, unsure if I could grant that last wish after everything that had happened between us. I felt Malo's grip weakening, the light fading from his eyes, and slowly I nodded, letting the last of the hatred I'd been carrying inside me go. "I forgive you," I whispered. "Go to the gods in peace."

Malo smiled then, and I could see the relief in his eyes. "The codex," he said softly.

I leaned closer, my heart racing. I'd forgotten all about my original reason for coming here. "Where is it, Malo?" I asked, breathless now.

The former House Agent fought to form words, but no sounds came out. I pressed my ear to his lips, finally able to register what he was trying to say, not hiding my surprise when I realized where the codex had been all this time. I should have guessed all along. Malo smiled at me afterward, both of us sharing in the irony before, with a wheeze of expelled air, he died. I slowly straightened, standing over the former House Agent for a long time as I stared down at his body, reflecting on everything he'd told me. Finally, I turned, crossing to the door and knocking on it. The door swung open immediately, revealing Walice's anxious face.

"Is everything all right, my lord?" the steward asked.

"Just fine," I said. I straightened my shoulders as I walked through the entrance. My fatigue was gone now, replaced with an unshakeable purpose that could not be denied.

I was going back to Mount Halas—back to Waldin's cave where it had all begun.

THE END

Author's Note

Thank you once again, dear reader, for your continued support of this series. I had a lot of misgivings and uncertainty when I started Codex, for though I had the beginning and end of this story already mapped out in my mind, the bulk of it remained unclear to me. I remember lamenting that very fact to my wife after the first few days of writing, telling her that this was probably going to be the shortest book in the series (excluding The Nine, of course) since, in my mind, I didn't have a solid story. My wife had laughed when I'd told her that, adamant that there was nothing to worry about and that knowing me, the story would come. I should have known better than to question her, for it seems she knows me better than I do, as The Wolf And The Codex turned out to be my longest book of the six so far. Go figure.

As promised a while ago, I am now turning my sights on my favorite little black-clad, wise-cracking, womanizing archer, Baine, who I think deserves to have his story finally told. Baine and the Outlaw of Corwick should be out in early spring, assuming all goes well. Until then, take care and stay safe.

Terry Cloutier, December 2022

Printed in Great Britain
by Amazon